The Amulet

The Amulet

How many coincidences have to occur without a rational explanation before one seeks an explanation elsewhere?

Clinton mhic Aonghais

(Clinton McInnes - Christchurch - New Zealand)
Author

FIELD SERVICE
TOP SECRET
PASSED BY CENSOR
No 3743

ISBN (NZ) 978-0-473-46302-1

FIRST EDITION

Published in 2018 by IngramSpark.
Additionally published as an e-book by IngramSpark
Contact
www.ingramspark.com
for special orders

Author's website
www.bestbooks.gifts

Cover and book design by
Timely Marketing & Promotions Limited
Christchurch - New Zealand

FIELD SERVICE
TOP SECRET
PASSED BY CENSOR
No 3743

Acknowledgements

To my wife Jane, and my children Carla, Duncan, and Samantha, for their patience in putting up with my literary wanderings; and to other friends Al Lester, Dave Findlay, Nickita Dobia, Smithy and Robert Polaschek for their encouragement and valuable input.

I also acknowledge all sources and contributors of photos and historic material including those from public domain sources and collections; the collections of The Seeds of Time, Fort Augustus, the D and S McInnes Historic Collections; and numerous others.

WW1 British War Medals

*Special limited issue collector stamps featured in this book
can be obtained at a special price from the
Chatham Islands Postal Service,
via the author,
by contacting
grandadmcinnes@gmail.com*

FIELD SERVICE
TOP SECRET
PASSED BY CENSOR
No 3743

Preface

It had been during the early months of the Great War of 1914-1918 that Commander Mansfield Smith-Cumming as head of Britain's Foreign Secret Service Bureau (SSB), (later known as MI6), employed a young female operative from Marseille, France.

At that time Smith-Cumming had additionally come to rely on Lieutenant Sidney George Reilly, MC, who would later be famously known as the 'Ace of Spies'. Reilly was a Jewish Russian-born adventurer and secret agent of dubious character who had been based in Saint Petersburg. He had been employed by both Scotland Yard and the SSB, although he is alleged to have spied for at least four nations. After Reilly's death in 1925, the London Evening Standard published a Master Spy serial in May 1931 imparting his exploits. Later, Ian Fleming would supposedly use Reilly as his model for James Bond, and in his account of Operation JB in WW2.

It has to be wondered, however, if the young Marseille prostitute, and MI6 operative, was not that inspiration. Named Jehanne Blanche, her pseudonym was 'Jane Blonde', a nickname given to her by Royal Navy sailors after their ship *HMS Blonde*. Perhaps, given the chauvinism of the age, a male entity was used by Fleming in her stead? Whatever the truth, the history of that age and the story of an 'Amulet' would bring Jehanne in contact with her true self, along with shaping the destinies of Acting Corporal Arthur Edgar Newcombe - 2/10th Battalion Middlesex Regiment, and the Ottoman mehmet and Moslem, Ahmed-oğlu Abdullah.

This tale, therefore, includes elements of the little known history and the activities of the British Intelligence Services during the Great War of 1914-18. It pertains to the pre-war discovery of an ancient amulet that impacted on the lives of several individuals, who, but for its recovery, would have more than likely gone completely unnoticed during that great conflict.

The story additionally covers military activity in what was then the Ottoman Empire - at Gallipoli, in Mesopotamia, in Egypt and the Sinai, and in what we know today as Palestine. As such it includes the unfortunate set of circumstances that became the foundation of the current ongoing Palestinian / Israeli conflict. A place where the use of power, politics and particularly religion continue to play their part to gain control over the land at the expense of the legitimate indigenous people and their promised self determination.

Clinton mhic Aonghais

Part I

Who led you through the great and terrifying wilderness, with its fiery serpents and scorpions and thirsty ground where there was no water, who brought you water out of the flinty rock, who fed you in the wilderness with manna that your fathers did not know, that he might humble you and test you, to do you good in the end.

(Deuteronomy 8:15-16 ESV)

The depths of the Sinai Desert with it's bare brownish rock masses, endless wastes of yellow and gray sands, sand storms, searing temperatures and scarcity of water, made it a foreboding place. Normally at night the only sounds heard that break it's monotony are the barks and howls of it's nocturnal children, the jackal and the hyena. This night, however, thrashing on its sands under a clear sky a young boy convulsed in the spasms of an epileptic fit while Bedouin who he was travelling with looked on in amazement and fear.

The Dead Sea

Foaming around his sand encrusted mouth, with eyes as wild as the hyena in the light from their night's fire, the boy lashed out uncontrollably in his contortions. This violent episode was spell binding and continued in severity until finally, with arched back and heels dug into the sand, the boy momentarily stared wild-eyed and rigid to the heavens before collapsing motionless.

To his entrusted Bedouin caregivers, who looked on from a perceived safe distance, he was being possessed by demons. Perhaps he was transforming into a *nasnas*, believed to be the offspring of a demon called a *Shiqq*, being half a human being; having half a head, half a body, one arm, one leg, with which it hops with much agility. The other unequally unsavoury possibility was that he was a *ghoul*; a  desert-dwelling, shape-shifting, demon that could assume the guise of an animal. This was especially true of a hyena, as his wild eyes had suggested, and that he was attempting to lure them further into the desert's endless burning wastes to slay and devour them. Very much aware that these creatures also preyed on young children, robbed graves, drank blood, and ate the dead to take on the form of the one they had just eaten, they wanted no association with one. Not of their making, and terrified at what they had witnessed, they would leave the boy where he lay out of fear that he would bring ruin to their tribe. Hurriedly packing up their tent and meagre belongings they loaded their three scrawny camels, and after leaving a small calabash of water as close to the boy as they dared, they quickly moved on.

By late afternoon wind-blown sand had already begun to build itself up in the folds of the boy's dirty thawb, along with partially covering half of a small amulet suspended on a rawhide thong that had fallen from his garments. The amulet's design incorporated a tubular pillar of ivory, fitted below the bronze effigy of a frog, above which was a worn open half crescent.

Born in the year 570 AD at Mecca the boy had been given to the Bedouin to teach him the ways of the desert. He was the son of Abdallah of the family of Hashim; and of Amina of the family of Zuhra, both from the powerful Arab tribe of the Quraysh, but of a side branch only, and therefore of little or no consequence.

His name was Mohammed…

The wastes of the Sinai Desert

Long, long ago, in a time that inspired mystical thought, a nomadic desert-dwelling Arabian tribal people had formed an impression of a Godhead that was manifest in their term *Ein Sof.* This was a place to which forgetting and oblivion pertained. It was a place where nothing could be said at all, and no thought could reach; where nothing could be known of it, for it was hidden and concealed in the mystery of absolute nothingness.

Millennia later, in an attempt to transcend these depths and the mystery of life, a Bedouin sage had stared trance-like, yet thoughtfully, at the heavens. He perceived of a being who could interpenetrate that outer universe of nothingness, and in so doing, he pondered that such a being had to be a manifestation of a God.

Logically, if this was so, then all existence must emanate from this God, with the entity's ultimate existence not dependent on anything else, or any other God. He concluded that this God had to be the absolute being, indivisible and incomparable, who was the ultimate cause of all existence. As the heavens were always changing he must also be eternal; the creator of the universe, and the source of morality that must also control the 'jinn', or spirits, who had been placed on earth to test mankind.

Whilst logical rational thought had led him to this conclusion, the implication concerning *Ein Sof,* where no thought could reach, was a revelation. This entity, as the divine origin of all created existence, had demonstrated his power to intervene in the mortal world through his thoughts. In this moment of enlightened clarity he knew that he, personally, must be divinely special in receiving this knowledge and message. Having been gifted this wisdom the sage then realised he needed to communicate it, along with any future revelation, or messages, to his people.

This one omnipotent God would be named 'Jehovah', and it would be the word of Jehovah, through him, that would guide his tribe. Being selected to receive divine enlightenment his people would consider that they were consequently divinely special. Within a short time the term 'Jehovah' had become an actual philosophic reality; not merely a projection of the sage's human psyche. As the singular God almighty, this entity communicated through the sage, as a prophet and intermediary, to God's 'chosen people'.

This original enlightened desert-dwelling Bedouin tribe with their single God, or monotheist religion, would be known as the Shasu of Yhw. Having emerged out of the Sinai Desert to begin pastoral farming in the Negev they inhabited part of the land known as Canaan. They were to develop into a Semitic Hebrew-speaking people who would later evolve as the Israelites. As Jews and Samaritans they would inhabit the territories of Judea and Galilee, and Samaria respectively. Then, during their monarchic period, their states of Israel and Judah would become related Iron Age kingdoms as part of an ancient Levant.

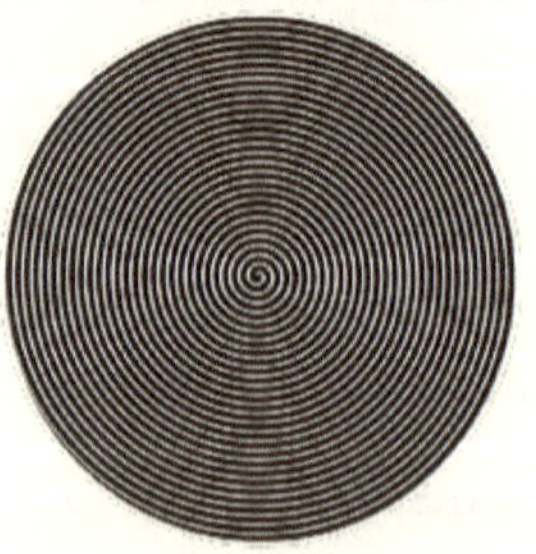

Is an end ever finite…?

Aged and almost completely bald, with a narrow remaining fringe at his temples the pharaoh Merneptah was fourth ruler of the XIX Dynasty of Ancient Egypt. His reign would extend for almost 10 years between early August 1213 BC and May 1203 BC. Whilst his appearance resembled that of his grandfather, Seti the Great, there the similarity ended; for Merneptah was a great believer in eternal life and in the coming of a future prophet that had been foretold in Arab legend.

Appearing in Egyptian hieroglyphs on a 1209 BC stone of Merneptah's is a brief inscription that reads…

Israel is laid waste but its seed is not…

During his conquering of the land to the north of Egypt, called Israel, Merneptah would visit and stay in the city that lay between the Mediterranean and the Dead Sea. It was known by its Babylonian name as Uru-Salim, 'the city of Salim'; shortened into Salem in the inscriptions of Merneptah's father, Ramses II. At that time it was the capital of an Egyptian vassal city-state that had existed for a number of generations; a modest settlement governing a few outlying villages and pastoral areas, with a small Egyptian garrison, and ruled by appointees under an appointed king.

In the time of Merneptah's father, and that of his grandfather before him, major construction had taken place in the city, and its prosperity had increased. Then following a visit from Merneptah he had presented the people with an amulet that exulted everlasting life and the foretelling of a future prophet. Shortly after he had bid the city good fortune, and returned to Egypt, the true message of the amulet started to fade from the consciousness of the people. Then with the construction of the First Temple on the Mount in Uru-Salim, by King Solomon, some 250 years later in 957 BC, the amulet would be placed under a stone in front of its alter to symbolise the importance of peace and the imbuing of goodwill on this Holy city.

The following century the Kingdom of Israel again emerged as an important local power before it fell to the Assyrian Empire, in 722 BC. Israel's southern neighbour, the Kingdom of Judah, in which Uru-Salim, or rather Jerusalem, resided with Solomon's Temple, had emerged to enjoy a period of prosperity as a client-state of first Assyria, and then Babylon. With each kingdom's rise and decline the people had taken, and continued to adapt, known myths and legends into their developing monotheist faith. By the 6th century BC, these were being employed as an ideal form of fanatical patriotism that dominated all their lives.

Hear O Israel, the Lord is our God, the Lord is One…

By now the narrow formalism of the Temple priests in Jerusalem, from the Jewish priestly families and orders of Kohanim and the Levites, had built a religious wall around the people inside which they now controlled communications with Jehovah. Accordingly it had also secured their wealth and comfortable lifestyle, where independence had been replaced by a fanatical belief that theirs was the 'Promised Land.' Used as a divine promise by the resolute energy of a theocratic party it now formed an integral part of their religion, philosophy, and way of life for the Jewish people.

In reality it was little more than part of a carefully cultivated form of insidious subjection to tie the people to that faith by not wanting them to express their own independence with freedom of thought. Extolling, in the name of Jehovah. *that any that were not with them, were against them,* they employed the fear of being caste out of their society as a form of control. As an ideal form of patriotism in fervently believing to be God's 'chosen people', few did; consequently following the required ritual of circumcision and other dogma of the priests. Carried to the extreme with their hatred of the stranger it was, in reality, a society that observed 'intolerance towards others' as its bi-line. Independent that all from the Levant generally were of the same blood originally, it was now not where one was born that was important, but rather their perceived superior moral links as Jews, along with their believed monopoly on being able to communicate with God as his 'chosen few', that set them apart. It had them believing that morally and philosophically they were superior to others, and it was to be their downfall.

Known as Judaism it is still the religious expression of a covenantal relationship established between their Jehovah, as God, and those they refer to as the 'Children of Israel'.

Solomon's Temple

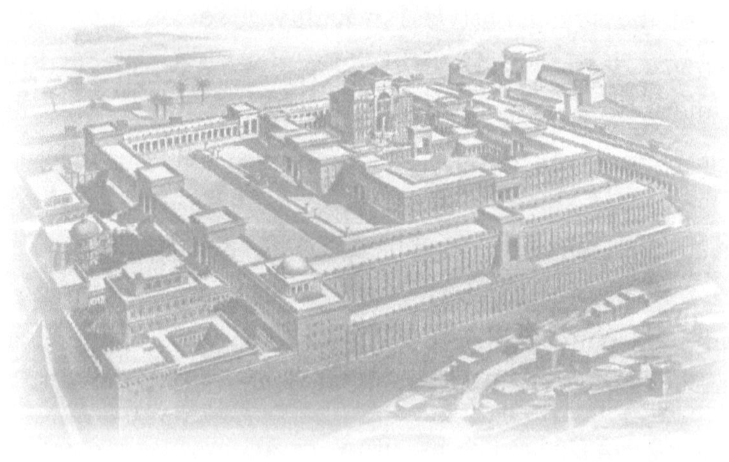

Depiction of Solomon's Temple – The First Temple on the Mount

Built between the Euphrates and Tigris Rivers in central Mesopotamia over a millennium earlier was the city of Babylon. Initially divided in equal parts along the Euphrates left and right banks, with steep embankments to contain the river's seasonal floods, it had sprung up from a small town that had flourished attaining independence with the rise of the First Amorite Babylonian Dynasty in 1894 BC. Claiming to be the successor of the ancient city of Eridu, Babylon had eclipsed Nippur as the 'Holy city' of Mesopotamia around the time an Amorite king named Hammurabi created the first short lived Babylonian Empire. This had quickly dissolved upon his death with Babylon then spending long periods under Kassite, Elamite and Assyrian domination.

In alliance with others, and under the Chaldean king Nabopolassar, Babylon eventually threw off Assyrian rule, destroying the Assyrian Empire between 620 and 605 BC.

The city that was Babylon

In so doing the city became the capital of a new Neo-Babylonian Empire. With its new found independence a new era of architectural activity would ensue with Nabopolassar's son making the city into one of the wonders of the ancient world, with the creation of the Hanging Gardens of Babylon. These gardens he supposedly built for his homesick wife Amyitis, evidently to remind her of her homeland of Medis in Persia.

The biblical 'Book of Jeremiah' contains a prophecy about the arising of a 'Destroyer of Nations' commonly regarded as a reference to that son, Nebuchadnezzar II. As king of the Neo-Babylonian Empire his reign would extend from c. 605 BC to 562 BC.

His Akkadian name was Nabûkudurri-uṣur, meaning '*O god Nabu defend my first born son*'.

Nabu was the Babylonian deity of wisdom, son of the god Marduk, and so Nebuchadnezzar II styled himself as Nabu's 'beloved' and 'favourite'. He would, however, be known to his troops as Bakhat Nasar, or 'Winner of the Fate'. For the Hebrews he would be recorded in their Old Testament Book of Isaiah as 'Helel ben Shahar', the shining one, son of the dawn. He was thus, Helel - 'son of the morning star' and he would conquer Judah and Jerusalem destroying its First Temple and sending the Jews into exile; but this is getting ahead in our story.

With the exuberance of youth, inthe fourth year of his reign, Nebuchadnezzar II engaged in several military campaigns designed to increase Babylonian influence in Aramea and Judah. His attempted invasion of Egypt in 601 BC was, however, repulsed with heavy losses that lead to numerous rebellions among the Phoenician and Canaanite states of the Levant, including Judah, which owed allegiance to Babylon. Thinking Nebuchadnezzar weak Jehoiakim, the King of Judah, along with his Temple priests, then badly misread the fall of the cards. In a game of life and death they had seen an opportunity to stop paying their required tribute to Babylon, and in siding with Egypt. Jehoiakim was to discover, however, that when he needed support from his new found allies that it was non-existent.

A Babylonian soldier

Nebuchadnezzar would deal with these rebellions by invading the Syrian / Palestinian lands of old Aramea, and then in 598 BC, in focusing on taking the city of Judah, namely Jerusalem.

His initial move in achieving this end was in sending assassins to kill the king. Not comprehending the danger he was in the leering expression of a Babylonian emissary's face in front of Jehoiakim would be the last earthly sign from Jehovah that he would witness, as behind him a well muscled soldier slashed downwards. The choreographed move of the glinting curved heavy scimitar struck the nape of the King of Judah's neck biting in deep, cutting to his breast bone. In an instant of realisation Jehoiakim faced nothingness before his body slumped to the ground in a gathering pool of his own blood. His mortal remains were gathered up quickly and thrown down to the dogs outside from the walls of the city.

Reporting back on their success, Nebuchadnezzar followed up by ordering that Jerusalem be placed under siege. Its capture early in the month of Adar, 597 BC, was, as it eventuated straight forward, along with capturing Jehoiakim's son, Jeconiah, who had only ruled for three months and 10 days. To complete the subjection the 18 year old Jeconiah along with his entire household, and 3000 Jews, were then exiled to Babylon.

Thinking this would solve his woes Nebuchadnezzar replaced the deposed son Jeconiah with his 21 year old uncle, Zedekiah, as tributary king of Judah, before continuing his campaigning further north. Zedekiah had exuded sympathetic peace-loving promises, however, no sooner had Nebuchadnezzar departed than he too revolted against Babylon, adding fuel to an already mounting fire by likewise entering into an alliance with Pharaoh Hophra, king of Egypt. Insurrection against Babylon and others on the land, instigated again by the Temple priests and ardent Jews against those they considered to be foreigners on their 'Promised Land', started to spread once more.

Later that year and enraged Nebuchadnezzar decided to draw a line in the sand having had enough over the continuing Jewish revolts. It was simply deliberate trouble and insurrection that continued to be instigated by a fanatical narrow minded people with an over inflated opinion of their own importance.

He had left these states with their own faith, and to their own devices, so long as they paid their required tribute. Not paying was bad enough, but in deviously conspiring with the Egyptians at his expense, and for the second time, along with continued revolt, was the final straw. This arrogant manipulative people would understand once and for all what 'intolerance of others' really meant. As the 'Destroyer of Nations' he would happily respond by invading and laying waste all of Judah, and in then applying pressure by laying siege to Jerusalem for as long as it took. He would not now be denied in delivering complete justice.

The exodus from Jerusalem

Let this be lesson to others that Helel, 'The Morning Star'... if that is what they now call me... will not tolerate treachery and intolerance. By the morning of the beginning of the month of Marduk, with the morning star's rising, all I want to see is flames and smoke!

Jerusalem was to be plundered with Solomon's Temple destroyed. The city was to be razed to the ground to put an end to the matter, and in sending a clear and unequivocal message. Most of the elite would also be taken into captivity. Along with the now blind Zedekiah they would be marched to Babylon where Zedekiah would remain a prisoner until his death.

For any I deem to spare they can reflect on what their religion has delivered them.

In January 589 BC, after a campaign on the land, the second siege on Jerusalem began, and after 30 months it was said that, *every worst woe befell the city, which drank the cup of God's fury to the dregs*.

A depiction of Nebuchadnezzar II

The siege continued while the resources of the people inside the city dwindled. Famine prevailed for those within its walls with no bread either for the people of the land. By the 11th year of Zedekiah's reign, in early 587 BC, with their walls hard pressed, the resoluteness of the survivors, now clawing at each other for food and water, began to break. With the greater part of Nebuchadnezzar's army still based further northeast at Riblah on the eastern boundary of Israel, inside the city, King Zedekiah decided, again unwisely, to escape with his forces. In so doing he would leave his people undefended to their own limited resources. With little thought for the thousands of starving women and children he was forsaking, the tributary king of Judah turned his back on the city to melt into the darkness via a gate at the end of the King's Garden.

As he stole off into the night he justified his action to himself.

Jehovah would look after them... After all they were his chosen people and he would surely not allow their demise.

Zedekiah's attempt at escape would be a lost cause for at the highest point of the sun he, along with his attendant army, was discovered on the plains of Jericho. Pursued by Babylonian troops they were overtaken and either killed or spread fleeing to the four winds. Zedekiah along with his sons were taken before Nebuchadnezzar at his headquarters at Riblah in the land of Hamath on the great road between Babylon and Palestine. Still smouldering over the second betrayal, and now Zedekiah's cowardice, Nebuchadnezzar looked into his dark brown eyes, and all he saw was uncertainty and fear.

This is no king to respect...! This is a self-seeking politician exploiting his people as some form of self appointed superior being based on religious decree.

After seeing his sons killed, Zedekiah was blinded, and bound, while Nebuchadnezzar's troops were once again on the move. With the fall of the city of Jerusalem the Babylonian General Nebuzaraddan was sent in to complete its destruction.

Tear down the walls; kill all remaining guards, the weak and especially the priests and their families; and round up those strong enough to walk and place them in slavery. Bring before me any other community leaders along with the spoils from the Temple, and then raise it and the city to the ground.

Pain and fury welled up inside the core of the High Priest's soul as he prostrated himself on the stone steps in front of the Temple on the Mount. Flames were starting to spread throughout its cedar structure and adornments as he continued to exalt Jehovah to strike retribution on the offenders. In not getting any heavenly or even earthly response, and no longer rationale, he exchanged his faith in Jehovah for spitting and screaming invective at any Babylonian soldier who was close by. Soldiers continued to herd any survivors into slavery, and carrying off spoils from the Temple, as flickering tentacles of flame extended skyward in the smoke and early morning light.

The destruction of Jersusalem

Babylon

For the High Priest his Temple and his income were no more. Reflected in the light of the mounting conflagration, with eyes as wild as a jackal and spittle running down his chin, his soul filled with a black hatred. He watched as a soldier made his way down the steps close to him with a number of King Solomon's gold plates and an amulet, that unbeknown to him, had been discovered under a flagstone at the Temple's altar. Without thought the priest seized his moment while the soldier's arms were full. Blinded with rage and solely focused on his target with the small dagger he had drawn, he failed to notice a soldier to his rear. With the dagger raised skyward the bronze spear tip that exited his diaphragm at his front was a revelation in retribution, but not the one he had anticipated. With mouth gaping in a silent message, he collapsed to roll down the steps dead; where his blood would flow to meet the congealing mass of others of his faith.

History tells us that after tearing down Jerusalem's walls and receiving rich tribute, Nebuchadnezzar set forth for Babylon with all remaining captured prominent citizens and craftsmen. Along with them was a sizable portion of the Jewish population of Judah, numbering around 10,000, who were all under pain of death if they did not comply. As Nebuchadnezzar had determined… *If they had time on their hands to rebel then perhaps their energies would be better employed working for him where he could keep an eye on them.*

Only a small number of people were permitted to remain to tend to the land, with Gedaliah made Governor over this remnant of Judah. Now as a Babylonian administrative division named the Yehud Province, it had a guard stationed at Mizpah.

This major Jewish diaspora, or historical exile and dispersion of

Jews from the region of the Kingdom of Judah, was not the first and it would not be the last. Having seen the writing on the wall prior to the destruction of Jerusalem, groups of more perceptive Jews had previously fled.

One group had migrated to Egypt where they had settled on the Nile delta; while another had fled via the Hejaz to settle in Mecca. Another large number would become mercenaries on an island called the Elephantine in Upper Egypt.

On hearing the news of the fall of the city Jews who had fled to Ammon in Moab, and other surrounding areas, now slowly returned to Judah. This land, however, would again be quickly depopulated after Gedaliah's assassination, and then after another unsuccessful revolt five years later. The few who remained, along with those who had returned, now fled to Egypt for safety.

Among those enslaved at Babylon was Ezekiel, the author of the biblical Book of Daniel, who wrote that, *none remained except the poorest people of the land.* Also taken were the treasures and furnishings of the king Solomon's Temple, the First Temple of the Mount at Jerusalem. Included were golden vessels dedicated by King Solomon, and the amulet.

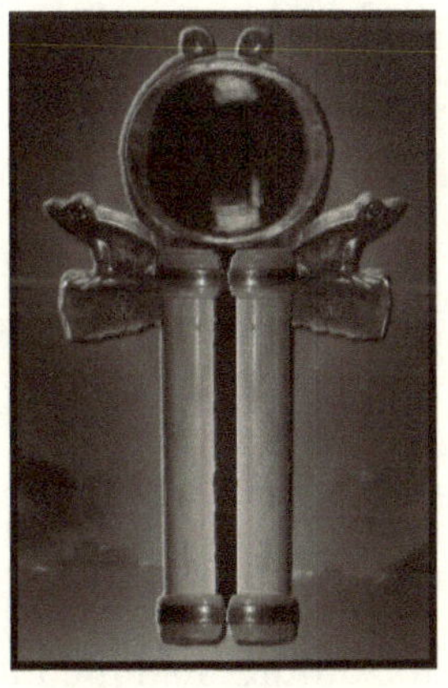

The Amulet

Once cleaned the amulet was presented to Nebuchadnezzar for his pleasure, and in the process of cleaning it had taken on a mystical quality. At the top of its bronze frame its central red jewel now transmitted a dull glow from it's elusive depths, while on either

31

side outward facing frog effigies guarded it above twin pillars of ivory. It was an unusual piece with two small identical etched symbols on each side on the rear of its frame that figuratively depicted the amulet's overall design. It looked to Nebuchadnezzar as though it was Egyptian in design and craftsmanship and he wondered what significance it held for the Jews. He decided to keep it before making up his mind what he would do with it.

Having completed the subjugation of Phoenicia and a further campaign against Egypt, with more slaves in tow Nebuchadnezzar set about continuing to rebuild and adorn Babylon. Undeterred he continued his father's work of reconstruction, aiming at making his capital one of the world's wonders. Other than the Hanging Gardens new edifices of incredible magnificence were erected to the many Gods of the Babylonian pantheon, and in completing his royal palace. Nothing was spared and naturally these undertakings, along with many others, required a considerable number of labourers. An inscription at the great temple of Marduk records that the labouring force used for the construction of these royal and public works was made up of captives brought from various parts of western Asia. Included were the Jews that Nebuchadnezzar had allowed to remain as a unified community in Babylon.

To Nebuchadnezzar, favoured of his God Nabu the son of Marduk, the amulet had meant little also and after a time he had bequeathed it back to the new Jewish leaders in Mesopotamia as a gesture of goodwill. Whilst they were slaves helping to build the grandeur that was Babylon he considered it wise to allow them their own faith and organisation; or at least to live freely while keeping a wary eye on them.

Unbeknown to Nebuchadnezzar the amulet held no special significance for the Jews either. No mythical, legendary or religious accounts or dogma had ever been mentioned by their Hebrew prophet Ezekiel in reference to it. They had kept it for a period all the same; that was until a renewed desire for wealth got the better on them.

Removing the amulet's central jewel from its frame they had sold it to a traveller from the west, to be richly rewarded. In so doing they established that the amulet frame came apart in two halves; each opposing the other with a half-crescent jewel frame, a bronze frog, and an ivory pillar. After the sale of the jewel, not seeing any importance in the frames, they simply caste them aside.

An Arab merchant caravan

Inscribed on a clay cylinder, dedicated to the chief Babylonian God Marduk and discovered in the foundations of the Esagila temple in Babylon, is the statement…

King of Babylon, King of Sumer and Akkad, King of the four corners of the world.

Today this artefact it is known as the 'Cyrus Cylinder' and its inscription refers to the rule of Cyrus the Persian.

After conquering the Babylonian empire in 540 BC, Cyrus had permitted Babylon's Judean descendants to return to their homeland. Many, however, had chosen to remain, retaining their religion, identity, holy artefacts, and social customs. Under both the Persians and Greeks, they had been allowed to conduct their lives according to their own laws. If they regretted the earlier destruction of Jerusalem it had been on account of the loss of the Temple.

What happened to Solomon's golden plates is unknown, however, it would be during this period of excavation that one half of the amulet came to light. The other was still buried somewhere within the city. Still holding no significance to the Jews this discovered half was eventually traded to an Arab merchant from the south. With the few silver shekels they received, Babylon's Jewish community were happy with the outcome. For the old Arab who had purchased it, he certainly was, for he had a suspicion that this was a piece of an amulet that was foretold in ancient Arab legend.

The demand for scents and incense by the empires of antiquity, such as Egypt, Rome and Babylon, made Arabia one of the oldest of all the trading lands of the ancient world. Controlled by the Arabs, the 'Incense Route' that brought frankincense and myrrh by camel caravan from South Arabia, enabled the villages, towns, and cities along the route, to grow rich providing services to merchants who rested at their oasis. They also served as international market places and

An Arab merchant

areas where knowledge was naturally exchanged and prophets extolled their beliefs.

Other than new inventions, artistic styles, religious faiths, cultures, languages, and social customs, in particular valued goods were transported for sale and exchange. One such object was the half amulet that had been transported south from Babylon sometime around 535 BC. How it came to pass that it found its way as far south to Mecca is a mystery. To the Hassimite family of the Quraysh, however, they would consider it destiny, for they knew it as part of an ancient sacred item that contained a divine message. As such they would hand it down through the generations, carefully adding their genealogy to it; that was until Mohammed bin Abdallah had lost it in the sands of the Sinai.

Arab merchants with their camels

The deserts of the Sinai do not generally grant wishes with many having disappeared into its strange and dangerous expanse. As a monument to the antiquity of life on earth, this triangular peninsular situated between the Mediterranean Sea to the north, and the Red Sea to the south, encompasses about 23,000 sq miles in area. As a vast mountainous desert historically traversing time, in its huge silence and solitude the simple presence of a human seems out of place. Yet over the millennia this long untamed land

has been frequented by nomads, hermits, prophets, saints, miners, slaves, soldiers and warriors.

Mohammed stumbles on

Appearing out of its shimmering haze, stumbled the form of Mohammed. Having recovered from his fit, and discovering he had been left by his Bedouin companions, he had lifted the calabash of water to his lips, shaken out his sand impregnated thawb and looked to the heavens. Taking his bearing by the stars he would stagger on. During the day sand blew growling in the distance, endlessly whirling, shifting and gathering. In the shade of the mountains and ravines it was bright enough to walk. With the sun not up for very long in any wadi they were the cooler paths to travel, but not a place to camp. Even with no clouds visible Mohammed was aware that each drained as much as a hundred square miles of desert during the wet season. As such they could deliver a wall of water that could barrel down upon the unsuspecting at any moment.

At night with the light from the heavens, with no sign of life, or the prospect of an oasis in sight, he began to climb. Onwards and ever upward to where his view of the surrounding desert would be the greatest. From the interface between land and sky, on the heights above the mountainous Sinai desert, the unimaginable canopy of the heavens took on a brighter appearance. Seated cross legged on

the edge of eternity the stillness of his surroundings was contrasted by the shooting stars that could be clearly seen every few minutes. The spiritually inspiring majesty of the firmament was Allah's domain that Mohammed knew he was part of. The more he stared skyward the more he was drawn towards its infinity. In an instant of self realisation his inner demons were at rest and he was at peace. Bigger than any dream he knew he was being summoned by Allah to be a prophet for his people.

Following in the steps of the son of Abdallah of the family of Hashim, the Sinai would be the path by which a contemporary of Mohammed would sweep down into Egypt 55 years later. He would be the Arab military commander Amr ibn al-`As, leading the conquest of Egypt in 640 AD, bringing Islam in his wake.

Even after this Moslem conquest, made with Mohammed's blessing, *Peace by Upon Him ...*, the monks of St. Catherine Monastery in the Sinai, founded in 547 AD, would be permitted to continue to greet pilgrims to the purported site of the Burning Bush. Tourism would be allowed to continue to flourish across the region, along with wealth also flowing into Mecca.

After the eventual fall of Babylon those 1000 years earlier it's lands had come under various rules, with the last extending from the end of the Roman Empire's crisis of the third century AD. Considered to have been one of Persia's most important and influential historical periods, it constituted the last great Iranian empire before the Moslem conquest, and the adoption of the Islamic faith that started in the mid 7th century with the settling of Islamic Arabs. These early Moslems had continued looking for both halves of the amulet that was sacred to them, and that they were hopeful still existed.

Having scoured all towns on the trail north from Mecca, including Petra and its surrounding Bedouin area, their endeavours would be just as unsuccessful as they had been in attempting to find Mohammed's lost piece in the Sinai.

The Sinai's wastes

FIELD SERVICE
TOP SECRET
PASSED BY CENSOR
No 3743

Part II

Jehanne Blanche

Jehanne Blanche was an attractive French girl who had grown up on the streets of Marseille, France, becoming involved in prostitution at a young age. At the turn of the century in 1900, Marseille's criminal activity lay chiefly in trafficking. Alongside local trafficking, international smuggling had developed in the 1880s and '90s with ringleaders able to exploit the port of Marseille's role as an interface. The most representative activity during this period was the trafficking of women to guarantee local and international establishments a regular supply of prostitutes.

A card promoting the girls of Marseille

These developments met initially with a strong reaction on the part of the public authorities. Dubbed the 'Chicago of France' by the French Press there had, however, been a growing disharmony between the local Marseille Police and Police de la Sûreté. This disharmony had been over the management of crime in the port city. It created an antagonistic culture fuelled by Police absenteeism, working conditions, and particularly the surveillance of foreign nationals over who should be reporting on them.

This was especially true of those involved in suspicious dealings in the sleazier quarters of the city and the attitude was not helping solve the 'white slave trade', particularly to North Africa and further East.

The 'Yellow Book' was a guide to the restricted quarter in Marseille filled with listings and details about 'les maisons closes' (whore-houses) and including photos of ladies hooking on the street.

It was published circa 1915 for 'tourists and visitors' to France's notorious southern seaport city.

Jehanne Blanche

Tied alongside a wharf in Marseille harbour displaying her reverse raking ram bow, the 400 feet length of the Royal Navy's Boadicea class, twin-screw, cruiser *HMS Blonde* was an impressive sight. With a complement of 315, and a top speed of 26 knots, she was every bit a support 'scout' for the destroyers that had recently become sea-going ships capable of escorting the fleet at sea. She had been sent to the Mediterranean as the senior officer's ship of the Seventh Flotilla, and her crew would frequent Marseille in 1911-1912.

HMS Blonde

Laid down in Pembroke Dockyard, and launched on 22nd July 1910, *HMS Blonde* had been completed a year later, around the time that Jehanne Blanche had also been laid down, losing her virginity at the tender age of 15.

In the same month as HMS Blonde had arrived it was reported in The Hague that brothels were to be banned nationwide in the Netherlands. Their parliament had voted in favour of a bill submitted by the Christian cabinet of Prime Minister Theo Heemskerk. The Social democratic opposition had additionally supported the bill even though they did not believe it would have any effect on prostitution. The party simply wanted to end the exploitation of women working in brothels. The Social Democrats believed that these women would be better off as independent 'window prostitutes'. It would be a ruling that would motivate another aspiring young Dutch woman, and spy, who would be later known as Mata Hari.

Prostitutes pose for a teaser photograph

Standing on one of Marseille's wharves Jehanne Blanche looked up at *HMS Blonde's* four funnels and clean lines, along with a number of the ship's crew on deck who hungrily looked back at her. With her soft olive complexion, part Sudanese blood line, and standing a little over 5' 10' with long blonde hair, and piercing

Teaser picture of Jehanne Blanche - Marseille

dark hazel eyes, Jehanne, or Jane in English, was strikingly attractive. Her loose fitting white dress revealed an ample, full and firm young bosom that from above had the sailors entranced. One of them on guard at the gangway called down to her....

Hey sweetie, how about you and me get hooked up when I get off on leave later this evening...?

It was as much a taunt in front of other young crew members than a serious proposal, and any reply was cut short by one of the ship's Lieutenant's appearing with a stern look of disapproval.

Looking up Jehanne reflected on how she had come to be standing at the bottom of a Royal Navy destroyer's gangway at the request of the ship's Intelligence Officer.

Marseille fashion advert

He had been under orders from the Admiralty to make enquiries and secure the services of a presentable, trustworthy, and street-wise working girl who could be of assistance to the ship. Initially wary, Jehanne had become that candidate, and was now employed, on an hourly retainer, conducting a confidential exercise in intelligence gathering. Her role was to report on the activities of the ship's sailors and officers while in port, along with any other untoward activity, or foreign visitors of dubious character, who may be associating with the crew.

As for the ship's crew, they did not know Jehanne's true role other than it had something to do with the senior officers on the ship. After a week of her visits, however, they had discovered her name through the ship's 'grape vine', and they had nick-named her 'Jane Blonde'. For them the name was an obvious one lines based on their ship's name given her blonde hair; likewise her attractive lines and that their sister ship's name, *HMS Blanche,* coincidently matched Jehanne's surname.

By 1913 both *HMS Blonde* and *HMS Blanche* may have already been at least 2.9 mph slower than the majority of destroyers, but that would not be the case with Jehanne as far as Mansfield Smith-

Jehanne Blanche

Below - The port of Marselle

When Commander Mansfield Smith-Cumming received his summons from the Admiralty in 1909 to head the new British Secret Service Bureau, (SSB), he had been testing sea boom defences at Southampton. Having retired from active naval service because of severe sea-sickness, this short, stumpy, 50 year old figure had an eagle eye that glared piercingly through a gold-rimmed monocle dominating his small, stern, mouth, and receding chin. He spoke no foreign languages, had spent the past 10 years languishing in obscurity, and seemed, at first appearance, an unlikely candidate for the job. Given a modest budget and a tiny office within a few years, however, he had firmly established his part in Britain's Secret Intelligence Service. Spreading a network of officers and agents to gather intelligence, and promote Britain's interests overseas by the most appropriate means necessary, he was now head of what would become MI6.

Captain Sir Mansfield Smith-Cumming

Forced to live a nomadic existence in its formative years, Smith-Cumming's Bureau Foreign Section would move twice before settling in a flat at the top of No. 2 Whitehall Court, close to its masters at the Admiralty, and to the Foreign and the War Offices. The building it was in was a regular maze of passages and steps with oddly shaped rooms, and was reached from an entrance hall by a private lift. The great unwashed who lived on the lower floors didn't realise the 'Bureau' above them even existed. For the few in government, or outside, who were privy to the secret work being conducted, they were aware that those who worked there were referred to by Smith-Cummings as his 'top mates', and that his agents, or operatives, he affectionately referred to as 'scallywags'.

Whitehall Court

From the outset, even though budgets were severely limited, Smith-Cumming had set about recruiting officers. They included the writers Somerset Maugham and Compton Mackenzie who, along with others, continued to sally forth in elaborate disguises, always armed with a swordstick, as a walking stick that pulled apart to reveal a rapier. But Smith-Cumming wasn't given funds for full time agents, scraping up only enough 'casuals' for piece work. With the balance of the Bureau's slender resources required to be directed entirely at Germany there would, however, be successes with these operatives, or spies, gathering important intelligence on German warships, zeppelins, and arms production.

Even obliged to go on missions personally, disguised and armed with the obligatory swordstick, Mansfield enthusiastically informed his newest operative, Compton Mackenzie, that.... *Spying was 'capital sport.*

Mansfield Smith-Cumming (right) meeting with several of his Royal Navy associates

As if in confirmation of his enthusiasm for disguise he kept a photograph of a heavily built individual in unmistakably German clothes' on his desk, and was exceedingly pleased when visitors failed to recognise that it was a picture of him.

Still under development, new initiatives were being tested by Mansfield Smith- Cumming who was always thinking of possibilities to counter a potential threat. Then when the SSB discovered that semen made a good invisible ink his agents adopted the motto…

Every man has his own stylo.

Also witnessing SSB's Home Section's use of teenage Girl Guides as couriers, it had not taken Mansfield long to astutely deduce that more sexually aware young ladies, with the right promiscuous qualities, might be a distinct advantage to the SSB. Testing his theory with Jehanne's unusual combination of talents he now had the Naval Intelligence Report from the Mediterranean Fleet before him regarding her activities. It confirmed the inkling of an idea that had begun to form in his ever active mind some months prior. This attractive female, with now proven initiative, and a liking for sexual freedom, could be groomed as a secret foreign operative. It would give Britain an ideal secret weapon to be employed on the unsuspecting; in times of war, or peace.

Prior to visiting Marseille to make Jehanne a formal offer Mansfield had secretly completed his background checks. He had discovered that Jehanne Blanche in reality had a British father of some standing who had enjoyed time in France in the 1890's as a British diplomat, and that she was oblivious to his identity. The fact that she was an only child, and that her father was still alive with a substantial estate, was retained information.

On her maternal side he had ascertained that her mother had been French with her grandmother, on her mother's side, Sudanese. Both were from respectable backgrounds.

With the dexterity of the diplomat Mansfield met with Jehanne. He informed her of her father, and that he had previously been in his employ, however, that he had been

killed at the hands of Franco–German revolutionists. This had taken careful timing and handling. With falsified papers that proved that a small pension was due to her, on top of an attractive wage for her services if she was willing to take his place, he had wooed her into his employ. The motivation of seeing justice prevail, and with full freedom in her new role ...; as freedom was something this young lady obviously enjoyed, Mansfield had got his way. Having proven to be articulate, quick witted, intelligent, very presentable, street-smart and trustworthy to date, it was now time to hone Jehanne's skills and cement her loyalty.

As for Jehanne Blanche, the role offered her by Mansfield Smith-Cumming had appealed to her risk taking mentality, along with the courteous way in which he had enlisted her help, and framed his offer. It was her chance to finally have a proper job, along with a new beginning away from Marseille; a role not constricted by chauvinist and political restrictions, where the money was also good. The news of her father had come as a shock, however, having grown up without one, and with a mother who had died of consumption in 1905, she was not one to look back. Knowing that men found her attractive, and having been in demand as a young higher class of escort, this was her chance to combine all her talents and desires while getting paid double for any extra-curricular activity.

Personally she certainly did not confuse 'freedom for women' that was currently the popular cry, with sexual licentiousness. Whilst 1913 may have been in the vanguard for women's rights, its tone to her was hectoring, and patronising. Life for her was more simple; it was a case of survival bound by a self-created code of ethics where loyalty begat loyalty. Unrestrained by law, religion, family ties, emotional connection, or morality, her one hate was that she had an absolute dislike for men who oppressed women. This was countered, just as much, with a dislike for women who were complicit in their oppression by being lazy, or unoccupied… married, or unmarried. For her this was especially true of those who hid behind a pack mentality with religion as their crutch, and as a result took no risks, and contributed little.

By late 1913, aged 18, Jehanne Blanche was in Mansfield's employ being groomed as an operative.

For the wider feminist public it was becoming increasingly clear that sexual exploitation of women in prostitution was an international phenomenon. Virtually all of them who did not indulge considered prostitution a terrible evil; an archetypical form of sexual subordination of the entire female sex. For the avid feminist, prostitution conveniently represented a profound antithesis of the ideal of freedom for women, but this was not the case for Jehanne. Most often seen as a 'forced' activity by others, and a tragic one on the downward slide to depravity, they were out of touch with Jehanne's views entirely. To her prostitution was simply another skill to be harnessed to achieve a desired outcome, and a well paying one at that. This suited Mansfield Smith-Cumming's plans admireably. He and his operatuves were soon to find that money and sex were usually the most effective inducements for obtaining information.

In this regard, as war with Germany loomed, one of his agents code-named Walter Christmas was charged with watching German naval shipyards. He would report on the trials of the new dreadnought battleships, the 'remarkable speed' reached by a new torpedo boat, and the continued construction of submarines. Walter always insisted that his reports should be collected by pretty young prostitutes paid for by the service, who would meet him in a hotel room to exchange intelligence, and where he could get an occasional 'Christmas' present early. It would be a partnership between the two oldest professions, spying and prostitution, that would endure throughout the service's history.

For Jehanne there was, however, still a clear-cut distinction between voluntary and forced sex, with her trade mark weapon of choice being a comfortable fitting brass knuckle duster that, she had come to master since 11 years of age. Jehanne kept it hidden in the folds of her skirt on a loose chord attached to her belt. It could be quickly fitted to her left hand and ripped free should the need arise; as her last Marseille patron, who had decided that he would like to indulge in rough sex, had found out to his detriment.

The ship, Jehanne had served prior to her recruitment, HMS Blonde, would go on to be attached to a variety of Battle Squadrons in the Grand Fleet, before being converted to lay mines, but would never be used in active service in that role.

Jehanne Blanche would not get to lay mines on active service either, but she would come close on several occasions.

Knowing that the Suez situation would be critical to British interests as part of his training procedure Mansfield Smith-Cumming had developed an association with Ernest Budge, the Keeper at the British Museum. He was one of several reliable contacts he had identified as having the skills to help educate his protégées. In Budge's case it was regarding Middle Eastern history, current politics, languages, and particularly philosophy and religion. Along with practical training and ongoing field work from the MI6 London office Mansfield wanted to ensure that a selected group of operatives in his employ were suited for what he now had in mind.

*Mansfield
Smith-Cumming*

Ernest Alfred Thompson Wallis Budge was a kindly, portly, man of medium stature with a love of nature and a good education. He had entered the British Museum in the renamed Department of Egyptian and Assyrian Antiquities back in 1883. Initially appointed to the Assyrian section he had soon transferred to the Egyptian, where he began to study the ancient Egyptian language under a senior mentor, the then 'Keeper for the Museum'.

Ernest Budge

Always interested in intrigue, and especially differences in religious doctrine, Budge had then been deputed by the British Museum to investigate why it was that cuneiform tablets, from various British Museum sites in Iraq, were showing up in the collections of London antiquities dealers. Supposedly being guarded by local agents of the British Museum, they were then being forced to purchase back collections of their own tablets at inflated London market rates. The Principal Librarian of the Museum wished Budge to find the source of the leaks and to seal them off once and for all. He also wanted him to establish ties to Iraqi antiquities dealers to buy whatever was available in the local market at appropriately reduced prices. Budge had travelled to Constantinople, (now Istanbul), during these years to obtain a permit from the Ottoman government to reopen the Museum's excavations at these Iraqi sites in order to obtain whatever tablets remained in them.

Max von Oppenheim

It was during one of these visits that he had met one of the last of the great amateur archaeological explorers of the Near East. He was a German named Max von Oppenheim, who was excavating the old site of the lost city of Babylon 130 miles south of Bagdad for financial gain. Budge had also sought to establish ties with local antiquities dealers in Egypt, and Iraq, so that the

British Museum would be able to obtain antiquities from them without the uncertainty and cost of excavation. It was a decidedly 19th century approach to building a museum collection, and Budge had returned from many of his missions with enormous collections of cuneiform tablets. Included had been Syriac, Coptic and Greek manuscripts, as well as significant collections of hieroglyphic papyri and tablets; the most significant of which were the Tell al-Amarna tablets.

Whilst Budge's prolific and well-planned acquisitions had given the British Museum arguably the best Ancient Near East collections in the world, the translation of the Tell al-Amarna tablets had opened a religious can of worms. They had caused a revolutionary change of opinion concerning the civilisation of patriarchal Palestine than that told as the evolutionary theory of Israel's history in the Old Testament.

Exodus - The Red Sea crossing

They highlighted an age old falsity that the people of Moses had, in any reality, possessed a 'Promised Land' as understood in

Western, or Jewish biblical terms. Rather, the truth was now unequivocally revealed that the Jews had Arabian nomadic ancestors from the Negev and Sinai, who had been the first to move into Southern Palestine where they had assimilated with others already on the land. They had settled there centuries prior to Moses, as tribal pastoralists, when it was an Egyptian outpost under Egyptian ownership and rule. From their Arabian roots, it additionally became clear that they had also developed the concept of a single God, that had been included in their myths and written into their legends. Up until, and including, the times of the line of David and the patriarchal kings, they had then been involved in war and intrigue ongoing, and in continuing to develop and mould their Jewish faith until well after the arrival of the Romans.

Confirming that there was a state of civilisation in Palestine with a faith believing in a single God theocracy prior to Moses, and well before the patriarchal age, questioned the validity of any Jewish belief in a 'Promised Land.' As such any Old Testament accounts were now proven to be simply mythical or ancestral religious stories.

As Budge put it …

The people of Moses were no more entitled to the grace of any God than any other of their co-existent, and similarly pagan, Bedouin and Arab brothers who believed in Yahoveh.

It was a view that was now being accepted by all classes of more enlightened scholars, from the most conservative on the one hand, to the most radical on the other. That was with the exception of the Judean and Christian churches where historical reality continued to interfere with their own dogma and political beliefs. Beliefs that continued to revolve around the ownership of Palestine by the Israelites as described in the Old Testament as a 'Promised Land' by Jehovah. With their continued denial, they had more at stake…. much more!

For his part, Mansfield Smith-Cumming had become aware of Ernest Budge's talents with antiquities, and Near Eastern relgion, several years earlier. As far as the antiquities were concerned Ernest's knowledge was also revered by several others including the British Army Royal Engineer, Stewart Newcombe, and the archaeologists T.E Lawrence, and Leonard Woolley.

Mansfield had recognised that archaeologists could move easily across borders and into the world's hinterlands, and being familiar with the attitudes of the people living where they excavated, they had natural opportunities that others did not. In that regard they were able to watch troop movements, note the distribution of military hardware and bases, and no doubt even commit sabotage if trained accordingly, and if the opportunity presented itself. Many would additionally be trained in deciphering dead languages, a skill also useful in mastering codes.

The British Museum

Now as confirmed 'Keeper of the Museum' specialising in Egyptology, Ernest Budge had, therefore, taken it upon himself to hold lectures for interested groups on the formation of early civilisations and religious beliefs. He had discovered he enjoyed particularly talking to young adults who were not constricted by preconceived ideas. His love of ancient language and the Tell el-Amarna tablets had also introduced him to the convoluted world of religion in which, both philosophically and historically, he had given a lot of study and thought. For some time now his talks had also been a curricular requirement for budding operatives likely to work in the Near East for the Bureau. Additionally he was working with Mansfield Smith-Cumming in vetting potential operatives to identify their true leanings and beliefs, particularly with regard to certain political or religious ideology. Jehanne Blanche was to become a friend of Ernest's whom she would consult with on Near Eastern archaeological, philosophical, religious and political matters.

Max von Oppenheim

Stewart Newcombe

Stewart Francis Newcombe had been commissioned into the Royal Engineers (R.E.) in 1898 attending the School of Military Engineering (S.M.E.) at Brompton Barracks in Chatham, Kent. On the eve of a new century he had been posted to the 29th Fortress Company based at Cape Town, South Africa, in time to participate in operations during the Second Boer War in the Orange Free State. He had seen action at Dreifontein, Karee Siding, and during the Relief of Kimberley for which he had been rewarded with the Queen's Medal with four clasps. Transferred to the Egyptian Army in April 1901, and posted to the Sudan Government Railways, he had soon built up a

Stewart Francis Newcombe in later life

reputation as an able surveyor. Following recommendations from an Arab guide, he and a fellow railway officer had then begun to reconnoitre a possible rail route between the River Nile and the Red Sea. With that survey complete Newcombe had switched his attentions to a proposed railway west of the Nile from Omdurman to El Obaid. Further surveys were carried out in subsequent years before he finally left the Egyptian Army after 10 years of field duty, departing Sudan in May 1911, and returning to the British Army in England. Here however, he soon found it boring sitting still, so he made plans in 1912 hopeful of a return to active overseas service.

To this end he sought assistance in returning to service in Africa, or Egypt, from Rudyard Kipling, whose acquaintance he had made some 12 years earlier during the South African War. A chance encounter with Rudyard Kipling had taken place during the Battle of Karee Siding when Rudyard was attached to troops in the field reporting on the slow progress of the war against a mobile and determined enemy. Stewart had informed Rudyard that some scrub in front of him was 'all clear' when it was anything but, forcing him to lie flat on his stomach for hours in great mental and bodily distress, until eventually saved. Having very nearly got Rudyard Kipling shot he recalled the encounter and again chanced his arm by seeking that author's assistance in helping him secure a more suitable posting.

Being well connected within military circles Rudyard had duly written to the Under Secretary of State for War, and in a cleverly crafted letter, put forward a request for assistance in securing for Newcombe a return to an overseas posting.

Isn't there any way by which you could set him on his return to Africa? he had written... *If he dies there I shall be revenged for his attempt on my life at Karree Siding. If he lives I fancy the service will be richer by his work.*

The letter had the desired effect and within a few weeks Stewart Newcombe had been making preparations to leave for an expedition to the desert region south of Beersheba in southern Palestine, in order to measure and map a strategic triangle of southern Palestine that was the Negev Desert. It was a secret survey being carried out on behalf of the British War Office, as a continuation of an original survey, carried out by Lieutenants Kitchener and Conder, for the Egyptian Survey Department.

The survey team, working under Stewart's direction, divided the assignment and worked meticulously throughout the cooler months of 1912. He was at last happy to be doing something of real value, and the work suited his organisational skills and planning, as well as his longing to be out in the field. With the survey party pushing this task through to near completion, there remained only one uncharted triangle of land south of Beersheba, including the Negev Desert, and down to the Gulf of Akaba. Known since biblical times as the Wilderness of Zin, this area was considered to be of military importance given the proximity of the strategic Suez Canal.

The military surveyors were now accompanied by two civilian experts, Oxford University graduates, Thomas Edward Lawrence and Leonard Woolley, who were to provide a suitable

T E Lawrence   *C L Woolley*

archaeological element to the survey to support the subterfuge. They would additionally later disguise the military intent with a published account of their findings describing the passage of the supposed Exodus led by Moses during its 40 odd year sojourn at Kadesh Barnea.

To complete the deception the survey work was being carried out under the auspices of the Palestine Exploration Fund. This academic organisation's mission was to promote research into 'the archaeology and history; manners, customs and culture; topography; geology and natural sciences of the Levant; the southern portion of which was conventionally named 'Palestine'. This initial encounter with Lawrence would set up a life-long friendship between the professional soldier and the young scholar-archaeologist.

Woolley and Lawrence would depart for Syria after six weeks, while Stewart Newcombe and his teams completed that season's surveys by mapping the Sinai Desert across to the Suez Canal.

T. E. Lawrence and Leonard Woolley (right) in Carchemish, spring 1913

Taking time off during his return journeys to Britain, Stewart Newcombe would explore Greater Syria along with sending back intelligence reports on the Berlin to Baghdad railway, and the Damascus to Medina line through the Hejaz Desert.

As team leader, Stewart used T E Lawrence's excavations with British archaeologist Leonard Woolley at a Carchemish site on the border of what is now Syria with Turkey to mix archaeology and surveillance. Lawrence's mission for Stewart Newcombe and British Intelligence was to monitor German progress on the railway to link Berlin and Baghdad which would circumvent the Suez Canal and secure means of shipping oil and other vital supplies during the war.

In 1914, Lawrence would write to his mother to say that these excavations were … *obviously only meant as red herrings, to give an archaeological colour to a political job.*

Lawrence and Wooley at Carchemish

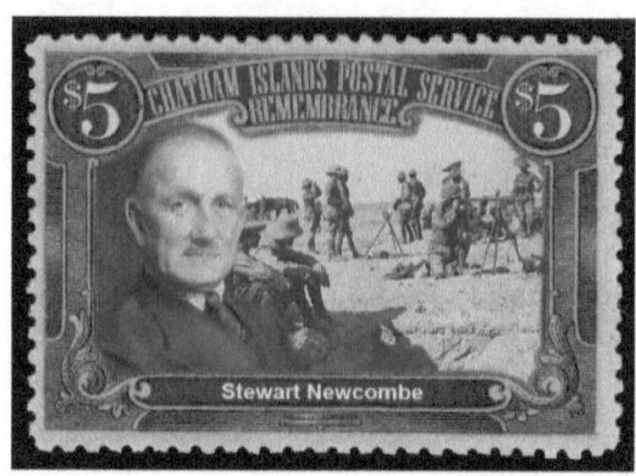

Stewart Newcombe

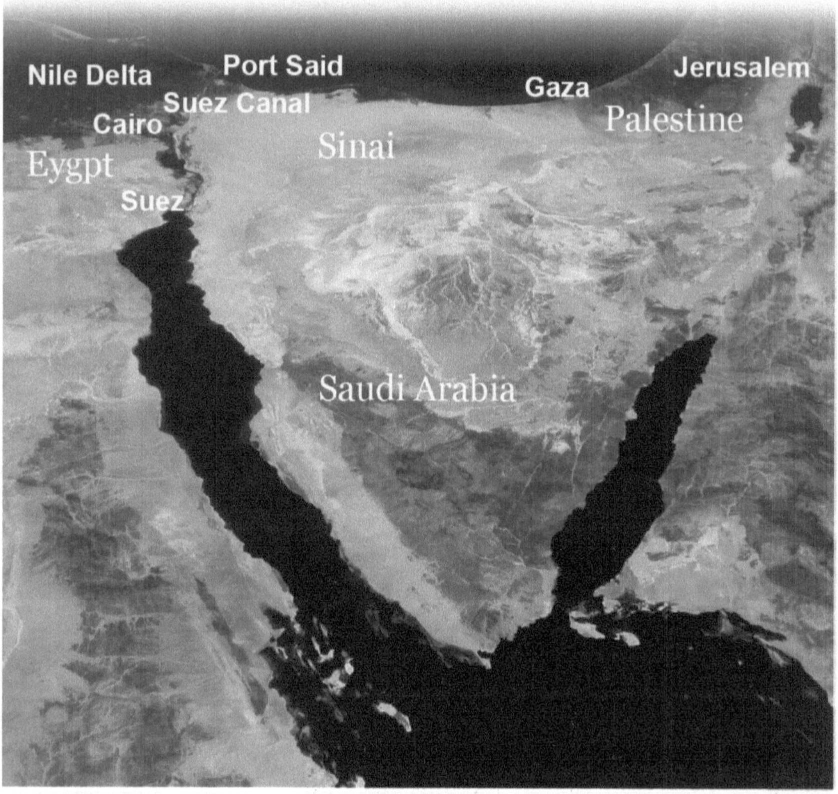

Overview of locations of Eygpt, the Sinai, and Palestine relative to one another

Part III

Sultan Abdul Hamid II

Before the turn of the 19th century Berlin's need to secure new markets and raw material to feed its booming industries had clearly lain in the east—specifically in the debt-ridden, ailing Ottoman Empire of Sultan Abdul Hamid II. The situation in Ottoman Turkey had become so extreme at that time that the Sultan had been forced in 1881, by his French and British creditors, to put the finances of the realm under the control of a banker-run agency. By the Decree of Muharrem the Ottoman public debt was reduced from £191,000,000 to £106,000,000, certain revenues were assigned to debt service, and a European - controlled organisation, the Ottoman Public Debt Administration (OPDA), was set up to collect the payments.

The OPDA subsequently acted as agent for the collection of other revenues and as an intermediary with European companies seeking investment opportunities. Its affairs were controlled by the two largest creditors—France and Britain, with the French being the larger.

The Germans had strategically set about to change that dependency of Ottoman Turkey on the British and French. For his part, Sultan Abdul Hamid II had been all too pleased to open his door to growing German influence as a welcome counterweight and a source of new capital to solve the economic problems of the empire.

Map showing the Black Sea and Asia Minor

Despite their mistrust of one another, Britain, France, and Russia had formed the Triple Entente alliance in order to resist Germany's explosive growth in industrial and military power. It was an expansion that had begun during the 1880's, and that continued to alarm countries in Europe and Asia. The signing of this Anglo-Russian Entente on 31st August, 1907, supplemented by agreements with Portugal and Japan, had been seen as a powerful counterweight to the Triple Alliance of Germany, Austria-Hungary, and Italy. Britain, especially, had been concerned about Germany's developing relationship with the Ottoman Empire. Especially the influence they could possibly wield in regards to the railway stretching across the Middle East from Constantinople to Baghdad. Giving direct access to the area, and points further south, it was considered that it could jeopardise Britain's colonialist endeavours in India.

In order to protect their assets, the British government moved to increase their control in Ottoman territories they already occupied. Within the Triple Entente, statesmen began to call for the dismemberment of the Ottoman Empire because of its alliance with Germany. The calls encouraged Britain to create a plan of destabilisation while establishing alliances with disgruntled Ottoman.

In 1888, the Oriental Railway from Austria, across the Balkans via Belgrade, Sofia, to Constantinople had been opened that had linked with the railways of Austria-Hungary and other European countries placing the Ottoman capital in direct communication with Vienna, Paris, and Berlin. It was a significant move.

By 1898, the Ottoman Ministry of Public Works had applications from several European

Work on the railway

groups to build railways in the Anatolian part of the empire. These had included an Austro-Russian syndicate, a French proposal, a proposal from a group of British bankers, and a proposal from the German Deutsche Bank. The Sublime Porte, however, had no desire to have significant Russian presence on its territory, because of continued Russian pressure for access for its navy through the Dardanelles.

Then British government backing for Ottoman bankers had faded away with outbreak of the Boer War in 1899

A train on a section of the new line

The French proposal, however, was considered significant enough that Deutsche Bank had entered into negotiations with the French Banks about a possible joint venture. Then on 27th November, 1899, the Ottoman Sultan, Abdul Hamid II, awarded Deutsche Bank a concession for a railway from Konia to Baghdad and to the Persian Gulf. It was based on the Sultan having previously assured the Anatolian Railway Company that it should have priority in the construction of any railway to Baghdad.

Building the Bagdad rail line

On the strength of those previous assurances, the Anatolian Company had conducted expensive surveys of the proposed route.

Additionally as part of the railway concession, the shrewd negotiators of the Deutsche Bank negotiated subsurface mineral rights 12.5 miles either side of the proposed Baghdad Railway line. Deutsche Bank, with the German government backing them, made certain these included the sole rights to any petroleum which might be found.

The Germans had scored a strategic coup over the British, or so it seemed. Mesopotamian oil secured through completion of the Berlin-Baghdad Railway was to be Germany's secure source to enter the emerging era of oil-driven transport. This German success was no minor event given the geographically strategic

position of
the Ottoman
Empire. It
dominated the
Dardanelles
Straits, and
Shatt-al-Arab at
the Persian Gulf,
from Aleppo to
Sinai bordering
the strategic Suez
Canal link to the
British Empire India
trade, down to Aden at the Strait of
Bab el Mandeb.

*German
Picklehaube
helmet*

General Liman von Sanders

The Ottoman flag

The German-
Ottoman agreement assuring
construction of the final section of the Berlin-Baghdad Railway
meant the shattering of England's hope of bringing Mesopotamia,
with its strategic location and its oil, under her exclusive
influence, and it meant as well a major defeat for France.

Sultan Abdul Hamid II was deposed on 27th April 1909 following
the Young Turk Revolution. He had been the 99th Caliph of Islam,
the 34th Sultan of the Ottoman Empire, and the last to exert
effective control. He was succeeded by Mehmed V who was
hailed by most Ottoman citizens who welcomed a return to
constitutional rule.

By now German engagement with the Ottoman Empire had taken

on an added dimension with a German-Turkish Military Agreement under which German General Liman von Sanders, member of the German Supreme War Council, was sent to Constantinople with the personal approval of the Kaiser to reorganise the Turkish army along the lines of the legendary German General Staff.

Liman von Sanders

In a letter to Chancellor von Bethmann - Hollweg, dated 26th April 1913, Freiherr von Wangenheim, the German Ambassador to Constantinople declared...

The Power which controls the Army will always be the strongest one in Turkey. No Government hostile to Germany will be able to hold on to power if the Army is controlled by us...

By the eve of World War I the following year, Germany would have established their Intelligence Bureau for the East. Known as *Nachrichtenstelle für den Orient*, or Germany's Intelligence Bureau, it was dedicated to promoting and sustaining subversive and nationalist agitations in the British Indian Empire, the Persian Gulf, and Egyptian satellite states.

*Max von Oppenheim
in Arab dress*

*Cartoon depicting
Max von Oppenheim*

Attached to the German Foreign Office, the Intelligence Bureau for the East was headed by none other than Ernest Budge's acquaintance, Max von Oppenheim. As an ardent German imperialist von Oppenheim classed himself as an ancient historian and archaeologist who had earlier abandoned a career in diplomacy to finance his own excavations at Tel Halaf in 1911-13. He had published his findings despite the fact that he had not trained as an archaeologist.

He had also developed a great interest in the customs and manners of the Bedouin tribes and published widely on this subject. Whilst he participated in professional conferences, some of his interpretations, however, were disputed by leading figures in the field. T.E. Lawrence, in particular, thought him stupid and disliked him.

Von Oppenheim had, however, been astute enough to keep one of his finds, made this at the old site of Babylon, secret. It was half an ancient amulet with a religious message hidden in it's single tubular ivory hirz. Having fermented and distilled his thoughts with regard to that message's significance shortly before the outbreak of war, he had advised Kaiser Wilhelm…

When the Turks invade Egypt, and India is set ablaze with the flames of revolt, only then will England crumble. For England is at her most vulnerable in her colonies.

In this regard he mentioned that he held an ace up his sleeve in the form of the ancient amulet's message. Having come to understand it's significance religiously, at the Kaiser's request he now tabled a short paper on his find, along with photographs of the artefact and the message text. Then on the outbreak of war, von Oppenheim penned a more complete German strategy to encourage Turkey to join with Germany and Austria and in

Mehmed V, the Sultan of Turkey, was then regarded as the Caliph by a substantial part of the Islamic world.

leading a Turkey-led Jihad, or Holy War, against the colonial powers of Britain, France and Russia. In his memorandum called the *Denkschrift,* he argued enlisting pan-Islamic support by using the amulet message that had historic Islamic relevance. With his strategy having found favour he now found himself heading the German Intelligence Bureau for the East, that was closely associated with German plans to initiate and support a rebellion in Egypt.

From an economic perspective the Ottoman, or rather the German, strategic goal was to cut off Russian access to the hydrocarbon resources around the Caspian Sea, and attempting to instigate instability in British possessions in Persia, Afghanistan, India, and the Middle East in Egypt. In this regard Von Oppenheim was to work intricately with the deposed Khedive Abbas II of Egypt, and Indian revolutionary organisations, including the Berlin

Committee, Jugantar, the Ghadar Party, and prominent Moslem socialists including Maulavi Barkatullah.

German Intelligence Bureau was to involve itself in intelligence gathering and subversive missions throughout the war, with Von Oppenheim's recruits to the Bureau including the likes of Gunther von Wesendonck, Ernst Sekunna, Franz von Papen, (who would later briefly be the Chancellor of the Weimar Republic), and others. Also included was a German diplomat named Wilhelm Wassmuss who would become known as the 'German Lawrence of Arabia'.

Sultan Memed V

Part IV

Having no family association to the engineer and surveyor

Stewart Newcombe, Arthur Edgar Newcombe had been born in the small fishing village of Paignton, Devon, in the parish of Stoke Damerel in September 1897. It had been a district that had been abolished a little over a year later to become part of the parish of Devonport. With its small harbour and origins as a Celtic settlement, like a lot of England, it was steeped in history. Originally only a small village, a rail line built by the Dartmouth and Torbay Railway had created links to Torquay and London and from that point in time the town's population had started to increase. With its main seafront area dominated by the 780 feet length of Paignton Pier the area had marketed itself as a location for family holidays. Having celebrated the first decade of the new century Torquay Tramways had then been extended into Paignton in 1911, and tourism had continued to flourish.

This, however, had not been enough for Arthur's father William Newcombe, who considered employment in the British Civil Service more appropriate for his son. As such Arthur had dutifully applied for registration with the Board of Trade in London, to be gazetted as a temporary boy clerk at the beginning of April 1913.

As a young lad with determination and initiative, Arthur Edgar Newcombe had relocated in August 1912 to board in London at Paddenswick Road, Hammersmith, shortly before his 15th birthday. Living opposite the walls and wrought-iron gates enclosing the Shakespeare Gardens of Ravenscourt Park had its benefits, along with the nearby rail link that transported him to his employment in central London.

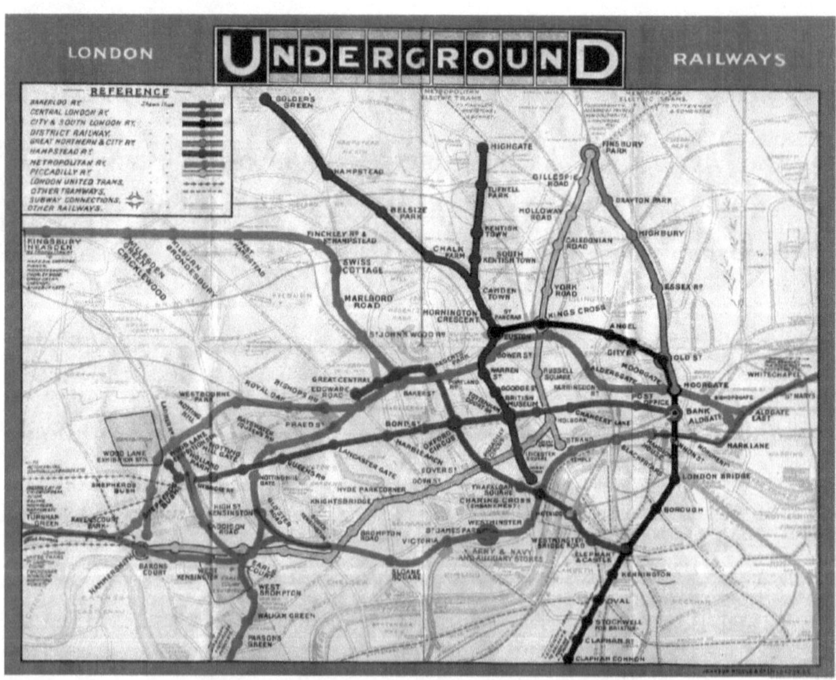

Map of the London underground in 1912

Catching the Great Northern, Piccadilly and Brompton Railway (GNP&BR) train at its western terminus at Hammersmith Station Arthur would disembark at Holborn, two blocks away from the British Museum.

In his spare time, from Paddenswick Road, he would visit the many nearby exhibitions at Shepherd's Bush. These attractions had continued following the large public fair that had been The Franco-British Exhibition of 1908.

His favourite pastime, however, was to walk through the mature elm and chestnut trees of Ravenscourt Park, to sit on a park bench in its old English scented garden. Here he would philosophically contemplate the origins of the universe and the antiquities he had been introduced to by the Keeper of the British Museum, Ernest Budge. Since his arrival in London he had availed himself of the opportunity to learn something from the fortnightly lectures offered by the museum. He enjoyed these immensely. They not only stimulated his inquisitive nature but also, more recently, an inner sexual desire that stirred within him brought on by one of the newer female attendees.

The British Museum

Seated in the front row of the museum's old auditorium, surrounded on all sides by high, timber-panelled walls, and four polished granite columns that culminated high above in a gothic arch, were several interested listeners. Other than Arthur two others in attendance were Jehanne Blanche, and another SSB contact, 43 year old Gertrude Bell. Most attending had an interest in Egyptology, early civilisations, religious history, philosophy, ancient languages, or a combination of those particular topics. Jehanne and Gertrude, however, were there at the behest of Mansfield Smith Cumming.

Budge's antiquities and religious philosophical addresses had previously stimulated Mansfield into realising that they were a good way of gauging potential operatives understanding and beliefs. Additional to that was instilling a broader historical knowledge, particularly of the Near East.

Gertrude Bell

Jehanne had been attending since her arrival in London the previous year, while sitting demurely to her right was Gertrude Bell who had recently returned from the Middle East. Her father was a 2nd Baronet, and as an archaeologist and adventurer Gertrude had already made her invaluable knowledge available to the SSB. Her years of Near Eastern excavations had already provided geographic information of importance. With reddish hair she had piercing blue-green eyes, with her mother's bow shaped lips and rounded chin, and her father's oval face and pointed nose. Her recent request for a Near East posting with the Foreign Service had been denied, however, like Jehanne that denial would not last.

Having received her early education from Queen's College in London, Gertrude had then attended Lady Margaret Hall, Oxford University at the age of 17. History was one of the few subjects women were allowed to study, due to the many restrictions imposed on them at the time. Gertrude had, therefore, specialised in modern history, in which she had received a first class honours degree in two years. In January 1909, she had left for

Mesopotamia; visited the Hittite city of Carchemish, mapped and described the ruin of Ukhaidir, and finally travelled to Babylon and Najaf. Back in Carchemish, she had consulted with the two archaeologists on site, one of whom had been T. E. Lawrence.

Gertrude Bell at a site in the Near East

There had then followed a difficult 1913 Arabian journey that made her only the second foreign woman, after Lady Anne Blunt, to visit Ha'il. Now as honorary secretary of the British Women's Anti-Suffrage League, Gertrude was deeply involved in politics herself, yet felt that women were not ready to vote while they remained confined to the domestic sphere. With her mother having died in child birth when she was six years of age, her stepmother had instilled concepts of duty and decorum in Gertrude. These, in some measure, had contributed to her intellectual and anti-feminist activities.

The archaelogical team at Carchemish

To Jehanne, Gertrude's beliefs seemed like reverse psychology and flawed thinking on her part. Whilst Jehanne did not support the over-zealous feminists in the ranks of the League she had no problem with suffrage and in women gaining the vote. As far as she was concerned she was the equal of any man, as her trusty knuckle duster had proved on more than one occasion.

Four years Jehanne's junior, Arthur Edgar Newcombe had also been attending the museum lectures. He had not got to know Jehanne personally like Gertrude, but that did not stop him glancing at her longingly on each visit, with a lust that only young hormones stimulated. To him she was beautiful; a bright ray in his dull life, and a fellow antiquarian. Any movement she made stirred a previously subdued desire within him. This desire had been noticed by Ernest Budge, but it would not be satisfied by Jehanne. Rather Arthur's natural virginal urges would be fulfilled in Ravenscourt Park by a neighbour's daughter shortly after he signed up to join the British army a few months later.

Work at the Nahr Rûd canal in southern Iraq - March 1911

From behind his lectern this over-caste Friday afternoon Ernest Budge surveyed his small band of listeners that included Jehanne, Gertrude and Arthur.

Today I would like to break from the norm to start a series of lectures that considers commonality in the Semitic religions of Judeism, Christianity and Islam; more particularly their common underlying theocracy and doctrine, and its consequent effect on history.

In this opening address I will postulate an opinion supported by some weighty evidence that hopefully stimulates your thinking and freedom of thought. It may, with any luck, have you wanting to return to hear more in subsequent addresses.

A slight smile creased his chubby friendly features….

Throughout their troubled history it has been the fate of the land that we call Palestine, or more particularly those who inhabited its lands, to be surrounded by, or controlled by, great empires. As such the people of that land have always struggled to maintain a precarious existence, generally at the mercy of the neighbouring great powers like Egypt, Babylon, Assyria, Persia, the Hittites, the Greeks and eventually the Romans. To these pagan empires with their free spirited approach to religion, the religious belief of several combined tribes from southern Palestine in the Negev must have seemed like an oddity.

Why...? You might ask.....!

From before the time of the story of Moses one of these nomadic tribes, known as the Shasu, had become pastoralists around the outposts of Egyptian rule in the area we know today as the northern Sinai and southern Palestine. We now refer to them as Jews, who by that time had come to believe in the rigidity of their new religion under One God that controlled every facet of their life. It was this idea of religion as the regulator of secular life with a sole civic spokesperson, that later formed the foundation of Judaism, Christianity and Islam.

This is what we call theocracy, where God himself is recognised as the head of the state. Its key feature has a human medium as the unquestioned and sole spokesman of God and ultimate authority, and it is the core building block of all three religions. Without it what is built would simply be built on shifting sand.

In order to understand its growth and effect in terms of theocratic Christianity, it helps to recognise that the exercising of secular authority over people in the name of one God was not a Jewish innovation traced to Moses. It was, however, supposedly Moses, referred to in the collection of books we know as the Old Testament, who demanded unquestioning obedience from his people in the name of one God of which he claimed to be the sole spokesman.

He, and subsequent patriarchal chief's, and then kings, established this claim. An example is the claim recorded in the Book of Deuteronomy of the Old Testament, in a passage from Chapter 18 verse 18; and I quote...

"I will raise them up a Prophet from among their brethren ... and will put my word in his mouth; and he shall speak unto them all that I shall command him..."

I put it to you that this virtually defines exclusivity, which implies that the intermediary is the exclusive spokesman for God - and there can be none other. It also follows that man cannot know God save through this intermediary; there being no direct access. By implication this exclusion of direct knowledge of God automatically shuts out alternative paths of exploration. It is the very antithesis of pluralism and freedom of choice and thought that our modem civilisation - like that of ancient Greece – should be valuing highly.

Of course in Judaism, Abraham is seen as that first intermediary, while in Christianity it is the apostles of Jesus as recorded in the

New Testament, and likewise both Isa as Jesus and the prophet Mohammed in the Islamic Qu'ran. There is, however, more to the story than that ...much, much, more...

For instance, consider the history of development of the various religious doctrines in which that decree of exclusivity has been carefully tended as being very convenient. A convenience not just in controlling the masses, but in expunging anyone with a contrary view, as is the case in Christianity; as either being a heretic, or conveniently by excommunication.

Let me be a bit more direct without intentionally targeting any Roman Catholics amongst us.

The Catholic Church, also known as the Holy Roman Catholic Church, is the world's largest Christian church. It is among the oldest religious institutions in the world and has played a prominent role in the history of Western civilisation both for good and bad. Its hierarchy is led by the Pope, and includes cardinals, patriarchs and diocesan bishops. This Church teaches that it is the one true church divinely founded by Jesus Christ, and that its bishops are the successors of Christ's apostles and that the Pope is the sole successor of Saint Peter, and as such has apostolic primacy.

As the self appointed intermediary since the days of Jesus's apostles, therefore, anything this Church's hierarchy consider to be politically or religiously fit is, by their self appointed divine definition and right, correct. It cannot be questioned, for it is the word of God. This is exactly what the Papacy has been telling their Christian believers since the Greek translation of the Bible. Ordering the faithful that their decrees were the word of God as communicated through their intermediaries. With the church's own doctrine, and convenient propaganda added, it still to this day excludes freedom of choice or thought.

Notwithstanding the good work of many Christian churches there is no escaping undisputed historical fact that the hierarchy of both Judeism and the Roman Catholic Church, and their clergy, have knowingly been hypocritically living a theocratic lie for nigh on two millennia. More importantly, they have been perpetuating their myths on their less educated brethren, with no doubt a number of ulterior over arching motives in mind.

Three that spring to mind are power, money and security of tenure.

With its hand equally in politics and misleading, controlled, divinity it could be construed from history that these religions pursue a cause of dwelling on the ignorant for power, financial gain, or security of tenure. A motivated methodology to increase their power base, property, and control, while covering up a record of persecution, damage, and in living a religious lie.

I contend that it is not just Judeism and Christianity, but also Islam that cultivate, deliberately or otherwise, an accepted state of ignorance. It is more correctly a state where parishioners are not required or encouraged to think but to blindly accept and conform to what they are being told.

What we all need, however, is freedom of thought, not restriction from it. Are we to believe Victorian church men who warned about building the London underground, when they claimed that the noise of the trains would disturb the Devil?

I for one would rather be an enlightened heretic than a brain dead believer.

He paused to let the words sink in…

I reiterate, there can be no freedom of choice without tolerance of pluralism. Exclusivity or 'exclusivism' has the opposite goal in its enforcement of uniformity of conduct and belief - and even thought. As history proves, this has been by whatever means their enforcers have seen fit. Uniformity, however, has proven to be unattainable, and, in that regard, I quote from Thomas Jefferson…

"Millions of innocent men, women and children since the introduction of Christianity, have been burnt, tortured, fined, imprisoned - yet we have not advanced one inch towards uniformity. What has been the effect of coercion? To make one half the world fools the other half hypocrites".

It is in the nature of every exclusivist doctrine, therefore, to divide humanity into two mutually exclusive camps of believers and non-believers - of us against them. This can be seen quite clearly in the contrast offered by the passage from Mathew in the Bible which at 12.30 states,

"He that is not with me, is against me".

The difference between exclusivism and pluralism could hardly be more clearly expressed. And this exclusivity as a division invariably leads to further subdivision, which does not stop at any predetermined point. There are no indivisibles as far as theology is concerned. This is clear from history also, as it is from the current state of Jewish, Christian, and Islamic societies.

Conflicts instigated by believers are also an inevitable consequence of this division. Again this has been the history of all three religions. The aggressor has always invoked his exclusivist doctrine as justification for his aggression. It is helpful, therefore, to recognise that exclusivism as a theocracy lies at the root of intolerance and ignorance. This is what Jefferson and other rationalists of the Enlightenment saw and objected to, and that we still see as human orchestrated theocracy that is part of the three.

Recognising the basis of this doctrine hopefully helps one understand the history of conflict that is so much a part of Judaism, Christianity and Islam. They cannot afford to let their followers explore unauthorised paths; hence the need for a truth-monitoring thought police calling itself the 'clergy', and in the case of the Roman Catholic Church stimulated also by more clandestine groups such as its SP and Jesuits.

Pausing again Budge studied every face in his small audience.

In closing let me quote you a number of biblical passages that reinforce what I am saying... The first is from Exodus 20.3,5... which states... "Thou shalt have no other gods before me...Thou shalt not bow down thyself to them, nor serve them: for I the Lord thy God am a jealous God, visiting the iniquity of the fathers upon the children unto the third and fourth generation..."

And further passages add to that contention... for example from Deuteronomy 12.2

"Ye shall utterly destroy all the places where-in the nations which ye possess served their gods, upon the high mountains, and upon the hills, and every green tree".

Then the ultimate prophetorial instruction... quoted from Deuteronomy 13. 6,8,9.

He picked up a copy of the Bible carefully …

"If thy brother, or thy son, or thy daughter, or the wife of thy bosom, or thy friend entice thee secretly, saying, Let us go and serve other gods, which thou hast not known, nor thy fathers; Thou shalt not consent... neither shalt thine eye pity him, neither shalt thou spare, neither shalt thou conceal him: But thou shalt surely kill him: thine hand shalt be first upon him to put him to death, and afterwards the hands of all people".

He closed the book with a thud…!

So the Tanakh, a name used in Judaism for the canon of the Hebrew Bible; the Christian Bible, and its close relative the Qu'ran, gives scriptural sanction to ignorance and intolerance. More importantly it makes it a sacred duty of the individual to destroy others of different beliefs, including perpetrating murder so long it is done in the name of God.

Consequently all believe in a personal, self-regulating, belief that makes espionage and spying on your neighbour regarding their beliefs acceptable. It is just as relevant in many minds today to justify their actions. Add to this, reward and punishment bound up in another human religiously introduced concept of heavenly 'peace', or eternal 'hell'; along with repentance and absolution for transgressions of the faith, and you arrive at the ultimate package. Absolution it should be noted as adjudicated by the clergy in a confessional who have no more right to absolve crime than I do.

This, therefore, is the apotheosis of exclusivism; division of the world into believers and non-believers, with non-believers deserving death and damnation. With this background the violence marred history of Judaism, Christianity and Islam I contend, becomes entirely understandable, as does the phenomenon of Holy War as Jihad.

Similarly as the great English magistrate of history Lord Acton observed regarding the Popes..... "They were not only murderers in the great style, but they made murder a legal basis of Christianity and the condition of salvation".

On the other hand is it not our freedom of choice that we should be fighting for?

The point was not lost on those in attendance.

German Colony Stamp - Turkey

Winston Churchill was a descendant of the first famous member of the Churchill family, John Churchill, 1st Duke of Marlborough. Being related to the Spencer family Churchill's legal surname was correctly Spencer-Churchill, though, starting with his father, Lord Randolph Churchill, his branch of the family stuck with the name Churchill in public life. Randolph Churchill's mother, like his grandfather's wife, and his great-grandfather's wife, was a Stewart, descended from James Douglas. Winston's mother was Jennie Jerome, the daughter of the American Jewish millionaire, Leonard Jerome.

Winston was a Scottish Rite Freemason, a member of the Ancient Order of Druids, and was eventually invested as Knight of the Order of the Garter.

Back in 1888 Lord Nathaniel Mayer Rothschild had been a keen proponent of increases in the strength of the Royal Navy, and as a consequence the London house of Rothschild had issued shares worth £225,000 for a Naval Construction and Armaments Company. Nathaniel was an intimate friend of Lord Randolph Churchill, the father of Winston Churchill, who would be appointed First Lord of the Admiralty. Winston vowed to do everything he could to prepare Britain militarily for what he referred to as the '*inescapable day of reckoning*'.

His charge now was to ensure that the Royal Navy, the symbol of Britain's imperial power, was to meet any German 'challenge' on the high seas.

As Jehanne, Gertrude, and Arthur descended the steps of the

British Museum, seated around their well appointed board table, only three blocks away, Anglo-Persian Oil Company (APOC) managers negotiated with a new customer, Winston Churchill. As First Lord of the Admiralty, Churchill sought to modernise Britain's navy as a part of a three-year expansion programme, by abandoning the use of coal.

Oil conversion of the British fleet dictated national security as a priority along with securing large oil reserves outside Britain. His problem was, however, that less than 2% of world oil production was produced within the British Empire.

Naturally, many thought that such a conversion was pure folly, for it meant that the Navy could no longer rely on safe, secure Welsh coal, but rather would have to depend on distant and insecure oil supplies from Persia. Oil was not only superior to coal, but the French branch of the Rothschild family were, together with the Rockefellers, supreme rulers of the oil business, having entered into a world cartel with Standard Oil.

Churchill wanted to free Britain from its reliance on the Royal Dutch-Shell oil company, but more particularly he did not want to see Britain dependent on Standard Oil.

On no one quality, on no one process, on no one country, on no one route and on no one field must we be dependent. Safety and certainty in oil lie in variety... and variety alone, he eloquently stated.

In 1901 the millionaire London socialite, William Knox D'Arcy, had negotiated an oil concession with the Shah Mozzafar al-Din Shah Qajar of Persia. He had assumed exclusive rights to prospect for oil for 60 years in a vast tract of territory including most of

Iran. In exchange the Shah had received £20,000, an equal amount in shares of D'Arcy's company, and a promise of 16% of future profits. D'Arcy had then hired geologist George Bernard Reynolds to do the prospecting in the Iranian desert. Conditions had been extremely harsh. It was country where small pox raged, bandits and warlords ruled, water was all but unavailable, and where temperatures often soared past 50°C.

After several years of prospecting, D'Arcy's fortune had dwindled away and he had been forced to sell most of his rights to a Glasgow-based syndicate, the Burmah Company (BP).

By 1908, having sunk more than £500,000 into their Persian venture and still having found no oil, D'Arcy and Burmah decided to abandon exploration in Iran.

In early May 1908 Burmah sent Reynolds a telegram telling him that they had run out of money and ordering him to cease work, dismiss the staff, dismantle anything worth the cost of transporting to the coast for re-shipment, and come home. Reynolds had delayed following these orders and in a stroke of luck, had struck oil shortly after on 26th May, 1908.

On 14th April 1909, Burmah Oil had created the Anglo-Persian Oil Company (APOC) as a subsidiary, and also sold shares to the public. Volume production of Persian oil products had just started from a refinery built at Abadan, that, for its first 50 years would be the largest oil refinery in the world.

Well No. 1 in 1908

At the board table, in exchange for secure oil supplies for its ships, the British government had just agreed to inject new capital into APOC and, in so doing they would acquire a controlling interest in the company. It was a contract that would hold for 20 years with the British government becoming the de facto hidden power behind the oil company.

While Germany had expanded toward Turkey, and South into Africa, her move eastward was restricted by Britain's control of important sea lanes. 'The British Round Table' had been especially alarmed about Germany's deal with the Ottoman Empire to build the railway from Berlin to Baghdad, as it provided direct German access to the Middle East oil, bypassing the Suez Canal controlled by the British. Britain had fortuitously precluded extension of that railway to the Persian Gulf by secretly concluding an agreement with tribes to establish Kuwait as British protectorate, thus effectively sealing it off from the Ottoman Empire.

Winston Churchill

The British Grand Fleet

Part V

Lying at the crossroads of three great religious traditions the ancient city of Constantinople, known today as Istanbul, sits astride the Bosporus Strait that separates Asia from Europe. Surrounded by the Adriatic Sea to the west, the Black Sea to the east, and the Mediterranean Sea to the south, the strategic Balkan Peninsula funnels down to meet up with the landmass of Asia at the Sea of Marmara. This strait provides the only outlet for shipping from the Black Sea to the warm waters of the Mediterranean.

From here the expansive Islamic world extended from West Asia into the Peninsula with a large concentration of Moslems in Turkey, Albania, Bosnia, Kosova and Skopje. Catholic Europe met up with the Islamic world along an axis linking Constantinople with Vienna. Bisecting it, at almost at ninety degrees, was the Orthodox Christian world running roughly along an axis linking Athens with Moscow. Compounding the mix of beliefs it is still a multiplicity of nationalities and ethnic groups; with Croats, Slovans, Czechs and Hungarians to the north; Bosnians, Albanians and Macedonians to the west; Serbs, Bulgars and Romanians to the east; and Turks and Greeks to the south. Throughout history, having seen a simultaneous myriad of religious beliefs, nationalities and ethnic groups, the area has produced a volatile mixture of competing interests.

As a result of Ottoman power, which had kept the Balkans united for more than 500 years under a single political umbrella, Islamic influence had extended deeper into Eastern Europe, northern Thrace and the territories around the Black Sea. Regression of that power was now encouraging the ambitions of the Hapsburgs in Austria-Hungary and Czarist Russia, with the Balkans becoming a powder keg that only needed a fuse lit to create a Great War.

In the years leading up to 1914, there was a powerful Scottish Rite Masonic Lodge in Belgrade, which was the capital of the Kingdom of Serbia. At the same time, Austro-Hungarian Emperor Franz Josef was certain that the French Freemasons were trying to

start a war between Austria-Hungary and Russia to destroy the great European monarchies.

His suspicions were almost prophetic.

In May 1911, 10 men in Serbia formed the Black Hand Secret Society. Early members included Colonel Dragutin Dimitrijevic, the chief of the Intelligence Department of the Serbian General Staff, Major Voja Tankosic and Milan Ciganovic. By 1914 there were around 2,500 members of the Black Hand with its main objective being the creation, by means

British stretcher bearers – Western Front

of violence, of a Greater Serbia. Its stated aim was…. *To realise the national ideal, the unification of all Serbs. This organisation prefers terrorist action to cultural activities, and as such it will, therefore, remain secret.*

As most will be aware, the immediate cause of the Great War of 1914 - 1918 was the 1914 assassination of the Austrian Crown Prince Franz Ferdinand in Sarajevo by a Serbian. Many Serbians aspired to see the formation of a large national Slavic state in the Balkans, which in reality was ill-suited for such unity. Opposing their aspiration were the Croatians, Slovenes, and many of the Herzegonians who were western, Catholic, and part of the Austro-Hungarian Empire. On the other hand the Serbians, Montenegrins, and many of the Bosnians were Eastern Orthodox Christians and more brutal.

There is no doubt that the assassination of the Austrian Crown Prince was carried out by a secret society with help from high-ranking officers of the Serbian Army. The Serbian Black Hand Secret Society by this time was mainly made up of junior army officers, but it also included lawyers, journalists, and university professors. About 30 of these lived and worked in Bosnia-Herzegovina.

Historians are divided as to whether the assassination was planned by the Belgrade Masonic Lodge or the secret society known as the Black Hand. The fact that all the conspirators in the 1914 assassination of the Crown Prince had military pistols may point to the latter, bu then testimony at the trial of the conspirators would implicate the Freemasons. Historians who wrote during the war tended to believe it was the Freemasons, however, more modern historians lean more toward the Black Hand. It is, however, suggested that the two groups probably had extensive overlapping memberships so perhaps the Masonic Lodge and the Black Hand were both involved.

What resulted we should be all historically aware of.

On 28th July, 1914, the Austro-Hungarians fired the first shots in preparation for the invasion of Serbia. As Russia mobilised to come to their support, Germany invaded neutral Belgium and Luxembourg before moving towards France, leading Britain to declare war on Germany.

The Great War had begun!

After the German march on Paris was brought to a halt, what became known as the Western Front settled into a battle of attrition, with a trench line that would see little change until 1917.

Meanwhile, on the Eastern Front, the Russian army was successful against the Austro-Hungarians, but was stopped in its invasion of East Prussia by the Germans.

In November 1914, the Ottoman Empire would join the war, opening fronts in the Caucasus, Mesopotamia and the Sinai. Italy and Bulgaria would not join the war until 1915; with Romania in 1916.

During the first two years of the war the Serbian Army suffered a series of military defeats. The Prime Minister of Serbia, Nikola Pasic, blamed the Black Hand for the war, and in December 1916 it was decided to disband the organisation. Dragutin Dimitrijevic and several of the Black Hand leaders would be arrested and executed the following year. By the end of the war, the King of

Serbia would get his kingdom of Yugoslavia with all the Balkans forced into it.

Serbia WW1

Top left - Austro/Hungary troops hanging Serbians in 1914
Top right - A serb grieves over a lost comrade
Bottom - Serbian defenders

Bowler hats blotched the sober, foggy, sulphurous, workday atmosphere of Fleet Street; on the steps of the drab stone buildings, or bobbed up and down in the human eddy of arcades as officials went about their business. As the capital of a motley yet picturesque empire, London was alive in the days following the news that war had been declared.

Between August 1911 and July 1914, MI1, had arrested just ten suspected spies in Britain, with Smith Cumming's attempts to establish a spy network in Germany meeting similarly with little success. This had not stopped the threat of Germany's growing militarism having created a climate in pre-war Britain in which popular novels about espionage thrived.

In these the actual small number of spies employed by the German navy active in pre-war Britain, was depicted instead as a sophisticated German intelligence network, laying the foundations for an invasion of Britain.

Whilst this triumph of journalistic fantasy had not initially been taken seriously by the government, immediate repercussions when war broke out, had rung bells in the highest government circles. For the general populace, however, their outlook was initially different. With the majority believing that the war would be over by Christmas 1914, many places up and down Great Britain held street celebrations. The War Office, in a hive of activity, would quickly deluge the public with numerous propaganda posters to encourage everyone in their nation's time of need. With the exuberance of youth men were now rushing to answer the call to arms. Many were too old to serve but wanted to show their patriotism before it was too late. The government had asked for 100,000 volunteers, and got 750,000 in just one month. With the vast bulk of the nation supportive, not only of the declaration of war, but also of any man who wanted to join up they believed that victory against Germany would be quick and a certainty.

It was in this period of national fervour that Jehanne Blanche realised that she would have her part to play.

Existing purely to ensure national security through counter-espionage, Jehanne's internal counterparts in the Home Section also made up a small staff who worked in conjunction with the Special Branch of the Metropolitan Police. Their service was responsible for overall direction and the identification of foreign agents, whilst Special Branch provided the manpower for the investigation of their affairs, arrest and interrogation. Almost as if to engender a sense of national pride, on the day after the declaration of war, the Home Secretary, Reginald McKenna, announced in reference to arrests directed by this service …

Within the last 24 hours no fewer than 21 spies, or suspected spies, have been arrested in various places all over the country, chiefly in important military or naval centres, some of them long known to the authorities to be spies.

Hopeful volunteers line up in the rain outside the Whitehall Recruiting Office – August 1914

In reality the actual number of suspects identified was 22 and the Home Section had started sending out letters to local police forces on 29th July giving them advance warning of arrests to be made as soon as war was declared. Portsmouth Constabulary had jumped the gun arresting one suspect on 3rd August, and not all of the 22 had been in custody by the time that McKenna made his speech.

The outcome was that 11 were executed with the incident recorded as a devastating blow to Imperial Germany depriving them of their entire spy ring, and in specifically upsetting the Kaiser. Their enthusiasm in support of national pride, however, had outshone the truth, for it would be later proven that only nine were actual spies; that there was no organised spy ring; and that the Home Secretary's efforts had effectively increased growing mass hysteria.

Following the balance of the arrests on 4th August, thousands of imaginary acts of espionage were now being reported to credulous police and military authorities as unprecedented 'spy mania' gripped Britain. Thousands of false accounts of suspicious 'night-signalling', by which German spies might be guiding Zeppelins or submarines towards their targets, were submitted. Homing pigeons, seen to be capable of carrying messages to the enemy, were killed by

Wilhelm II, German Kaiser

enthusiastic patriots. Fabricated systems of German espionage, ranging from German operatives in the ranks of prostitutes around Piccadilly Circus, to 'naturalised' businessmen of the highest social standing, encouraged anti-German sentiment. With imagination running rampant the truth, however, could be construed as more prosaic.

Specialising in foreign target espionage, the role of the Foreign Section (MI1) of which Jehanne was now a trained operative, moved quickly to expand its network of agents across Europe and Russia. It was imperative to know where Germany's troops were heading and what armaments they were developing. Many civilians in Belgium and northern France would risk their lives to provide details of enemy troop movements by watching the trains on which they travelled to the front.

In his office Smith Cumming had taken up the habit of often dropping the 'Smith' from his surname in routine communication, typically now only signing correspondence with his initial 'C' in green ink. Whilst other operatives had their disguises, at the suggestion of Smith Cumming, Jehanne Blanche had reverted to her naval nickname in written communications as 'Jane Blonde' with her telegraphic code reference as *HMS Blonde*. This delighted Smith Cumming who jokingly referred to her as 'His Majesty's Blonde Spy'.

Kaiser Wilhelm

Located in this massive neo-Baroque building, with its thousand rooms linked by 2½ miles of corridors spread across seven floors, was the War Office in Whitehall, London. From the warmth and safety of its interior the dull, grey, over-caste of that blustery autumn afternoon epitomised the depressing significance the announcement that war had brought.

British War Office, Whitehall, London

Jehanne was preparing for her first trip back to France since leaving those two years earlier. Staring out at the plane trees across Horse Guards' Avenue they reminded her of those on Marseille's elegant, tree, lined boulevards that rushed up from her quayside. As she reflected on how fortunate she had been the falling autumn leaves outside were being choreographed by some hidden hand to flutter momentarily before a stronger, cold, northerly gust picked them out. Blown against the uprights of the black, cast iron, fence in front of the building opposite; down the footpath and gutters, or under the wheels of the passing conveyances, their withered forms would again come to rest to await their next dance of nature. Maybe some unforeseen hand was steering her destiny also, or did humanity create its own?

By 5th September the First Battle of the Marne had been underway that had stopped German troops at the gates of Meaux in Northern France. This heroic action had not only prevented the city from being taken by the Germans but also changed the course of the war. A week later it had resulted in an Allied victory against the German Army under Chief of Staff Helmuth von Moltke the Younger.

French troops defend a position on the Marne River

This battle effectively ended the month long German offensive that had opened the war and reached the outskirts of Paris. The counterattack of six French field armies and one British army along the Marne River would force the German Imperial Army to abandon its push on Paris and retreat northeast, setting the stage for four years of trench warfare on the Western Front. It was an immense strategic victory for the Allies, wrecking Germany's bid for a swift victory over France and forcing it into a protracted two-front war.

Now, early October, and a Rolls-Royce Coupe driven by the 24-year-old intelligence officer Alastair Smith-Cumming sped along the road through the woods outside Meaux. With a love of fast cars his father, Mansfield, sat beside him with Jehanne in the back seat. Mansfield had come out to France to visit his son, and to meet with, and introduce Jehanne to Captain Stewart Newcombe RE who had been sent to France with the Royal Engineers in support of the recent Allied retreat at Mons. They had just left their meeting with Captain Newcombe when, suffering a blow out in one of tyres, the open-topped Rolls suddenly veered off the road to smash through undergrowth and into a tree on the edge of recently ploughed field. Here the car overturned pinning Mansfield by his left leg, almost severing it at the ankle, and flinging his son out onto his head.

Rolls Royce coupe

Jehanne was catapulted over the screen to land unceremoniously, and remarkably without injury, 20 feet further on in the field between two recently ploughed furrows.

Hearing his son moaning, and in severe pain himself, Mansfield tried to extricate himself from the wreckage to crawl to him but despite all efforts he was unable to free his leg.

Picking herself up, after discovering nothing was broken, Jehanne arrived at his side to help. Not wanting to compromise her position, or his own, any further, Mansfield ordered her to quickly depart the scene. Her instructions were to anonymously advise local gendarmerie of the accident, and then get herself discreetly back to Britain. After cleaning herself up she would make the call from a nearby town before blending back into the countryside on a stolen bicycle.

Back at the crash site, popular history has it that taking out his penknife Smith-Cumming began hacking through his tendons and bone until, completely severing his lower leg, he was free of any restriction. Hospital records show, however, that while both his legs were broken, his left foot was only amputated the day after the accident. He did, however, free himself, managing to drag himself over to spread his coat over his dying son. He would be found sometime later unconscious by the body of his boy. His extraordinary act of bravery, sacrifice, and a willingness to use whatever means necessary, however unpleasant, to achieve an end, was to make him a secret service legend.

No mention was ever made of the female operative who had placed the anonymous call.

Later Smith-Cumming would later often tell all sorts of fantastic stories as to how he lost his leg, and shock people by interrupting meetings in his office by suddenly stabbing his artificial leg with a knife, letter opener or fountain pen; also as a test for new aspiring agents to see if they flinched.

Sidney Reilly

Carl Hans Lody

By the time of Jehanne's return from France activity within MI1 had increased dramatically with her just in time to be party to the verdict and fate of the first German spy captured on British soil. He was the German Imperial Naval Reserve officer Carl Hans Lody. Found guilty of all counts against him, he was shot at the Tower of London on 6th November 1914.

Jehanne had studied his supposed methods, arriving at the conclusion that many of his espionage attempts had, in fact, been amateurish and inaccurate. This bizarrely included incorrect information about the alleged landing of large numbers of Russian troops in Aberdeen, on 2nd September, 1914 bound for France.

As one of his last acts before his execution Hans had been permitted to put pen to paper to write to his loved ones.

London, Nov, 5th 1914
Tower of London
(To relations in Stuttgart)

My dear ones,

I have trusted in God and He has decided. My hour has come, and I must start on the journey through the Dark Valley like so many of my comrades in this terrible War of Nations. May my life be offered as a humble offering on the 'alter of the Fatherland'.

A hero's death on the battlefield is certainly finer, but such is not to be my lot, and I die here in the Enemy's country silent and unknown, but the consciousness that I die in the service of the Fatherland makes death easy.

The Supreme Court-Martial of London has sentenced me to death for Military Conspiracy. Tomorrow I shall be shot here in the Tower. I have had just Judges and I shall die as an Officer, not as a spy.

Farewell. God bless you…. Hans.

Now on the old oak desk to Jehanne's side an opened file revealed another letter, along with a series of photographs on early Egyptian amulets, with one that was of specific interest.

Discovered by the German archaeologist Max von Oppenheim in central Mesopotamia at the site of the ancient city of Babylon, the bronze and ivory object in the photographs had evidently been in German hands in Berlin for some years. More importantly the ancient information it contained was only now being secretly shared. Their agent had advised, via German Intelligence, that by order of the Kaiser it was now being used to encourage the Ottoman Empire to join the Central Powers in the war and to instigate a Holy War, or jihad, in the East.

This intelligence had recently been received from an operative working inside the Austrian embassy in Berlin who, risking considerably more than his pension, had managed to get a copy to interested Entente parties. With it had come a short message in French that had been translated into English … not that Jehanne had any need of that. It read….

Amulet with hirz containing 1400 BC text reads…

"I will raise them up a Prophet from among their brethren, as Hashim ha-meshuggah the son of Abdullah ... and will put my word in his mouth; and he shall speak unto them all that I shall command him". Stop……Dynamite… Stop... Being used by German Intel to woo Turkey to join CP and start jihad.

Amulet half and note

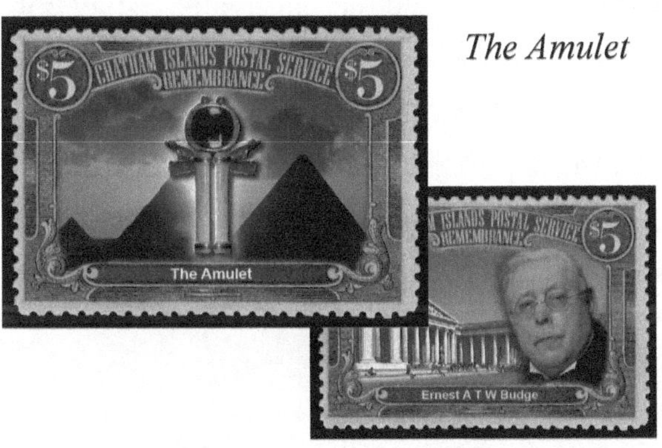

The Amulet

Jehanne picked up the photo again and studied the object. To her it looked like half an amulet of some kind and it certainly looked very old. Its design incorporated what she now surmised to be an ivory stem fitted below a metal effigy of a frog, above which was a worn open half crescent. No doubt previous owners had assumed the stem to be to be solid, and this must have been where its ancient message had been hidden. The note and photograph had been delivered to her desk with a simple instruction.

Confidentially find out background information on object's authenticity with the true relevance of its message. Refer to your acquaintance Budge at British Museum; along with anything concerning archaeologist Max von Oppenheim.

With the outbreak of war, and with her knowledge and skills developing, Jehanne's desire to risk take on a field assignment had been heightened. Her unfortunate experience in France with the loss of Mansfield's son likewise made her feel as though she should be doing more, and it was this desire that Mansfield needed her to understand and control. Further training and work in support services, therefore, was all that was currently on offer.

Remembering Mansfield's wise counsel that it was all in her best interests Jehanne positively continued her specialist education. With his ability to expand her thinking with his philosophy and political rationale; both current and ancient, she would consult with Ernest Budge. He also kept her focused, and Jehanne looked forward to her time with him. For some inexplicable reason she now had the unmistakeable feeling that she was going to need his wise counsel and information in future.

The British Museum, London

Mansfield and Ernest were, however, only two sources of knowledge and experience Jehanne was introduced to.

Ernest Budge

Jehanne Blanche

In the confines of the small oddly shaped upstairs room in Whitehall Jehanne listened with intent to a tall, pipe-smoking Naval Intelligence officer, whose enthusiasm and mannerisms, in the blue haze he created, reminded her of a runaway train at full speed. He had been called in to give MI1 a briefing regarding the enemy's military communications and British success in enemy code-breaking, while out in the English Channel in a swirling, cold, squall of salt spray, a cable ship attempted to stay on station in a rising sea.

While the Naval Intelligence instructor darted his pointer over a map back in London, the ship's oil skin clad seamen fought the elements on deck. They manned a grapple and winches on board that was straining to lift a clamped undersea cable. With the sea racing over the ship's aft deck the seamen perservered at their task while water washed down the scuppers back to be released back to the mounting sea's dull grey depths. This cable was another of Germany's telegraphic cables that, freed from the bottom, would be cut the same as others had been.

Cable ships working in the English Channel

As the barometer continued to drop the seamen worked as fast as they dared, hopeful that they could complete their task so their ship could make the haven of a sheltered port before the storm hit.

Back in London the instructor steamed ahead with his oratory sucking intermittently on his now glowing pipe.

A cable laying ship

More spectacular has been the expansion of the international telegraph network, mainly through the laying of submarine cables. Each cable comprises many individual wires, and every major power owns its own commercial network of cables. These have now been placed under direct government control, or close supervision, with much of Germany's telegraph connection to the world beyond the Central Powers, ordered to be destroyed.

As he continued his gesticulations appeared, amusingly to Jehanne, as though he was inflicted with 'St Vitus' Dance.

Technology has advanced to the point where primitive forms of multiplexer and code compressors are in use to allow a single wire to handle multiple messages. Switching equipment, although fundamentally mechanical, had become complex and expensive. The destruction or damage of an international telegraph station or relay can cause considerable disruption and take a long time to replace, especially if complex equipment has to be transported to it by sea. Such stations have, therefore, become important strategic targets, with our worldwide spread empire and trading interests also vulnerable to damage to our cable network.

In the stuffy smoke filled atmosphere Jehanne and the others learnt that on 4th August Britain had opened the telegraph war by initially cutting the German submarine cable that ran from Borkum in the North Sea to the Spanish island of Tenerife in the South Atlantic.

Once the cable was ashore it ran from a cable shed to the Cable Station

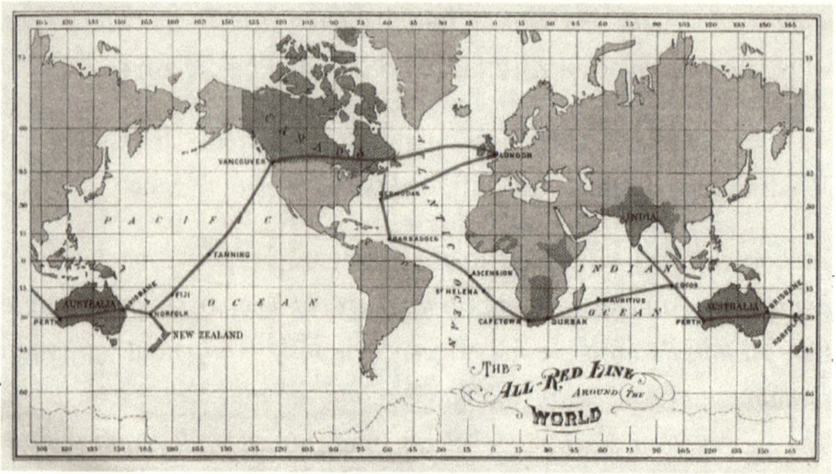

There was a substantial German research station on the coast of Tenerife and there were fears that it was being used as a cover for espionage and potentially U boat support. As Tenerife lies close to the sea routes our ships take to Britain's West African colonies and South Africa, the 1st Lord of the Admiralty, Winston Churchill, ordered the cutting of the communications link.

The next step has been to address the remaining German cables running through the English Channel. Many of these are simply being grappled, raised, and cut, with some that link to neutral countries patched into the our British cable network. This provides us with additional capacity, and in the short term allows for the intercepting of incoming messages for Germany from the remote terminus of these cables.

With Germany now lacking direct telegraphic access to the Western hemisphere it has forced them to either use radio over shorter distances, or use our British or American cables instead, despite the risk of interception. Any messages passed over cables that touch on British soil are of course capable of being intercepted by us at British Intelligence.

Don't we have cables that come ashore that the Germans' can get at ? enquired Jehanne.

Good point! ..... In fact our German friends have not been idle. Recently, we were advised that they have struck back. Their cruisers SMS Nurnberg, accompanied by SMS Leipzig, under cover of the French flag, landed on the tiny Pacific territory of Fanning Island on 7th September. Fanning Island's only importance is that the submarine cable from Canada comes ashore there to a cable station that provides the switching capacity to route messages to and from two connecting cables, one to Australia and the other to New Zealand. The landing party from the Nurnberg wrecked the station and cut the cables. They also found time to raid the local post office and steal some stamps... the instructor grinned.

Maybe one of them is a stamp collector and thinks they will be valuable after the war...

He laughed, continuing in his same enthusiastic manner ...

Maybe you already know that earlier this year the teletypewriter was invented. This has meant that an incoming electric signal can be automatically decoded and typed onto a strip of ticker tape, which clerks then glue to a blank form for delivery.

Now for the special bit....

Formed only a few weeks ago by our chaps in Naval Intelligence, we now have 'Room 40'; also known as Old Building 40, or 40 O.B. It is here that the section in the Admiralty most identified with the British crypto-analysis effort now resides. At the Admiralty's insistence its operators are only permitted to decrypt, but not to interpret the information they acquire, and, I have to say, they are doing a sterling job.

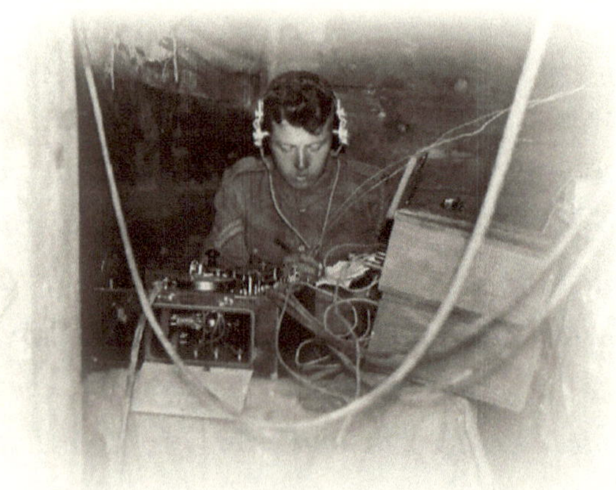

British wireless communication in the field

The section began unofficially some time back when intercepts from the German radio station at Nauen, near Berlin, were given to our Director of Naval Education Alfred Ewing, who constructed ciphers as a hobby. Ewing recruited a translator of theological works from German, and a publisher to assist him in his deciphering. The basis of this room's operations have since evolved around a German naval codebook that was passed on to us by the Russians. Known as the 'Signalbuch der Kaiserlichen Marine (SKM)', it includes maps containing coded squares. The Russians managed to seize the book from the German cruiser Magdeburg when it ran aground off the Estonian coast on 26th August. Two of the four copies that the warship had been carrying were recovered; one has been retained by the Russians, while the other was thankfully passed into us.

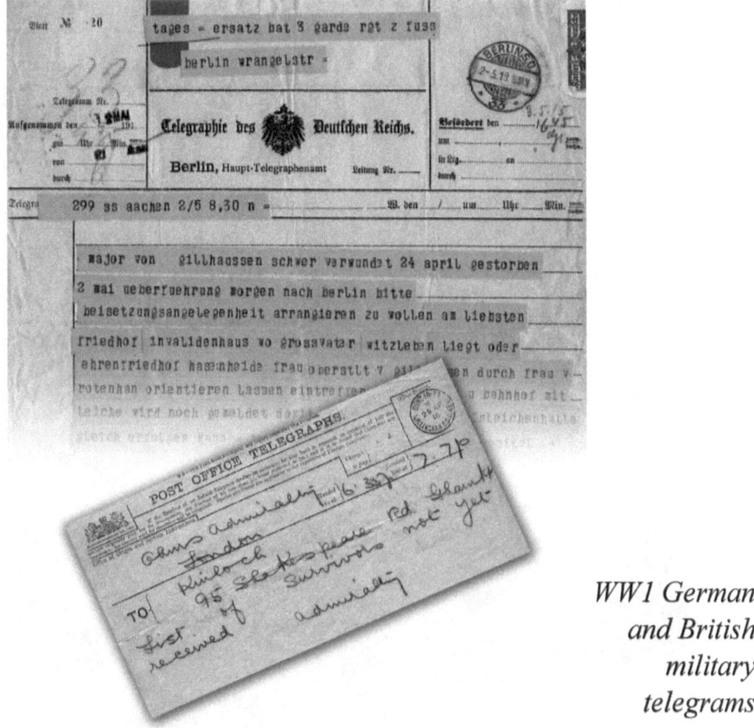

*WW1 German
and British
military
telegrams*

More recently we obtained the Handelsschiffsverkehrsbuch (HVB), or Imperial German Navy's codebook used by German naval warships, merchantmen, naval zeppelins and U-Boats. This was captured from the German steamer Hobart by the Royal Australian Navy.

As the communications presentation came to an end Jehanne started to apply her thoughts to meeting with Ernest Budge two days later on the 9th November. Her priority was now the amulet and its use by Germany in attempting to incite Holy war in the East with the Turks. That was, she mused to herself once she stood, if she could see to make her way out of this smoke laden room. Its now open door with an escaping blue haze highly likely had already inspired some concerned resident ringing the local fire brigade.

Right - Early 1915 vacuum tube receiver

Below - Onboard ship transmitter and receiver

For British Naval Intelligence and Room 40, luck would compound on luck, for on 30th November a British trawler would recover a safe from the sunken German destroyer S-119. In it they would find the Verkehrsbuch (VB); the code used by the Germans to communicate with naval attachés, embassies and warships overseas.

German Iron Cross 1st Class

Part VI

Arthur Newcombe

 ith the outbreak of war, and much to the disgust of his father a young confident, 16 year-old, Arthur Newcombe entered the recruitment office at Stamford Brook Hall on the outskirts of London to sign on for King and Country.

Name, followed by age...? asked the enlistment sergeant from behind a shabby oak desk.

Arthur Edgar Newcombe, and I'm 17... was Arthur's cautious reply.

With his 17th birthday the following week Arthur had calculated he might get away with stating he was 17, but that he would probably not fool the sergeant as being a year older.

Without raising his head the sergeant curtly responded …
I suggest you walk round the block and rethink that age, as 18 is the legal age for enlistment!

Taking this to be an affirmation

Enlistment poster

that he should return to try again, Arthur simply followed military instructions. He walked round the block, entered the office for a second time, gave his name, and this time confidently stated his age as 18. Signing his name on the Middlesex Regiment's enlistment form, he was accepted, subject of course to the cursory medical which, as it transpired, he would pass with flying colours.

Following the 'First Line Battalions' of the Middlesex Regiment having quickly been sent off to their overseas war stations a surplus of volunteers sought to enlist in Territorial Battalions. It had become quickly obvious that the First Line Battalions would need reinforcements almost at once, and the War Office had given permission to raise Second Line Territorial units.

Lining up to recruit

General Kitchener was not in favour of these 'Territorial' units, although he and other critics would be silenced after they fought so well with the British Expeditionary Force (BEF) after Mons.

The War Office wanted these 'Territorial' volunteers to transfer to the Regular Army, or Kitchener's New Army. The majority, however, loyally elected to remain with the Territorial Battalions that had enlisted them.

Private 2806 Arthur Edgar Newcombe

One of these was the 2/10th Battalion of the Middlesex Regiment that had been formed at Stamford Brook in September 1914, and into whose ranks Arthur Newcombe had enlisted just short of his 17th birthday. His battalion had then moved to Staines to be attached to 2/Middlesex Brigade, (later the 201st Brigade of the

Home Counties (67th) Division).

The small town of Staines lay on the east bank of the Thames, on the border with Surrey, and across which there has been a bridge since Roman times. Located on the main road west from London it was 17 miles east north-east to Charing Cross, on the outskirts of the city. To the north and south of the town lay fields and meadows that were now dotted with canvas bell tents. Up until the army's arrival an increase in heavy traffic through Staines had helped to support its 27 inns and hotels. Now they were additionally doing a brisk trade hosting new recruits of eligible age, with money to spend during their few hours off from training.

British soldiers retiring with their wounded to the trenches

Predominantly in the larger cities, those who were fit enough, of eligible age, who had not wanted to join the military were considered fair game to be targeted as cowards. Many were being handed white feathers, while others were being refused service by shops and pubs.

This enthusiasm and associated scare mongering thankfully did not last, for after the Battle of the Marne it had become obvious, as trench warfare in northern France took hold, that there would not be a quick victory. The true reality of a modern war would become obvious to all as war-weariness set in with the government not able to hide the fact that many thousands of men had been killed or severely wounded. The return of wounded soldiers to London rail stations late at night would do nothing to detract from the knowledge that casualties were becoming horrendous. A chaplain would later write…

We had imagined ourselves then to be living in an age of enlightenment; and that a civilised nation like Germany should wantonly provoke a war with her European neighbours came as a shock both to the intelligence and to the conscience. The nation sprang at once to arms; so too did the peoples of the British Empire. There is no adequate parallel in history, before or since, to the upsurge of stern resolution that the need aroused. The response came from every section of the community. And it was for long an entirely voluntary response: despite the desperate character of the struggle, conscription was not introduced till two years later. Above all there was an idealistic ardour, a sense of unity, and a comradeship which a later generation has found it hard to understand.

With his surname coincidentally the same as Arthur's, Major Stewart Newcombe had returned from France and was now working with T E Lawrence at the War Office in London to complete the reports and maps of the surveys he had undertaken of Southern Palestine and the Sinai Peninsula.

On 9th December, 1914, both Stewart and T.E.Lawrence were ordered to Egypt to be joined by Woolley and other specialists in Middle Eastern affairs. Based in Cairo under Gilbert Clayton, **as** Director of both the Military and Political Intelligence Services, Stewart would be tasked with organising a new Military Intelligence Branch.

It would not be long before Jehanne Blanche joined them.

Arthur Edgar Newcombe

Cairo

Captain William Shakespear

In the December 1914 the British Government attempted to cultivate favour with Ibn Saud, the future king of Saudi Arabia, via their secret agent, Captain William Shakespear.

The captain had been an English civil servant and explorer who had mapped uncharted areas of Northern Arabia, and become military adviser to Ibn Saud. Having held that post since 1910 he would be shot and killed in the territorial battle of Jarrab by one of Ibn Rashid's men on 24th January 1915.

As a proxy battle of World War I this territorial scrap was effectively between the British-supported Sa'udis and their traditional enemies, the Ottoman-supported Rashidis.

British interest in the Sa'udis would be abandoned after Shakespear's death. Instead, the British would transfer their support to his Ibn Saud rival Sharif Hussein bin Ali, leader of the Hejaz, with whom the Sa'udis were almost constantly at war. It was at this juncture that Lord Kitchener appealed to Hussein bin Ali, Sharif of Mecca for

Abd al-'Azīz Āl Sa'ūd

assistance in the conflict. Naturally Hussein wanted political recognition in return.

Known as Tirabin al-Sana, the Tarabin Bedouin were the most important Bedouin tribe in the Sinai Peninsula during the 19th century and destined to become the second largest inside Mandatory Palestine. They could trace their ancestry to one by the name of Atiya who had lived at Turba, east of Mecca, as a tribal member of the Quraysh. This was the tribe of Mohammed the prophet, and it is believed that Atiya had migrated to the western Sinai in the 14th Century.

A Bedouin camp

The descendents of Atiya's son Nijm had then shifted north into the Negev to settle around Beersheba. Nijm had brought up two sons from whom the two branches of the Negev Tarabin trace their line; the Nijmat and the Ghawali. The first of these was regarded as the paramount clan, and tradition had it, that at times of war, that the Nijmat would lead the whole tribe into battle.

In the first months of 1915 their leader was Hammad Pasha al-Sufi, and he would lead his force of 1,500 Negev Bedouin, under overall Turkish command, in an attack on the Suez Canal.

Later, seeing the writing on the wall other Bedouin, and Arabs further east, would wisely withdraw from the conflict.

Since the early Islamic period the vast majority of Bedouin had been Sunni Moslems. Their Five Pillars of Islamic faith included the five daily ritual prayers, along with almsgiving, fasting, and the pilgrimage to Mecca. As a declaration of faith most Bedouin societies observe the fast of Ramadan, perform the obligatory prayers, and celebrate the two major Islamic holidays. Some groups endeavour to make the hajj, or pilgrimage to Mecca, more than once in a lifetime, with individual piety sometimes reflected in the number of pilgrimages an individual manages to undertake.

For the Tirabin al-Sana they variously believed in the presence of spirits, in the form of playful or malevolent 'jinn' that interfered in the life of humans. In this regard the 'envious eye' was very real to them, with their children

An Arab in prayer

believed to be particularly vulnerable.

Other Bedouin groups postulated the existence of ogresses, and of monstrous super-naturals. For both reasons they often had protective amulets attached to their clothing or hung around their necks.

Handed down through his family, Ibrahim Sulaiman Bin Ghanim al-Sana, with the wisdom of years upon him, wore one such amulet. If reality it was only half of an ancient amulet. It was not just a symbol of his faith, in the presence of 'jinn', but it was also known to ward off the ahl al-ard or 'people of the earth' who were known to sometimes meet lone travellers in the desert with dire consequences.

Moslems face Mecca in prayer

Also known to Ibrahim Sulaiman Bin Ghanim al-Sana was that many generations ago in the Sinai the dark gnarled hand of an ancestor had brushed away the remnants of a parched goat's hide covering to discover his tarnished bronze and ivory tube-shaped half amulet. With its ancient bronze frog, it had not hung from the more common pyramid-shaped network of interlocked silver rods and loops, on three long strands of heavy silver chains. Neither was it decorated with ancient Arabic calligraphy, but it did have a symbol inscribed in a chasing technique that indicated that this was only half of an original more complete amulet.

Whether half or whole, to Ibrahim and his Bedouin followers, they had known that it was very special, of a very early type that kept protective religious verses, or incantations. This one they knew to be was old, also knowing that its ivory tube was highly likely hollow that it hid a message. The family had handed it down over the generations with the instruction that it was dangerous to open it, and as a consequence no one had dared to remove its ancient script.

A Bedouin tribesman

Since its opening in 1869 the Suez Canal had featured prominently in British policy with it deemed an important, if not vital, artery for the Empire. An international convention signed in 1888 by the European Powers had then guaranteed freedom of navigation of its channel, while the equipped ports at Alexandria and Port Said, along with their military bases had made the region

Armed constabulary

particularly useful as a British foothold in the Near East.

British troops on the Suez Canal

To re-cement and protect that foothold, with its line of communication, by August 1914 it was defended by a force of 5,000 British soldiers based in Egypt.

Kress von Kressenstein

British troops - Suez Canal 1915

Abbas Hilmi, the reigning Ottoman Khedive, who opposed British occupation, had been out of the country when the war had started. Then when the British declared Egypt a Protectorate on 18th December 1914 they had deposed him and created Prince Hussein Kamel as the Sultan of Egypt in his place.

Going against British sentiment, however, was the undeniable fact that by 1914 British popularity had been in decline in Egypt. The majority of the populace disliked their occupation, the imposition of their race and religion, and their control over Egypt. Whilst not having a like for the Turks or Germans either, while the outcome of the war was unknown and the fighting continued, the population would live ever hopeful that the British would be evicted, along with the Turks.

Abbas Hilmi

Turkey had formally entered the war on 28th October 1914 with the bombing of Russian Black Sea ports. When their Ottoman armies mobilised Brigadier General Zekki Pasha, commanding the Ottoman IV Army at Damascus, immediately planned an attack on the Suez Canal. This plan was orchestrated with the support of Djemal Pasha, Commander in Chief of Syria and Palestine.

The Bavarian Colonel Kress von Kressenstein had been appointed Chief of Staff of the VIII Corps, IV Army on his arrival from Constantinople on 18th November 1914. His VIII Corps in Sinai and Palestine comprised five infantry divisions; - the 8th, 10th, 23rd, 25th, and 27th They included contingents from the Sinai Bedouins, Druzes, Kurds, Mohadjirs, the Circassians from Syria, and Arabs. It was envisaged that these Moslem contingents would foment revolt against the British in Egypt.

Eyüp Sultan Mosque

An Arab merchant caravan

With the advent of Turkey entering the war orders had been sent to the rulers and governors around the Ottoman empire to pray for victory. Prayers were now being recited in all the holy places, including mosques and monasteries throughout the empire, along with the reading of the Surah Al-Fath, and Al-An'am.

Scholars and hafizes in Constantinople gathered at Eyüp Sultan Mosque with each taking a part from the Quran to read. After the whole Quran was read they would then pray for the army's triumph. In the following weeks the city's inhabitants gathered in their neighborhoods on Mondays and Thursdays, while scholars, hafizes and mudarris, (religious professors), gathered in the mosques. Ulamas and the statesmen would recite Surah Al-Fath, and the prayer Salat-ı Munciye, 1,001 times after the Maghrib prayer, while the Ayat al-Kursi was recited in the department of Hırka-ı Şerif in Topkapı Palace. Ever confident in victory the Quran was then read in the mosques after the Fajr prayer twice a week.

Ottoman troops

Colonel Kress von Kressenstein
Chief of Staff of the VIII Corps, IV Ottoman Army

On 20th November, 1914, hostilities in the Sinai had commenced when a 20 man patrol of Bikanir Imperial Camel Corps service troops from India was attacked at Bir en Nuss, 20 miles east of

Kantara, by 200 Bedouin.

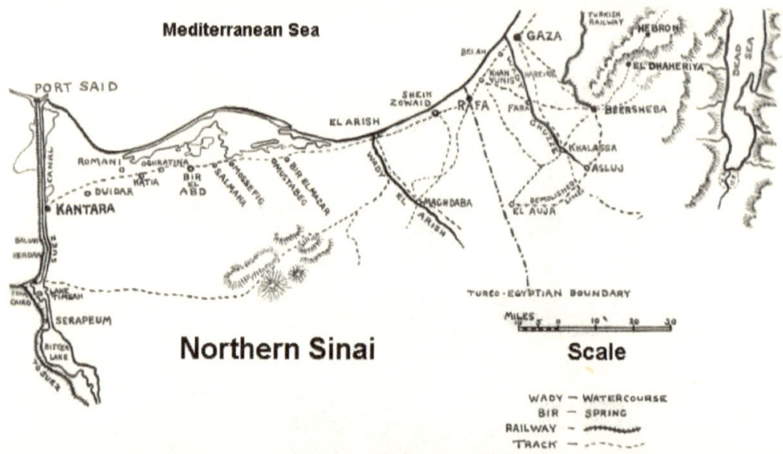

Slaughtered without a quam the patrol had lost more than half their number.

By December El Arish on the Sinai coast had been occupied by an Ottoman force while an organised defence by the British of the Suez Canal was underway. Whilst there had been a pre-war suggestion that a force of camels could hold Nekhl to the south of the Egyptian - Palestine frontier, on the western side of the Suez Canal in central Sinai, the decision had been made that a more appropriate and obvious line of actual defence of the eastern frontier of Egypt, was the Suez Canal itself.

Ottoman troops and artillery

In January 1915 Kress von Kressenstein concentrated 20,000 men in southern Palestine with nine field batteries and one 5.9 inch howitzer. The force comprised two echelons, including approximately 1,500 Arabs. Included in their ranks were the Bedouin of Ibrahim Sulaiman Bin Ghanim al-Sana.

Its task was to cross the Sinai and attack the Suez Canal.

Once there, the plan was that a single infantry division, supported by Ibrahim's Sinai Bedouins, would cross the canal to capture Ismailia before being reinforced by a second infantry division. They would be supported on the east bank of the canal by two additional divisions, with a further division also available to reinforce the bridgehead on the west bank.

To aid achieving their objective, during the autumn of 1914, the Ottoman Empire had fortuitously constructed a branch railway line extending from the Jaffa–Jerusalem railway at Ramleh. It ran south to reach Sileh about 275 miles from the Suez Canal.

Just nine months from the start of this section's construction the 100 mile stretch of the railway to Beersheba had been opened in October 1915. Any attack on the Suez Canal would, however, still require artillery and a bridging train to be dragged across the Sinai desert.

Hammad Pasha al-Sufi at the head of his Bedouin force at Beersheba (above and below)

The two Ottoman divisions, plus the reserve with camel and horse units, were ready to depart in mid-January. It was intended that German aircraft stationed in Palestine would aid the Ottoman force flying bombing missions in support of their main attack. Their 10 day advance across the Sinai, however, would be tracked by British aircraft.

Arab irregulars of the Ottoman army heading south from Jerusalem

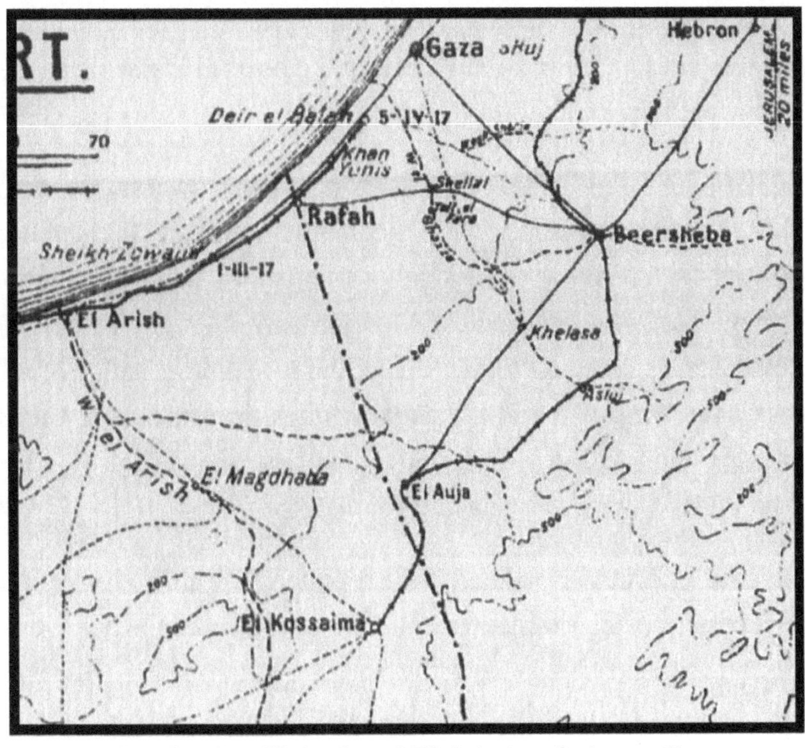

Map showing El Arish and El Auja in relation to Gaza

Kress von Kressenstein's force moved south by rail, continuing on foot to el Aujah that would become their principal desert base. With them they transported iron pontoons for crossing the Suez Canal at Serapeum and Tussum.

Back at British Headquarters in Egypt it was known that the Ottoman's had assembled three divisions near Beersheba. By 11th January it was established that Nekhl had been occupied by a small Ottoman force, and on the 13th that strong columns of Ottoman troops were passing through el Aujah and El Arish. On 25th January a regiment was reported to be approaching Qantara, while the next day a force of 6,000 soldiers was sighted 25 miles east of the Little Bitter Lake, at Moiya Harab. It was on this day that British defenders at Qantara were first fired on by part of the approaching force. Then on 27th January the El Arish to Kantara road was cut five miles to the east and the posts at Baluchistan and Kubri were attacked.

The Ottoman forces had moved ever closer towards the Suez Canal in three echelons, with the main group making its way along its central route, while smaller forces were advancing on the northern and southern routes. Moving only at night Kress von Kressenstein's Suez Ottoman Expeditionary Force had by now established themselves in a camp 16 miles from the Suez Canal, believing they had not been noticed as their forward scouts had observed British officers playing football.

For those at British Headquarters a reported forward movement of the central attacking force made it clear that the main attack would come in the central sector, to the north or south of Lake Timsah. An armoured train with four platoons of New Zealand infantry was, therefore, hurriedly sent to reinforce the 5th Gurkhas post on the East bank.

Carrying pontoons and rafts, the Turkish infantry with a number of their Bedouin supporters approached the east bank of the canal in the early hours of 3rd February. It was to be an ill-fated attempt as Indian machine-gunners cut swathes through those on the water and through men massing in the gullies on the eastern canal bank.

Ottoman camp in the Sinai

Below - Turkish troops preparing to move out

Turkish troops moving across the Sinai towards their objective

The bullet that ripped into the chest of Ibrahim Sulaiman Bin Ghanim al-Sana as he stepped from the pontoon boat with his sword raised above his head, stopped him in his tracks with him tumbling face first into the water by the shore. Panic ensued with many Arab and Bedouin troops on the Ottoman side surrendering

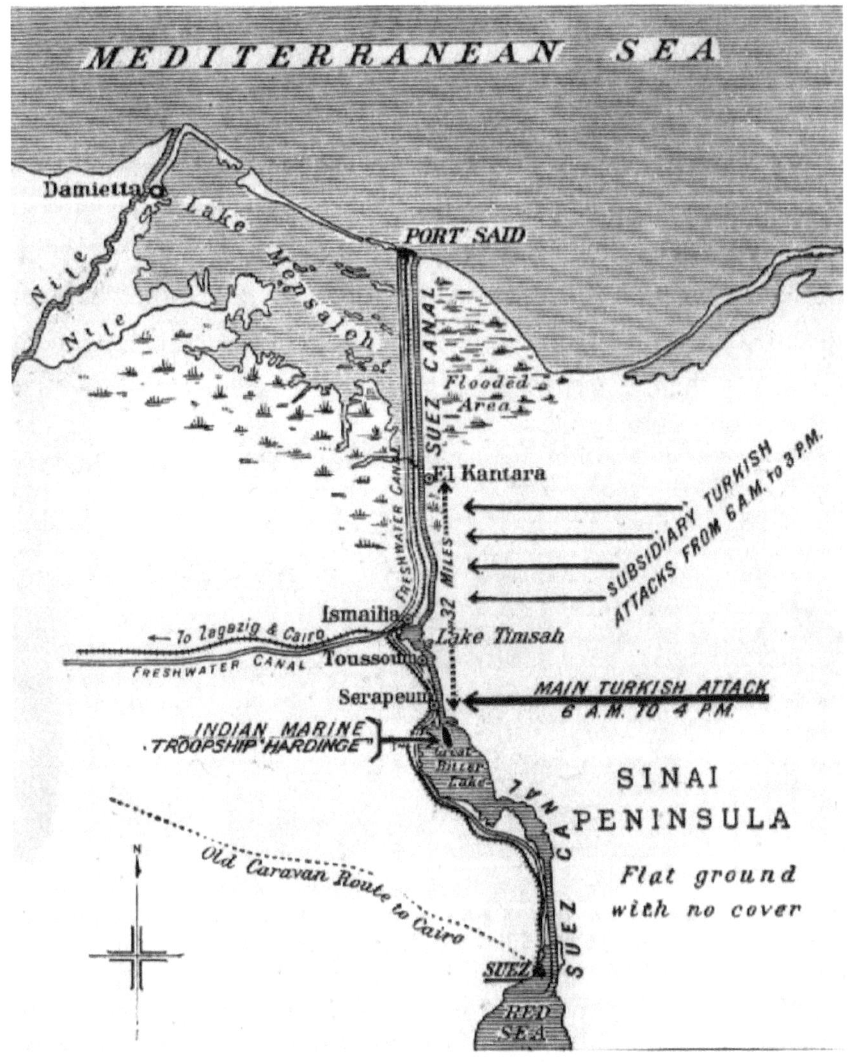

A map showing locations of the Turkish attacks

much to the disgust of the Turks. Undeterred the Ottoman attack was renewed that morning, with additional diversionary attacks launched at Kantara, and near Ismailia. The Ottoman force advancing from the southeast occupied entrenched positions 800 yards from the canal defences, while two of their field batteries went into action in support of their infantry attacks. They fortuitously started to hit shipping in the canal, but after the location of the Ottoman howitzer was identified, 9,200 metres away, one of the British Navy ship's turrets took out the howitzer with their third round. Shelling, along with continued staunch resistance by Allied troops in defensive posts, resulted in an end to the fighting by mid afternoon. As a consequence the entire Ottoman force was forced to withdraw back across the Sinai towards Beersheba. They were unmolested by the British who did not follow them in any force.

Indian troops defend the Canal

As an outcome this unsuccessful attack by the Turks had lost them 1,500 troops, with no sign of any local Egyptian Arab insurrection.

Ibrahim's body would remain until stripped eagerly by expectant local Arabs seeking his garments and effects. As for his half amulet, within two days it would be traded by local Delta Egyptians back in Cairo for needed supplies, and not so needed relief.

The Suez Canal

Indian troops - Suez Canal

FIELD SERVICE
TOP SECRET
PASSED BY CENSOR
No 3743

Part VII

Before the events of August 1914 reports speaking of a war that could shake humanity had reached the Roman Catholic Church's Holy See in Rome. Then with war's outbreak those in power in the Church had feared an ominous sequel to the assassination of Archduke Franz Ferdinand of Austria.

Pope Pius X

In the interim, Pope Pius X in his hatred of the Orthodox Church had worked with true Catholic diplomacy, and Christian charity, behind the scenes to continually incite Emperor Franz Joseph of Austria-Hungary to eliminate the Serbs. After the Sarajevo assassination, Baron Ritter, the Bavarian representative in the Holy See had written to his government ...

The Pope approves of Austria's harsh treatment of Serbia. He has no great opinion of the armies of Russia and France in the event of a war against Germany. The Cardinal Secretary of State, Rafael Merry del Val, does not see when Austria could make war if she does not decide to do so now.

By the 15th August, 1914, the Pope had begun to feel unwell, and by the 19th his status had been critical. On the 20th, at 1:15 a.m., almost two months after Archduke Franz Ferdinand's assassination, he had died holding the hand of his loyal collaborator Cardinal Rafael Merry del Val. Whether Pope Pius X had a direct hand in the Archduke's assassination or not is unknown. He was, however, certainly complicit in creating an environment that had achieved that end, and the resultant division of European nations and empires into two sides locked in war. It was now a Great War that would continue in an unprecedented manner over the next four and half years, resulting in over 37 million military and civilian casualties.

Pope Pius X

Following those ill-fated first shots having been fired the two great Central Powers of Austria-Hungary and Germany had confronted the so-called Entente, or Allied, Powers of France, Russia, and Great Britain. They had met in secret on 5th September, 1914, agreeing that none of them would sign a separate treaty of peace to end the conflict.

Italy, on the other hand, had declined to join a Triple Alliance opting instead to remain neutral, even though its allies were Germany and Austria-Hungary when war was declared. In spite of the difficulties imposed by the war, cardinals in Rome had assembled to choose Pope Pius X's successor.

On the afternoon of 31st August, 57 of the 65 members of the College of Cardinals had first met, and on 3rd September, 1914 they had elected Giacomo della Chiesa as Pope. He had chosen the name Benedict XV. Curiously he had been raised to the elevated position of cardinal only four months prior to Pius X's death, thus making him eligible to vote in the conclave that elected him.

One of the new foundation blocks of this new Pope was the acceptance of religious 'modernism' by the Roman Catholic Church. In its 'dogmata', which its members were required to believe, it was now decreed that dogmata could conveniently evolve over time, not only in expression but also in substance, rather than remaining the same in substance for all time. Previously someone who believed, who had been taught something different from what the Church had ordained and believed, was labelled a heretic. This invariably involved the heretic claiming that they were right, or at least closer to the truth, and that the rest of the Church was wrong, or had been mislead.

Invariably also it was because the purported heretic had received a new revelation from God, or that they had understood the 'true' teaching of God which had previously not been understood, or had been lost. Both scenarios had almost inevitably led over the centuries to organisational separation, or a schism within the Church, while in true compassionate Roman Catholic style the offenders were excommunicated and ejected from the Church.

Adopting the new idea that doctrine could evolve it was possible for the Roman Catholic Modernist to believe that both the old teachings of the Church, and any new seemingly contradictory teachings could be correct. Each would have its time and place. Other than just showing a modern face to the world, any acceptance of this would be convenient politically in allowing almost any type of new belief the Roman Catholic Church, might wish to introduce, thus continuing to control freedom of choice. A truely magnanimous gesture that allowed the Church to focus on its power and control, with its added need for the accumulation of wealth.

As one of the old school the previous Pope Pius X had staunchly held to the view that modernist thinking was… *the synthesis of all heresies.* He had issued edicts in 1907 condemning the growing modernist movement within the Church as exactly that…. heresy! To ensure enforcement of the edicts of the Holy See, during his reign, his designated Monsignor had been required to organise, through his personal contacts with theologians, an unofficial group of censors who had reported to him those thought to be teaching condemned doctrine. This group was called the Sodalitium Pianum (SP), or the Fellowship of Pius (X), which in France was known as La Sapinière. It had never had more than 50 members, and from the outset its frequently overzealous and clandestine methods included not just the opening and photographing of private letters, but even the checking of the records of local bookshops to see who was buying what. This stance had hindered, rather than helped, the Church's drive to combat the new beliefs.

By WW1 the Sodalitium Pianum had become something else entirely. Branded more commonly as the S.P. it was now the Holy See's counter-espionage agency with British Intelligence fearing that it was highly likely that German or Austrian spies had managed to infiltrate both it and the Holy Alliance.

As for the Italian Government, at the outbreak of hostilities the Italian political left became severely split over its position on the war.

Pope Benedict XV

The Italian Socialist Party (PSI) opposed the war on the grounds of internationalism, but a number of Italian revolutionary syndicates supported intervention against Germany and Austria-Hungary, on the grounds that their reactionary regimes needed to be defeated to ensure the success of socialism. Opposing them was a German agenda, with the Roman Catholic Church in the centre. Impacting on this was now Pope Benedict XV's desire for the Church to adopt his more 'modernist' approach attempting to institute measures intended to break with the past. It had naturally signalled a new course for papal politics, and while reports of casualties and destruction poured into the Secretariat of State from its embassies in Brussels, Berlin, and Vienna, the new more enlightened position was adopted.

For political and financial ends the Roman Catholic Church now conveniently allowed acceptance of almost any type of new belief which they might wish to introduce under the guise of open acceptance publicly of all competing views.

Unbeknown to the British, whilst the new Pope was seen as their ally he would see particular benefits in the Holy See justifying its willing acceptance of large sums of money from the Imperial German State, via secret Swiss bank accounts.

With regard to Italy's involvement in the war, Church spies' continued their furtive encounters in dark Roman alleys that would soon give way to social gatherings in palaces and mansions in sympathy with one side or the other. Huge sums of money continued to flow into secret Swiss bank accounts from Germany to grease the palms of Catholic clergy and officialdom at the Holy See's acceptance. It was to be used to buy the Church's and Press's influence in Italian politics to either have Italy join the Central Powers, or keep Italy out of the war. In the latter case there was an incentive also in keeping the Holy See, and its bureaucracy of inflated ego driven officials, from the midst of a battlefront, while others tried to entertain the Allies as though the Church had no hand in domestic or military politics.

The clandestine affairs of several Cardinals and many high Church officials in Rome were complicit with the Germans and Austria in inflating the Roman Catholic Church's coffers while a minority were supporting the Allied cause. All were unaware of the tidal wave of fate that was descending upon them.

For Allah, the Compassionate, the Merciful, would be in the temple of God, to cast out all those that sell and buy in the temple, and to overthrow the tables of the moneychangers, and the seats of those that sell doves, and he would say to them ... It is written, My house shall be called the house of prayer; but you have made it a den of thieves. And the blind and the lame will come to me; and I will heal them ...

Initially for the Germans the war had unfolded in accordance with its strategy as laid out in 1906 in their Schlieffen Plan; a strategic roadmap for troop movements that had believed in guarantee quick victory for the German Empire. This prediction had not come true. After September's battle at the Marne the Germans had been forced to pull back their forward troops, which had changed the nature of the military conflict. By early 1915 what had been a lightning war of rapid movement and strategic strikes had turned into trench warfare, as a cruel, long, seemingly endless struggle with attendant loss of human lives. Both sides now needed new allies to reinforce their defensive lines, or simply to provide replacements for troop units that had now spent months fighting under awful conditions. It was logical, therefore, that both sides, now tried even harder to lure Italy into the war.

Although Italy was a member of the Triple Alliance with Germany and Austria, its leaders were determined not to expose their citizens to the hazards of war. In the first months of 1915 the embassies of both sides mounted full-press efforts to win Italy's support for the Entente on the one hand, or the Central Powers on the other.

With its hands firmly in politics the Holy See and the Pope felt a duty to seek a solution with Rome becoming an objective, but not a military one, as a strategic location for spies and conspiracies.

Germany and Austria had diplomatic representation in the Papal Court. Germany had been very well positioned since the 19th century counting on two ambassadors; one representing Prussia and the other representing Bavaria. Count Otto von Mühlberg, the Prussian diplomat, was energetic in his work while his Bavarian counterpart, Otto von Ritter, was especially admired by the Holy See's administration for his moderate nature. Austria was represented by Prince Schönberg, scion of a noble family who had served state and church for centuries. All three diplomats were experts in relations with the Roman curia, especially with bishops and cardinals, and more particularly with the Italian press.

In contrast, the Allies' diplomatic corps had been relegated to rubbing shoulders with lower-ranking levels of the papal administration. The only Allied ambassador with any ties in the upper realms of the Holy See was the Belgian envoy, but he preferred the good life to bad diplomacy, which annoyed his Russian equivalent, Tsar Nicholas II's representative. This Russian was not so well regarded in Rome, because of his country's religious politics, which made Orthodox Russia one of the great defenders of Protestantism within Catholic Europe.

Sir James Rennel Rodd

The main counterweights to the Central Powers' diplomacy were the British Ambassador to Italy, Sir James Rennell Rodd, and in the Holy See the English Cardinal Francis Aidan Gasquet, and his secretary Dom Philip Langdon. The latter now worked for the Holy Alliance in the capacity of an Allied propagandist. Langdon was better known as an expert on English monasteries than as a Holy Alliance spy.

Though he carried out-missions for the papal espionage services, it was said that the cardinal was behind these operations and that his secretary was merely following his orders. Patriotic and loyal to Benedict XV, Cardinal Gasquet had never doubted the need to support the Allied cause over the warlike Central Powers.

With the aid of the loyal Langdon he continued to gather information for the Holy Alliance and send copies on to London. In one of his early reports he had included a letter to the British Foreign Office describing the Central Powers espionage efforts to win the Holy See's sympathy to the German-Austrian cause. The letter had urged the Foreign Service to immediately name an ambassador to the Holy See. As a consequence in November, 1914,

Sir Henry Howard

London had sent Sir Henry Howard, a retired Catholic diplomat. In his first report back he had described the pro-German atmosphere, offering that the Holy Alliance agent inside the Holy See, Cardinal Gasquet, would continue funnelling information on everything inside the Holy See that related to the war unfolding outside.

Gasquet lived in the Palazzo San Calisto, a building in the Trastevere district belonging to the Holy See, and it soon became a centre for Allied sympathisers. Unfortunately it became so obvious that Pope Benedict XV had to summon Gasquet requesting that he keep his meetings more under cover. He feared that if an ambassador of the Central Powers were to learn of the cardinal's 'goings on', papal neutrality in the war would be jeopardised, along with the flow of finance. The Pope had additionally ordered the cardinal to pass on any information on Central Powers spies in the Holy See to the Holy Alliance, before sending it to the British. He reminded the cardinal that his first loyalty was to the papacy, not the English.

German and Austrian spies, just like their diplomats, worked openly to win over the Pope's sympathies and his aides to their cause in order to gain justification for their war policy, and to undermine the Allied Powers opposing them. Gasquet feared that German or Austrian spies might have managed to infiltrate the Holy Alliance and the Church's counter-espionage agency,

Cardinal Francis Aidan Gasquet

the Sodalitium Pianum, and he knew they needed to fight against that outcome.

In the first months of the war, Berlin and Vienna had sent not only ambassadors to the Holy See but also large contingents of diplomats and secret agents. These diplomats frequently requested audiences with Benedict XV.

The Holy Alliance had already reported to the Pope and his Secretary of State, Cardinal Pietro Gasparri, about the intentions of Italy's leaders.

Cardinal Pietro Gasparri

Papal spies also knew of meetings between representatives of the Roman government and the Austro-Hungarian Empire to negotiate Italy's entrance on that side.

Rome's opportunist position placed Vienna in a tight spot. The price of Italian support for Austria and Germany would be the so-called '*terre irredente*'; the Italian-speaking lands in the Trentine districts that belonged to the Austrian Empire.

Pope Benedict XV

On the other hand, the Holy Alliance had also reported to the Pope about the Italian government's contacts with the Allies. Papal espionage services had learned that the government in Rome was simultaneously negotiating its neutrality with the Entente. If Italy stayed neutral and the Entente won the war, the kingdom would likewise be rewarded with lands previously belonging to Austria.

Pope Benedict XV quickly ordered his spy service and Secretariat of State to devote themselves, body and soul, to preventing Italian entrance into the war in support of Austria and Germany. The Pope doubted the Italian state's ability to survive the storm of war, either politically or economically. This was especially if Italy, and therefore Rome, became a target for bombing attacks. Just as important he did not want to see the Holy See at the centre of any Italian conflict.

Vatican Lateran Cross

A problem emerged, however, when it was discovered that many high church officials in Rome favoured Italian intervention on the side of the Central Powers, which were the leading Catholic powers in central Europe and a barrier against the advance of the Russian Orthodox religion and pan-Slavism. These leanings encouraged German espionage to undertake still more intrigues within the Holy See, often with the support of papal counterespionage, the Sodalitium Pianum.

*Matthias
Erzberger*

It would not be long before Holy Alliance agents in Rome detected the arrival of another German. His name was Matthias Erzberger and he was already well respected in the upper spheres of the Holy See, and a familiar figure to the Pope.

Over the following months Erzberger would visit the Italian capital on several more occasions, maintaining relations in the Austrian and German embassies and keeping up continual visits to the Holy See's palaces. The German politician did not know he was under strict surveillance, not only by the Italian Secret Service, but also by the Holy Alliance who were more sympathetic to the Allied cause and the arguments of Cardinal Gasquet, than the Sodalitium Pianum, that was close to the Central Powers. It was clear that Ezberger was in Italy doing covert work for the Central Powers, but only the Holy Alliance knew the true intentions of this leader of the Catholic Center Party

Matthais Erzberger (left) in Rome

and the organisation Zentrum, which had been persecuted in Germany by Otto von Bismarck for many years.

With careful orchestration Erzberger had managed to be appointed to Rome, on Kaiser Wilhelm's orders, to offer Benedict XV the *'terre irredente'* aimed at the unification of Italian speaking peoples, and territories deemed to be Italian lands, in return for his convincing Italy to remain neutral in the conflict. Germany and its ruler had come to the conclusion that they preferred that Italy did not intervene in favour of Austria, because that would make Italy a theatre of war requiring both the Central Powers and the Entente to divert troops from other fronts. Kaiser Wilhelm likewise did not want Italy to intervene in favour of the Entente, which would bring an open Austrian-Italian conflict over the Trentine lands.

The formal proposal that the politician and spy brought from Kaiser Wilhelm to Benedict XV was the automatic transfer of Trentino from Austria to the Pope himself. This would allow the creation of an independent papal enclave near the Holy See, including a corridor to the sea. The proposal had the support of the S.P. while the Holy Alliance recommended that Cardinal Gasparri reject the proposal.

Pietro Gasparri

Both Benedict XV and his Secretary of State, Gasparri, knew that saying yes to Erzberger would in fact end papal neutrality in the war. Both the supreme pontiff and Gasparri doubted that, at the end of the war, either Austria or Italy would permit papal representatives to set up Church administration in Trentino. Still, it was now becoming clear, for the first time since the outbreak of the war, that Germany and the Roman Catholic Church had parallel interests, and that Matthias Erzberger provided a secure channel for the flow of messages between Rome and Berlin. Suddenly, by way of papal diplomacy, the Kaiser's spy had become an ally of the Holy See. Under the protection of the papal spy service by order of Gasparri, and Benedict XV himself, Erzberger carried diplomatic proposals from one side of Rome to the other. He also became a source of Holy See financing, because on Kaiser Wilhelm's orders, he was contributing sizable sums to the papal treasury as supposed 'donations'.

Matthias Erzberger

Since 1914, the Holy See's coffers had been in a sorry state; in fact they were nearly empty because of the war's effect on the economies of Europe in general, and Italy in particular. The Pope had thought that pilgrims' donations, along with contributions by parishioners abroad, could support not only the Holy See's expenses, but also the broad structure of the Church around the world. But the war had killed off tourism and interrupted the flow of donations from pilgrims to Rome. The Holy See may not have been bankrupt, but it was in a delicate financial shape that would endanger the operation of the papal bureaucracy in the not-so-distant future.

Recognising the opportunity for Kaiser Wilhelm to ingratiate himself with the Pope, Erzberger had encouraged the Kaiser to send sizable amounts of money through him to give the Holy See treasury breathing room. What began as small sums had by now turned into millions in secret funds coming from several Swiss banks. As the Pope's senior administrator Cardinal Pietro Gasparri then ordered that these funds show up in the Holy See's accounts as part of the contributions from parishioners abroad, to avoid upsetting the nations of the Entente.

As liaison for undercover German finance operations a pro-German priest, Father Antonio Lapoma, assisted working in the city of Potenza. Father Lapoma and Erzberger had joined hands in Operation Eisbär, or 'Polar Bear', that would become the code name by which German espionage agents in Rome referred to Pope Benedict XV.

Operation Eisbär's first step had been to raise money for the Holy See from private citizens of the Central Powers, with them told that the money was going to those wounded in the war. Erzberger had returned to Berlin to organise this nationwide network for fundraising, not only among Catholics, but also among Lutherans and other Protestants. With Erzberger's encouragement Kaiser Wilhelm's government now required businessmen, bankers, and even housewives to actively participate in the fundraising, without their ever knowing that the eventual recipient of their donations was the Holy See, after their money had passed through Swiss banks.

Believing that Benedict XV had inherited empty coffers from the papacy of Pius X in 1914 Italian Intelligence now surprisingly discovered, part way into 1915, that the new Pope had mysteriously rescued the Holy See's finances. With this information the Entente's Secret Service set out to prove their suspicions that the Pope had fallen under the sway of the Central Powers, at least economically.

In the meantime the Kaiser had given Erzberger complete freedom to turn over as much money as he could. He was now working alongside Franz von Stockhammern in the German Embassy in Rome, who had taken over direction of Germany's intelligence services in Italy when the war broke out. Erzberger and Stockhammern worked closely together on covert operations, along with the Holy Alliance's Father Antonio Lapoma who was in charge of countering any attempts by politicians, parties, grass-roots movements, or organisations, to bring Italy into the conflict on either side.

Knowing that Italy's neutrality brought them millions of German marks Pope Benedict XV and Cardinal Gasparri promoted the Holy See's neutral position. Other than his weekly meetings with the Pope, Gasparri organised additional meetings with his aides, and hosted dinners for high-ranking members of the Roman curia along with the Italian press. It was little wonder, therefore, that Catholic newspapers, who proclaimed to be mouthpieces for the citizenry, were firm defenders of Italian neutrality.

It had been in early 1915 that the Austrian Embassy in Rome had reported to Vienna that close to 50 Italian Catholic papers were expressing the opinion that Italy, as the Central Powers' only friend, opposed entry into the war. Austrian spies knew from various informants that Italy's mass media were getting subsidies from mysterious sources and that perhaps the German Embassy was involved. In fact, this money came from the same funds sent by Kaiser Wilhelm to the Holy See via Swiss banks, and from where The Holy Alliance's agent Antonio Lapoma channelled money to the newspapers' publishers.

Britain's ambassadors, Sir James Rennell Rodd and Sir Henry Howard, had both received reports about sinister meetings in Franz von Stockhammern's private rooms in Rome's elegant Hotel Russie. Here the German diplomat wined and dined his guests with French champagne and Russian caviar. These guests included cardinals, abbots of Roman monasteries, and some bishops from important Holy See departments. They graciously undertook to write newspaper articles, and sometimes advise the German diplomat about the propaganda campaign that formed part of Operation Eisbär. Their campaign was bringing about a shift in public opinion in favour of the Central Powers and Italian neutrality that was opposed to any support for the Entente.

Naturally Sir Henry Howard presented a formal complaint to the Roman Catholic Secretary of State, Cardinal Pietro Gasparri, but without success. Gasparri, however, promised to ask any publishers he knew for a more measured tone in articles and editorials. Perched precariously on his high perch Pope Benedict XV instructed Cardinal Gasparri that if the press kept attacking the Entente that he should write an article in L'Osservatore Romano, chastising the editors and publishers of those media, and that appeared to balance the position. As the media criticism grew sharper, Gasparri occasionally, therefore, paid small 'subsidies' to one paper or another to keep it from publishing particular articles, or drawings, that were overly critical of the Entente. This money also came from the funds sent from Germany to the Holy See.

While Franz von Stockhammern worked closely with the press, Matthias Erzberger did the same with Father Lapoma, spreading neutralist propaganda in still more communications media to change the minds of any who wanted to see Italy enter the war on the Entente side. When the British became aware of this it became clear that now was the time, both politically and religiously, to use the existence of the amulet's hidden secret message. Realising that its message had powerful connotations particularly for the Roman Catholic Church, and Italy as a people, MI1 had a shelf plan devised to counter any German and Austrian inspired efforts.

It was obvious that the Germans had not made the Roman Catholic Church aware of the existence of the discovery of the amulet, and that they were playing with a double edged sword in that they were secretly also inspiring Moslem faithful at the Church in Rome's expense. Several minds back in London had been quick enough to realise that with the Pope having adopted his new supposedly enlightened Modernist position, that the amulet's message could not now be construed as a heresy in that seemingly contradictory teachings could be correct.

Alternatively, the only other stance he could take would be for the Church to hypocritically revert to old Pope Pius X's position, refuting the message. Taking that tack would no doubt immediately be construed as a political 'U' turn by the press and the masses. It would simply be seen to be a convenient decision based on expediency and power, and completely at odds with modern Christian teaching.

Then of course there were the payments made by Germany that would be seen as the Church accepting a bribe. This along with Operation Eisbär condoning the fleecing of a gullible flock and the collapse of Catholicism would be assured.

Placing the Roman Catholic Church in jeopardy, with a lot more unsavoury historical acts perpetrated in the name of God being exposed at

Italian soldier WW1

the same time, would not be an option the pope and the Holy See could afford. The solution, even though it maybe unpalatable to them, would be to request Britain to keep the amulet and its message secret, and the price for that support would be in them convincing the Italian Government to ratify Italy in joining the Allies in the war. The revelation of the amulet's existence, therefore, would hopefully leave the Roman Catholic Church with no room to manoeuvre, and place enough weight politically on the Italian parliament to carry the day.

The Basilica, Rome

To subtly make their point clear and apply pressure London had decided they needed to instigate their plan in Rome rather than dealing remotely via the Italian ambassador in London.

They had also come to the conclusion that they needed an appropriate operative on the ground in Rome to support both their ambassadors and Cardinal Gasquet. That operative would also monitor any media shift, and gather any other relevant intelligence. What better than a female agent who spoke fluent French and Italian who could operate undetected.

Victor Emmanuel III

The first part of the plan involved having the two British ambassadors in Italy leak the fact that their government were in possession of authenticated intelligence that threatened the Roman Catholic Church. In particular what the verified contents of the amulet's ancient message implied for both their Church religiously, and also in a broader sense for both the Church and Italy politically and financially. This included getting this information, along with the amulet's photograph, in front of the King of Italy, Victor Emmanuel III, the Italian Prime Minister Antonio Salandra, and Pope Benedict XV, so they were all perfectly clear of what could transpire if they did not acede to the Entente's wishes.

The carrot in them joining the Entente was that Britain was prepared to support Italy with the acquisition of previously lost territory to Austria on winning the war. This was along with gifting the amulet and its message to the Holy See to protect its foundations into the future. As Britain's ambassador to the Holy See, Sir Henry Howard needed to confirm with Cardinal Gasquet that, with the Pope's

Italian PM Antonio Salandra

support, that Britain would lend weight in securing the complete amulet for the Roman Catholic Church.

The second part, and just as important, was in ensuring that Cardinal Gasquet got the message to the Pope that Germany and Austria were using the half amulet and its message to instigate a

Moslem inspired jihad, or Holy war, in the Near and Far East, that was to the detriment to the Church of Rome. This, they needed to be aware, was a Holy war that not just threatened Italy but also Roman Catholic Church's interests globally. Gasquet's role, therefore, was to make the Pope aware, unequivocally, of the outcome should both the Church and Italy not support the Entente.

The final part of the plan would be down to Jehanne Blanche in having her stimulate public support for the Entente, while monitoring and reporting on any Italian media change in attitude. While the ambassadors kept pressure on the King, the Prime Minister, Italian politicians, and the Holy See, Jehanne was to additionally glean intelligence regarding German activity in Rome.

Matthias Erzberger

Gabriele D'Annunzio

During the period leading up to the last week of January 1915 Jehanne finalised a plan that including the Italian writer, poet, journalist and playwright Gabriele D'Annunzio. His daredevil lifestyle had forced him into debt by 1910, at which point he had been forced to flee to France, from Italy, to escape his creditors. Jehanne was aware that in 1911 Gabriele had collaborated in France with the composer Claude Debussy on a musical play Le martyre de Saint Sébastien. Known as 'The Martyrdom of St Sebastian', it had been written for the Russian ballerina and actress Ida Rubinstein. Because of its content Jehanne was aware that at the time the Holy See had reacted by placing all of D'Annunzio's works in the 'Index of Forbidden Books'. More importantly intelligence had also now identified that Gabriele was supportive of the Triple Entente of Britain, France and Russia, and that he was highly motivated in

Monumento Vittorio Emanuele II - Rome

Gabriele D'Annunzio

to do something to help.

From its beginning in the 1870's, the Italian Nationalist Movement had dreamed about Italy joining the modernised world powers. In the north of Italy extensive industrialisation had commenced with the added building of modern infrastructure that had been well underway by the 1890s. Alpine railway lines now connected Italy to the French, German and Austrian rail systems, with two south-going coastal lines also linking Rome with the rest of Europe.

A Paris - Lyon - Mediterranean railway poster

Meeting D'Annunzio in Paris Jehanne and Gabrielle would travel by train to Rome. During the trip it was decided that as Gabriele was a well known public identity that he would make public speeches in favour of Italy's entry into the war on the side of the Triple Entente. In response to any enquiries from others concerning Jehanne, they would be told that she was simply on holiday from

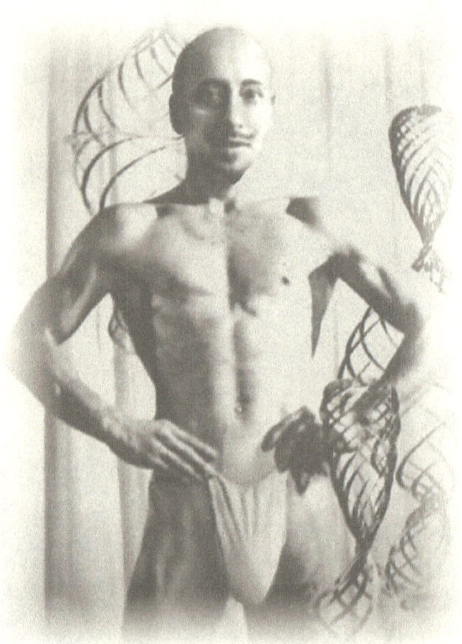

Gabriele D'Annunzio

Marseille, and that they had struck up a friendship on the train.

By dawn on the 26th January their trip found them beside the great Sâone in Beaujolais. Not having travelled widely Jehanne was enraptured by the scenery. Down the long, lovely valley beneath the Cèvennes, and over the Isêre, till that evening they saw the high snows of the Dauphiny. On past the chalet style houses of a newer type, and into a bright sun buoyant sparkling air, with olive and orange trees, cypresses and aloes, white hard roads, and those lovely bays. Onwards the rail ties clacked towards Rome where Jehanne and Gabriele arrived in late January 1915.

After delivering a package to Sir James Rennell Rodd at the British Embassy with intelligence concerning the amulet, Jehanne struck up a relationship with several in the Italian media.

Once German and papal spies became aware of Gabriele's arrival, and activities, they knew they needed to try and disuade him and enlist his support. To this end they decided to ingratiate themselves with him in an attempt to woo him to their cause.

Jehanne Blanche - Rome

On Gabriele's arm Jehanne would attend several of the Franz von Stockhammern's dinner parties at the Hotel Russie, along with with visiting Gasquet's Holy See residence in the Palazzo San Calisto. Gabriele D'Annunzio played his part well appearing to papal envoys, diplomats, and spies alike to waiver in his views when in their company. The Church's counter-espionage agency, the Sodalitium Pianum, were not so sure. They, however, did not suspect Jehanne. To them she was a mere slip of a French girl on holiday, and an attractive one at that. Whilst she no doubt supported her country's losing cause, they saw nothing else to worry about.

As for D'Annunzio's relgious affiliations, he was an atheist and had little interest in the politics of the Roman Catholic Church. As such he was more than happy to see their tail in a crack with their lies of convenience and their manipulation exposed. More particularly he had a dislike for German arrogance, but with all the skill of the actor he did not show it. In making light conversation at the dinner table at the first of von Stockhammern's invitations, he had whimsically offered that …

Since taking a flight with Wilbur Wright in 1908, I have developed an interest in aviation, and then plausibly stated, *and I hope to be reincarnated as a bird.*

This had placed a grin on Cardinal Francis Aidan Gasquet's usually stoic features, but Jehanne would also notice that it was an expression that could change in an instant if he was goaded. Jehanne had noticed that shift in a reply to Cardinal Hartmann, the archbishop of Cologne, who had reflected to him ….

Eminence I will not insult you by talking of the war... to which Gasquet had quickly replied…. *Eminence… I will not mock you by talking about peace.*

Jehanne liked Gasquet; he had an elegant courtly bearing, an upright carriage, a direct manner, and a handsome demeanour. He was of medium height, 5 feet 6 inches with a full head of grey hair. His tendency to pomposity was ameliorated by his sense of humour and in the Irish jokes that she now discovered he told with eloquence. For all of that she discerned that he was staunchly patriotic to the British cause, tending to be bullish in his manner and attitudes. Following his curt reply to Cardinal Hartmann, Gasquet had abruptly turned to Jehanne enquiring pleasantly as to whether she had interests in aviation also. Her reply had been less pointed, as she simply stated…

One day I hope to take a flight in an aeroplane…. that is if there are any left after the war; … otherwise I will have to build my own.

Her humour had brought a laugh to all present and warmed the obvious chill that existed between the cardinals. What Jehanne had not informed them was that she has in fact been taken for a ride in an aeroplane back in 1913. It had been for services rendered, and it had scared her witless at the time.

With Jehanne accepted as simply an attractive female, and D'Annunzio as a suspected threat, Franz von Stockhammern got Jehanne to one side after dinner to see what she knew of her escort. Mingling with others over a further glass of champagne he quietly quizzed her on how long she had known D'Annunzio. Jehanne had replied that they had only just met, but that she had known of Gabriele's plays when she had been younger, living in Marseille. Working on the premise that the truth was easier to remember and that it could be validated if checked, Jehanne had added that they had met on the train to Rome. As they both shared the same interest in plays Gabriele had invited her to partner him to the dinner. Following a discussion with others on the merits of Italy remaining neutral in the war Jehanne had pleaded her

Jehanne in the pilot's seat - 1913

ignorance and excused herself. Demurely thanking her host for his hospitality, she moved back to talk with Cardinal Hartmann who she had noticed was taking an obvious interest in her youthful femininity. Then moving onto Cardinal Gasquet she was in time to be entertained by his newest joke…

One of my Irish friends Murphy dropped some buttered toast on the kitchen floor. It landed butter-side-up, he was extolling. *He looked at what he had done in astonishment, for he knew that it was a law of nature that buttered toast always falls buttered-side down. He rushed round to his local presbytery to fetch the priest, to tell him that he thought a miracle had happened round at his house. He would not say what it was but he wanted Father Flanagan to see it with his own eyes. He brought the Father into his kitchen and asked him what he saw on the floor.*

"Well," said Father Flanagan, "it's pretty obvious what we have here. Someone dropped some buttered toast, and then for some reason flipped it over so that the butter is on top."

"No, Father", Murphy replied, "I dropped it and it landed like that."

"Well," said Father Flanagan, "it's certainly a natural law of the universe that dropped toast never falls butter side up. But it's not for me to say it's a miracle. I'll report the matter to the bishop, and have him send people round, to interview you and take a photograph."

An investigation of some rigour was conducted, not only by priests of the archdiocese, but after contacting me, and then by ecumenical scientists sent from the Curia here in Rome. The final ruling was a negative, however. The report from the miraculous investigating committee here in Rome; that I am in possession of a copy of, states…

"We agree that it was certainly an extraordinary event that occurred in Murphy's room, quite outside the normal run of normal phenomena. Yet we have to be very cautious before ruling

any happening miraculous, ruling out all possible natural explanations. In this case we have declared it not to be miracle… for it was possibly the result of Murphy buttering the toast on the wrong side."

There was general applause although a number in the room looked on in distain. Then quietly to Jehanne, Gasquet said…

So, my dear …. You just have to make sure you have your toast buttered on the right side!

By mid-March, after establishing that the Pope had been fully informed of the existence of the amulet message and its ramifications, Jehanne Blanche was on her way back to Marseille. It was where she had been instructed to return after her supposed holiday, to wait further instructions. Supplied with additional funds by the British Embassy in Rome Jehanne boarded a train for Lyon to catch the Compagnie des chemins de fer de Paris à Lyon et à la Méditerranée, or PLM, that operated chiefly in the south-east of France, with a main line which connected the Côte d'Azur from Lyon to Marseille.

In late spring 1915, papal spies informed the Germans that the Italian Prime Minister, Antonio Salandra, and his minister of foreign affairs, Sidney Sonnino, were getting ready to pressure the cabinet and parliament to ratify an accord they had secretly signed in London in April. In that accord they had agreed to bring Italy into the war on the British and French side.

Father Lapoma put Erzberger in contact with Pasquale Grippo, the Minister of Education in Salandra's cabinet. Father Lapoma had told Matthias Erzberger of his secret meetings with Grippo in Roman churches, where the education minister revealed that after

Salandra and Sonnino presented their war proposal that several ministers had come out against intervention. These included Vincenzo Riccio, head of the Italian Postal Service, and Gianetto Cavasola, the Minister of Agriculture. Riccio and Cavasola had remained both firm defenders of neutrality at any price. Pasquale Grippo's information, therefore, suggested to Vienna and Berlin that Italy's government must be divided. The German Secret Service and the Austrian government pinned their hopes on Giovanni Gioliti, an important politician with great influence in other social circles, and in the Italian parliament. Erzberger implored Stockhammern and Father Lapoma to stall for time or, and if necessary, buy it. To this end Berlin sent him five million lire to distribute among Italian parliamentary deputies.

The Austrians also had bought several deputies, and the Germans, through Stockhammern, paid various journalists to ratchet up their attacks on the Entente. Father Lapoma was supposed to gather signatures of bishops and cardinals against the war. In this task he had the aid of Father Fonck, director of the Jesuit Biblical Institute and former member of the Holy See's counterespionage service, as well as Monsignor Boncompagni, a high Holy See official with important ties in the Roman curia and aristocracy. Finally, by order of Kaiser Wilhelm, the German embassy reacted as might have been expected. Benedict XV's support was essential, and on the night of 6th May, Franz von Stockhammern, with the aid of the pope's secretary Monsignor Giuseppe Migone, he won entry to the Holy See. Although the Swiss Guard had closed the gates at 9 p.m. and the Italian police and secret service had all entrances under surveillance, Monsignor Migone managed to bring Stockhammern to the Pope's residence. Benedict XV was waiting in a small room. The supreme pontiff was now playing a dangerous game with the Holy See's survival in the balance. He may have thought that Sidney Sonnino, the Italian Foreign Minister, was playing that with Italy's future, but now the Catholic Church had other priorities.

In this secret meeting, Stockhammern openly offered the pope Austria's Trentine lands if he could keep Italy out of the war. With other priorities on his mind, Pope Benedict XV, howeverm simply offered the German spy a platitude, before giving him his blessing.

King Victor Emmanuel of Italy

Whatever support the Holy See can muster in the next cabinet meeting I will encourage ... he had stated.

Stockhammern knew there was now likely to be little support. There was no need to mention Pasquale Grippo's name aloud, or any other more recent developments that had changed things entirely. None of the secret bribes, manoeuvres, clandestine meetings, propaganda operations, or any other efforts by Franz von Stockhammern, Matthias Erzberger, Father Antonio Lapoma, or the German spy service were going to avoid what appeared now to be the inevitable.

Pressure from Britain and France had swayed Italy to sign the secret Treaty of London on 26th April 1915. In that agreement, Italy promised to leave the Triple Alliance and declare war against its former allies within a month in return for territorial gains after the end of the war. What many were unaware of was the significance the amulet's contents on the decision makers, and that the Holy See had another expectation given their back door support of the agreement.

With most Italians opposing entry into the war, the Italian Chamber of Deputies had managed to force the Italian Prime Minister Antonio Salandra to resign. King Victor Emmanuel, however,

Victor Emmanuel III (right) with Albert I of Belgium (left). This photograph shows Victor's small physical stature.

had declined Salandra's resignation and personally made the decision for Italy to enter the war. He was well within his rights to do so under the Statuto, popular opposition to the war notwithstanding. This effectively shut the door on the Germans once and for all, and on 23rd May, 1915 Italy declared war on Austria.

When Italy entered the war, Germany and Austria closed their embassies in Rome, recalling their emissaries to Berlin and Vienna. From now on Germany's and Austria's new ambassadors to the Holy See would operate out of the Swiss city of Lugano. Franz von Stockhammern likewise moved his spy operations to neutral Switzerland. From the safety of Lugano, Germany and the

Holy Alliance, who was still having a bob each way, would organise covert operations against Italy and other members of the Entente. One of these would take place in Ireland, and would be financed with some of the funds still in the secret Swiss bank accounts that Kaiser Wilhelm had sent the Holy See.

Soon afterwards, the Italian espionage services discovered the contacts established between the German Secret Service, the Papal one, and Pope Benedict XV himself in their goal of influencing Italy's political decisions prior to Italy's mysterious change of heart. They would take this as evidence of the Holy See's connivance with the Central Powers.

WW1 Italian Soldiers

Saint Peter's

Part VIII

*Wilhelm
Wassmuss*

Working under Max von Oppenheim as a German consular official Wilhelm Wassmuss, along with a number of his followers, had sailed down the Tigris River in the first days of February 1915. Travelling on the Turkish manned river steamer *SS Pioneer* they had arrived at a point below Kut al Amara in Mesopotamia; a town about 100 miles southeast of Baghdad. From here Wassmuss' party moved eastward into Iran to begin the grandiose mission of ending Anglo-Russian domination in the Near East by raising up all willing Islamic people against the Central Powers enemies. To inspire them, with him Wilhelm carried Max von Oppenheim's piece of the amulet along with its original message as validation of the authority of Mohammed.

Described as physically stocky and philosophically short, Wassmuss was in fact a broad, heavy set, megalomaniac mystic, and fanatic, who was fervently patriotic to Germany. With his bull neck, slightly melancholic mouth, high forehead, and blue eyes that generally looked

Wassmuss in Arab attire

upward, his appearance in no way indicated his dreams. As a European who had come to love the Mesopotamian desert he had educated himself into an intimate knowledge of it, its people, and their customs and languages. A a relgious zealot he was both a skilled liar as well as a man of deep principles. As one who enjoyed wearing the flowing robes of a desert tribesman he was in reality a consummate actor and spy. Known as 'Wassmuss of Persia' he was charged with successfully organising and leading an Islamic revolt against the British.

With oil from the Persian Gulf flowing to Britain from its new refinery and port at Abadan, and with a need to protect its interests in India, Britain outposts in Persia and Kuwait, were exposed. Wilhelm Wassmuss along with his German Foreign Office officials knew that they could achieve victory over these British interests if they succeeded in bringing Iran into the war on the German side. Failing that they could at least organise revolts by Iranians against their British occupiers.

Based in Bushehr, Wilhelm initially succeeded in organising the Tangsir and Qashghâi tribes to revolt against the British in the south of the country. Then moving into Iran, he first passed through the market towns of Dezful and Shushtar where he conferred with local chieftains and distributed pamphlets urging their tribesmen to revolt. Once he started on his mission any secrecy quickly dissolved with the local police at Shushtar trying to arrest him. Warned, he managed to escape but he would soon be in peril again.

Travelling south some 100 miles to Behbahan it was here that a supposedly friendly local chieftain invited him to dinner, and then promptly placed him under armed guard. Knowing there was likely to be a good price on his head, to this chief his detention simply made good business sense.

Planning to sell Wassmuss to the British the chief sent a messenger to them to the effect that he held a person they were looking for going by the name of Wassmuss, and that his release to them was negotiable. Fortuitously the chief's messenger met a British detachment on the road who excitedly told its mounted officers of his master's captured visitor. Galloping to Behbahan the British detachment would, however, lose valuable hours over the required politeness of Eastern protocol in negotiating the chieftain's price for Wilhelm. This time wasting, as it turned out, was critical because when the officers went to get the prisoner he was gone.

That evening, telling his guards his horse was sick, Wilhelm Wassmuss had requested to be escorted under guard to the stables to check on his horse's condition. This he had demanded every hour until eventually by early morning the guards had become sleepy and grown tired of escorting him across the small courtyard, so they didn't bother. Being inherently lazy and thinking he could not escape they had allowed him to visit the stable alone.

Saddling his stallion quickly Wilhelm had led it into the courtyard before climbing into the saddle. The horse had reared before, landing stiffly on its forefeet nearly throwing him. That morning there could be no thought for a mere horse, so he had yanked on the curb with his full strength while bringing his fist down hard between the horse's ears. After several blows of similar encouragement the stallion had stretched his splendid muscled body into a short hard gallop, exiting the yard into the early morning gloom.

Whilst the tribal chief who had captured him was out of pocket, Wilhelm had, unfortunately, been forced to leave his luggage behind. It would be found in the chieftain's courtyard that morning along with a bag of propaganda leaflets. Reading the pamphlets the British realised he definitely had to be stopped. As the days passed, however, Wilhelm Wasmuss rapidly became increasingly famous throughout Iran. It became obvious that his capture was not going to be as easy as it may have first seemed, with him having organised the Bakhtiari tribes in the name of Mohammed, and then having purchased the loyalty of others.

Wassmuss rides off towards the rising sun.

Although successful he continually raged about his lost luggage, going as far as insisting to see the Governor at the Persian provincial capital of Shiraz to formally protest about it, and to demand its return. This, of course, was impossible since it was by this time held by the India Office in London. What his ranting did

achieve, however, was that it drew attention to it. Opened by MI1 staff in April 1915, in it they discovered Wassmuss's German Diplomatic Code Book, Code No. 13040, and even more fortuitously Max von Oppenheim's half amulet, along with its ancient message. The Code book was now with Room 40 and the amulet was being made ready by the Foreign Office for urgent despatch to the Cairo Museum for authentication. It would travel by troop transport, escorted by a Royal Navy destroyer.

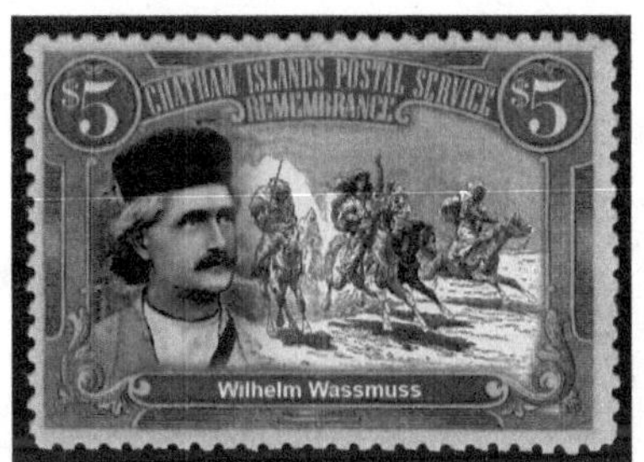

Whilhelm Wassmuss

A Royal Navy destroyer – WW1

With spies and other Government operatives largely working behind the scenes, espionage, along with the information created and transmitted by agents and informants, has historically played a major role in the tactical decision making of states since time immemorial. With regard to the Near East there has historically been a false assumption that spies were agents with some sort of particular regional or communal allegiance. The information they gleened was, in fact, a resource to be fought over, or bought, and sold. Like translators, converts, and merchants, in the Near East they in fact bridged the gap between the Mediterranean's various polities.

A back street in Cairo

With Smith Cumming very aware that the image of prostitution, as humanity's 'oldest profession', obscured the fact that its class harboured it own spies and informants. He was also aware that this occupation also carried a different social meaning, and economic value, in the Eastern Mediterranean, and that it could be exploited to MI1's advantage. Having a British Foreign office in Cairo where the white slave trade out of Marseille thrived along with native whores of a lower class, it gave him an opportunity.

As the brightest gem in the handle of the green fan of Eygpt, Cairo had been founded in 641 AD by Amr the Mohammedan, conqueror of that land, and close to the Roman fortress of Babylon. It had been initially named El Fustat or 'The Tent' because it had been erected on the spot where he had encamped.

Old Cairo

Remains of this, the oldest Mohammedan capital, were still present in the old Cairo in the form of early Coptic churches that had been built inside the old fortress. With expansion over the course of the next 1250 years that city had grown considerably. Then, in its 1915 form, with the accession of Mohammed 'Ali' and his dynasty in the early 1900's, Cairo had been greatly enlarged on its west side, with the space between the city of

Saladin and the Nile covered with villas and palaces of European construction.

It had not been until the Triple Entente, or Allied Powers, declared war on the Ottoman Empire on the 4th November 1914 that Eygpt was declared a British Protectorate. Until then it had nominally been under Ottoman rule with de facto British involvement. This had been before the Ottoman Empire joined the Central Powers to form the Triple Alliance with the signing of their August 1914 Turco-German Alliance. As an inevitable outcome Shepheard's and the Continental hotels' were now jammed with British staff officers with suede boots, fly whisks and swagger sticks. More relevant, perhaps, was that the city had become a hub for agents and diplomats; including German and Turkish, as well as local spies and disaffected Egyptians and Moslems, while also being the British Headquarters' for a forthcoming Dardanelles Campaign. Placing an agent who was a higher class Marseille prostitute into this environment, in the right establishment frequented by the upper class, Smith-Cumming saw as a good move strategically.

With the arrival of the British thawb wearing street Egyptians had begun to invent a thousand new ways of getting a few piasters out of the pockets of red-faced British soldiers. And it was not just the street Arab who were getting the pickings, but European and Levantine speculators, black marketers, rich Egyptians, and even the British, who were making bent on making their fortune.

To complicate matters, out of convenience, many foreign born residents, and Egyptians of foreign ancestry, claimed the protection of foreign consulates. This had been made possible with a system of 'capitulations', under which they were subject to the laws of their protective country, not Egypt. For the British Deputy Chief of Police for Cairo, Sir Thomas Russell, known as Russell Pasha to many of Cairo's residents, he now had the unenviable task of settling disputes with Egyptian nationals in a system of 'Mixed Courts'. This whole system naturally created complex jurisdictional issues for law enforcement that could be exploited to the advantage of the unscrupulous.

Cairo

As for Cairo's licensed brothel quarter, it had been developed in the late 19th century, while beyond this licensed quarter there were areas where prostitution was semi-tolerated. With ongoing problems Russell Pasha tried to keep a lid on things.

One particular house of some size and popularity, he stated, *defied Bimbashi Quartier, our chief detective officer. For months both him and I had found ourselves dealing with changes in the nationality of the padrona, or Madam. Our police could not enter a foreigner's house without the consent and presence of the*

Consul or his representative. When we arrived with the French consular cavass to demand admission from the French padrona,

The Madam

the spy-hole in the front door would be opened and a husky voice announce that Madame Yvonne had sold the business to Madame Gentili, an Italian subject, without whose Consular representative we could not enter. Next week we would arrive with the Italian cavass to be met by another change of nationality by the padrona. Picqued beyond the ordinary, one night Quartier assembled seven Consular cavasses at the fast-closed door, and one by one the fictitious landladies were defeated, entry gained, with the law enforced.

Developed as a contact zone between the wealthy area round Lake Ezbekiyya and an expanding central city, by 1915 the Wagh El-Birket had become the entertainment and red-light district of Cairo. This Red Blind Quarter, or 'The Birka' as it was colloquially known, included the once-elegant colonnaded street of Clot Bey, along with other streets to the north of the Ezbekiyya Gardens. It had been named, ironically, after the French doctor who introduced European medicine to Egypt during the rule of Muhammad 'Ali.

Above - Clot Bey Street, Cairo
Below - Marseille harbour

Trembling on the verge of 40 the married businessman Andre Faberge was the only man throughout the war that Jehanne Blanche regretted duping and causing physical harm. With her plan of leaving Marseille on a departing early morning tramp steamer, she needed a cover to establish her credibility in fleeing to Cairo. Enticing Andre from a bar on the waterfront with the promise of discounted sex she had fondled him affectionately, allowing him to ejaculate, before levelling him in an alley with her trusty knuckle duster and stealing the contents of his wallet. Calculating that local Gendarmerie would not discover his body till later in the morning she had jumped the departing steamer, with a down payment and a promise to the 1st mate to allow her the use of a cabin. It was a promise she, also, had not kept, as shortly before dropping anchor in Port Said, to quell the expectant enthusiasm of the 1st mate, she informed him that she had syphilis, gave him a final payment, and encouraged him to keep quiet about her arrival and condition. Jehanne had a fair idea that he would not keep that information secret.

Shortly after the Central Powers supposedly surprise and abortive February 1915 attack against Britain's 'jugular vein', the Suez Canal in their attempt to stir the passions of the locals, Jehanne Blanche had blended into Cairo society.

Two months prior to her disembarkation in Port Said, in a pre-emptive strike, London had landed an Anglo-Indian force at Basra, near the estuary of the Euphrates and Tigris rivers. It had been instigated to protect the Anglo-Persian oil pipeline, vital to the British Navy, and to show the Union Jack in this strategically important area in the Persian Gulf. Progress north by this force would, however, be stopped for two years by Turkish forces at

Kut. The British would suffer over 20,000 casualties, with them unable to take Baghdad or Mosul until later in the war.

British troops and artillery on the move

As for Jehanne Cairo was blossoming as British soldiers seeing sun, desert and clean air for the first time in their lives, looked hungrily at the girls of Clot Beys brothels. They were by now filled to overflowing with soldiers before they were ordered to meet their destiny on the Gallipoli Peninsular. Many of the troops had come from appalling conditions in the black and grimy back streets of British cities and never seen before what they now could enjoy during their time off in Cairo. For the Colonials, including ANZAC troops, they had better judgement knowing when they were being ripped off. They also enjoyed a better rate of pay that afforded a better class of woman.

Up until the late 19th century Ezbekiyya, Cairo, had been a partail lake. It had been in an area to the west of the city that had mostly been flood plain. Then under the rule of the Khedives, Isma'il and Tawfiq, the area had been filled in becoming the Ismailia Quarter, with

Shepheard's Hotel, Cairo

Ezbekiyya Lake developed into the Ezbekiyya Gardens. This area of formal gardens with promenades had been surrounded by foreign consular quarters and big foreign hotels, including Shepheard's Hotel, opposite its northwest corner. Ezbekiyya had remained fashionable, with Shepheard's Hotel now being the HQ of the ANZAC command.

North of Ezbekiyya was known as Wagh al-Birka. It had once been a place of glorious palaces and villas that had fronted the lake. Wajh al-Birkat and the streets to its north, though once fashionable, were in the area where the new city of Cairo, with its elegant foreign hotels, rubbed up against the older quarters of town, with Shepheard's Hotel only a couple of blocks away.

The tolerated brothel quarters around Clot Bey and the Wajh al-Birkat had merged into a greater unregulated area known as the Wasa'a, that literally meant the 'wide area'. It had apparently once referred to the old fish markets when the Nile had run much farther east.

The Wajh al-Birkat was populated with European women of all breeds and races, other than British, for whom it was illegal under their Consular authority to practice the licensed trade of prostitution, even in Egypt. Most were considered to

Clot Bey

be of the third, or economy class ticket 'type of ride', and for whom Marseilles had no further use. They would eventually be passed on to Bombay and Far East markets who were less discerning. Here they were still Europeans, however having not yet fallen so low as to live in the one-room shacks of the Wasa'a which had always been the quarter for purely native prostitution of the lowest class. It was here that their clients more satirically, rode outdoors.

The Wagh al-Birka was ruled by a huge, fat, sweaty self appointed Nubian 'king' named Ibrahim al-Gharbi who enjoyed small boys, dressed in women's clothes, and wore a white veil. He lived and worked in a street named Darb al-Muballat, keeping two guards of his own proportion on the street outside while he administered and pimped his affairs from a small office on the first floor.

The Nubian Ibrahim al-Gharbi

Following her arrival in Cairo Jehanne had been pointed in the Nubian's direction, also being warned that he was an Ottoman spy.

Most cunning animals are masters of disguise who can fool even the most beady-eyed passer-by into believing they are not, and the moment Jehanne set eyes on the Nubian she was on her guard. To her he epitomised a panther in search of prey, and he did not hide it. His yellow piercing eyes, sweaty complexion, cruel mouth and corpulent frame added to her feeling of disgust. The thing that mesmerised her for an instant, however, was not his appearance or his leering deportment, but rather the half amulet that hung from his neck. Was this just coincidence? It appeared to be the other half of the amulet that she knew Ernest Budge had recently sent to Cairo for evaluation. Knowing it had not arrived yet she then considered whether it might be a fake, in which case were they both such? In her wildest dreams she did not believe that this was the matching genuine half, yet the quick glance she had initially got of the object suggested that it might just be.

From that point on Jehanne had not concentrated on the artefact, but rather in holding the Nubian's stare until she received a meagre offer for her employment. He had snarled it out with a wave of his hand, with spittle gathering at the edge of his mouth. Not inclined to bargain she had simply excused herself from his threatening presence. The claustrophobic stench of the room pervaded her nostrils for minutes after she was back on the street. There was no way she was working for a bastard like that, and with money in hand Jehanne decided to bide her time as she now had another more important opportunity to consider.

A statement Mansfield Cumming had made to her a few months earlier drifted into her mind.

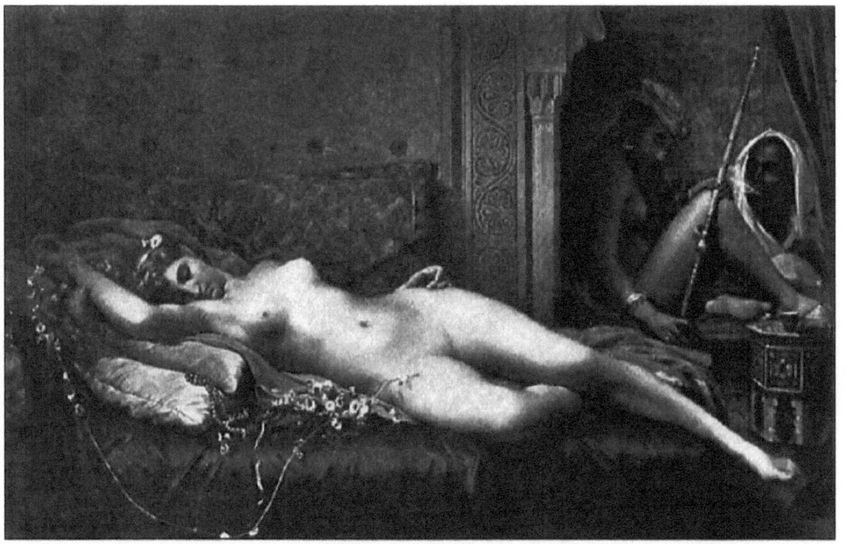

Was it little wonder that in the long process of time, after fortune had taken its course, that coincidences could spontaneously occur?

The coincidental discovery of the potential second half of the amulet had transported her thoughts to a different plane entirely as she tried to logically think through her luck, and to wonder whether it was destiny. Was her destiny simply shaped by the vagaries of fate, she wondered, or was it all part of some greater predetermined yet unexplained course of events? Was it conceivable that her find had been predetermined, and likewise her future? Jehanne had not previously thought too much about God or Allah, or believed that there could be some sort of pre-ordained order in the cosmos, but she was starting to wonder. Was it simply coincidence that over the space of three millennia that two long missing objects forming an single amulet had both been revealed to her within the space of three months? It was amazing to say the least, however, whether coincidence or otherwise, it was going to be very important to MI1 that she secure this second half to determine whether it was in fact genuine. With that objective in mind a smile creased her complexion as she considered that it might also be a way of getting rid of that fat, disgusting, Nubian.

The following morning Jehanne's short message to her local Foreign Office MI1 controller positively read …

Other half of amulet with Ottoman spy - Nubian, Ibrahim al-Gharbi. Formulating plan for recovery with Z.

Prostitution - Cairo

Like their British counterparts ANZAC units of Australians and New Zealanders found themselves in Cairo being trained in camps near the Pyramids. With a great many never having been far from their own hometowns before they, not unnaturally, enjoyed their free time in Cairo. Other than sightseeing many spent their time drinking and seeking women; especially the sort whose virtue was negotiable. With penicillin not yet discovered, houses of prostitution were subject to medical checks, and though the inspections were tolerated the rate of venereal disease had become enough to create a major problem for the British and Colonial forces. ANZAC units were reporting an average incidence of VD across the Corps of 12%, or one man in eight, with one unit said to have a rate of 25%.

A Cairo dancer

It was in this environment, and much to his surprise, that one British soldier from Manchester discovered his sister in one of Darb al-Muballat's establishments dancing perfectly naked with a dozen or so other women. He was in what they called a 'Can-Can Hall' where he was also witnessing other girls exposing their person to every kind of indignity from a number of onlookers, while others also fought to also participate.

After her act the soldier managed to have a talk with his sister, learning that she had left England as a servant to some supposedly well-to-do lady who had taken her to Egypt and left her there. The soldier tried to get her away, as she was only too willing to leave, but those who now employed her had other ideas and would not let her go. When challenged they had thrown the brother out a window which resulted in him being hospitalised for nearly a week.

Knowing of the colonial troops' desire to exact revenge for past grievances arising from dealings with this district's denizens; such as diluted liquor, exorbitant prices, high rates of venereal infection, wild rumours of stabbings of ANZAC men by locals, and the behaviour of local tram conductors, Jehanne and the Bureau decided to use their emotional state over perceived injustices to its advantage to acquire the second half of the amulet.

With the tramways not designed to carry such volumes of men, some were compelled to sit on the roof of the carriages. In Cairo itself it was a bizarre sight as bemused pedestrians looked at the progress of any loaded tram. Less entertaining was the desire of Eygptian tram conductors to check every ticket, regardless of the time it took to

Loaded tram, Cairo

perform, or the crowded nature of the tram.

As a consequence catching the last tram to Mena Camp was always precarious for everyone. If the men did not get back to camp before their leave ran out, which was usually midnight, they were charged as Absent Without Leave, (AWL), which usually cost the unlucky man a couple of days' pay. Naturally this led to tension between the men and any tram conductor's officious behaviour, as it often resulted in a tram load of men each being placed on a charge because of the delay. Particularly officious, lugubrious and unsympathetic conductors would, therefore, cop it with follow-up complaints lodged at Mena Camp Headquarters by conductors who had been assaulted for supposedly carrying out their duties.

On other occasions conductors were simply physically tossed off the tram if it was felt that the conductor's behaviour would result in the tram arriving late.

Dressed in the uniform of a Manchester sergeant, and taking the last tram to Mena an associate Cairo based MI1 male agent was ready for what was to transpire. Also onboard expressing their subversive fears and frustrations were several ANZAC soldiers who were drunkenly and rowdily singing an old Naploeonic war song they had just learnt from a number of newly acquainted British mates…

I don't want the Sergeant's shilling,

I don't want to be shot down;
I'm really much more willing
To make myself a killing,
Living off the pickings of the Ladies of the Town;
Don't want a bullet up my bum hole,
Don't want my cobblers minced with ball;
For if I have to lose 'em
Then let it be with Susan
Or Meg or Peg or any whore at all .... Gorblimey!

On Monday I touched her on the ankle,
On Tuesday I touched her on the knee;
On Wednesday such caresses
As I got inside her dresses,
On Thursday she was moaning sweetly;
On Friday I had my fingers in it,
On Saturday she gave my balls a wrench;
And on Sunday after supper,
I had the fucker up her,
And now she's got me up before the Bench, ... Gorblimey!

A soldier's more graphic keepsake card

Instigating a scene amidst the singing the agent physically ejected the conductor off the tram and then ordered the driver at gun point to drive nonstop for the camp. Supporting this action the song had stopped immediately to be replaced by the hoots and whistles from the incumbent troops, who signalled their pleasure at what had just transpired.

Selecting a respectable looking corporal who appeared to be one of the only one's not completely drunk, and with not much time available, the agent quickly explained the predicament of the young English lady who was being detained in one of the Nubian's establishments. He suggested the colonials might like to help, additionally outlining the condition of her brother who was in hospital with injuries sustained by a number of that establishment's 'wogs'. He went onto suggest that they may like to visit the brother to validate the story, and the predicament he faced in setting the girl free. Before disembarking the agent handed one of the more rowdy ANZAC occupants a plain brown sealed manila envelope, with a number of photos and a message that simply read…

Mena Camp

You and your mates may find these interesting and want to do something about them also, as well as the girl. The pictures were taken in Darb al-Muballat, Wajh al-Birkat.

The photos taken by the agent showed local Arabs urinating in the troops intended Good Friday beer, with the notated offending location and date on the back.

The MI1 agent had correctly calculated that confidentially requesting help to recover the soldier's sister from her predicament, along with the added impetis in seeking retribution based on the photos, would be enough to create the desired effect. Their action was intended to be a smoke screen for a planned operation to recover the second half of the amulet. The outcome, however, was to far exceed both Jehanne, the agent's, and the British Foreign Office's less sanguine expectations.

MI1 along with Jehanne both knew that the Australian & New Zealand Army Corps (ANZAC) had received news that their period of training was at an end, with orders for them to embark for long-awaited action. More importantly they had discovered that there would be no training on Good Friday, 2nd April, with large numbers of men being given final leave. As such the scene was now set to allow all the soldiers' resentments to come to a head.

News of the Manchester soldier's sister's strife, along with the photos content, had spread across the various colonial camps like wild fire over the previous few days. To them it definitely now gave them justification to take action so .... *if the Gypo's and their wog mates wanted to learn the hard way then so be it!*

On Good Friday, as predicted a hardcore group spent the day drinking and stewing on the injustices that had been heaped upon them. At first the ANZAC troops could not find the sister but eventually, later that afternoon, they discovered her in a dive on Darb al-Muballat.

Witnessed by the MI1 agent they began their attack soon after 5 p.m on the house at Number 8, Darb al-Muballat. Entering the premises they knocked the overseeing pimp down the stairs, after which several took the liberty of urinating on him for good measure. Soon soldiers were evicting whores and their pimps into the street, and tossing their possessions out after them. Bedding, furniture and clothing were thrown from windows of buildings several storeys high. These materials along with sofas were piled in the road and set alight. As the soldiers moved to other premises the two guards of the Nubian king's offices a few doors away from the MI1 agent entered the fray, to be swiftly dealt with by several New Zealanders who were in no mood for any discussion. The town picket, drawn from the Australian 9th Light Horse Regiment, came on the scene and tried to clear the men out of the houses being attacked. Five arrests were made, although the crowd, growing larger by the minute, refused to let

Darb al-Muballat

these men be taken away. They snatched the rifles from some of the troopers and threw them onto the fires while also successfully freeing four of the prisoners.

During the confusion the MI1 agent took the opportunity to quickly scale the stairs through the now vacant front door to access the office of the Nubian king. Down below a growing crowd of as many as 2000 Australian and New Zealand troops were torching brothels and fighting with natives and each other.

Sitting up from stuffing his ill-gotten gains into a leather valise from a large open black caste iron safe to one side of his desk, the Nubian attempted to ooz charm. A momentary flash of his black eyes from under his raised veil as he sat upright gave away his intention. He could not disguise the sweat on his brow, or in that instant, the sneer that appeared on his corpulent countenance. As his finger tightening on the trigger of the luger pistol he hid under his desk he would be an instant too slow. Passing through his airway and voice box the sword stick that now protruded from his fat neck had partially severed his upper spinal cord freezing any defence he was attempting. Having registered a momentary realisation his now bulbous eyes were glazing over in death.

Quickly extracting the blade the agent removed the chain with the amulet from around the Nubian's blood soaked neck. Dropping his veil over his face he proceeded to tip a bottle of blue liqueur that was on the top of the safe over the body, the paper strewn desk, and the room's shabby curtains. He finished with a trail across the floor to the door. Moving back onto the inner landing he quickly threw the now empty bottle back into the room before striking a match.

Outside British Military Police had been summoned with about 30 having arrived on horseback to a chorus of abuse and a shower of stones and bottles. As the MI1 agent appeared on the street he was almost hit by a piano that had been thrown out of a neighbouring buildings second story window. On hitting the pavement its internals exploded like a bomb to also send its woodwork and keys spewing across the street. An ill-advised effort by the MPs to gain control by firing their pistols, supposedly over the rioters' heads, resulted in the wounding of four men in the throng now estimated as having grown by another 1000 in number. It only served to further inflame matters, forcing the police to withdraw hastily and in giving the agent the opportunity to do likewise towards Ismailia Square.

Darb al-Muballat showing damage

Back in Darb al-Muballat efforts by the Egyptian Fire Brigade to douse the bonfires and burning buildings were also frustrated by their hose-lines being cut. Its members were also being manhandled after they had turned a hose onto the crowd, and their engine itself was finally pushed into the flames. All in all it was turning into a very enjoyable and successful evening until more unruly elements began to loot some shops and to torch a Greek tavern.

Shortly after 7 p.m. a second fire engine arrived, this time under cavalry escort which exercised extreme tact, and the various fires were tackled while a still sizeable crowd looked on. Since the 'Wassa' was close by Shepherd's Hotel where the ANZAC commander had his headquarters were established, armed troops had also been called out.

About 8pm 500 Manchester troops were ordered to charge with fixed bayonets. They charged alright but they wouldn't go far with these troops giving up their rifles which were also added to the street fires. Then, knowing of the rescue of the girl, they turned and ran with the crowd following them up with sticks. Sometime later the South Australian Light Horse came but their horses wouldn't face the fire and smoke. After Lancashire Territorials, who were non-regular British troops and who were popular with the colonials, were drawn across the road and it was at this point that the rioters wisely began to disperse.

A little after 11pm the affair came to an end as the Westminster Dragoons advanced down the street. With their swords drawn their horses went straight through the fire and smoke. This cleared the street allowing troops to go for the houses and in taking everybody prisoner they found that still remained. Included were 50 Australians and some New Zealanders.

The following day a formal inquiry was convened under Colonel Frederic Hughes, commander of the AIF's 3rd Light Horse Brigade. Its task was to investigate the cause of the riot and establish responsibility for its outbreak. Many New Zealand officers attempted to disclaim that their men had played any part, although the evidence of their presence was quite conclusive.

To counter the allegation an officer leading the Australian picket was adamant that the New Zealanders had predominated. In any event, nine-tenths of those present had been merely spectators and apportioning blame was next to impossible. With other priorities, and few of the 50 witnesses able, or willing, to provide precise information, it was a lost cause. As the number of men injured by the MPs' bullets, was roughly in proportion to the size of the respective contingents, it could be said that the 'honours' were about equally shared. So too was the damages bill of £1,700.

Darb al-Muballat showing the damage after the riot

The girl who had been the cause of all the trouble would be sent to England. The British Embassy ensured she was taken charge of by the Y.M.C.A. while the men in camp collected over £40 to pay her passage and expenses back to England. Of course the money was handed over to the Y.M.C.A. without them being the wiser as to the true story of her fortuitous escape.

As if to reinforce the rioters' feelings another incident occurred the following night in the canteen at Abbasieh Camp. Somebody caught an Arab, who was employed in his canteen, also urinating in a tub of beer. The Arab was at once pulled from the place and half killed. All the beer casks and tubs were broken and spilt along with all the groceries and dry goods stolen, with the place burned down. By the time the guard got there the incident was over with the camp quiet, except for the crackling of the flames.

Then as if to prove that Easter celebrations came in threes, on Sunday evening, prior to a promised resurrection on Monday, the New Zealanders burned down a moving picture show. The man running the establishment had advertised a boxing match, doubling the admission charge accordingly and then foolishly proceeded to show the same pictures as he usually did, with the inevitable consequence.

For the prepared force of about 30,000 Australian and New Zealanders they were destined for operations in the Dardanelles with the Mediterranean Expeditionary Force. The landings at Gallipoli on 25th April 1915 would begin the illfated Gallipoli Campaign, during which Egypt would continue to support the fighting as the closest major base.

ANZAC Cove, Gallipoli Peninsular

Cairo 1914

Part IX

James Quibell

Between collectors for the museums of Europe, and the British Empire, there was tremendous competition for Egyptian and Iraqi antiquities, so having the best collection of Egyptian and Assyrian antiquities in the world was as a matter of national pride.

Egyptian Museum of Antiquities, Cairo

These museum officials and their local agents smuggled antiquities in diplomatic pouches, bribed customs officials, or simply went to friends or countrymen in the Egyptian Service of Antiquities to ask them to let their cases of antiquities pass unopened. Ernest Budge from the British Museum had become expert at trading on the same level, but his greatest strength had been in diplomatically building relationships that would grease the wheel of progress.

One, who he had recognised as being of material use to Budge's worthy ends was James Quibell, the newly appointed Director of the Egyptian Museum. On a recent visit to Cairo he had reached agreement with him over the use of diplomatic pouches for any smaller items of perceived value.

Housing the world's largest collection of Pharaonic antiquities, including the many treasures of King Tutankhamen of Eygpt, and the Near East, the Egyptian government had established and built the Egyptian Museum of Antiquities back in 1835 near Ezbekeyah Garden. The museum, however, had soon moved in 1858 to Boulaq, because the original building had become too small to hold all of the artifacts. Then in 1855, shortly after the move, Archduke Maximilian of Austria had been given all of the artifacts. He had hired a French architect to design and build a new museum to be constructed on the bank of the Nile River in Boulaq. In 1878, however, it had suffered irreversible damage due to flooding of the Nile River which again caused the antiquities to be relocated to another museum. This time it was one at Giza where they had remained until 1902 when they were moved, for the last time, to the current museum in Tahrir Square.

Educated at Adams' Grammar School and Christ Church, Oxford, and fascinated by the antiquities, James Edward Quibell had been newly appointed as the Director of the Egyptian Museum the previous year. On arrival in Cairo to take up his new role he had quickly come

James Edward Ouibell

to understand several of the early beliefs of the Arabs. One had been that the oral transmission of religious knowledge, in particular, carried greater moral and emotional weight when information was passed person-to-person, and where its integrity depended on the integrity of the transmitter. He had initially, therefore, been mystified as to why the small fragile leather scroll he was now being shown was an important ancient religious find. It had been carefully removed from an ancient amulet half delivered to the museum by Jehanne Blanche from MI1, with a request from Ernerst Budge that it had to be kept secret.

Measuring 5.11"in height and 0.86" wide it, weighed only 4.25 oz. James knew the museum had a similar example of a message hirz displayed downstairs from his office in the museum, and that had been used to keep protective Koranic verses or incantations, but it was nothing like this amulet half quality or age. Without truely knowing the significance of its contents the artifact had been left to be carefully opened by museum staff with its early cuneiform script translated by qualified translators. With them sworn to secrecy the most experienced of those translators was now briefing James about the amulet, and the message's translation.

As you are aware, he began, *before the advent of Islam, memorisation was the primary means of conveyance of information amongst the Arabs. There were, however, some instances of writing at that time, including promissory notes, personal letters, tribal agreements, and some religious literature. There were very few Arabs that could read or even write, with the majority unlettered, as they still are today. Interestingly according to Sunni tradition, so was Mohammed.*

The translator paused for breath in the close confines of the office, before continuing.

So, in early Islamic Arabia, memory was, therefore, considered a more trustworthy mode of preservation than writing. Many feared that written documents were similar and could be confused; that there was no way of telling a draft from a final version; and that once information was set down in writing, it could be manipulated and taken out of context. Based on experience these observations have been rather prophetic when it comes to religious documents, as is the case with the Bible.

Writing was most commonly used as a mnemonic aid, or for legal documents; however, even such legal documents were still often as mnemonic aids for their oral testimony, which was a necessary component of evidence. Yet here written in Arabic by an unknown scribe on a very fine papyrus, and dated sometime around 500 AD, are the words....

"Itaq-ullah... Keep your duty to Allah... this is what is faithfully recorded..., habl-Allah... held fast by covenant with Allah..., al-Ahad, the one and only..., the Compassionate, the Merciful, as

recorded in the book of the generations protected for Mohammed ... the Prophet of Allah, and transcribed in the month of Rajab".

As you know there is no month as great or noble in the sight of Allah, to the Moslem, as the month of Rajab. Even Arabs today refer to as 'The Time of Ignorance', holding this month in great esteem as the coming of the religion of al-Islam at the hands of the final Messenger of Allah, Mohammed, as the Prophet of Allah.

Nothing needs to be added to it for an Arab, to increase its greatness.

Very much older in origin, however, written in Akkadian hieratic script reading from right to left, is an earlier text. Its accompanying translation I have recorded on a high quality non toxic parchment. This text reads...

"To your descendants I give this land, from Aššur to the km.t. I will raise them up a Prophet in the land of Chorev from among your brethren. From the son of Abdullah, I will make you into a great nation, and I will bless you; I will make your name great, and you will be a blessing".

The translator let his words sink in before continuing....

The part of the message that is quiet clear is the piece that reads ... "To your descendants I give this land, from Aššur to the km.t."

Aššur was home to the Aššuri people. It was one of the capitals of ancient Assyria wholly known as the Empire of Aššur. The remains of the city are situated on the western bank of the river Tigris, north of the confluence with the tributary Little Zab River. The city was occupied from around 2600 to 2500 BC through to the 14th

Century AD when a massacre occurred of its population. Aššur is also the name of the chief deity of the city. He was considered the highest god in the Assyrian pantheon, and the protector of the Assyrian state. In Mesopotamian mythology he was the equivalent of the Babylonian god Marduk.

Km.t, probably pronounced 'ku mat' in ancient Egyptian, on the other hand, refers to Egypt.

And so the message suggests a covenant with a god, or the God, who bequeathed the land from the Tigris River to Egypt to his chosen people. They will then have a prophet who is the son of the servant of God, who will become great with God's, or Allah's blessing.

There was silence in the room as James Quibell sat with his mouth partially agape. Not getting a response the translator once again continued…

As for the overall artefact itself, given that a hieroglyphic depiction of the object is partially inscribed on its back, it seems to be a matching half to an object which in the remotest period may have been used as an amulet, and chiefly employed as the pendant of a necklace. With regard to the overall hieroglyphic depiction, the Egyptian frog-headed icon is of the goddess Heqt, the wife of Khnemu, who was associated with resurrection. I believe that this amulet, therefore, when laid upon the body of the dead, was intended to transfer to it, her power.

As you are aware from other pieces we have here in the museum downstairs the frog is represented on the upper part of much later Greek and Roman terra-cotta lamp examples that were found here in Egypt. One of them has a legend written in Greek that translates ... 'I am the resurrection'. ... so the question is what do two frogs mean with regarding to 'God' eternal, if the second half matches this half?

Before James could interject, and as if anticipating his question he went on...

Let me explain...

The hieroglyph that connects the frog hieroglyphs is still unknown; however, all the suggestions which have been made concerning it previously, none is more likely than it symbolises 'life' as every Egyptian god from antiquity carries it. I strongly believe, therefore, that those carved in the form of this ankh hieroglyph were understood to impart the mystical properties of 'everlasting life'.

In an abstract sense, it may be construed as a hieroglyph which is simply translated as 'the Giver of Life' or possibly 'God eternal.' When combined it may, therefore, relate to multiple resurrections in relation to God eternal?

The fact that this ivory message pillar, or hirz, looks like it fitted together with another matching half to form a complete amulet, based on the complete inscribed heirogyph, and judging by evidence of worn oval clasps at the top and sides, I would hazard a guess to suggest that it may also have had a gem of some kind at its connected centre.

Let me finish by saying I am not going to ask the obvious question that arises, but simply say that the evidence, combined with the initial translation of the message, should be left to more experienced minds than mine to conjecture over, along with its likely origin, and true relevance.

James's first impression was that the fine scrolls must be fraudulent. His mind was now focusing on the fact that it made reference to the prophet possibly being fortold as Mohammed. It was clearly in connection with a verse from the Old Testament, but written 1000 years before the known earliest rendering of that biblical text. In his mind he backtracked to the time of Moses and accounts of what were known of the origins of the Old Testament book of Genesis. Whilst tradition credited Moses as the author of the books of Genesis, Exodus, Leviticus, Numbers and most of Deuteronomy, he also knew that some scholars had recently started seeing it as a product of the 5th and 6th centuries.

This find was reinforcing that theory, yet with this much older message having been altered to prepare the later account.

Taking each scenario in turn both James Quibell and his senior translator postulated that given the wisdom of the Egyptians, that as Moses had supposedly been taught in Egypt, that he may have originally gathered about him a number of faithfully protected clay tablet accounts that had been recorded in cuneiform over the generations. In the name of Jehovah he could then have been the initial editor of the book of Genesis, but in using his own characters.

This, however, then posed the question, if Moses had been both writer and editor of the Pentateuch, and the five books that they represented in the Old Testament, then why had the final result been changed from what was now being revealed?

The only logical conclusion that could be drawn, given the authenticity of the amulet half, was that a number of ancient tablets must have had their passages and messages conveniently and selectively altered, either by Moses or when they were redacted in the 5th and 6th century, to create the book of Genesis.

Whichever way they looked at it, and whatever the motive, as a supposed combined record of the people of God, with their continuation of preserving those records as knowledge of the word of God, it was now obvious that parts of Genesis had conveniently been altered. The obvious motivation appeared to have been for early Judeans to have conveniently changed extracts to make a single God their own with the name of Jehovah, as was already being proven with other increasing archaeological evidence. Having rechecked the dating of the artefact's message it was not just proof that biblical writers then, in their attempt at promoting an account and belief in Christianity, used the Jewish faith's flawed foundation and manipulation of the truth.

And that simple truth could be that Mohammed's life was preordained, and that the Jews were not God's chosen people.

James read the translation of the message out again…

To your descendants I give this land, from Aššur to the km.t. I will raise them up a Prophet in the land of Chorev from among your brethren. From the son of Abdullah, I will make you into a great nation, and I will bless you; I will make your name great, and you will be a blessing.

After a moment he added …

Correct me if I am wrong but this then clearly indicates that whoever wrote this considered that approximately 1400 years from the time it was written in circa 900BC, that the son of an Abdullah was going to be great in the eyes of an early God, or God eternal. It refers to lands from the Sinai to Mesopotamia, but more importantly says to me that this maybe a very early verse that was then recorded in redacted form in the Old Testament. If so it is stating that the Israelites were not the promised people, but a tribe of an Abdullah, as the servant of God.

Looking at the interpreter he asked…. *Do I understand that correctly?*

Yes that is broadly correct ... and there was again quiet in the room until the translator was asked to expand on his translation…

In this context given its age it more than likely relates to the son of 'Abdeel', or 'the servant of God'. This is also cognate to the Arabic name 'Abdullah', who along with reference to the land of Chorev means, I suspect, the mountain of God, as either Har Horeb, Har Sinai, or Har ha-Elohim, where the Torah was supposedly given to Moses by God, or it may just mean the Sinai.

Simply put it is referring to a prophet who is a son of an Abdullah, as a servant of God, who will receive God's word in the Sinai at some unspecified time in the future. Whilst that could fit with the account of Moses, it likewise fits with Mohammed. If that was the case then the Arabs were God's 'chosen people', at least in terms of an early belief, and that their Promised Land stretched from Mesopotamia to Egypt.

The million pound question is, however, how would this have been known over 1400 years before Mohammed's birth, unless it had been ordained and recorded correctly as the word of God? Was he accepted 1400 years before his coming to resurrect God's faith as his prophet on earth, and was he the actual foretold resurrection?

The message, therefore, poses more questions than it answers, but given its authenticity it certainly brings into question the origins of a promised people, or a promised land in terms of the Jews, unless of course they originally were descended from Arabs of the Quraysh. If that is proven to be the case then Mohammed was the true prophesised prophet, and not Jesus Christ.

It also leads to another mystery, and that is how the messages came to be included in an ancient Egyptian amulet symbolising eternal life. More interestingly, however, I suggest, is what the other matching half of the amulet contained, and where might that have got to?

Unbeknown to James Quibell one of the museum's archaeological staff had overheard part of a conversation regarding the find, and had taken the liberty of transcribing a copy of both scroll's Arabic and Akkadian translations onto paper. Now being told to forget about the find and return any script on its existence, it had heightened his suspicions. As a practicing Christian of the Coptic Church of Alexandria, with a dutiful Christian spirit, he would hand his copy of the text over to his church to see if it held any significance for them, for as his elders had always counselled…

As with most things that are attempted to be kept secret they set barriers between men, but in all cases they offer up the seductive temptation to break through the barrier by confession, where the opportunity arises.

Two days later a more complete and corrected text translation of the amulet's contents had been revealed like a bolt of lightning to the elders and bishop of The Coptic Church of Alexandria. This came along with the authenticated dates, and a brief explanation as to why the Arabic written word may have been used with this unique religious artefact. They now comprehended that this amulet hirz contents were a theological time-bomb that not just appeared to validate the prophet Mohammed, but also placed under severe scrutiny the validity and rights the Christian Church and the Jews had built their faiths upon.

Firstly there was Judaism that had established a purported, and now proven incorrect, right over any Land of Promise. Secondly, it brought into question the authenticity of the first book of the Old Testament - Genesis; and then subsequently elements of what Jesus's disciples had recorded to be compiled later in the New Testament when they recorded that Jesus had been the son of God on earth, as he is in heaven. Whilst it validated the Coptic Church's stance, bringing into question the eternal nature of Jesus as the eternal son of God; a view they had long held that they continued to be at odds with Catholicism over, it certainly placed under direct threat not just their Church but many others. For several of them who were now privy to the discovery they could see the irony in what was unfolding given the historical manipulative and dishonest nature of both the Roman Catholic and Jewish churches.

More to the point was that for the Moslem it would be seen as final validation and retribution to unbelievers. It was certainly true for them that the Catholic faith, with its Church of Rome and image of a pontiff as some fictional representative of God on earth, had been insulting Mohammed for nearly two millennia.

Maybe now they would get to see the divine, blinding, light of truth, with its rays lighting up all those who had continued unabated through the centuries in attempting to sell a God, on their terms, to the uneducated and the ignorant. It also meant that it would additionally shine on the rabbinical egotism and ill founded beliefs of the Jews, and all other supposed Jews and Christians. It would be an ultimate judgement that would certainly rock their hypocritical, increasing, self indulgent, power based foundations. If it did not bring their empires crashing around their ears, they would at least see that truth, that was Allah, was non-negotiable.

That was if the half amulet and its message were ever made public.

Whilst the Coptic faith had a historic dislike of the Roman Catholic Church philosophically, this was a different matter entirely, as it was that church that had the resource and manpower to hopefully do something about it.

Having received a communiqué, that had arrived via the British Embassy in Cairo, Jehanne was by now aware that the first half of the amulet, that she had seen the original photograph of, had been fortuitously obtained. With it in now in British hands she was advised that it was being sent to her for matching and validation also at the Egyptian Museum in Cairo, alongside the second half. In that regard she was instructed to meet the ship transporting it, and to get it safely to James Quibell for cleaning and authentication.

Up until now Jehanne had been instructed not to make anyone in the Near East aware of the initial half of von Oppenheim's amulet find. Whilst it had been used to lever the Italians to fall into line, it was not something London wanted known in the Near East given the Central Powers desire to leverage it to their advantage. Consequently James Quibell was only aware of the second half. Now he be needed to be briefed on the discovery of the first half, and his new role in authenticating and matching it after being sworn, under oath, in preserving the object's secrecy.

The Cairo Museum

In the congested port of Liverpool, England the armed merchantman *Empress of Britain* had been re-commissioned as a troop transport. Now boarding reinforcements for Egypt she would go onto carry more than 110,000 troops to the Dardanelles, Egypt and India. On this, her first troop transport duty, she was also to carry the German half of the amulet, and to protect her from coming to grief she would be escorted by a Royal Navy light cruiser destined for the Dardenelles.

HMT Empress of Britain would arrive at Port Said without incident 20 days later on 5th June 1915 to hand over a small confidential package containing the amulet to a waiting British MI1 operative.

HMT Empress of Britain

Port Said harbour

Located at the northern entrance to the Suez Canal, by the late 19th century, Port Said had become the world's largest coal-bunkering station, catering almost

Port Said

exclusively to canal traffic. Then, with the coming of the rail it had become Egypt's chief port after Alexandria. Initially for the traveller there had been no road from Cairo, with only a single standard-gauge railway track that crossed the 30 miles of desert from Cairo to Ismaïlia on the Suez Canal, before branching north to Port Said, and south to Suez. This line had opened in 1904 with the trip from Port Said to Cairo now taking around four and a half hours.

As the designated operative, on her way to collect the package Jehanne sat looking out over the Nile Delta from her airy carriage. The trip had given her time to reflect on what could transpire over the discovery of the amulet's two messages. Would Britain now use it to force the hand of either Moslem, Christian, or Jew? Its existence certainly created a powerful inducement for the Roman Catholic Church, or the Jews for that matter, to want to get their hands on it. If they did they no doubt would either destroy it or keep it hidden. As for any Moslems, if it's messages became public, they would no doubt incite jihad across all Moslem nations, as had already been attempted with the first half. Politically, Jehanne thought, it was certainly worth a lot more than its weight in gold as had been evidenced with the Italians, so who else could be looking for it?

At Ismailia Jehanne's train had been ushered onto a siding while another with labour Corp workers bound for Cairo steamed past. These workers were employed working on the branch military railway line that was extending itself across the western Sinai from Kantara. This feat, along with an accompanying water line, was a triumph for the railways companies of Royal Engineers, officials of the Egyptian State Railways who had become part of the military staff, and the construction gangs of Sikh Pioneers and Egyptian Labour Corps.

Troops passing on open wagons

The latter were proving themselves the finest navvies in the world with them having to build the railway right under the enemy's nose. Protected only by a thin line of outposts these 'gyppy' labourers worked under continual threat of ground attack and from aerial bombardment. Bombs often sought them out, and at El

Arish one bomb would kill and wound 39 of them. Working under British, and some Syrian, officers the heat affected them little, and with the example set by the Sikhs, the line was progressing exceptionally well.

Troops arriving at Port Said

Incentivised by a much better rate of pay than that available on the Nile Delta, along with a plentiful supply of good food, uniforms, blankets, and tents to sleep in, they were a motivated bunch. The real bonus, however, was the 10 days leave they received every three months with free passes issued on the rail.

For Jehanne this passing train of packed cheerful labourers, off on leave with pockets full of money, was a sight to behold. Waving flags of all shapes, colours, and hues, they hung out of the carriage windows singing, clapping hands, and waving at anything, and anyone, they saw as they had past, to start their well earned break.

Following the Labour train passing several soldiers boarded the train for the leg to Kantara and onto Port Said. They inspired Jehanne for some reason to think of Private Arthur Edgar Newcombe and in wondering what he was up to, before reflecting on the talks of Ernest Budge that had opened another world to her with regard to religion and antiquities. Her personal experiences with the duplicity and extremes of the Roman Catholic Church, along with the many extremist zealots she had come in contact with in Egypt over recent months, had also opened here eyes. Most were neither sincere nor honest; not at all like a good number of her old Marseille clientele or the average soldier like Arthur, who were at least that. The patronising, non enlightened, stance of some with rank and station she had also now become wary of. This included any who continued to extol that God was on their side, like politicians and church leaders. Understanding all too well that there was a war to be won Jehanne was beginning to perceive that there was now a larger game being played with a subtly different agenda.

Disembarking at Port Said Railway Station Jehanne kept her eyes open for foreign or local spies in case they were aware of what she was collecting. Over previous months of routine daily surveillance she had, along with others, managed to create a list of potential, and known, German and Ottoman spies in and around Cairo. Keeping a low profile she had blended into the bazaar cafes at night where the underbelly of Egyptian society organised its nefarious affairs.

This was different, for the close confines of the harbour was congested with merchant, and naval vessels of all types, while alongside the wharves a hospital ship discharged wounded to a waiting line of ambulances. Here there was a bustle of activity with soldiers, gyppo porters, labourers, and traders of all races, scurrying about their business. Closer to her a transport was loading fresh reinforcements for the killing grounds of the now infamous Gallipoli peninsular. Several who were boarding were looking further along the wharf and the casualties being discharged, no doubt wondering if they would return the same way; or not return at all. This simple picture epitomised the futility of war in that it was always the innocent youth like Arthur who had to bear the brunt of the nightmare of others desire to exterminate their largely unknown enemy.

Hospital Ship alongside the wharf at Port Said discharging patients to the waiting ambulances

Preservation of freedom was no doubt a just and honourable cause, but the stupidity of two sets of related royal families

Reinforcements off to Gallipoli

fighting each other using their subjects as cannon fodder was not lost on her.

Moving further along the wharf Jehanne she could see a manned Navy cutter below alongside a small barnacle encrusted jetty and steps. The British Naval officer in white uniform, flanked by two armed guards, on the wharf was no doubt from the transport. Checking her pocket watch, and waiting momentarily for the exact rendezvous time, she approached the officer showing him her signed Embassy letter with photo of identification. Satisfied that all was in order she received the package with the amulet and quickly slipped it into a small Egyptian tourist bag she had bought for the purpose.

Jehanne's train

Charged with monitoring all activity on the wharf the German operative had picked Jehanne out of the crowd for her attractiveness and had witnessed her receive the package. For him it had happened by chance and now as she passed him again he paid particular attention to her appearance. Briefed on all Cairo based British Intelligence personnel he knew instinctively she had a connection, recalling her as possibly one of the Embassy's clerical staff. Her receiving the packet had initially surprised him until he realised that who better to send than someone that was not likely to be identified. It was only luck that he had looked at the Cairo Intelligence file on suspected British Embassy staff only a few hours earlier, and that her picture had been included. Now suspecting that the package highly likely contained the amulet that he had been ordered to intercept if the opportunity presented itself, he followed at a safe distance.

Boarding the train after Jehanne he stood at the back of the carriage until its departure to check out each of the other passengers. All were local Egyptians with the exception of one young soldier sitting to his left. Realising that Jehanne had no support he determined that her master's had likely made a fatal error. With few others onboard in the confines of the carriage he slipped into a seat opposite the soldier to wait until they were well past the silos at Kantara before making his move.

Silo and water pumping – Kantara 1915

With no one boarding at Kantara he could not believe his luck.

An hour later he lazily stood, stretched his arms, and moved down the carriage to quickly sit next to the British operative. Jehanne was initially surprised by the jab of the long barrelled German naval luger pistol that was being pressed into her side. Not looking at her attacker she simply listened to his instructions.

Get up junge Dame and move to das end of das carriage oot onto das footplate. Don't try anything foolish or it vill be your last endeavour in ihre life… Raus!

Nodding in acknowledgement Jehanne got carefully to her feet. Slipping in front of the German operative, she made her way forward, with him close behind. Moving slowly with her hands hidden she quickly removed the package from her bag with her left hand, placing it in one of her front facing skirt pockets. Then, transferring the bag to her left hand, within two more steps she slipped the knuckle duster that comfortably hung in the folds of her skirt, onto her right knuckles. Still grasping the bag that now only held a half eaten bunch of grapes she slowly opened the carriage door. Stepping out onto the footplate that led to the forward carriage she immediately turned to face the German spy in the increased rush of wind and noise. In his desire to cover his intentions the German agent had momentarily looked behind himself to close the door, and in that instant Jehanne made her move.

Dropping the bag she grabbed the spy's lapel with her left hand and jerked him forward. With his left hand occupied with the door handle it had the affect of swinging her attacker side on to the footplate, at which point the knuckle duster connected solidly with his face smashing his nose and splitting his upper lip. It had all happened so fast his German's mind was still catching up with what was occurring when a well directed kick to his scrotum sent him reeling backwards off the footplate. With his gun hand pointing off into space he got off one shot before discarding the pistol to try and grasp the metal carriage handhold as he fell. Clutching at fresh air he momentarily got to witness Jehanne's set features before his scream, along with his body, was carried off on the wind as the train drummed over the rails. The last that was seen of him was by the young British soldier at the rear of Jehanne's carriage who witnessed his look of terror a split second before he hit a metal railway distance marker on the side of the track. It would break his back and almost sever his head from his quivering torso.

Smoothing herself off Jehanne re-entered the carriage this time to sit beside the rather nervous looking young lad from the Northumberland Regiment.

Port Said

Locomotive drivers on the Cairo to Port Said line

Part X

After reporting her experience to her superiors a series of telegraphic exchanges was made with others in authority in London. Their decision to do so was based on the undeniable fact that the amulet was not safe in Cairo and the British Foreign Office wanted to get it out of Egypt as soon as possible. Jehanne was instructed to have the museum conduct their assessment as quickly as possible so the complete amulet could be returned to London for safekeeping. To her, knowing its importance, it seemed astonishing that they would keep sending pieces backwards and forwards with the cat now definitely out of the bag.

With no known U-boat threat having manifested itself in the Mediterranean, and with no Royal Naval vessel available, London, again astonishingly, considered it safe enough to have the artefact transported with urgency in a diplomatic pouch by British merchant ship as far as Gibraltar. Here it was to be handed over to the Admiralty who would ensure its safe return to Britain.

The only ship due to depart for Gibraltar over the next two days, was out of Alexandria. It was the *SS Clan Aonghais,* so Jehanne and James Quibell were consequently now working to a tight deadline.

At the Egyptian Museum James had received the second half of the amulet with excitement and some trepidation. He could not remember when in his career he had been so much on edge, and help couldn't help wondering where this second remaining piece had come from…? It was like a lifetime's achievement had suddenly arrived in the space of three months. Like Jehanne he did not like coincidences any more than others in his profession, and it left him with an uneasy feeling.

Repeating the procedure of authentication with this amulet half and message he now stood looking down on the completed amulet on his office desk. The two halves had been fitted together and there was no doubt that they matched, and he tried to visualise the artefact with its missing central stone. Polished, in its day it would have been magnificent and an intricate piece of craftsmanship for its time. As he gazed on its beauty the museum's translator interrupted his thoughts by knocking on his door to reveal his findings.

With a select group seated at his desk the translator began by summerising the initial message they had already authenticated …

I will begin, he quietly stated, *by reading the message from the first half of the amulet that we received to refresh our joint memories. After that I will then introduce the second.*

We all remember the first recorded message….

"To your descendants I give this land, from Aššur to the km.t. I will raise them up a prophet in the land of Chorev from among your brethren. From the son of Abdullah, I will make you into a great nation, and I will bless you; I will make your name great, and you will be a blessing".

James will remember that we both wondered who the prophet may have been, and that in our minds it likely referred to either Moses or Mohammed…. Well the second half reads….

"I will raise them up a prophet from among their brethren, as Hashim ha-meshuggah the son of Abdullah … and will put my word in his mouth; and he shall speak unto them all that I shall command him".

There was a deathly hush in the room. Those present already had an inkling of what was coming next…

Let me start with the prophet's name, Hashim ha-meshuggah, as the son of Abdullah. In this context Hashim ha-meshuggah is 'the madman of Hashim' with Abdullah literally meaning 'the servant of God' as I previously mentioned to James. As such he is recoreded as an intermediary for God, or Allah, and he cannot be confused, I believe, as anyone other than the prophet Mohammed.

The interpreter continued….

I have done some more delving since we investigated the first message, and more specifically I can advise that Hashim ibn 'Abd Manaf lived from 464 to 497 AD. He was the great-grandfather of the Islamic prophet Mohammed and the progenitor of the Banu Hashim clan of the distinguished Quraish tribe in Mecca. His true name was 'Amr al-Ulā, but he was given the nickname 'Hashim' which supposedly, in one account, translates as 'pulveriser' in Arabic, because he initiated the practice of providing crumbled bread in broth for the pilgrims to the Ka'aba in Mecca.

A more likely version of the story of this naming is that Hashim comes from the Arabic root Hashm, meaning, 'to save the starving, because he arranged for the feeding of the people of Mecca during a seasonal famine, and he, therefore, became 'the man who fed the starving.'

Interestingly his father was 'Abd Manaf ibn Qusai who, according to Islamic tradition, is a descendant of Ibrahim through his son Ismail, or Ishmael. Known as Abraham in the Old Testament, Ibrahim is also recognised in Islam as a prophet and apostle of God; or God in Arabic as 'Allah'. Ibrahim is also known by the title Khalilullah, or friend of Allah, and he supposedly lived around 2000 BC. Originally Abram, in an Old Testament sense, he is the first of the three Patriarchs of Israel whose story is told in chapters 11–25 of the Book of Genesis. According to that account Abram, as he is recorded, was called by God to leave his father Terah's house and native land of Mesopotamia in return for a new land, family, and inheritance in Canaan; the 'Promised Land'. This of course is the land the Jews claim to be theirs, through the line of the Israelite kings.

As an aside the father of Ibrahim, Terah or Térach, means 'Wanderer'. He was supposedly a wicked idolatrous priest who manufactured idols, and tenth in line of descent from Noah. The meaning as 'wanderer' may refer to him being like the Bedouin, and then Arabic in lineal descent to tribe of Hashim.

Given that both messages' age are clearly much early than any recorded version in the Old Testaments book of Genesis, it clearly identifies that the 'Promised Land' was being bequeathed to the Arabs, with Mohammed as their future prophet, who had God, or Allah's blessing.

Before you interject, let me state that this, to me, leads to one particularly interesting line of thought.

I know, for instance, that previously several academics have conjectured, and then argued, that the Arabs and Bedouin were the original founders of monotheist religion, not the later Hebrews? This for me seems to validate that scenario also, as it confirms two very important points.

Firstly that an Arabic tribe had a covenant with a single God over the land from Mesopotamia to Egypt, over 1000 years before any Old Testament tablet was recorded and, secondly, that Mohammed as a prophet of Allah was foretold over a 1500 years before his birth.

The silence in the room was defeaning. With its high eves and imposing dark book cases the walls seemed to be closing in on James Quibell. He needed time to think about what he had just been told without letting his emotions show. The phrase '*Peace and blessings be upon Him*' seemed to be repeating itself over and over in his head as he tried to grasp the probable implications of the amulet's messages. Getting up James walked from his office on the first floor and past the artifacts from the final two dynasties of Egypt. Included were those from the tombs of the Pharaohs Thutmosis III, Thutmosis IV, Amenophis II, Hatshepsut, and the courtier Maiherpri from the Valley of the Kings. As he walked he thought that if this was not a hoax, or fraudulent, then it made everything in his immediate surroundings insignificant. He made the ground floor still in a state of shock to gaze on the extensive collection of papyrus that represented material originating from the Ancient world. The numerous pieces were small fragments due to their decay over the past two millennia. Several languages were found on these examples including Greek, Latin, Arabic, and the Ancient Egyptian written form of hieroglyphs. There was hieratic and cuneiform script on clay tablets such as that recorded on the fine amulet's scrolls, and gathering his thoughts he turned to artefacts from the New Kingdom of Eygpt. They were all from the estimated time period of 1550 to 1070 BC, and the one he was looking for immediately caught his eye.

On his return to his office the trusted museum's senior translator had wanted advice as to what should be done with the completed find given, and its analysis, given its validity and translations. James advised, as he had been told, that it was required be to sent back to England as soon as possible for further evaluation, and to see what Ernest Budge thought about it at the British Museum now that it had been translated, as it must be considered a fraud. This surprised the translator, however, he kept quite sensing that their was more to this find than met the eye.

Not being one to seek glory, to James Quibell's simple way of thinking, having both halves of the amulet out of his hands would achieve two things. Firstly, it would be back in British hands, removed from any threat of theft in a war zone; and secondly, he could see that that the longer it remained here, the word could surely get out about its message and authenticity. This, he deduced, would result in the not improbable outcome of the museum being ransacked to discover its whereabouts, with his staff also being placed in danger. Having grasped the amulet's wider significance he was considering the immediacy of the museum's position with a find of this nature. As a political and religious time bomb in terms of a full blown Moslem jihad in the name of Allah, if the messages were made public he knew it would play directly into the Central Powers hands.

He was also scared to what ends other interested parties might extend their endeavours to get their hands on it, to either make use of it politically, or to smother its existence.

After agreeing with the translater on the urgent need for tightened security, he advised museum staff that the amulet and its messages were dangerous, but in fact that they were a hoax and forgeries. This was even after several had authenticated its age and origins, placing them in a positions as to motivations of the museum's director. He had ordered all who had worked on it to deliver up all copies and working transcripts of its texts, and any other supporting papyri, even though the translating had not yet been fully, or accurately, completed. The original minutely fine messages were to be carefully returned to the now partially cleaned ivory pillars, and resealed with wax, as they had been, with the amulet delivered to the director for wrapping carefully in cotton cloth and oil paper. The complete was to then be finally sealed for collection by Jehanne Blanche from the British Embassy.

The first railway in Egypt, between Alexandria and Cairo, had been the first on the African continent. It had opened in 1856, with

Mena Camp, Cairo

Mena Military Camp in the vicinity of the pyramids

the policy of the State Railways Administration up until 1914 having been the gradual absorption of private lines, and the improvement of services, so that by 1915 there were express trains operating daily in either direction between and Cairo and Alexandria. With the advent of war, the associated large volume of traffic arriving and departing from Alexandria, had developed it into the largest goods' station in Egypt.

The journey of 120 miles was covered in three and a half hours and Jehanne now made it in the company of James Quibell, along with a burly looking associate male operative, also employed by MI1. During the journey James was noticeably on edge, even though he was relieved to be rid of any responsibility for the amulet. Still, now knowing only too well its significance historically, religiously, and politically, and having pondered what effect it would have on the Christian and Jewish faiths, his nerves were on edge.

Sworn as a British subject under the Secrecy Act he had been given very clear instructions in needing to keep up the façade that the amulet was a fraud.

The Cairo to Alexandria railway

Fortunately the trip went without incident and Jehanne located the Indian crewed *SS Clan Aonghais*. Going onboard she personally expressed to the ship's captain the importance of ensuring the that diplomatic pouch reached its destination at the offices of the Royal Navy in Gibraltar.

Four days later a telegram sent from the desk of the C in CE Indies, Egypt would read … *Have you any news of the SS Clan Aonghais - departed Alexandria on the 25th May bound for Gibraltar.*

The reply to the C in CE Indies simply stated…. *Clan Aonghais has not yet arrived Gibraltar.*

Cairo to Alexandria Railway

SS Clan Aonghais

With its white-washed houses fanning down a gentle slope to its superb enclosed harbour the Turkish port town of Bodrum was tucked into a peninsula of the same name. It lay pristine in the south-western Aegean directly in the line of travel for vessels plying between Egypt and the Dardenelles.

Bodrum from Pola

Oberleutnant zur See Werner

After arriving at Bodrum from Pola on the 20th May, Oberleutnant zur See Werner of UB7 had his submarine topped up with fuel and stores before again putting to sea. Heading towards Alexandria in search of shipping three days later he had found that his main engine was defective, with it stopping as soon as the clutch was engaged to the propeller. Forced to rely on electric motors, even on the surface, his engineer and engine room crew had worked furiously to repair the fault.

261

Using only the main engine for charging was not a satisfactory state of affairs as they drifted on the surface in a war zone, and it

A crew member on UB7

had also meant care over economy with the batteries. After a day and a half of hard work the fault had been rectified.

On the 25th May, they fixed their position as only 100 miles due north of Mersa Matruh on the North African coast, and only 180 odd miles from Alexandria. With a slight relocation they had been able to monitor the westerly shipping lanes to and from Alexandria, and Port Said, and they were to be in luck.

On the afternoon of the 26th a day out from port, they sighted a ship steaming towards them on the horizon. It was *SS Aonghais.* With the weather fine and clear, and wind in the west, there was a slight sea, and she was steaming a full speed making an average of 10 knots.

With lookouts in her crow's nest, and two on her foc'sle head, the chief officer on *SS Aonghais,* Frederick James Hawley, had just been called as he was to go on duty at 4 pm.

262

Submerged to wait his prey in the control room of UB7 Werner and his first officer calculated the likely shooting angle, and speed of the oncoming ship. They couldn't believe their luck as with little manoeuvering they knew that she would pass across their bows at close range. Viewed through the periscope the oncoming ship's bow wave could now be made out along with superstructure. With her 45cm torpedo tube doors open and tubes loaded Werner counted down the minutes before he gave the order to fire.

Feuer!... resonated around the U-boat's control room before confirmation was received from the torpedo room... *Torpedo lose!*

The sinking of the SS Clan Aonghais

The outcome was almost inevitable with the torpedo running towards the doomed ship at high speed. Werner followed its course through the periscope by the light streak of bubbles that it left in its wake. He also witnessed the torpedo's bubble-track being discovered on the bridge of the steamer as frightened arms pointed towards the water. The captain of the *SS Aonghais* simply put his hands in front of his eyes and waited resignedly for the frightful explosion that followed.

Several seconds later the crew of UB7 were thrown against one another by the concussion of the blast. Then, like Vulcan, a huge and majestic column of water 50 metres broad, and terrible in its beauty and power, shot up 200 metres towards the heavens.

Hit abaft the funnel…. Werner shouted through the control room intercom.

As soon as the torpedo struck, on board the doomed SS Aonghais the Chief Officer Frederick Hawley ran on deck into a mountain of descending water. He discovered the hatch cover and tarpaulins of No 5 hatch blown off and several of the temporary deck timber horse stables damaged. With the cargo breaking up and starting to float out of the steamer's side he immediately gave orders to man the life boats. With the ship's increasing list only the port side boats were operable and there was now increased panic onboard to get away from the stricken vessel. The starboard life boats were simply let go from their davits with two managing to reach the surface undamaged, but empty. The Captain had reappeared with a small pania including the ship's log and the diplomatic pouch he had been entrusted with. Quickly conferring with the master Hawley ordered 'Abondon Ship' before searching the forecastles to make sure no one was in them. With it growing dark the ship was quickly beginning to settle by the stern, and after surfacing Werner's later record of events stated what he witnessed from UB7's conning tower….

All her decks were visible and from all hatchways a storming, despairing mass of men had fought their way on deck; grimy Indian stokers and crew, officers, groom, cooks. Numbers of the Asians appeared to be running screaming for boats. They tore and thrust one another from the ladders leading down to them, fought for the lifebelts and jostled one another on the sloping deck. Amongst them a rearing, slipping horse was wedged. The starboard boats could not be lowered on account of the list; and many, therefore, ran across to the port boats, which in the hurry and panic, had been lowered with great stupidity either half full or overcrowded.

The men left behind were wringing their hands in despair and running to and fro along the decks to finally throw threw themselves into the water to swim to the boats.

Then - a second explosion, followed by the escape of white hissing steam from all hatchways and scuttles. This white steam drove the horses on deck mad. I witnessed a beautiful long-tailed dapple-grey take a mighty leap over the berthing rails and land into a fully laden boat.

At that point he had been able to bear the sight any longer, and he had lowered the periscope to dive deep.

Amazingly, for the crew of the *SS Aonghais,* by 5.15pm all remaining hands had been recovered by the remaining boats and rowed clear. All the boats were made fast astern of the master's boat to keep them together during the night.

Oberleutnant zur See Werner
and the crew of UB7

A few minutes later UB7 surfaced and came alongside the lifeboats where Werner asked details of the steamship before steering eastwards. After this exchange, masts were stepped in the lifeboats, sails broken out, and a course set for Crete, which was thought to be 55 to 60 miles away to the north.

The remaining crew of the freighter sailed all night and in the morning it fell calm. The boats were separated and the men rowed until 10.00 am when a light northerly wind sprang up. They set sail again and continued until 5 pm when the boats were all made fast again. Again they sailed all night. On May 28th at 8.00 am they made the north-east end of Crete; but the wind and sea increased and the boats were blown to the south-west along the coast. Land was only three or four miles distance but it was impossible to make headway.

A depiction of the blighted crew of SS Aonghais

At 10pm that night the third officer's boat parted the tow rope. The second gunner's boat was attached to this one, and they were both swallowed up in the darkness. The master's boat caste off and went in search of them while Hawley's boat lay to with the others. It was a terrible night. With a good number of Indian natives in boat's crews, they suffered greatly from exposure. One by one, in the dim light of the lanterns they gave up the fight for life pathetically slipping into the water that swilled about their feet. For those still clutching to life their wild eyes, always aloof, flashed like those of frightened wild animals while they murmured deliriously, no doubt about some distant Eastern home. Five of them died in Hawley's boat to be lifted dripping from the water that had been shipped, and slid over the side into the dark sea. A sixth died in the second officer's boat.

At daybreak the master's boat was sighted; a black dot amongst the distant white caps, and by 8.00 am he had managed to rejoin them. He told them he had been unable to find the missing boats and that three natives in his own boat had also died during the night.

At 4pm that afternoon they decided to abandon No.1 boat, transferring the fourth engineer, with six natives, to Hawley's boat, and two natives to the master's boat. The wind and sea had increased in an orchestrated symphony of waves and salt spray , before half an hour later the rudder on the master's boat was carried away. With further effort fighting the sea, his crew made fast astern of the second officer's boat. By 5.30 the wind and sea had increased so much that the master was forced to let go. They watched as he set a reefed jib, however, by daylight the following morning, the 30th May, there was no sign of him.

At 2 pm he was sighted again sailing westward. Hawley set sail and tried to follow but he had the second officers' boat attached and could not catch up. The last they saw of the master's boat was at sunset. It was heading approximately WSW before finally vanishing into the evening light.

In Hawley's boat sails were stowed and the boats lay to. A sea anchor was used that night, then at daylight they attached a bucket to the sea anchor to increase its drag.

At 1.00 am on the 31st it was decided to abandon No.4 boat and transfer the second officer, third engineer and seven natives, with their remaining food and water, to Hawley's boat. It was a perilous task in the wind and boisterous sea, and during the process their rudder was broken and unshipped. They were now forced to use an oar with a goose winged jib as a jigger, to keep their head to the sea. During the afternoon the wind increased to a gale with a resultant increasing sea. The boat laboured heavily shipping water with heavy seas and spray continually bursting over the men as they baled. Oil was used to try and settle the sea around the boat while baling went on without a break. Soaked head to toe by the

cold seas exposure continued to take its toll for at noon on the 1st the cook died and was slipped overboard. Half an hour later the officer's boy died, to be followed the same bleak morning by a

ship's fireman. The burial of the dead, with a heave and that brief plunge of each body that lightened the boat, were the only interruptions to the long monotony of baling.

The following morning the wind and sea moderated a little and at noon they sighted the smoke of a steamer away to the SE, but she drew no nearer, and the smoke died away.

It was now that Hawley decided to set a reefed lug-sail and make ESE for Alexandria, though it was about 200 miles distant. At 4.15 pm another native died and was slipped overboard. They sailed all night and at 5.00 am on the 3rd June the wind shifted to the NW and freshened with the sea increasing again. At 6 am the captain's boy died having fought hard for life throughout the night, and his burial made the boat lighter still. At 7.30 am they put a second reef in the lug sail and changed course to steer SE.

At 8 am they sighted a steamer on the port bow, only about three miles distant. Cries broke out from their blackened lips while they made signals of distress by waving some of the dead men's clothing on an oar. Fortuitously the steamer sighted them and made for them blowing her steam whistle.

At 8.30 am they were alongside and by 9.00 am they were aboard.

Rescue at sea

On the way to Malta two more of their number passed away. Hawley telegrammed requesting a search for the missing boats, one of which had been commanded by their master in whose care was the diplomatic pouch.

The telegram reply of the 5th June, 1915, simply stated… *No ships available!*

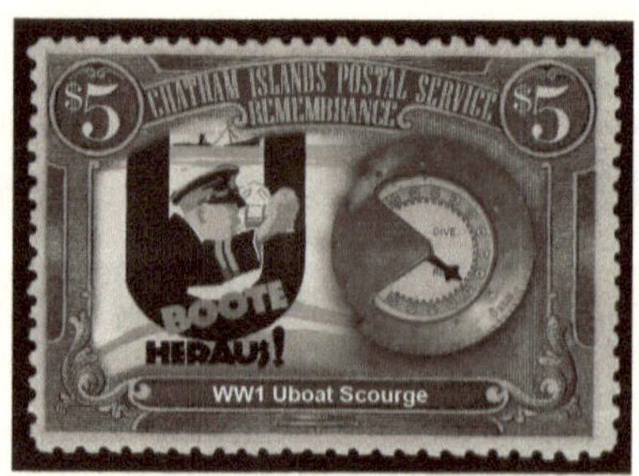

The U boat scourge

Part XI

King George V

With an overwhelming sense of pride Private Arthur Newcombe stood to attention while King George V inspected the 2/10th Territorial Battalion, Middlesex Regiment, along with others of the division at Cambridge on 11th February, 1915.

Two months later, following the Gallipoli landings at the end of April, Arthur's battalion was joined by other Home County battalions to form the 160th Brigade of the 53rd Division. When the division was fully up to strength in May it moved to Bedford, to continue training. They would remain there until early July when the order came to refit for service in the Mediterranean.

The King inspects his troops

Since joining the battalion Arthur had been teased about his obvious youth and had been jovially been nicknamed the battalion 'Batman'. As a form of endearment that had been accepted, as his training progressed older incumbents had come to realise that skill had nothing to do with age. Whilst not adjudicated the best shot in the battalion Arthur was above average in marksmanship. Physically capable of holding his own he had earned their respect and was now on an equal footing with those around him. Likewise they were all equally excited about where they would be heading, and whilst most were apprehensive about their futures, Arthur saw it as a chance to prove his worth.

One of his new friends was Private John Richard Bestonso who was three years Arthur's senior. John had been born on 28th January 1896, in St. Giles. He was the eldest son of Mary Bestonso and Italian-born wood carver Giacinto of London. He had followed his father's trade and had been living at 27 Cobbold Road, Willesden, London, before the war, and not far from Arthur. With his love

John Bestonso

of art and history the two had hit it off and had by now become firm pals.

It had been John who had first made Arthur aware of the First Lord of the Admiralty Winston Churchill's plan to use the Royal Navy to force a way through the Dardanelles to attack Constantinople, in an attempt to link up with the Russians. Both of them were now aware that the March naval attack had failed to get past the minefields and artillery overlooking the Dardanelle Straits. The plan had been subsequently changed to land the army on the Gallipoli Peninsula and they had both read about the two landings made on 25th April; one at the tip of the peninsular at Cape Helles by British and French forces, and the other by Australian and New Zealand forces part-way up the west coast, at what was now referred to as Anzac Cove. They were also very much aware that both groups had become trapped on their beach-heads, and were being constantly shelled by the Turks from the surrounding hills with their casualties continuing to grow.

What do you reckon with happen to us? surmised Arthur to his friend.

We'll be OK ... You are too good a shot to let me be hit, John had jokingly replied.

Unbeknown to them the Dardanelles Committee had met in London on the 7th June, 1915 under the guidance of Lord Kitchener. At this this meeting it had decided to reinforce the Mediterranean Expeditionary Force of General Sir Ian Hamilton with three New Army divisions, along with two more Territorial Army divisions later that month. This, it was considered, would hopefully give Hamilton the numbers required to reinvigorate the campaign.

It had been a long-standing plan to attempt to break out of the Anzac bridge-head and had first been proposed in late May by the commander of the Australian and New Zealand Army Corps, Lieutenant-General William Birdwood.

Just as the original landing site at Helles back in April had insufficient space to land all the available troops now, in July, there was insufficient room to accommodate all the new troops within the congested Anzac perimeter. Nor was there room to manoeuvre them in battle, and so a new landing at Suvla Bay was planned which would link up with the forces at Anzac.

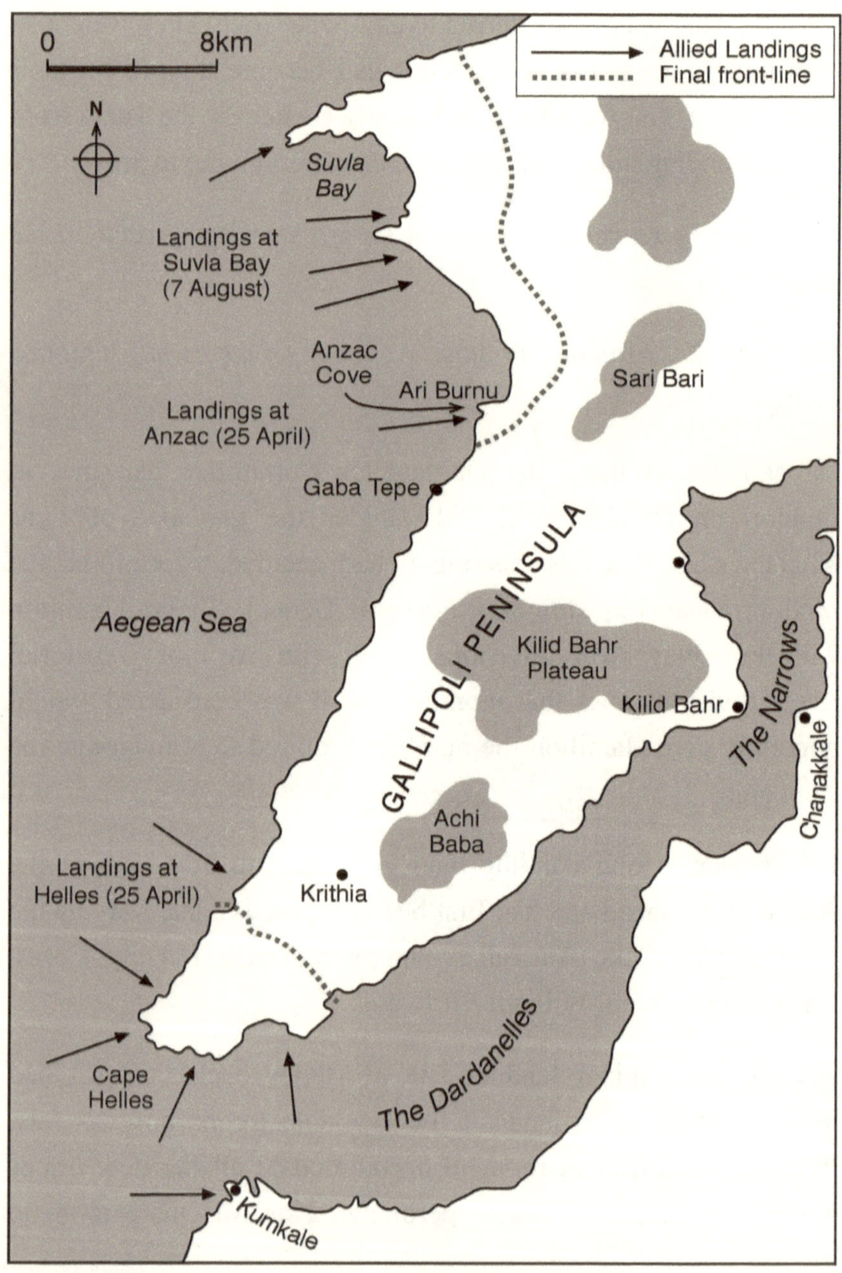

Suvla Bay in relation to Anzac Cove

A new landing further north at Suvla Bay was now planned for August, with the intention of providing a base to gain control of the local hills in order to relieve the Anzac forces to the south.

With a growing sense of excitement mixed with apprehension Privates' Arthur Newcombe and John Bestonso, along with their other newly found chums, embarked on the 14th July, 1915 for the Near East. They were to make themselves at home on HMT *Minneapolis* as one of eight transport ships waiting at Devonport to carry the nominated divisions to war.

HMT Minneapolis

Departing on 18th July they sailed down the Bay of Biscay, passing Gibraltar, and stopping briefly at Malta. Continuing through the Mediterranean they reached Alexandria on the 26th, before leaving again on 4th August to head for Lemnos Island, about 50 miles off the coast of Turkey.

Back in Britain during the course of their trip the Intelligence Bureau had stepped up its surveillance of enemy comminiques. Censors had intercepted four sheets of music being sent to Norway. Within these it was discovered by code-breakers in MI1's Room 40 that they contained 'secret writing'. This writing revealed detailed information about various aspects of the British war effort such as strikes, conscription, and possible military targets for German aircraft. The writer of the code, who had signed himself 'Cecil', had also asked his paymasters in his message for more money so that he could gain further information from his brother concerning 'Royal Navy movements'.

In October 1915 an enemy agent named 'Cecil', whose real name was Courtenay de Rysbach, would be sentenced to life imprisonment for his espionage activities. The same, unfortunately, would not be the case for the incompetent commander appointed to lead Arthur and his battalion in battle.

Arthur and John's arrival at Lemnos on 6th August, 1915 had been occasioned by a considerable amount of renewed excitement. Along with several others onboard Arthur had rushed to a porthole as they approached the island. He could see that the

53rd (Welsh) Divisional emblem

sky to the east was a brilliant purple and the sea a gentle calm with submarines, destroyers, and battleships passing to and fro. Gradually, as they neared the harbour entrance, to pass through its boom, the full grandeur of moored shipping was displayed to view. Others troops of their division, direct from Alexandria on

HMT Wiltshire, had arrived shortly before them. They dropped anchor near her with Arthur and John continuing to dominate a porthole taking in the surrounding sights. Viewed to the left was a large village behind which two rocky promontories rose majestically upwards. Arthur surmised that the village must be that of Mudros, and to its right was what appeared to be another village around which there were many encampments. Further right again a number of sheep were grazing on the land near the sea while a few farm houses dotted the surrounding hills. As his eyes wandered inland the land seemed more barren with little or no vegetation apparent. Anyway, the climate seemed equable with a beautiful fresh breeze through the open port light invigorating his somewhat sluggish constitution.

Mudros harbour

They would stay at anchor all day with conjecture rife within their ranks that they were to shortly see their first action against the Turks on the Gallipoli Peninsula. Their grape vine, as it turned out was correct for once, for they would shortly be shipped via Imbros to land at Sulva Bay, Gallipoli on 9th August, 1915.

New Zealand Troops

Mudros harbour

When Lieutenant-General Sir Frederick Stopford had first been shown the plan for the Suvla Bay offensive on 22nd July he had simply declared …

It is a good plan. I am sure it will succeed and I congratulate whoever has been responsible for framing it.

Lieut. General Sir Frederick Stopford

Brigadier General Hamilton Reed (right)

Stopford's chief-of-staff, Brigadier General Hamilton Reed was not so supportive, and his doubts and prejudices would succeed in swaying Stopford. Reed was an artillery officer who had won the Victoria Cross during the Boer War, and having served on the Western Front, he believed no assault on entrenched positions could be made without artillery support. Even while reconnaissance revealed that there were no prepared enemy fortifications at Suvla Stopford proceeded to limit the objectives of the landing based on Reed's advice, and Hamilton failed to stop him. The final orders issued by Stopford along with the 11th Division commander, Major General Frederick Hammersley, were additionally imprecise, requiring only that the high ground be taken *'if possible'*.

Stopford and Reed also wanted one brigade to be landed within Suvla Bay itself.

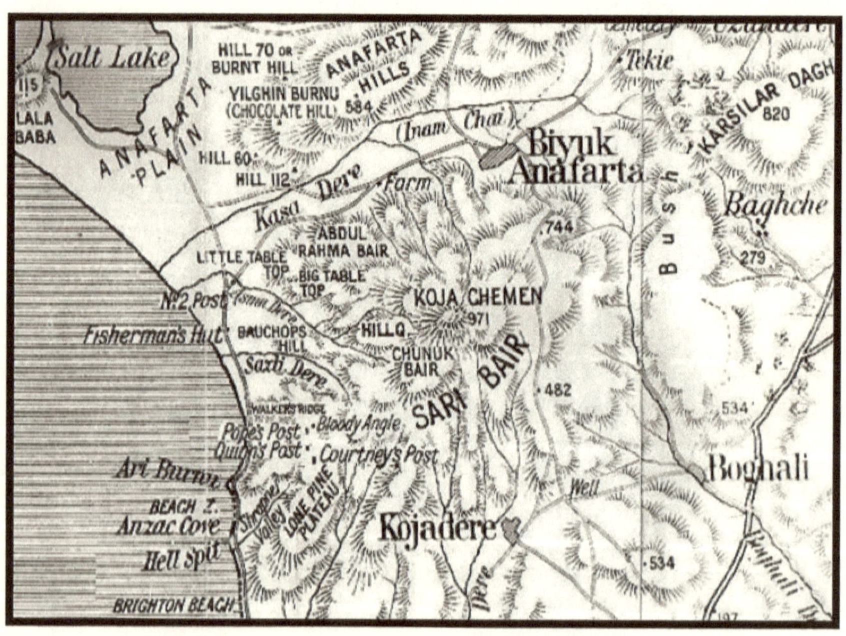

Map showing the location of Suvla Bay at top left

Unlike the April landings, the Corps was supplied with purpose-built landing craft known as 'Beetles' which were armoured and self-propelled. This fleet of landing craft was commanded by Commander Edward Unwin who had captained the *SS River Clyde* during the April landing on V Beach at Cape Helles.

The planned amphibious landings commenced on the night of 6th August with the intention of supporting a breakout from the Anzac sector, five miles to the south. As part of their August Offensive it would be the final British attempt to break the deadlock of the battle of Gallipoli.

Looking north towards Suvla Bay from the Sari Bair ran

For those approaching Suvla Bay by ship on the left Suvla Point stood out, with Nebrunessi Point on their right. Enclosed between both, a mile and a half across, was the small bay known as Suvla that included the beaches now designated 'A' and 'D'. To the right of Nebrunessi Point a long gently curving sandy beach, four or five miles in extent, terminated where the Australian and New Zealanders position at ANZAC rose steeply to the Sari Bair range. Along this stretch, closer to Nebrunessi Point, were the designated landing positions 'B' and 'C'.

Inland, immediately in front of Suvla Bay, was a large, flat, sandy plain covered with scrub with a dry salt lake that showed dazzlingly white in the hot morning sun. Immediately beyond was Chocolate Hill, and behind this lay the village of Anafarta, four miles from the shore. As a backdrop the Anafarta Ridge ran practically parallel with the sea, gradually sloped down to the coast. To achieve these objectives, the newly formed corps was made up of six divisions, including the 53rd.

Looking towards Suvla Bay from the Sari Bair range, northeast of ANZAC Cove

With command of the corps being in the hands of the 61 year old British military historian, Lieutenant-General Sir Frederick

Stopford, who had retired in 1909, it quickly became obvious that he had no concept of what general-ship meant. Lacking the energy and enthusiasm required for such a venture he had simply been appointed to his position based on the British army list of seniority, and with little combat experience having never commanded men in battle.

At dusk HMS Talbot shells Turkish positions ashore

In overall command, General Sir Ian Hamilton had requested either Lieutenant-General Julian Byng, or Lieutenant-General Henry Rawlinson, both experienced Western Front corps commanders. Both, however, were junior to Lieutenant-General Sir Bryan Mahon, commander of the 10th Division, and so by a process of elimination, and with true administrative efficiency, Stopford had been selected.

Gen.Sir Ian Hamilton

The Suvla Bay landings

From a military perspective, the prime objective of the Suvla Corps was to seize the ring of hills that surrounded the Suvla plain; Kiretch Tepe to the north along the Gulf of Saros, Tekke Tepe to the east, and Anafarta Ridge to the south-east.

The offensive opened on 6th August, 1915 with diversions at Helles with the battle of Krithia Vineyard, and at Anzac with the battle of Lone Pine. The initial landing at Suvla was planned to commence at 10 pm, an hour after the two assaulting columns had broken out of Anzac, heading for the Sari Bair heights.

The original plan was to initially put one division ashore south of Nebrunnesi Point, as the southern headland of the bay. It was not considered safe to land in the dark within the bay itself where there were uncharted shoals, so two other brigades of a further division, would land their the following morning.

Packed like sardines in lighters, the first two brigades had started to come ashore at 'B Beach' south of Nebrunnesi Point shortly before 10 pm. on the 6th August. Except for a few bullets whizzing about that occasionally struck the boats, there was very little to get excited about. After jumping ashore, the troops extended out in line with fixed bayonets, with the order given that no man was to fire. They advanced inland about a quarter of a mile, with little eventuating other than one poor chap being shot clean through the head. They were then ordered to make a good trench and dig themselves in till morning. Without orders they would stop there all the next day rather than taking possession of the hills where so many lives would later be lost.

The British dig themselves in

Lighters taking troops ashore at Suvla

On the opposing side the commander of the Ottoman forces, General Otto Liman von Sanders, was well aware a new landing was imminent. He had received reports of troop build-ups in the Greek Islands, however, he had been unsure of where the landing would be made. British deceptions made a landing on the Asian shore possible so three of his divisions had been located there, while three more were currently stationed 30 miles north of Suvla at Bulair, on the neck of the peninsula.

Suvla itself was only defended by three Ottoman battalions known as the' Anafarta Detachment'. They were under the command of a Bavarian cavalry officer, Major Wilhelm Willmer, whose task was to delay any enemy advance until reinforcements arrived. He, however, had no machine guns and only a few field artillery pieces, but he had constructed three strong points. One was on Kiretch Tepe to the north, one on Hill 10 in the centre, and the third on Chocolate Hill near the southern end of the salt lake and plain that lay behind the beach. Small pickets and snipers were positioned elsewhere, including on Lala Baba, a small hill between the beach and the salt lake.

When the attack at Lone Pine commenced above Anzac Cove, Willmer was ordered to send one of his battalions as reinforcements. This stacked the odds heavily in favour of the British at Suvla given that they had 20,000 British troops capable of landing that were only initially opposed by 1,500 Ottoman troops.

Anafarta Spur marked the southern edge of the Suvla sector, comprising Scimitar Hill, so named because of its curved summit, and the neighbouring 'W' Hills to the south. Its capture was part of the British first-day's objectives but General Stopford had become exceedingly hesitant about making any major advances without artillery support.

In the first action fought by a New Army unit, two companies drove the Ottoman defenders off the small hillock of Lala Baba which overlooked the beach. It was an inauspicious start with all but two of their officers becoming casualties, as were a third of their men.

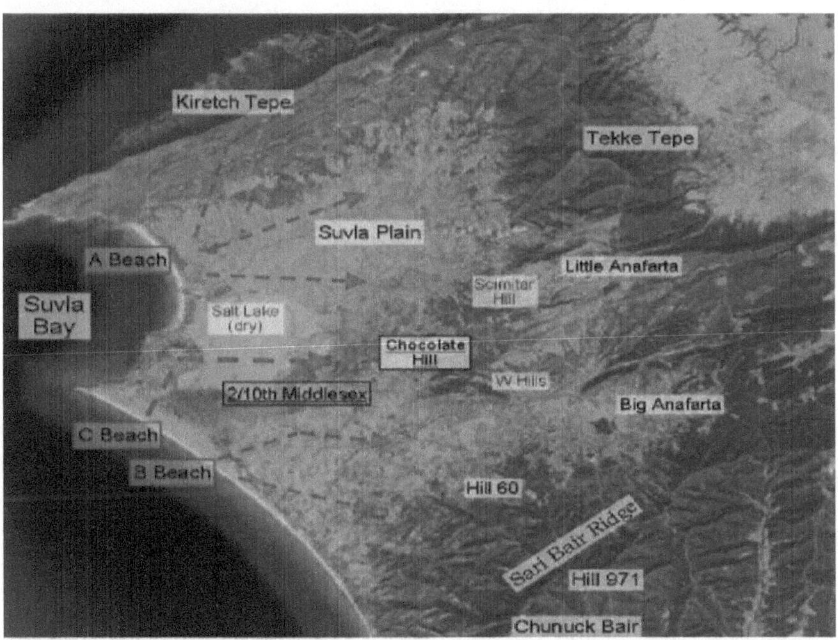

Image showing the general location of features in the Suvla Bay area.

Shortly after the first two brigades were ashore another brigade attempted to land at 'A Beach', within Suvla Bay, but the landing went awry from the start. The destroyers conveying the brigade anchored 1,000 yards too far south, facing shoal water and on the wrong side of the channel that drained the salt lake into the bay.

Two lighters grounded on reefs and the men had to wade ashore submerged up to their necks.

Lighters transporting troops ashore

Another battalion was forced to wade ashore in darkness and were pinned down between the beach and the salt lake by sniper fire and shelling. Their CO was shot in the head around dawn and the battalion lost six other officers killed and seven wounded.

Yet another battalion, having come ashore from the destroyer *HMS Grampus*, had the greatest success of the landings, managing to find its way to the Kiretch Tepe Ridge and fight its way some distance along it to the east, for the loss of 200 casualties.

Elsewhere the landings were in chaos, having been made in pitch darkness which resulted in confusion with units becoming mixed and officers unable to locate either their position or their objective. Later, when the moon rose these British troops became targets for Ottoman snipers. Attempts to capture Hill 10 failed because no one in the field actually had a clue where Hill 10 was. Shortly after dawn it was eventually found and taken after an Ottoman rearguard had withdrawn during the night.

Stopford had chosen to command the landings from the sloop *HMS Jonquil,* but as the landings were in progress he had gone to sleep. The first news he received was when Commander Unwin came aboard at 4.00 am. on 7th August to discourage further landings in Suvla Bay.

For Arthur and his chums still onboard the transport *Minneapolis,* while they could hear fighting continuing at Anzac, Suvla was comparatively quiet. Unbeknown to them no firm hand controlled the mass of men already dumped on that unknown shore, and with it now broad daylight the situation was verging on chaos.

Stopford did not go ashore from the *Jonquil* on 7th and by the end of the day the chain of command had completely broken down.

Troops landing on the Suvla shore

Progress that first day had been minimal with another two brigades having come ashore, that had added to the confusion. In the heat of the day, the soldiers had also become desperate and exhausted from lack of drinking water.

Dehydrated, and under constant shrapnel and sniper fire, they suffered 1,700 casualties in the first 24 hours, a figure exceeding the total size of the opposing Turk commander Willmer's detachment. At 5.00 pm. Willmer was able to report to Von Sanders ....

No energetic attacks on the enemy's part have taken place. On the contrary, the enemy is advancing timidly.

Towards evening two hills east of the salt lake had been captured, and these represented the sole gains for the first day ashore. As a consequence of Stopford's reticence the two initial divisions landed would not advance from the immediate environs of the beach until 8th August.

What seems to be an overwhelming force landed at Suvla Bay

Sir Ian Hamilton

Wounded being evacuated from Suvla

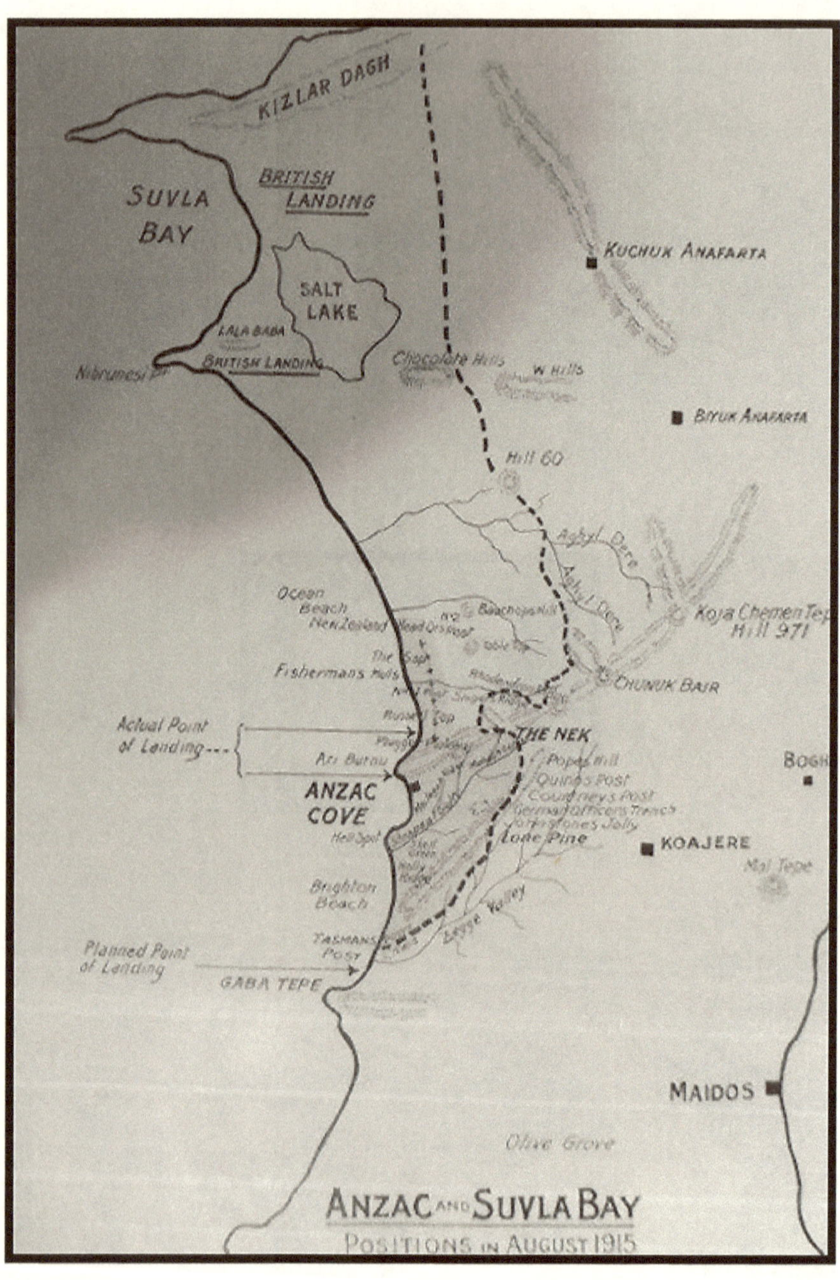

KIZLAR DAGH
SUVLA BAY
BRITISH LANDING
SALT LAKE
LALA BABA
Nibrunesi Pt
BRITISH LANDING
Chocolate Hills
W Hills
KUCHUK ANAFARTA
BIYUK ANAFARTA
Hill 60
Aghyl Dere
Aghyl Dere
Ocean Beach
New Zealand
Head Quarters
No 2
Beachojanik
Koja Chemen Tepe
Hill 971
Table Top
The Sari
Fishermans huts
Rhododendron
CHUNUK BAIR
Actual Point of Landing
Russell Top
Plugges Plateau
THE NEK
Ari Burnu
Popes Hill
Quinns Post
ANZAC COVE
Courtneys Post
German Officers Trench
Johnstones Jolly
BOGH
Hell Spit
Lone Pine
KOAJERE
Mal Tepe
Brighton Beach
Legge Valley
Planned Point of Landing
TASMANS POST
GABA TEPE
MAIDOS
Olive Grove
ANZAC AND SUVLA BAY
POSITIONS IN AUGUST 1915

Part XII

When the Gallipoli campaign first commenced the Ottoman Fifth Army under the command of the German General Otto Liman von Sanders had comprised two army corps; one was defending the Gallipoli peninsula commanded by Mehmet Esat Bülkat, while the other was defending the Asian shore. In addition, another division was positioned north of the peninsula under the command of the First Army.

Mehmet Esat Bülkat

Ahmet-oğlu Abdullah

Ottoman Troops Attack

Gallipoli historians tend to focus on the role of General Liman von Sanders, and on Mehmed Esad's subordinate Mustapha Kemal Pasha who is better known as Atatürk, the founder of modern Turkey. It was, however, Mehmed Esad who prepared the Ottoman defences and who actively commanded the Ottoman army on the peninsula during the battle.

In October 1915, Esad would be appointed CO of the First Army succeeding Colmar Freiherr von der Goltz who was dispatched to the Mesopotamian front. Following Willmer's reports of the British landings and their limited progress at Suvla, von Sanders had ordered the two divisions from Bulair to move south down the peninsula to urgently reinforce the hills surrounding Suvla Bay. They were under the command of Feizi Bey, and in the ranks of one of these was a young soldier named Ahmet-oğlu Abdullah.

Ahmet was a simple hard working rural lad with little education who came from a small rural village 15 miles from the nearest town of Bursa, south of the Sea of Marama.

British troops - Suvla Bay

At Anzac the New Zealanders with British units in support had finally captured Chunuk Bair and held it despite strong Turkish counter-attacks. A small unit of Gurkhas briefly captured another summit to the north of Chunuk Bair known as 'Q', but they had been driven off by the Turks, while an Australian Brigade had failed to make any progress towards Hill 971.

As for Stopford at Suvla, he was satisfied with the results of the first day and on the morning of 8th August he signalled Hamilton.

Major-General Hammersley and troops under him deserve great credit for the result attained against strenuous opposition and great difficulty. I must now consolidate the position held.

It was obvious he had no immediate intention of advancing to the high ground. With success considered doubtful given that it was now known that Turkish reinforcements were moving up rapidly, the morning's dawn attack planned for the 8th was delayed.

British troops on the move, Suvla Bay

Paralysed by inaction in not knowing if at any moment the enemy might sweep down from the hills in a desperate effort to drive the invaders back into the sea, Stopford and Hammersley now planned to order an advance for the morning of the 9th August after the situation became clearer. Beyond a small advance by part of a division between Chocolate Hill and Ismail Oglu Tepe, and some further progress along the Kiretch Tepe Ridge by troops of another division, the day of the 8th had also been lost.

British staff officers estimated that it would take the reinforcing Ottoman divisions at Bulair 36 hours to reach Suvla, and that they could be expected to arrive on the evening of the 8th. Hamilton was, therefore, naturally dismayed by the lack of progress so far with the absence of any drive from Stopford or his subordinates to capture the high ground. He dispatched Captain Aspinall to discover first-hand what was happening on the ground accompanied by Lieutenant-Colonel Maurice Hankey, Secretary to the Committee of Imperial Defence, who was to report on the progress of the campaign to the British Cabinet.

When he received Stopford's signal, however, Hamilton decided to see Suvla for himself.

Aspinall and Hankey were initially encouraged by the ease and inactivity at Suvla, assuming it meant the fighting was now far away amongst the hills. Once on the beach, however, they were warned to keep their heads down as the front line was only a few hundred yards away, and that Stopford was still aboard the *Jonquil*. Aspinall found Stopford in excellent spirits, well satisfied with progress. When Aspinall pointed out that the men had not reached the high ground, Stopford replied …

No, but they are ashore!

Aspinall and Hamilton both converged on the light cruiser *HMS*

Chatham, the flagship of Rear-Admiral John de Robeck who commanded the landing fleet.

Finally, on the afternoon of 8th August, nearly two days after the landing commenced, Hamilton gained a clear picture of events. Accompanied by Aspinall and Commodore Roger Keyes he crossed to the *Jonquil* to confront Stopford who had finally been ashore to consult with Hammersley. Stopford and Hammersley planned to order an advance the morning of the 9[th,], however, Hamilton insisted that an advance be made immediately. At 6.30 pm on the evening of the 8th, therefore, a brigade was ordered to march the two and a half miles to secure the high ground to the east, called Tekke Tepe Ridge. Scimitar Hill which guarded the approach to this ridge from the southwest along the Anafarta Spur, had been captured unopposed by a battalion earlier that day, but that position had then been abandoned.

As Feizi Bey's troops began to arrive on the evening of 8th August, von Sanders wanted them to attack immediately. Feizi Bey objected, arguing that the men were exhausted and without artillery support. Without a quam, von Sanders dismissed him and in his place he put Mustafa Kemal, the commander of the Ottoman 19th Division which had been fighting at Chunuk Bair. Kemal now assumed authority over the 'Anafarta section' which spanned from Suvla south to Chunuk Bair.

Mustafa Kemal Ataturk

Ahmet-oğlu Abdullah arrived on Tekke Tepe ridge along with his regiment on the morning of 9th August at 2.00 am, and whilst they were tired, they were immediately put into the line.

The British brigade ordered to secure the high ground had marched in darkness over unfamiliar rough terrain. They had found it exceedingly difficult in the dark with them not approaching the summit of Tekke Tepe Ridge until two hours later, at 04.00 am. Here the Ottoman reinforcements, including Ahmet, met the exhausted British infantry with a bayonet charge. The outcome saw the British brigade virtually broken in a matter of minutes, with the remnants of the battalions stumbling back towards the beach before managing to regroup.

Kemal was proving he was easily a match for Stopford. Ruthless and decisive, he now held the high ground and was content to remain on the defensive at Suvla while he dealt with the threat to the Sari Bair Ridge.

Looking towards Suvla Bay from ANZAC Cove

As Ahmet was entering the Turkish front line on Tekke Tepe Ridge, young Private Arthur Edgar Newcombe with his Middlesex chums and the balance of the 53rd Division, had been landed without mishap to wait the coming dawn. They sat or lay about the beach with the grim silence of the hills in front of them, broken occasionally by the sharp crack of a rifle. Few knew what was happening in the frontline that was still only 1000 yards away.

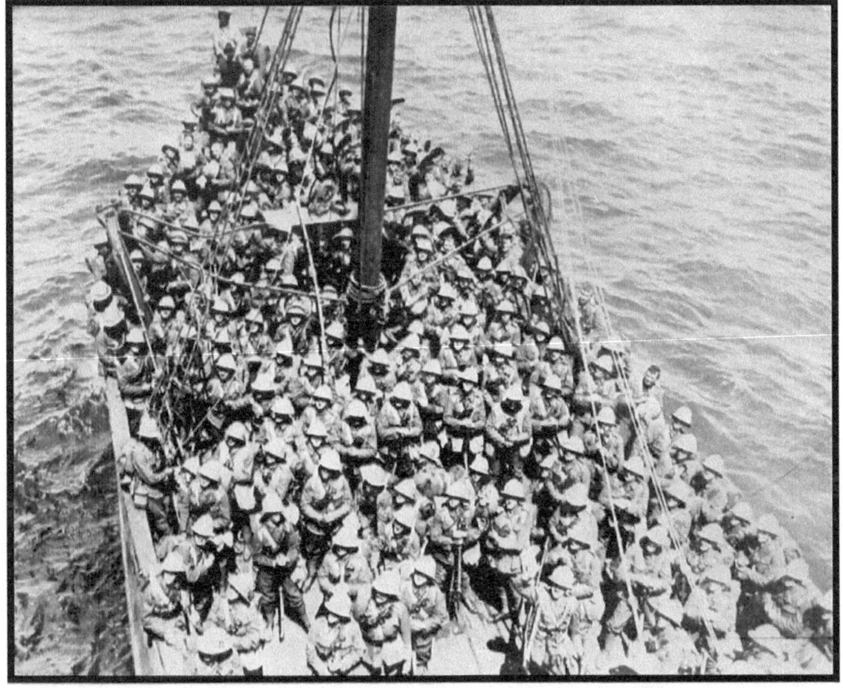

Private Arthur Newcombe's regiment landing at Suvla Bay

Further afield Tekke Tepe ridge had then erupted in the rattle of musketry and the boom of guns, with the Turks' attack underway. A British attempt to recapture the hill resulted in further intense fighting with the hill's possession changing hands a number of times before the British were forced off it around midday. The intensity of the fighting would escalate at Suvla that day, but despite the arrival of reinforcements the opportunity for the British to make a swift advance had disappeared. In reality any hopes they had of a quick victory at Suvla were now gone as the Ottomans consolidated their hold on the surrounding ridges.

Above - Lala Baba hill from where commanders had a good view of the advance on the hills. Below - An attack underway.

Hamilton who had watched the battle from *HMS Triad* wrote in his diary…

My heart has grown tough amidst the struggles of the peninsula but the misery of this scene well nigh broke it... Words are of no use.

Ottoman artillery

Cooks, batmen and signallers from the Finsbury Rifles behind the lines at Suvla Bay.

All through the day of the 9th the New Zealanders from Anzac Cove held on to Chunuk Bair, and in the evening they were relieved by British units. The following day, however, Ottoman troops led by Colonel Mustafa Kemal would drive the British from the heights, but they were unable to push the British, Indian, and New Zealand troops back down the valleys to the beach.....

Chunuk Bair

By nightfall on the 9th the situation at Suvla was confusing with the 53rd Division scattered in all directions. Divisional headquarters was at Lala Baba; one brigade had the Herefords in action southeast of Lala Baba; while another was inextricably mixed up with a different brigade west of Sulajik, with their exact position unknown to their brigade staff. Two of the battalions of Arthur's brigade were in action about Hill 53, while his Middlesex battalion was on beach duty, and a fourth was still aboard ship. There was no transport, the Royal Engineers and one Field Ambulance were being landed without stores, and the Signals

Company had not yet arrived. And then their Divisional Commander, General Lindley, received orders that he was to attack the next morning.

Whilst some 53rd Division troops had been involved in fighting on the 9th, the Welsh Field Ambulances would only begin to struggle ashore in confusion over the next few days, with the 3rd Field Ambulance not landing until Wednesday 11th. Fortuitously for Arthur the 2/10th Middlesex had not been destined to take part in operations on the 9th; instead they had been detailed to unload of stores and ammunition, and also pump water from barge tanks into canvas troughs on the beach.

British troops on the beach

The beach was in full view of the Turks whose guns searched the whole area where the Middlesex men were working. It was a trying experience for raw troops under fire for the first time, and it was now that the battalion suffered its first casualties, although they were not heavy. All day long the 2/10th carried on their work exasperated at being shelled heavily, and unable to fire a shot in reply. Rumours drifted back from the firing line, while information was gathered from wounded men that the advance was hung up a few thousand yards away. Mercifully night fell, shielding the men on the beach from the enemy's artillery observers.

It was to be a short lived peace for later that night they were ordered to move to the western slopes of Lala Baba to join another brigade of the 53rd. The following morning they were both to attempt to drive home an attack on Yilghin Burnu, or Chocolate Hill as it was by now more commonly known. An operational order, issued from the 53rd Divisional Headquarters at 10 pm on the night of the 9th, had outlined the current state of affairs along with orders for the following day.

The 11th and 53rd Divisions are holding the line Yilghin Burnu-Hill 50-1 of Sulajik-last A of Anafarta Ova. The 10th Division holds the line Bench Mark 200 on Kiretch Tepe Sirt - about sq. 135 Y.6- about sq. 118 a.7

Enemy have shown strength on ridges Ismail Oglu Tepe-Anfarta Sagir and have opposed steadily the 10th Division's advance to-day.

The 158th Brigade, with the addition of 2/10th Middlesex from 160th Brigade, and the 159th Brigade will carry out an attack tomorrow against the ridge from points where the road cuts contour 100 about 105 p.5 to the point where the road cuts contour 100 about 106 G, half-way between points 3 and 6.

Ordered to capture the first objective on the 10th one of the designated brigades, that had been fighting hard the whole of the previous day, had its units scattered. The work of collecting and reorganising, therefore, had gone on through the night, so that by the morning of 10th all battalions, bar one, were assembled in their jumping-off positions ready for 'Zero Hour'.

As if to signal the onslaught to come 53rd Division's Casualty Clearing Station had been established near the entrance to the Salt Lake, and as dawn broke the 2/10th Middlesex, with Arthur in its ranks, joined the attacking brigade about 4.00 am. Their attack was to begin two hours later at 6.00 am.

Dutifully on time the guns of the 11th Division, and aboard the naval boats in Sulva Bay, opened fire on the Turkish positions, and their advance began. The country over which they were advancing was flat, and while it was covered with scrub, trees and hedges, it still afforded little cover. There were few landmarks also. With the absence of previous reconnaissance and the poor nature of the maps supplied it was extremely difficult, if not impossible, for battalion commanders to locate their exact positions, or those of the enemy. Roughly the objectives of the attack lay between Scimitar Hill on their right, and Baka Baba on their left.

Being the reserve battalion in the brigade Arthur took part in the advance over the Salt Lake in an easterly direction, and almost at once they came under heavy shrapnel fire. Receiving their first actual experience of war the men encouraged each other on never wavering.

One would later write in his diary…

At dawn on the 10th August, we advanced across the intervening plain that was named on the map as 'Salt Lake', but at this time of the year was a dry plain with marshy edges. We ploughed across the stinking mud on to the hard bed of the lake, and for the next thousand yards of the advance there was not a scrap of cover. The shelling was terrific, and towards the far side the battalion came into the zone of machine-gun and rifle fire. I stayed steady with the others around me watching others hit and fall. I could hear the fall of shot and simply accepted my fate whatever it maybe.

The advance across the salt flat.

Once among the foothills there was more chance of cover than in the scrub, but their advance was hampered by the volume of enemy fire. Beyond the plain a number of stunted oaks gradually became more dense further inland. These formed excellent cover for enemy's snipers, as a mode of warfare at which the Turk was demonstrating he was very adept. Officers and men were continually shot down, not only by rifle fire from advanced posts of the enemy but by men, and even women, from behind their own firing line.

As one wrote …

The stunted oak, lent itself to concealment, being short with dense foliage. Here the sniper would lurk, with face painted green, and so well hidden as to defy detection. Others would crouch in the dense brushwood, where anyone passing could be shot with ease. When discovered, these snipers had in their possession enough food and water for a considerable period, as well as an ample supply of ammunition.

Advancing up the slopes of Chocolate Hill the various British companies managed to get out of touch with one another, and near the top they became merged into a firing line made up of many units. From then on anything like control by battalion commanders was out of the question. The heat was awful, the hill was already a shambles, and to add to their misery their want of water became a serious matter. They had suffered severely due to a lack of it since the initial landings.

*Stretcher bearers move down
to the salt flat*

*Drawing: R Caton Woodville impression of the fire on Scimitar Hill,
August 1915.*

While Arthur and his 2/10th Middlesex chums remained pinned
down by enfilading fire, to add to the torment of those off to the
right, around midday, gunfire set the scrub alight. Those watching
from Lala Baba, saw the British wounded trying to escape the
flames. Many were unable to even though a super-human effort
was made to rescue some of them. Mostly the effort was to no
avail with the screams of those caught in the conflagration carried
on the wind. Even though their overall line remained steady,
Arthur's battalion unable to push on, or do anything about those
caught in the flames. He was forced to watch the approaching
flames as injured caught in its grasp screamed; …. crawling,
clawing, figures trying in vain to escape the flames before
disappearing amidst dense clouds of black smoke. When the fire
eventually passed little mounds of scorched khaki marked the
spots where numerous mismanaged soldiers of the King had
returned to mother earth.

At one stage there was panic when two battalions broke, believing that they were being attacked by the Turks. They had streamed back from the line with one man shouting at an oncoming Middlesex soldier...

You bloody well don't want to go up there!

This rout was stopped by an officer and they once again surged forward unsupported.

The dead on Scimitar Hill

With maturity belying his years Arthur would later reflect ....

How could anyone blame us; direct from England as 'Territorials', we all found ourselves on an unknown shore that morning, fighting an almost invisible enemy. With no maps and no orders we had been sent blindly forward to be lost in this new scrub covered land, most of which was by now ablaze or shrouded in smoke, combined with the screams of the trapped and dying.

During the afternoon isolated attempts were again bravely made by officers to lead on parties of their men, but all were doomed to failure, and night came without any progress being made.

For Arthur his mind was racing with confusion.

This was not what we expected, nor was it sane. To be thrown against an enemy firing from behind clumps of bush at close range, and in then having young and innocent wounded on both sides incinerated alive. What was so important about this God forsaken parched piece of country anyway. Hell I am parched... and he again subconsciously reached for his water bottle even though it was empty.

Meanwhile the Turks were still doing their utmost to drive them from their position, but they too were beaten to a standstill, and so the two forces were in a state of stale-mate.

He would later write in his diary … *The order came from the Corps Commander that we were to dig in on the line held and prepare for trench warfare. It was a bitter disappointment but it seemed to be the only alternative other than being killed or driven off the peninsula,*

With the battalion dispersed in the line it was impossible to ascertain the casualties that night, but Arthur knew that a number of their officers had been killed, or wounded, amongst many others. He had witnessed Captain Foley falling mortally wounded and had then watched as Captain Britten had gone to his assistance, to then be shot and killed himself by a sniper while giving his fellow officer a drink of water.

He was just thankful he was still alive, but he was changing his perspective on God being on their side. He had obviously been misinformed, for this was not God's work as far as he could see, although his hand must be evident like the selfless action of Captain Britten, otherwise it was all simply futile.

The words of Ernest Budge came back to him....

Is it not our freedom of choice that we should be fighting for?

The trench line

All that night Arthur and the others did their best with their entrenching implements to scratch out some sort of cover. No picks or shovels had come up to the line and the scratching was simply that. During the night their tireless Quartermaster, by the name of Wallis, also toiled to bring us up food and water. Arthur had noticed that he had gallantly attempted this several times during the day but that it had been impossible to bring his mules across that deadly Salt Lake. The fighting had ended for now. With their corps, as well as the Turks, utterly exhausted it allowed the 11th August to pass uneventfully for both sides. Arthur surmised that the Turks probably thought the offensive was over, but unbeknown to him his commanders were already planning another attack. As for the Turks they retained the high ground, leaving the British to their gains along part of Kiretch Tepe, Lala Baba, Hill 10 and Chocolate Hill.

As disorganised troops they had all achieved little. With everyone eventually required to pull back to the start line it was a worrying beginning. In these first days of fighting 26 'rank and file' of the 2/10th Middlesex were killed, along with Captains Foley and Britten, Lieutenant Pope and Second Lieutenant Hollingsworth, and with Lieutenant Snowden and Second Lieutenant Reid-Todd wounded. On their right flank Chunuk Bair had been captured and lost, with the Anzacs fighting themselves to a standstill. At Helles the diversionary attacks failed to keep the Turks in the area engaged.

Arthur in the line

Encapsulated in a nutshell the plan had failed, on all three fronts, with an estimated 25,000 British, and 20,000 Turkish losses all that was to show for four days of fighting.

Having collected the remaining troops in their companies more or less during the night of the 11th, Arthur's battalion was now ordered to take over another sector of the line a few hundred yards to the left of their existing position. When ordered to move Arthur got out of the trench followed by a number of soldiers from another battalion who didn't seem to like the idea of staying in the trench and seeing them leave. They were ordered back but hesitated momentarily, showing a distinct lack of discipline. Arthur realised the poor buggars were just about on the point of breaking.

The relocation of the remaining Middlesex boys was eventually achieved by noon on the 12th with great difficulty, and from then on till late on the night of the 13th they remained dug in, suffering many more casualties, but keeping the line intact.

Ottoman Gallipoli Star

FIELD SERVICE
TOP SECRET
PASSED BY CENSOR
No 3743

Part XIII

Following the appointment of Wing Captain Frederick Sykes to command Royal Naval Air Service units in the eastern Mediterranean in July 1915, plans had been put in place for air reinforcements to be made available in support of the ground troops. The landing at Suvla Bay, however, had begun before those reinforcements had arrived, nonetheless Sykes's aviators did succeed in destroying several Ottoman ships. This had hindered the re-supply of enemy troops forcing the Ottomans to depend on land re-supply over an extended route.

In June, 1915, the converted Isle of Man cross-channel packet steamer, *HMS Ben-My-Chree,* or 'the Woman of My Heart', had arrived in the little bay of Iero off Lesbos Island carrying aircraft. She was twice as fast as the Royal Navy's carrier *HMS Ark Royal* but held half the number of aeroplanes. On arrival in the Aegean Sea her complement of seaplanes comprised three Short Folder, and two Sopwith Schneider, variants.

HMS Ben-My-Chree

By 12.30 pm on the 12th August, as Arthur fought off another Turk counter-attack on Chocolate Hill, Short Folder Seaplane No. 842 had been lowered into the water. The weather was fine and the sea again like glass. Equipped with a 10 inch mark 14 inch torpedo it had then been flown across the isthmus north of Gallipoli by Flight Commander C.H.K. Edmonds.

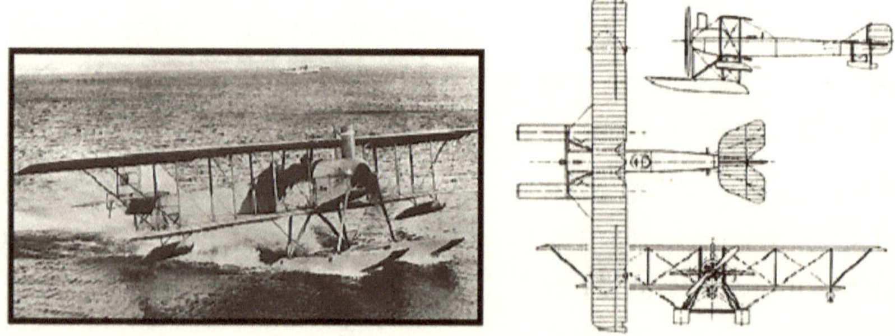

The Short Folder Seaplane

The day previous Turkish transport ships had been pouring reinforcements into Ak Bashi and Kilia Liman, from Chanak on the Asiatic shore, for new attacks against Suvla and Anzac fronts. Simultaneously a British counter action had been underway to impede this transference of the enemy troops across the straits, and to harass their movement down the Gallipoli peninsular. *HMS Ben-My-Chree's* aircraft had been spotting for the monitor *HMS M16*, and it was now, while both ships were in the Gulf of Xeros, that a new technique in warfare was about to be introduced that would impact on the life of Private Arthur Edgar Newcombe.

While young Arthur lined up another Turk in his sights Edmonds had sighted a 5000 ton steamer off Injeh Burnu. Arthur squeezed the trigger of his .303 rifle as Edmonds glided down to successfully launch his torpedo. Watching its track it hit the ship causing it settle down by the stern. This, as it transpired, was the first successful aerial torpedo attack in history, notwithstanding that it was later determined that the target had been immobilised previously by the British submarine, *HMS E14*.

Above - A Short Folder seaplane from HMS Ben-My-Chree

A torpedo heads for the water

Edmonds was now reflecting that the foresight of United States Navy Officer Bradley Fiske, had been correct.

Following the Russo-Japanese War of 1904-1905, Fiske had fuelled new theories regarding dropping lightweight torpedoes from aircraft. Awarded a patent in 1912, he had worked out the mechanics of carrying and releasing an aerial torpedo from an aeroplane, including defining tactics that included a night-time approach so that the target ship would be less able to defend its self. He had also determined that a notional torpedo bomber should descend rapidly in a sharp spiral to evade enemy guns, then when about 10 to 20 feet above the water the aircraft would straighten its flight long enough to line up on the torpedo's intended path.

HMS Ben-My-Chree

As Arthur finished his morning duties, this time clinching his claim to fame Edmonds of No.3 Squadron R.N.A.S torpedoed another supply ship while again flying Short Folder Seaplane No. 482. During this second flight he had been accompanied by a second Short Folder also equipped with a torpedo, and flown by Flight Lieutenant G.B. Dacre. Due to engine trouble Dacre had been forced to alight in The Narrows of the Dardanelle Straights, near a Turkish hospital ship which he gallantly waved on to safe passage. He then sighted a large Turk naval tug in False Bay, taxied towards it on the surface, pointed his aeroplane in its general direction and released his 14 inch torpedo, which, running true to mark sunk the vessel. Then in an attempt to fix his float plane's engine problem he noticed

The partially submerged lifeboat

what looked like an almost totally submerged lifeboat about 50 feet away in his anticipated flight path off his starboard pontoon. With the sea lapping over its gunnels he could only occasionally make it out. Normally he would have simply taxied the aircraft to avoid any object like this but with noone in the vicinity, and with the sea calm, his inquisitiveness was peeked enough to find out from what vessel it had come.

HMS Ben-My-Chree with her Short Folder seaplanes

Gabbing a short paddle from behind his cockpit seat, and positioning himself centrally under his aircraft where the torpedo had previous been suspended, he carefully paddled his way toward the sunken lifeboat. As he got closer he could see that there was nothing of interest inside, not even a life vest.

He was just about to turn away when he noticed what looked like a partially floating tag and chord that came from the lifeboat's forward locker under its bow. Manoeuvring the aircraft upwind alongside the submerged boat's chine he managed to get into a position, with his starboard pontoon pushed against submerged boat, to be able to reach the cord in an attempt to remove whatever it was attached to. After several attempts his prize was free and he lifted it onto the pontoon for closer inspection. It was a diplomatic pouch with the makings of the British Embassy in Cairo.

With the engine repaired, and now less the weight of the torpedo but with the pouch, he took off after a take-off run of two miles, to fly back to his carrier ship.

Back onboard *HMS Be-My-Shree* an urgent message was transmitted to Cairo informing them of the find. The reply via Mudros Naval Intelligence advised the captain of the carrier that a ship was urgently en-route to collect the

Flight Cmdr. Edmonds and his Short Folder Seaplane No 842 being winched aboard HMS Be-My-Chree

item. Pre-empting actual receipt of the pouch, in their exuberance the Cairo Bureau had used their Alexander station to telegraph London with news of the discovery. The method of communication used was classed as 'open station to station' that went via the Daily Telegraph office in London. With a designation of '14' at the beginning of any message it meant to the London Telegraph office that the message was to be passed onto MI1 urgently.

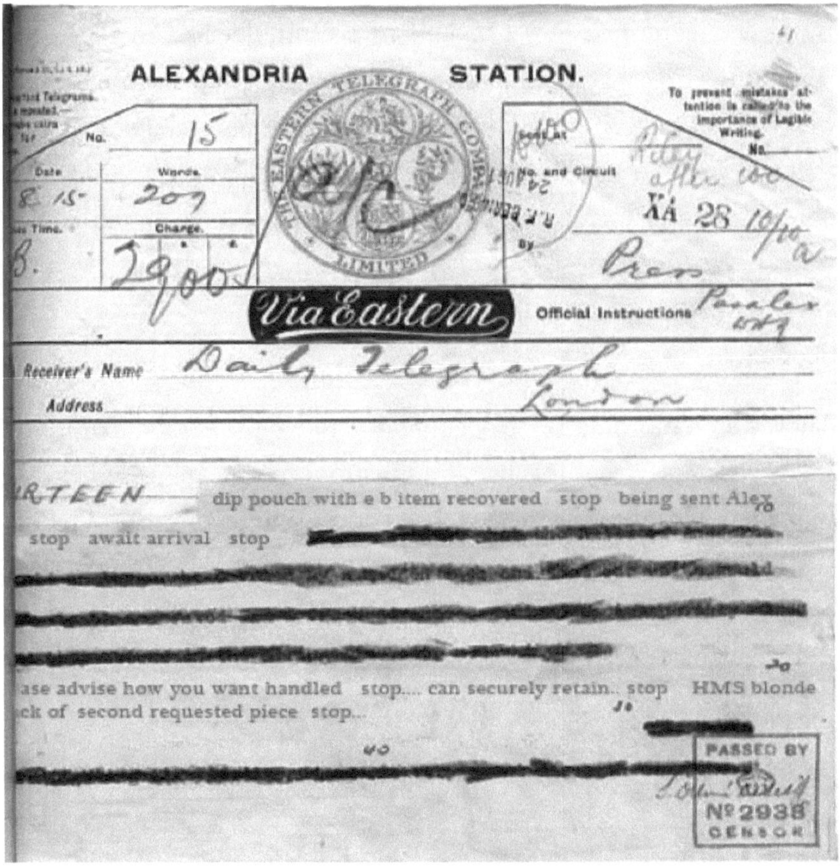

ALEXANDRIA STATION.

No. 15

Date 8 15 | Words 207

Time 8. | Charge 29.00

Via Eastern

Official Instructions

Receiver's Name Daily Telegraph

Address London

RTEEN dip pouch with e b item recovered stop being sent Alex

stop await arrival stop [redacted]

ase advise how you want handled stop.... can securely retain.. stop HMS blonde

ck of second requested piece stop...

[redacted]

PASSED BY

Nº 2938

CENSOR

The London telegram

A month earlier, thinking they were politically offering a courtesy to the Church in Rome, the British Ambassador to the Holy See had advised Church officials that the amulet and its message had gone missing. He had advised them, truthfully, that the ship carrying the amulet had been sunk by a German submarine in the Mediterranean. The British had not, however, told the Holy See of their recovery of the second half of the artefact.

With scepticism born out of their political and religious insecurity the Jesuit Black Pope, along with his SP agents in Rome, had been of the opinion that they were being duped by the British. They had by now ascertained that one half of the amulet had in fact been sent to Cairo, where it had been matched with a second half obtained in that city. Being naturally suspicious they had decided that the story given them was just too convenient to be true. Still smarting from the British having blackmailed them initially they now decided to despatch their own operatives to secure the complete amulet and its messages, by whatever means they deemed necessary.

They were not going to be accountable to any politician or foreign intelligence service for the administration and management of God's work on earth, as the protection of their one true Church was infinitely more important than that.

Short Seaplane

Within only two days of its landing the massive failure that had been the attack against Chocolate and Scimitar Hills at Suvla Bay on the 10th August had effectively ruined the 53rd Division as a fighting unit. Whilst further reinforcements had been landed it was pointless. The remaining Middlesex men were almost spent and thankfully, at around midnight on lucky Friday the 13th, they were relieved by a battalion of the Royal West Kent Regiment.

Arthur along with the other survivors stumbled back to 'A' Beach hopeful of a rest but instead they were inspirationally given 12 hours work per day at fatigue duty on the beach.

Cleaning up after coming down from the trenches on Chocolate Hill

The chaos and confusion of orders and counter orders, lack of maps or briefing, and the linked curses of heat, thirst and exhaustion had seen a drastic effect on all three brigades of 53rd Division. They had been thrown into the battle piecemeal across the British lines to be shattered in the fighting, and by now they had sustained approx 2,300 casualties. With Stopford still justifying his inaction with a statement … *that the Ottomans had inclined to be aggressive*, Hamilton had finally had enough. He cabled Kitchener that his Corps generals were 'unfit' for command.

Kitchener swiftly replied on 14th August….

Lieut. General Sir Frederick Stopford

If you should deem it necessary to replace Stopford, Mahon and Hammersley, have you any competent generals to take their place? From your report I think Stopford should come home. This is a young man's war, and we must have commanding officers that will take full advantage of opportunities which occur but seldom. If, therefore, any generals fail, do not hesitate to act promptly. Any generals I have available I will send you.

Before receiving a response, Kitchener made Lieutenant-General Julian Byng available to command IX Corps. On 15th August Hamilton dismissed Stopford, and while Byng was travelling from France he replaced him with Major-General Beauvoir De Lisle, commander of the British 29th Division at Helles. Hammersley was also dismissed, but Hamilton intended to retain Mahon in command of the 10th Division. Mahon, however, had been incensed that de Lisle, whom he disliked, had been appointed above him and he quit, stating….

I respectfully decline to waive my seniority and to serve under the officer you name.

He had effectively abandoned his division while it was in the thick of the fighting on Kiretch Tepe.

The commander of Arthur's 53rd Division, Major-General John Lindley, had also voluntarily resigned and responsibility for this debarkle ultimately lay at the feet of Lord Kitchener who, as Secretary of State for War, had appointed the elderly and inexperienced Stopford to an active corps command. Blame also needs to be apportioned to Sir Ian Hamilton who initially accepted his appointment and then failed to impose his will on his subordinate.

On 13th August Hamilton wrote in his diary…

Ought I have resigned sooner than allow generals old and inexperienced to be foisted upon me.

By then it was too late and Stopford's departure contributed to Hamilton's downfall which would come on 15th October when he was sacked as the commander of the Mediterranean Expeditionary Force. Under General de Lisle's command, the Suvla front would be reorganised and reinforced with the arrival of a division from Helles along with the 2nd Mounted Division from Egypt,....less their horses.

An Ottoman war stamp

British soldiers on the shore at Suvla Bay - August 1915. Behind them is the ordinance dump and pontoon pier at Kangaroo Beach

The *Laforey*-class destroyer *HMS Louis* carrying the recovered diplomatic pouch with the amulet forged ahead heading south away from Imbros. At 25 knots her bow wave cut clean white against the depths of the opal green Aegean Sea. With the Gallipoli peninsular and Anzac Cove away to port she would steer clear of the coast. The day was clear and fine with no wind, and the sea stretched away in all directions as flat as glass.

The Laforey-class destroyer HMS Louis

The day previous the ship's captain had been ordered to rendezvous with the float plane carrier, HMS Ben-My-Shree, to uplift the discovered diplomatic pouch and get it to Alexandria as quickly as possible. Now with the pouch on board, and with visibility at a maximum, the ship's lookouts scanned the horizon for smoke, forgetting about waters closer to the ship. Unbeknown to them, and all others onboard HMS Louis, was that they were to be the first victim of a recently laid mine field directly in their path. Entering the mine field at 25 knots one submerged mine hit the side of the ship a glancing blow, port side forward, with a metallic thud. In the few seconds it took for its detonator to activate the ship's bow wave pushed it partially to one side. It was *this movement of the mine by the bow wave at speed that was all that saved HMS Louis from the full effects of the blast, and an likely immediate watery grave for her crew.*

H M S Louis

The ship shuddered and reeled violently to starboard as the concussion transported the ship on the edge of a mountain of water that erupted alongside it. Her helmsman and captain on the bridge were knocked to the deck and drenched by the ensuing deluge that cascaded through the open bridge wing door engulfing them along with those also in the open on the forward port quarter of the ship. Grasping the bridge door surround the captain pulled himself to his feet with his mind racing.

His first thought was that they had been torpedoed, but with the ship still on a level keel it then dawned on him that they had highly likely hit a mine. With her hull plates staved in below the waterline the bridge the helmsman, at the captain's direction, immediately telegraphed the engine room crew to 'All Stop'. Yelling down the engine room speaking tube the first officer, who had appeared out of nowhere, attempted to ascertain the extent of the damage. Experience also told him that a torpedo would have ripped into the bowls of the ship. Thankfully receiving a reply it did not appear to be the case and that the damage, therefore, may not be fatal, yet both him and the captain both knew the ship was more than likely mortally wounded.

With the precision and discipline of Royal Navy training, those below decks in the engine room had begun jacking stays in place over makeshift canvass patches. It was an attempt to stem the incoming flow of the sea through the ship's split seams. Forward and aft bulk head doors were then dogged closed while in the engine room's bilge scavenge pumps worked overtime to compete with the rising water.

On being radioed of their fate naval command on Imbros had quickly decided to have her captain attempt to beach *HMS Louis* on a forgiving bottom. The captain was ordered to reverse course and make a run for Suvla Bay where a beaching may result in the ship being salvageable. There was little room at Mudros and risking having the ship sink in the harbour entrance, or in the harbour itself, was not an alternative. With the August offensive operations underway at Anzac Cove further east the logical place, therefore, was Suvla; that was if the ship could make it.

Following further inspection onboard *HMS Louis* it was fortunate that none of the hull plates had ripped away from the side of the ship. Whilst a number of her seams were split they still had power and were able to make way. Working in calf deep water with a calmness belying their inner feelings, the stokers and engine room ratings below deck kept up the needed coal to the twin boiler furnaces. Others continued to work on stemming the incoming water while the Chief Engineer monitored their headway. With the ship's increased speed it then became obvious that the rate of flow into the ship was easing as the hull lifted. It encouraged a cheer from the exceedingly apprehensive seamen while the ship's speed was increased to 10 knots.

It took several hours to make the entrance to the bay off Nebrunessi Point, to then steer to port towards the proposed breakwater and boat dock at West Beach. They could see as they approached that both bay and beach were receiving an ongoing barrage of enemy high explosive and shrapnel fire. With it obvious to the officers onboard the ship that they were highly likely to become the next target the destroyer's lifeboats were unshipped and prepared. Orders had also been given to be in

H M S Louis beached at Suvla

readiness to lower the boats and abandon ship in an orderly fashion as soon as they struck the bottom.

HMS Louis in Suvla Bay

With a wrenching sound they hit hard bottom 100 yards from the shore to keel over to starboard almost immediately. The ship's telegraph had been set to register 'All Stop' 300 yards from shore to give those below a chance to get on deck.

The Chief Engineer had just made the deck when the first shell struck killing two ratings and damaging one of the boats on the port side. The destroyer's crew were tumbling into the lifeboats now that the Turks had found their range. Others jumped into the sea to swim to shore. Grasping the diplomatic pouch and ship's log the First Officer had those on the oars in the boat he had boarded steer clear of the ship to head for shore. None of them heard the incoming shell that exploded alongside shattering the boat and killing the majority of those onboard, instantly. Several troops on the beach who witnessed the mayhem, and growing carnage, reacted instantly. One of these was Arthur Newcombe who had been sheltering behind a pile stores since the Turks' evening barrage began. Without a thought he plunged into the water to drag survivors ashore. Shells continued to explode raising columns of water along with shattered remains, while the odd round continued to hit the ship. The confusion created by the cacophony of deadly explosions was not the welcome those of the Royal Navy onboard *HMS Louis* had expected.

The wreck of HMS Louis

Within 15 minutes it was over and the shelling had ceased. With the dead and injured removed from the sea, amongst the casualties were the Captain and his First Officer.

It was early the following morning, as Arthur walked the beach viewing the aftermath, that he came across a ripped Cairo diplomatic pouch. Inside he was amazed to find a small sealed oilskin package addressed to Ernest Budge at the British Museum.

The Mounted Division moving up from reserve the area of the Salt Lake on 21st August to join the battle.

The wreck of H M S Louis

The hopelessly mismanaged attack at Sulva Bay, that climaxed on 21st August with the battle of Scimitar Hill, was the largest battle of the Gallipoli campaign. When it failed, activity at Suvla subsided into sporadic fighting. Even so living conditions continued to be atrocious with the flies still as bad as ever.

Arthur had learnt to be ready should any pot of jam be opened, for it was now that another battle would instantaniously commence between flies and soldiers as to who would get the larger share.

Sunday 22nd August was a busy morning with wounded coming in regularly, but not in such large numbers as the night before. There had been continuous shelling again for two hours that morning. The 2/10th Middlesex Battalion's Reserve Company who had rejoined them from Alexandria the day prior were now enjoying the treat of having a large number of high explosive shells dropped amongst them. Fortunately they did little damage and they were again heavily shelled in the evening, mostly by high explosives, with one soldier killed alongside Arthur. Three shells also landed plum in the midst of the 3rd Welsh Field Ambulance wounding a lot of men.

For Arthur and his mates the only consolation was that the weather remained fine. Were it otherwise, he reflected, life would be totally miserable. Just as the thought entered his head the boys of the Field Ambulance received a further shell, again right in their midst. Two patients were killed, with their Colonel wounded and now in great pain with his heel shattered.

As August gave way to September the summer conditions that had been marked by the appalling heat, flies, and lack of sanitation, changed as the weather became cooler. As if to signal this seasonal shift an increasing number of patients now started passing them daily, suffering from dysentery.

The Scottish Horse bivouacking on the beach a Lala Baba on landing on the 3ʳᵈ September. The beach soon came under shell fire from a 6" gun with casualties soon occurring.

The Royal Australian Navy Bridging Train had landed to assist the British force with the construction of piers, the control of water supplies, and other similar tasks. This unit was based at Kangaroo Beach and they would have the honour of being among the last to leave with the eventual evacuation in December.

Bridging Train tourists, seven bob a day
Unloading lighters at Suvla Bay,
If they should grumble, the jaunty would say
Away to the guard shed, and stay there all day.

Amid the construction of a tramway to transport stores and equipment to and from Kangaroo Point Arthur celebrated his 18th birthday on the beach with others of his Middlesex battalion. It was like coming of age with him being teased that he had now finally of legal age to join the army. At dusk he visited his friends in the Welsh Field Ambulance to find them all in cheery mood and still fit. As the evening's shadows descended over the camp the Welsh boys offered up a fine selection of songs to celebrate his birthday.

During his next stint in the front line Arthur wore the amulet around his neck as a symbol of good luck. He had decided on opening the package and once he discovered the artefact he had decided that it was safer on his person than in an oil skin wrapper

Arthur and other British troops dug in on Chocolate Hill

that could be misplaced. After several hours in the front line, with no activity occurring, he removed the amulet to study it. He wondered if some other soldier in the dim distant past had likewise worn it in a similar manner. A vision of armies of old attacking each other using swords to hack off limbs and disembowel their foes entered his thoughts. In a moment of clarity he realised that mankind had not learnt a thing since he stood on his hind legs. His mind wandered back to happier times that he had enjoyed those few months earlier, then…

What about that uninspiring speech given by that bloody Catholic Archbishop before leaving England that had ended with the words…"Always remember that God is on our side!"

I bet he is tucked up safe. Nice and cosy, with his silver tea service, no doubt writing further platitudes for the next group of unsuspecting trainees.

Thinking again of Ernest Budge he remembered his words relating to the scripture on a supposed God…

"Whoever is not with me is against me…"

Well these Moslems up this hill no doubt think the same way with their exclusivist faith also, so where does that leave us? Are we both fighting for the same God because he has a different name on either side… or because the bloody Pope thinks he can con people that he, along with his mates, exclusively receive God's messages and that as such they can perform miracles; or that Muhammad, on behalf of Allah, decreed some Holy jihad. Bloody ridiculous… We might as well be still worshipping rocks or the sun!

His mental journey then brought him back closer to his present reality…

Bloody Churchill and his grand ideas …. Greed, power, and mans' everlasting, ignorance, ego, and arrogance is all this affair is about; as it certainly isn't justice or respect for humanity.

As he sat in contemplation a soldier close by him in the trench noticed his thoughtful look as he clasped the amulet, and commented to one of Arthur's mates.

What…? Is 'Batman' a wog Moslem or something..?

No, it's his lucky charm that he wants to get back to some chap in London ….

He had just finished that observation when bullets started kicking up dirt around them. The fusillade snapped Arthur back to reality and he instinctively ducked. *Jesus... that was close….* was all he managed to utter before a high explosive shell erupted directly behind him with a rock hitting his pith helmet knocking him out cold.

As he slipped sideways the amulet fell from his grasp.

Due to the level of casualties the fighting units' stretcher bearers were not able to cope so the RAMC had to take on a role which was clearly dangerous and extremely hard work. Unlike the Western front it was not a question of whisking the patients away from the sphere of operations to comparative safety. Here, from the firing line, any wounded soldiers had to be carried to field dressing stations in slow and difficult stages under continuing shell-fire. To complicate matters the Advanced Dressing Stations, (ADS), near the fighting were little more than semi-sheltered areas where the wounded were collected. From here they had to be carried across the dry salt lake in mule-drawn ambulances.

ADS serving Chocolate Hill next to armament stores

On coming to, Arthur found himself being carried face downwards on a stretcher by others of his platoon. Suddenly another shell burst close-by showering them with lumps rock and clay. One bearer stumbled, recovered, and they we went on to deposit Arthur with the Field Ambulance at the bottom of the hill, where he was initially inspected. Close-by a mules attached to an ambulance cart stood patiently waiting to convey wounded to the beach. While four injured waited to be lifted into the cart, a shell burst killing the two lead mules. Whilst these were cut away from the two survivors it would be an hour before new ones could be procured.

Meanwhile, more wounded were accumulating. It was one of the most uncomfortable few hours Arthur would ever spend, lying on his face on a stretcher unable to move. He was getting stiffer by the minute, not knowing where the next shell would fall, with the mules that had been killed about ten yards from where he lay.

Mule drawn ambulances on the salt flat

Eventually they were off at last; four lying and four sitting cases, jolting over the bed of the salt pan. The blinds were drawn so

Arthur couldn't see out. Twice shell exploded near the wagon but the good little mules plodded on eventually bringing them to the Welsh Casualty Clearing Station. Here they each received an injection of anti-tetanic serum, and where their wounds were properly dressed. The worst cases had to wait to be carried on to the barges in the morning.

The accommodation at the main Dressing Stations was very basic being small shelters dug into the low dunes along the beach with a few tents used for the 'operating theatres' and for dressing the wounded. Even these were in short supply and makeshift structures had been erected with very little protection from the blazing sun during the day, or the bitter cold at night. Most of the arriving casualties were simply lined up on the beach as close as possible to the pontoon jetty to wait their turn for evacuation on barges that would be towed out to the hospital ships waiting offshore.

The Casualty Clearing Station – A Beach

53rd Division's Casualty Clearing Station (CCS) was located on 'A' Beach. Like others it was a grim place with a dressing tent packed full of shattered men, while others had little option other than to tolerate conditions out in the open. Inside at night it had an eerie feeling where a sleepy orderly sat by a medical table at one end overseeing rows of stretchers in front of him from the dim light of two poor lamps. For him the reality was that the lack of light was rather a blessing as it hid the true effects of the white bandages now stained a dull red, while the continual groaning and whimpering of many in great pain was amplified in the cold night air.

Don't make me leave... was Arthur's first comment to the medical orderly who was inspecting him. *I don't want to let my mates down...*

You'll be OK. You have grazing, bruising, concussion, and a lump on the back of your head about half the size of a hard boiled. It's nothing that a day or so won't fix.

As he cleaned the wound, applied antiseptic, gauze, and wrapped a bandage around Arthur's head the two made small talk and for whatever reason Arthur commented..... *And to top it all off I lost an ancient amulet on that hill that was meant to go to London. I'll get it though the next time I am up there...*

In the dim light another injured soldier nearby pricked up his ears and listened intently. After Arthur had left the tent that patient had quizzed the orderly as to the Arthur's name and what he had been talking about.

Following Arthur's discharge to recover on the beach the outside air was once again bitter for those in the open. With dew forming like rain 200 odd wounded were lying on open ground close to the dressing station. As Arthur walked amongst them, one who had

A sandbagged dugout known as 'The 'Wardroom', used by the officers of the 1st Royal Australian Naval Bridging Train at Kangaroo Beach, Suvla Bay - September 1915.

been shot in the stomach was yelling for morphia while another, who had got it through the head, was lying with a blood soaked bandage round his forehead. A third had been shot through both cheeks with his tongue taken off at the same time. He was coughing blood continuously and couldn't lie down. Several would die before morning, while those not suffering so much from pain were forced to tolerate the cold. Although many would have little time to feel it, others were simply praying for the sun to rise as they sat shivering waiting for attention.

Back on Chocolate Hill after Arthur had sustaining his head injury from the opening salvos of the Turkish artillery barrage the trench he had been in had been evacuated. The 2/10th Middlesex boys had hung on as long as they could but with further casualties they

were forced to follow Arthur shortly after he had been carted off
the hill.

Landing at Suvla Bay

*West Beach at Suvla Bay after the construction of a boat harbour by
the 1st Royal Australian Naval Bridging Train -October 1915.*

Following up their barrage with a counter attack the Turks had
easily re-taken those front line positions before putting out further
snipers to discourage any immediate British attempt at a counter-
attack of their own.

Leaping into the trench and sliding to a stop in a cloud of dust
Ahmet-oğlu Abdullah had begun to help two fellow mehmets set

*Ahmet-oğlu
Abdullah*

up a maxim machine gun to cover the slope below. As he hefted its heavy tripod from the edge of the trench he looked down to discover the amulet that had fallen from Arthur's hand. Recognising its religious significance, and that destiny had brought it in contact with him… *praise be to Allah*, he too would wear the amulet around his neck as a symbol to ward off harm.

*The 1st Royal Australian Naval Bridging Train towing a hulk into
place to form a breakwater for the boat dock at West Beach, Suvla Bay
- September 1915.*

Similar to the British term 'Tommy' or the New Zealand and Australian term 'Digger', Mehmetçik or 'Mehmet' was used in a similar way by Turkish soldiers as an affectionate Turkish nickname, or form of endearment for a fellow brother in arms. Mehmet was simply a respectful contraction of the name 'Muhammad' used by many Moslems, and consequently one of the most popular male names in the Ottoman Empire.

In many respects the lives of all rank and file soldiers of any army have similarities. To the British and their allies Ahmed and his fellow Turkish soldiers were known as either 'Abdul', 'Johnny Turk' or 'Jacko'. They were all human beings usually from basic backgrounds like Arthur or Ahmed, and each was required to place his life on the line to fight for causes that were not always understood.

Like the English, as Ahmed referred to them as, he too had feelings and aspirations relating to loved ones, his faith, and his fears. He also had a sense of compassion even if his masters did not always display the same. As Ahmed's short experience in the war had progressed he too had lost fellow mehmets. The 'dog-eat-dog' mentality required for survival that reared its head daily tested his faith and he too would question the 'them or us' mentality that had placed him in the situation he found himself in. And so he clung

Turk soldiers on the Suvla plain

to his belief and faith in Allah and the teaching of Mohammed.

A Turkish soldier's life was not an easy one with many developing heightened fears, while others simply resigned themselves to whatever cards Allah dealt them.

The machine gun squad and fellow mehmets
Below - Turk soldiers

Al Waliyy ... Behold, your only helper shall be Allah, and His Apostle, and those who have attained to faith - those that are constant in prayer, and render the purifying dues, and bow down before Allah

In 1914 all male subjects of the Ottoman Empire aged between 20 and 45 had been liable for military service. Every March the young men who turned 20 that year were drafted into the army as a group cohort, or class. They served two years as full-time soldiers, or *Nizamiye*, in either the infantry or cavalry, or three years in the artillery. After completing this obligation they were transferred to the reserve, or *Ihtiyat*, in which they remained until the age of 38. Reservists returned to civilian life but could be recalled to full-time service in the event of war. On turning 38 they transferred to the territorial force, or *Mustahfiz*, for a further eight years of service. Territorials could also be called up if the empire went to war, but they were expected to serve only as local garrison or fortress troops.

Like Ahmed his fellow mehmets came mostly from rural peasant backgrounds, had little or no formal education, and little knowledge of the world beyond the nearest market town. Even the majority of those recruited from the cities were illiterate. Many who had been sent to the Gallipoli Peninsula thought at first that they were once again fighting the Greeks. Most had never heard of New Zealand or Australia and referred to all Entente troops as the 'English'.

If their upbringing left them somewhat ignorant concerning the wider world, it had given them a stoic outlook on life and the ability to endure great hardships. It was just as well because life in the Ottoman Army was harsh, even by the military standards of the day. Ottoman Army officers expected blind obedience from their men, with an officer having no need to explain or justify his orders to those below him, and strict discipline was imposed to ensure they got it. Ottoman commanders who had recently trained under the Prussian model could also be extremely ruthless with the lives of their men in battle.

Turkish commanders at Suvla

Out of the front lines, though, most officers did their best to look after mehmets under their command and help ensure that their basic needs of food, shelter and clothing were met. This, as it was turning out, wasn't an easy task. With more than a million men under arms the Ottoman Army's supply chain had begun to buckle under the urgent and competing demands made upon it. The empire's primitive rail and road network struggled to move troops where they needed to go, and then to keep them supplied when they got there. For mehmets on the front lines, they would suffer constant shortages of ammunition, replacement weapons, equipment and even food.

Unlike the British it was also very hard for soldiers to keep in touch with their loved ones back home. Even those who could read and write found that their letters and those sent to them often went astray. It could be months, even years, before news from home reached them. Turkish soldiers at Gallipoli and in the Caucasus received occasional visits from village spokespeople who had committed messages from fellow villagers to memory. They personally would deliver them to the front line and return home with the soldiers' replies.

But there were no such visits for those serving on the distant fronts of Sinai or Palestine with leave to visit home unheard of. Once a soldier reached the front the only legitimate way to see home again was through evacuation due to wounds or illness. Mehmets soon learnt that secondment to this front wasn't a desirable option as being wounded or falling sick in Palestine was often a death sentence. With the medical services of the Ottoman Army having been badly neglected prior to the war there was a shortage of doctors, nurses and modern medical supplies that condemned thousands to premature and unnecessary death.

The more up-to-date facilities that did exist were in larger cities that were many days, if not weeks, from the front lines. As a consequence many wounded or sick soldiers died in transit. This lack of medical staff and poor practices was also reflected in poor hygiene and sanitation standards generally across the army that additionally contributing to the death toll. Thousands were now dying from preventable diseases such as enteric dysentery, cholera, and malaria.

More Ottoman soldiers would die of disease during the war than would be killed in combat, or die of wounds. It was far from ideal and it could have been avoided.

Suvla Bay 1915

Looking towards Suvla Bay

Part XIV

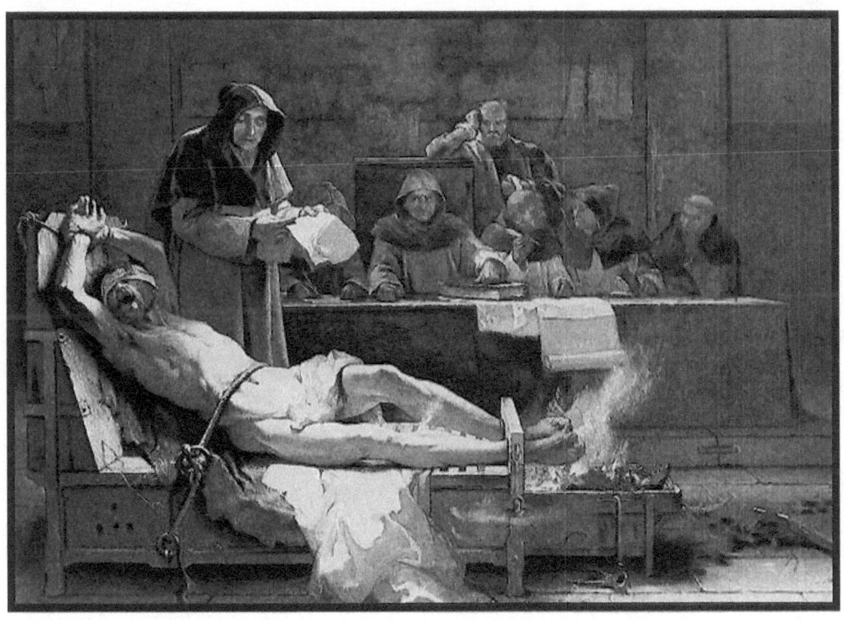

Up until 1904 when Pope Pius X renamed it The Supreme Sacred Congregation of the Holy Office in Rome had been known in many Catholic countries as 'The Supreme Sacred Congregation of the Roman and Universal Inquisition'. It was the oldest among the nine congregations of the Roman Curia, and it was also called in an abbreviated form as either the 'Roman Inquisition', 'Holy Inquisition', or simply as the 'Holy Office'.

Purging by fire during the Holy Inquisition

In early 1915 it had come to the attention of this Supreme Congregation that certain persons, even from among the ecclesiastic assemblage, were disregarding the decisions of this Holy Congregation. They were those who, contrary to the orders of the Holy Office, had continued to proceed to discuss and examine books, other small works, and articles edited in periodicals that were deemed unacceptable by the Church in Rome, and regarded by them as heretical teaching. Their instruction had been quite clear as…. *whether signed, or without a name, concerning the so-called Secret of La Salette, its diverse forms and its relevance to present and future times; and, this not only without permission of the Ordinaries, but, also against their ban.*

So that abuses that were deemed to oppose true piety and that greatly wounded ecclesiastical authority might be curbed further orders had been issued to the clergy and masses.

The same Sacred Congregation orders all the faithful of any region not to discuss or investigate under any pretext, neither through books, or little works or articles, whether signed or unsigned, or in any other way of any kind, about the mentioned subject. Whoever, indeed, violates this precept of the Holy Office, if they are priests, are deprived of all dignity and suspended by the local ordinary from hearing sacramental confessions and from offering Mass: and, if they are lay people, they are not permitted to the sacraments until they repent.

To ensure enforcement of their decisions a Church historian in Rome going by the name of Monsignor Umberto Benigni organised through his personal contacts with theologians an unofficial group of censors. They were to report to him on all those thought to be teaching condemned doctrine. Once again it was an apotheosis in exclusivism by the Catholic church that segregated believers and non-believers.

This clandestine group was called the Sodalitium Pianum, or 'Fellowship of Pius (X)'. In abbreviated form it had become known as simply the SP, or in France as 'La Sapinière'.

This Fellowship never had more than 50 members, who

Monsignor Umberto Benigni

through its frequently overzealous and secretive methods, included opening and photographing private mail and checking out the records of the local bookshop to see who was buying what. Naturally it had helped the Church in combating Modernist teaching at that time, but now it was hindering it.

Paralleling the SP, and founded by Pope Paul III back in 1542, around the time of the Holy Office, had been 'The Society of Jesus', whose sole objective was similar to the Holy Office and SP.... *to spread sound Catholic doctrine and defend those points of Christian tradition which seem in danger because of new and unacceptable doctrines.*

As a Consecrated Christian male religious order of the Roman Catholic Church, this Jesuit Society also has its headquarters, or General Curia, in Rome. Its members were called Jesuits and whilst the Society promoted evangelisation and apostolic ministry around the world one small sect had aligned itself to the SP. In so doing it had retained its clandestine military methodology. These Jesuits had been founded by Ignatius of Loyola with a special vow of obedience to the Pope that committed that…

We may be altogether of the same mind and in conformity…. if the Church shall have defined anything to be black, which to our eyes appears to be white, we ought in like manner to pronounce it to be black.

With regard to its military background the opening lines of this Society's founding document would also declare that it was founded for ….

Whoever desires to serve as a soldier of God… to strive especially for the defence and propagation of the faith and for the progress of souls in Christian life and doctrine.

Penances and sentences for those who confessed, or were deemed to be found guilty by this group, were generally pronounced together in a public ceremony at the end of all of their inquisitorial processes.

Known as the *sermo generalis,* or auto-da-fé, its penances generally consisted of a pilgrimage, a public scourging, a fine, or the wearing of a cross. The wearing of two tongues of red, or other brightly coloured cloth sewn onto an outer garment in the form of an 'X' marked out those who were under investigation.

Sentences and penalties in serious cases, however, ranged from confiscation of property, to inquisition, imprisonment, or even death. The first of these had been conveniently used with false charges being laid against an individual with the resultant confiscation of the property of those over a certain income bracket. Those trageted were particularly rich maranos. The last three generally involved various forms of torture to purge the soul.

As such it was a Society based on its members' unquestioned willingness to accept orders anywhere in the world, and to live in extreme conditions when

Simon the Redeemer

required to achieve the Society's objectives.

In matters requiring assassination the church had deferred to a special select, historically prepared, breakaway group within The Society of Jesus, who reported to the society's Black Pope. Referred to colloquially as 'God's Soldiers' this secret sect of assassins had been practising the literal interpretation of the Holy Roman Catholic faith, with the preservation of their interrogation techniques since the days of the Inquisition.

Simon the Redeemer

One such member, whose mask of sanity was veneer thin, was known simply as 'Simon the Redeemer'. Feeling no genuine emotion he had developed a narcissistic personality throughout his life by mimicking other Jesuits and Catholic hierarchy. Sexually abused by various clergy from a young age he had been programmed to follow literal religious doctrine without question. Overlaying his already strong psychopathic and inferiority tendencies he had developed to a point where he totally lacked empathy, compassion, remorse, or guilt. He saw himself as God's soldier and as such in being exonerated for any action he committed. As such he was emotionally shallow living in a world of denial while failing to accept responsibility for any of his actions instructed or otherwise.

Over the years several in the Society had attempted to cure his sadistic tendencies, however, their methods had simply empowered Simon further. He had reacted by improving his cunning manipulative methods along with his ability to conceal his true personality, even from trained eyes. For the few who could be construed as his controllers he was their ultimate instrument of redemption. A religious zealot with a disdain for close attachments and empowered by callous exploitative tendencies combined with the use of extreme cruelty. To any singled out that were unfortunate enough to cross his path Simon simply saw his behaviour as him purging the victim's soul as a genuine act of piety.

With a mind that retained detail he could recall when he had first been conducted into the Chapel of the Convent of the Order those many years ago. There had only been three others present; the Superior standing in front of the altar with a monk on either side.

One of the monks had held a banner displaying the Papal colours of yellow and white while the other held a black banner with a dagger and red cross above skull and crossed bones.

This also displayed the initials INRI, or *'Iustum Necar Reges Impios*, meaning … *It is just to exterminate or annihilate impious or heretical kings, governments, or rulers.*

Upon the floor was a red cross on which Simon had knelt as the prospect and where the Superior had handed him a small black crucifix. This he had taken in his left hand and pressed to his heart while the Superior at the same time presented to him a dagger which he had grasped by the blade holding the point against his heart. With the Superior still holding it by the hilt he had addressed Simon.....

My son, here-to-fore you have been taught to act the dissembler among Roman Catholics, to be a Roman Catholic and to be a spy even among your own brethren; to believe no man and to trust no man. Among the Reformers, to be a Reformer; among the Huguenots, to be a Huguenot; among the Calvinists, to be a Calvinist; among other Protestants; generally to be a Protestant, obtaining their confidence; to seek even to preach from their pulpits, and to denounce with all the vehemence in your nature our Holy Religion and the Pope; and even to descend so low as to become a Jew among Jews, that you might be enabled to gather together all information for the benefit of your Order as a faithful soldier of the Pope.

You have been taught to insidiously plant the seeds of jealousy and hatred between communities, provinces, or states at peace, and incite them to deeds of blood; involving them in war with each other, and to create revolutions and civil wars in countries that are independent and prosperous, cultivating the arts and the sciences and enjoying the blessings of peace. To take sides with the combatants and to act secretly with your brother Jesuit, who might be engaged on the other side, but openly opposed to that with which you might be connected, only that the Church might be the gainer in the end, in the conditions fixed in the treaties for peace in that the end justifies the means.

Since taking his vows Simon had developed the fanatical code of this Jesuit sect. Given the title 'Simon the Redeemer' after several less savoury clandestine Church inspired escapades he was now being sent on a highly important mission, along with another of their small band; an ex criminal Jesuit named Peter.

Following Italy's decision to join the war on the side of the Entente the Holy See had come to the conclusion that the British had no intention of having the amulet and its historic message gifted to them. They had consequently decided that what they had not been able to achieve by diplomacy they would now locate and acquire by stealth and force. The two candidates were briefed on details of the amulet and its damaging script, and most importantly, their need for success. Nothing was to stand in their way in the name of God in seeing the amulet and its message recovered for the Roman Catholic Church. That included the annihilation of those suspected of being in possession of the artefact to ensure that they could not communicate its hidden messages in future also.

In support of their decision the SP had continued in its attempts to trace the whereabouts of both halves of the amulet through their counter espionage contacts. After obtaining a copy of a photograph of half of the object that had been held by the Germans it now became clear that they too had been playing a double hand with their joint German - Ottoman instigated Moslem inspired jihad in the Near East. It was then discovered that the German agent by the name of Wasmuss had managed to lose the German half of the amulet at the time of his capture and escape and it was this piece that they suspected to have been in British hands.

The next piece of valuable information had surfaced through a spy in the Coptic Church of Alexandria, who had confirmed that the missing half along with a second damaging text had been discovered. This had naturally peaked the Holy See's motivation in recovering both halves and their messages. As they saw it, at that time, they effectively had a double threat on their hands.

It was around this time that they had a break from a Catholic informant inside the British Museum who communicated that the German recovered piece had been obtained by the British who had studied it before forwarding it to the Egyptian Museum of Antiquities in Cairo. Checking this intelligence with their Coptic Church spy in Cairo they determined that this original half of the amulet, along with its text, had arrived in Cairo where it had been matched with the second piece to form the complete amulet. The disturbing news, however, was that both halves and their messages had been proven to be

authenticatic and that the messages the ancient amulet contained, therefore, legitimately undermined everything they had built their

Catholic Rome

Church on both religiously, politically and economically since the 4th century. Just as important was that it would take away their power in promoting their religious doctrine in being the one true Church and in having any intermediary status as the sole communicator with God. Seen very much in old biblical terms as being a case of 'them or us' that undermining was not going to happen as far as they were concerned. After almost two millennia of manipulation of the masses their good works had brought them to the grandeur and property ownership they now enjoyed and they were going to protect their position at all costs.

With advice from the British Ambassador to the Holy See that the ship on which the artefact had been travelling back to Britain had sunk with the amulet and its message lost, the SP had incorrectly surmised that the British were again up to no good. They were aware the British had not mentioned their acquisition of the second half of the amulet to them, or of the second message, and they weren't going to be conned again as the German's had obviously been doing to date. While they awaited further intelligence from their Coptic Church contact in Cairo they became aware from a Catholic agent on Mudros of a British naval communication that indicated that a diplomatic bag with an item fitting the description of the missing amulet had been recovered in the Aegean. The field contact involved had then gone onto communicate that he suspected that the artefact had to be somewhere on the Gallipoli Peninsular as the ship it had been carried on had also been sunk in the vicinity of Suvla Bay with the crew abandoning the ship.

Was this another ploy by the British and if so it left them no closer to getting their hands on the object. They were going to have to check the beached ship and then be patient until further news of the diplomatic pouch came to light.

The grandeur that is the Holy See in Rome

The 1913 built Royal Navy destroyer *HMS Louis* that now lay derelict in Kangaroo Bay was off limits to any and all servicemen. Partially submerged the hulk was considered a hazard to other shipping and an eye-sore to the troops on shore. To both able seaman and private alike it additionally stood out as a beacon of failure that was part of the overall ill-fated Gallipoli Campaign.

A heavy Turkish shell lands beside a pier at Suvla - October 1915.

Hey, Batman... I bet those sailor boys left some of that Navy rum onboard that ship out there in their hurry to get off that tub ...?

It was as much a statement as a question with his platoon mates having already worked out that Arthur was the best swimmer. As such they had organised the drawing of straws so that he would end up with the shortest piece.

How about we draw straws to see who swims out to check it out...?

With all of them enthusiastically supporting this proposal as a grand idea, and already dreaming of the prospect of heart warming liquor, Arthur was enticed to join in.

The rail line to Kangaroo Point

HMS Louis

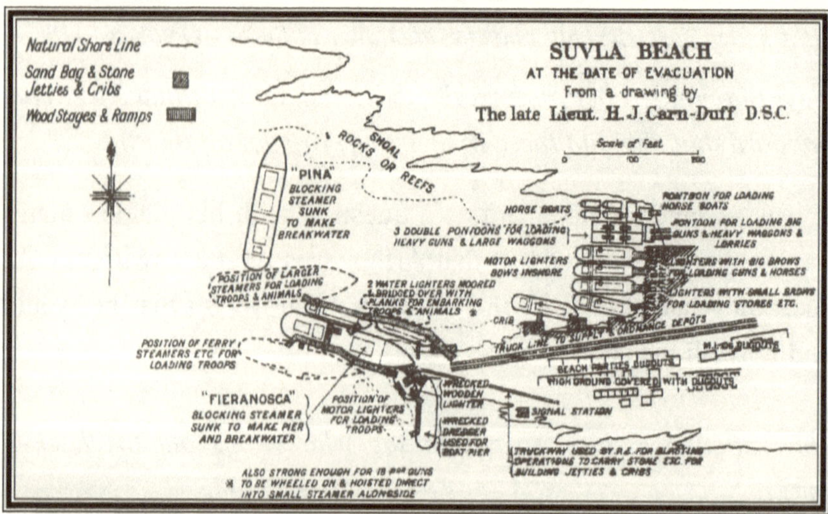

Having literally drawn the short straw over the past hour Arthur had managed to quietly manoeuvre his way along the embankment that sheltered the narrow gauge rail line from the northern shoreline of the bay. It was here that he would step into the sea before the Navi and HQ huts, close to the end of Kangaroo Point that separated it from Little West Beach. Adding to the tenseness gripping his insides the cold night air sent a chill through his body as he fixed the position of the wrecked destroyer *HMS Louis* in his mind before entering the water. With the ship's half submerged hull barely discernible at sea level he slipped beneath the surface coming up for a breath 50 feet further out in the bay. He could not, however, now make out the wreck against the blackness of the peninsular towards Anzac Cove. He took another deep breath and proceeded again underwater before finally surfacing to resort to his favoured side stroke. Heading in the general direction of the ship he silently made progress until its dark rusting hulk towered above him. Manoeuvering further down its hull he managed to slide onto *HMS Louis's* aft deck from its submerged stern.

Pausing, to try and settle his breathing, 18 year old Arthur Edgar Newcombe now wondered what the hell he was doing. He was about to climb up the sloping deck when he became aware of movement above him to his right. He lay still and waited until from the side of an aft bulkhead the clear form of a silhouetted figure appeared. His heart was pounding in his chest with an increasing sense of foreboding, before whoever it was clung to the starboard rail for a moment, as if listening, before slipping over the side of the ship to disappear in the darkness. Arthur lay silently where he was for a further 10 minutes. His mind was alive with thoughts as to why another person would be onboard. Maybe they had beaten him to the booze, yet the form he had seen had not been carrying anything so logically they must have been after something else. He had not expected anyone else and with his heart still beating inside his chest like a hammer it dawned on him that if he had arrived a minute earlier he would have run into the unknown identity with it highly likely that any meeting would have ended in dire consequences.

Deciding that the way was now clear he cautiously instigated a search of the ship's superstructure to strike his jackpot in a now smashed cupboard in what must have been the Officers' Mess. With his spoils of war in a canvas navy kit bag Arthur again slipped into the water to make it back to the beach.

He was glad to be away from the ship and its unforeseen danger yet whilst his return was uneventful he was still on edge. He made the shore without too much effort, crossed the tram lines, to appear out of the darkness at the dugout approximately three hours after he had left. In his possession were two dark bottles of rum, and the prize of all prizes, a bottle of single malt Scotch whiskey.

Pontoons in use as a bridge on Kangaroo Point beach, Suvla Bay, August 1915.

After nine months of intelligence duties in Cairo Colonel Stewart Newcombe had been sent to Gallipoli to command an Australian Division of Royal Engineers attached to the Imperial Army at Anzac Cove. It had become obvious to the overall campaign commanders that there was a need to adopt a fixed set of place-names for the ever-enlarging trench system on the peninsula. It had, therefore, fallen to experienced mapmakers, including Newcombe, to supervise the creation of a definitive and annotated map. During his stay he was to make a rescue attempt in a tunnel where his men had been overwhelmed by an ammonia gas explosion. For his effort on both counts he would later be awarded the Distinguished Service Order (DSO).

A group of men recovering from hypothermia following the great ice storm, in a hut made of biscuit crates.

Back at Suvla Bay on the 15th November the rain came down in cold torrents. With their supply of rum and whiskey long gone Arthur and his mates had to endure another major storm on the 26th and 27th that flooded trenches up to four feet deep. If this was not bad enough this deluge was followed by a blizzard of snow with two nights of heavy frost. The outcome was that 220 men drowned or froze to death, along with 12,000 cases of frostbite or exposure. With no words capable of depicting the horror of the situation they all now faced Arthur now wished they had kept those bottles. With the lack of shelter for the sick, or overworked doctors, and no winter clothing they huddled together half frozen. With no boats able to approach the Gallipoli beaches until the fury of the storm had abated there was also no means of evacuating the stricken. Like a final straw that can break a camels back the combined effects of the fighting with few reinforcements, along

Suvla - November 1915

with dysentery, heatstroke, jaundice, other ailments, and now this dreadful blizzard, it naturally led to their ranks being decimated.

By December, in contrast to the campaign itself, plans were underway for the overall withdrawal from Gallipoli. In contrast to the campaign itself these would be well planned and executed. To prevent the Turks from realising that a withdrawal was taking place many successful deceptions were executed that resulted in minimal losses, with many guns and other equipment also being recovered.

Before Arthur had been evacuated from Suvla's shores he had visited the graves of some of his fallen comrades, while others were still lost in the hills as his amulet had been. Private Arthur Edgar Newcombe had been one of the lucky survivors in a division reduced to just 162 officers and 2428 men. This compared to the 556 officers and 13,559 men who had sailed from Devonport 18 weeks earlier; a reduction of 85%.

Troops and artillery being evacuated - December 1915

A British soldier farewells a fallen comrade

Suvla Bay was evacuated in the second week of December and on 11th and 12th Arthur along with the remnants of the 2/10th Middlesex battalion were shipped to Mudros. Here they were transferred to *HMT Karroo* which sailed at 5.00 pm on the 17th for Alexandria. They arrived at 3.00 pm on 19th December, 1915 to be disembarked the following day.

Mudros harbour

HMT Karoo

Turk officers witness British ships withdrawing from Gallipoli – December 1915

As the Gallipoli campaign had wound down, an Anglo-Indian force in Mesopotamia had been cut off and surrounded at Kut-el-Amara, a town about 100 miles south of Baghdad. Their limited, defensive action at Basra had evolved into a distant and risky advance up the Tigris toward Baghdad and this had been the result.

Troops on the move

Once again political considerations had again trumped military ones with the Anglo-Indian force not having had the necessary reserves or logistical support to retain Baghdad, even if they had been able to capture it.

Whilst a strong British presence in Mesopotamia had no connection with ultimate defeat of Britain's primary strategic rival Germany the Indian government were still concerned that a Holy War might be ignited in Persia and Afghanistan thus threatening India. As such they continued to pressure for British prestige to be upheld in the Islamic world to avert such a war.

For the troops involved in Mesopotamia a more difficult theatre in which to fight is hard to imagine. Having to overcome the heat during the summer and the freezing cold at night, while flies and mosquitoes continually attacked the troops with many becoming sick when dust turned to mud or when the banks of the Tigris overflowed during the rainy season, was no picnic.

British troops in Mesopotamia

Not liking the taste of another defeat London reacted to the retreat from Gallipoli and the eventual surrender of the Anglo-Indian force at Kut-el-Amara in April 1916 by redoubling its efforts against the Central Powers in the Near East. After all, as a wealthy industrial power, Britain had the resources that the Ottoman Empire, even with German assistance, could not hope to match.

In Mesopotamia a new commander, General Sir Stanley Frederick Maude, would assemble a large force of some 150,000 men equipped with the latest weapons of war. Basra would be transformed into a modern port, a railway and a metal road constructed, with river transportation on the Tigris dramatically expanded.

Maude would capture and enter Bagdad in March 1917

In Egypt too its defence would evolve to an eventual invasion of Palestine, but first the Sinai Desert with its sand storms and searing temperatures had to be crossed. This was proving to be a test of endurance as well as of engineering for the troops involved with access to water dictating what could be achieved. Tens of thousands of camels and drivers were required to supply the thirsty soldiers while the water pipe and a railway were being extended to the borders of Palestine.

Arthur with the remainder of the 53rd Division were now located at Wardan Camp situated near the village of Beni Salama about 25 miles North of Cairo. It was here that they would spend the next few months recovering, re-equipping and re-training. The last decimated infantry units of their division had reached the camp shortly after Arthur, and just shy of Christmas 1915. Whilst celebrations had been austere it had meant a lot to those survivors just to remember their lost mates and for them be able to give thanks in still being alive. Their divisional artillery would rejoin them at Wardan in February.

Captain Davidson of HMS Cornwallis, (the last ship to leave Suvla Bay), meets in January 1916 with General Byng, who was in commander at Suvla and who had arranged the evacuation.

It was here that Arthur wondered again about the amulet; if anyone had found it, and if so, to whom were they praying. Was it a Christian God, Jehovah, or Allah. Personally Arthur now had serious doubts that there was any God at all, yet something knawed at him that both fate and creation were not just random occurrences. Just in case there was he made an ethereal request for another bottle of single malt, like the one they had enjoyed shortly after he had lost the British Museum's artefact. As he stared at the stars he wondered if there was some form of order in this chaos and came to the simple conclusion that there had to be more to life on earth than simply just survival of the fittest. For some unknown reason the initial apprehension and then feeling of pleasure he had experienced the first time he had sex in Ravenscourt Park came into his head. In his mind he still carried the reminder of the musky smell of the young girl he had been with that had excited him so much. He then thought of Jehanne and wondered where she was, and then whether Budge was still holding his lectures back at the British Museum. After the war he knew he had a long list of questions he was going to ask both of them. Anyway for all of that survival was now a day by day affair even if life was now a lot more idyllic than being on any Suvla shore.

By this time there had been a change of plan regarding defence of the Suez Canal. A commission under Major-General Sir Henry Horne had recommended that the defensive line should be moved forward from the west bank to the east, as far enough away from the canal for it to be beyond the range of the enemy's heaviest guns. Three new defensive lines were now being constructed with the supply railways from Cairo doubling in capacity. This construction effort was again being largely undertaken by locally-recruited workers, organised as the Egyptian Labour Corps.

36th Turkish Field Hospital El Arish

It had been stated that 12 divisions would be required to defend the canal from the quarter of a million Turks believed to be massing in Palestine. This, as it eventuated, proved to be a gross over-estimate as even if they had of had that size of force the railways and the water supplies in Palestine would not have supported them. The Ottoman Army did, however, maintain advance troops and outposts on the Sinai Peninsula on a line between El Arish and Nekhl. Combined with the forces at Gaza, and with 30,000 troops in the vicinity of Beersheba, they still presented a considerable threat. Once again Kress von Kressenstein, Djemal Pasha's German Chief-of Staff, had been assigned to command a number of mobile units designated to launch a series of further raids and attacks to disrupt traffic on the canal.

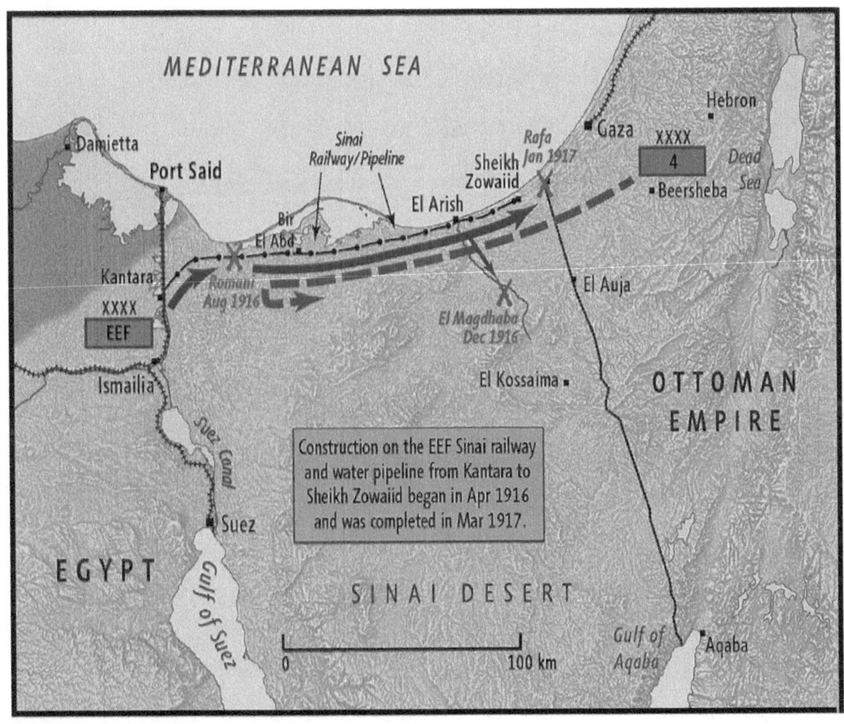

A map showing the construction of the EEF Sinai railway and water pipeline from Kantara towards Palestine that began in April 1916 and that was completed in March 1917.

For the British, the Egyptian theatre was now placed under the command of Lieut-General Sir Archibald Murray, recently arrived after being Chief of General Staff to Sir John French on the Western Front.

Murray had proposed to the War Office to undertake limited offensive action to be able to control the area in the vicinity of El Arish. While it would require continued major construction of railways and water supplies, it would effectively prohibit

Lieut-General
Sir Archibald Murray

the Turks from using the coastal route to the canal, and also put British troops in striking distance of any central route, well away from the canal.

To this end CIGS Sir William Robertson had given his cautious approval in March 1916.

In April 1916, at the General Headquarters of the Commander in Chief in Cairo a rearrangement of British commanded Egyptian forces was made in conjunction senior commanding officers. Included was the reorganisation of a Levant Base with a needed Headquarters with administrative services and departments.

The field reorganisation included the formation of a Western Frontier Force, made up of North Western and South Western Sections under the command of Major General W. E. Peyton. The South Western Section was commanded by Colonel (temp Brigadier General) H. W. Hodgson, while the North Western Section was commanded by Colonel (temp. Major General) A. E.

Dallas. Arthur's 53rd Division were in the North Western Section and were still being brought up to strength after their severe losses at Gallipoli.

Above- A sign of things to come…. a German Rumpler C.I and Pfalz E.I flying over Beersheba Airfield, April 1916.
Below - The Suez Canal

As one of the division's Gallipoli survivors Arthur could now genuinely call himself a 'Die Hard'; a colloquial title given to the regiment in 1811 during the Peninsular War. Over the coming months, with 6000 fresh troops from the UK arriving, the reconstituted battalions would post troops to a number of different locations to assist with local policing. As a part of this redeployment the 53rd Division was moved to the Suez Canal in May 1916.

Camped beside the Suez Canal

Egyptian Rail WW1

By April 1916 the Black Pope and SP in Rome had finally secured their last piece of valuable intelligence regarding the whereabouts of the amulet from a Catholic spy in Cairo. According to his report it's general vicinity had been located by an injured soldier who had been in the British forces in the field at Suvla Bay prior to his evacuation. His intelligence indicated that a British soldier with the surname of Newcombe had been in possession of the object until he lost it on Chocolate Hill. The spy believed that it may have since been recovered by this same soldier, but that he unfortunately had no idea as to what battalion or regiment he had been in, or whether he was still alive.

To those in the SP they now arrived at the conclusion that if the amulet was not lost then by now it had to be back in Egypt with a soldier named Newcombe if he had survived. They determined their first job, therefore, was to narrow down the field by instructing their obedient Church contacts in Britain to ascertain in what battalions and regiments in Egypt soldiers with the surname of Newcombe existed.

From the underbelly of all British Roman Catholic churches, the spy's of God, who usually did little and said lots, crawled from beneath their rocks. Clinging to obedience as their justification of personal piety, purity, and a belief that God had a reason for everything that happened, they pointed their moral compass in the desired requested direction. Without those in Rome having to get involved in anything distasteful they let their priests and parishioners supply the needed intelligence in the belief they were doing the work of God. Those in Rome knew that it was likely to not be a quick process but it was their only lead. As it transpired their loyal devotees did an excellent job without thought of any consequences or the damage they were about to cause.

By November 1916 the SP had established a shortlist of British non-commissioned soldiers in Egypt with the surname of Newcombe. Simon the Redeemer had been briefed along with a second supporting agent and both had been set loose on their mission of redemption and recovery. Liaising with German Intelligence in Constantinople the Church in Rome had additionally arranged for supportive native inhabitants to also help. Those selected had an appropriate axe to grind and were descendants of a North Caucasian ethnic group native to Circassia who had been displaced after the Russian–Circassian War of 1862. They were Circassians from Moab who had a vehement hated for Arab and British alike.

Circassians

A Circassian warrior

Part XV

ollowing the British evacuation from the Gallipoli Peninsula various Ottoman regiments had been removed to the rear for rest and recuperation. One of these was Ahmed-oğlu Abdullah's whose battalion ranks had likewise been decimated in defence of their positions.

Constantinople 1850

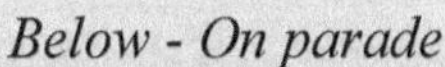

Below - On parade

Fortunate to come out of the experience unscathed Ahmed had come to put his survival down to Allah the Merciful, and in some obscure unexplainable divine way to his possession of the amulet that he still kept close under his tunic.

Winter in Constantinople was long and disagreeable not because of its cold which was rarely severe but because of its darkness and penetrating dampness. Not being able to count on the sun between October and April these six months were considered the rainy season.

On his arrival in the city Ahmed's was reminded of his first visit here during the empire's revolutionary days. There were still a few window frames in otherwise good repair that were still bullet hole riddled, while one iron shutter he noticed still remained hanging nearly perforated by dozens of small round holes. Many walls were still curiously pockmarked and he remembered that before the war he had seen a shell embedded in one. That first introduction and impression of conflict had by now changed dramatically with his experiences at Suvla Bay, paricularly the screams of those burning British troops on Scimitair Hill that still haunting him. In late January 1916 Ahmed and his fellow mehmets had been marched through the suburbs to reach the vicinity of the Taxime Artillery Barracks in semi darkness, having first passed the stately forms of trees in Taksim Gardens.

Training in Constantinople

Back in training in Constantinople Ahmed was placed on the establishment of reinforcements, and allowed an amount of leave as part of his rest and recuperation. Looking out over the city all appeared still suggesting all was at peace yet nothing could be further from the truth. Within its streets and bazaars German,

Austrian, Turkish, Arab and other forces bound for Mesopotamia, the Caucasus, Arabia, Sinai and Palestine, enjoyed the city's sites and pleasures before being sent to be disciplined on those harsh Ottoman fronts. In the surrounds of the harbour below the barracks marine traffic on the Bosporus and Sea of Marmora continued to busily ply amongst the resting hulls of transport and naval ships of all sizes. Later each day from his post in the barracks he would watch the smaller dowers load supplies in their shadows or glide in their wakes. The Turkish Navy could be found here for the greater part of the year having found enough deep water quite close to the shore.

With a liking for the sea it was this foreshore that Ahmed would visit as one of his favourite places during in his time off. Here he would sit and contemplate under the distant large orange dipping sun before meeting up with fellow mehmets.

Constantinople - WW1

Turkish Constantinople lay on the southern side of the Golden Horn where the courses of old stone and red brick delineating the location of old Byzantium still showed that the city still occupied much the same area as it had in the days of the first emperor Constantine. On the northern side of the Bosporus lay Christian Constantinople that was connected to the south by a number of rude but effective bridges. It was from the larger of these that steamers started for various points on the Bosporus or the Sea of Marmora.

This particular evening Ahmed along with a number of his friends had decided on making their way into the city centre to see the sights. Minarets and mosques, silhouetted against the skyline, merged lazily in a yellow haze of winter twilight as they descended the narrow lane of stone steps that led to the Grand Rue of Pera. This was the main street of the city where the fashionable

One of the major bridges across the Bosporus

shops were located and where they easily blended in with the diverse ethnicity that was the soul of the city. Being early evening the promenade of the Grand Rue was filled with people. Turks sat outside the cafes tranquilly smoking their cigarettes while watching the passers by, while poor men sat at the street corners, sweating and idle. Camals, staggering under their burdens, competed with grape-sellers weighed down with deep hampers of grapes, while the open tawdry shops displayed dark young men lounging in their doorways. Red fez passers with distrustful, disdainful, anxious eyes under them, jostled along with other soldiers in this crush and tangle of races. Each was elbowing the other over the slime of the street or against the shoulders of the trotting tram-horses.

The Grand Rue of Pera

Ahmed was not interested in buying goods here, although he observed several soldiers immersed in haggling. Buying at either wholesale or at retail prices was a slow process with prices definitely not fixed. With the seller always asking more than he expected to get, and the purchaser offering less than he expected to give, the negotiating would continue for some time. Each was making concessions to the other until finally an agreement would be reached.

After coming out of the café where he and his friends had enjoyed a meal with coffee Ahmed noticed that only a few shops remained open, with a few men sitting on their chairs outside of other cafes, and a few passers-by. Heaps of refuse lay in the gutters, which mangy dogs now nosed in, or lay asleep in the holes on the road or jags of the pavement. As Ahmed and his fellow mehmets passed a strange dog was being led on a leash through their midst and a howling began which was caught up and continued along the street with dog after dog getting up slowly to begin to bark.

Dogs being fed in the streets of Constantinople

It was a dense, uninterrupted noise, which he would soon come to know as the un-resting inarticulate voice of the city. This first evening out had been an experience and they bought oranges and coffee before going back to their barracks.

A week later as the sun again departed for the day Ahmed made his way to meet his fellow mehmets for coffee. On this occasion long-horned oxen, pulling a heavy cart over the rough cobblestones of the street, competed with the occasional truck, while donkeys with panniers strapped to their backs went by in single file guided by their Turkish drivers. Most of the people were Turks but the population still included almost every race imaginable, including those now considered as belligerents. Men with deceitful faces seemed odiously regular. One that paid particular interest to Ahmet and the amulet that hung from his neck was a Catholic priest. His slow steady passing and stare made Ahmet uncomfortable. He had stood out over the other Europeans, Levantines, French, and the occasional Greek, and Ahmet wondered what had peaked his interest.

Constantinople

After an hour with his friends Ahmed excused himself to make his way to the Haydarpaşa Railway Station where he could dream alone and gaze at the functionality of the trains. After the war he wanted to be an engine driver. They held an obvious fascination for him that also took his mind off the war.

Bazaar coffee shop

Ahmed's dream

On this visit he studied the large map on the station wall that showed the railway's existing destinations along with those currently under construction. He wondered when he would get a chance to travel by train, as it was not an experience he had been fortunate in having the pleasure of to date. Staring up at the map he knew that the line ran from Constantinople to Konia via Eskişehir where the railway workshops were located that had been built when he was young. Celebrated at the time this had been the first section of the Baghdad Railway. Then another railway, known as the Hejaz Railway had been commissioned by Sultan Hamid II and built by German engineers. From 1912 to the outbreak of the war an aggregate of 330 miles in different parts of the country had been opened for traffic.

Ahmed knew that the total time to travel the 1,255 miles from Constantinople to Baghdad was 22 days. He had also been told by a railway worker that breaks in the railway meant that the Ottoman government was still having difficulty in sending supplies and reinforcements to the Mesopotamian and Palestinian fronts. Workers were supposedly urgently labouring to complete a narrow gauge section through tunnels and over viaducts that negotiated the Taurus Mountains. Ottoman authorities had wisely chosen to place the line outside the range of the British Navy guns with the coastal way from Alexandretta to Aleppo avoided. This had meant that the line had to cross the inland Adana and Amanus ranges also at the added cost of expensive engineering.

Ahmed could see that north of Aleppo in Syria the line from Constantinople to Aleppo branched off for Baghdad at Mouslimiie Junction where there was another railway station. Further delays related to work being urgently conducted on the Bagdad section from Mouslimiie Junction, while the line travelling south that connected ultimately with the Hejaz line was evidently passable for military purposes.

Map showing the relative locations of the Taurus and Amanus ranges.

A study of the place-names on the map established a fairly well-defined line, running from about Jerablus on the Euphrates to the sea near Antioch, south of which the Turkish names gave way to Arabic. From here Arabian Syria extended southward with the broad-gauge line running through Aleppo, Hama Homs, to Rayak Junction in the Lebanon Valley, where it branched to Damascus, and Beirut on the coast of Lebanon.

South of Damascus the Hejaz Railway established a connection between Constantinople and the Hejaz region in Arabia giving the army better control of the far-flung empire. The line had got no further than Medina; a distance of 825 miles. This was 250 miles short of Mecca due to the interruption of construction works caused by the outbreak of the war. It did, however, pass through Transjordan in Az-Zarqa, Al-Qatranah, Amman and Ma'an before reaching north western Arabia that was known as the Hejaz region.

A more recent effort was the military railway branching off the Hejaz line, that ran to Beersheba in southern Palestine. It was here, Ahmed had heard from a military engineer, that many of the rail sleepers were made of iron because of the shortage of wood, and to also avoid rapacious locals from stealing them for firewood.

Before the Taurus Mountains

Map showing various Ottoman railways including the dotted British line from Kanatara to Gaza, and the Hejaz line heading south to Medina from the junction at Deraa.

Lying on the Asian bank of Bosphorus along with some of Constantinople's inner city forests was the suburb of Kandilli in the neighbourhood of Üsküdar. One of Ahmed's aging aunts lived here and on his third leave period he decided to visit her.

Instead of focusing on political issues and the plight of others while on the tram there he simply took delight at looking at the dark women and girls both on the tram and on the pavements. Not paying much attention to anything else he tried looking at their profound yet empty faces. Tightened in their smart dresses they sat or walked slowly by with their free cynical hard roving eyes; young girls with combed hair and finely cut mouths and neat, small firm figures.

After disembarking he made the decision to walk up Kandilli hill to his aunt's via a shortcut he had used before the war. The track was still there and on his climb up through the trees he reflected that maybe one day he too would have a smiling girlfriend or in then thinking that ... *maybe that enjoyment will be saved for Paradise... Allah be Praised.*

In a quiter section of the track, in a larger stand of trees and not far from his aunt's, Ahmed was confronted by a knife weilding assailant. Immediately on guard for others with him this one looked to be alone and of Greek or Italian origin. Something niggled in that instant that this face was familar but Ahmed could not remember where he had previously seen him. There was no time to think on that score with little pleasure expressed on Peter the Jesuit's face as he snarled in Turkish… *Bana muska ver !* *(Give me the amulet!)*. In that frozen moment between stand off and death Ahmed knew what his attacker was after and he was obviously ready to kill him for it.

Allah için koruyorum, (I am protecting it for Allah)… was Ahmed's simple reply. *Allah has reason to defend me as I am young and strong*, he silently reasoned to himself while holding the Jesuit's stare.

There was no invitational smirk the instant the Jesuit lunged at Ahmed with the knife but things would not go the attacker's way. In the split second Peter made his move Ahmed side-stepped and grasping the Jesuit's upper arm with one hand, and knife wrist firmly with the other. Applying his weight with the Jesuit's forward momentum he twisted his forearm arm up to forcefully drive the knife into his assailant's throat.

It was all over in a split second with Peter the Jesuit slumping to the ground gurgling in shock and the throws of death. There was no butchery just an expertly severed jugular with the flow of his blood now darkly staining the ground amongst the trees where he lay mothionless. Ahmed looked impassively down at the body. His training had held up despite this being this unexpected kill. Taking him for an unlucky thief Ahmed would not report the attack, neither did he search the corpse; he simply rolled the body to one side before moving on.

Since his initial military training and experiences on the Gallipoli Peninsular he had become quite skilled and unsympathetic at the criminal acts of others, whilst he was still ignorant of the many political events that surrounded him, or what had been occurring generally throughout the Empire. Satisfied inwardly that crime did not pay he praised Allah for his deliverance. He had no time for theives, or anyone else who broke Allah's code. Quite frankly he was not worthy of worrying about and anyway he had other things on his mind.

It would be from visits to his aunt that he was to learn of some of the Empire's more repressive measures, becoming aware of the hard bitten crime, racism and persecution that was the underbelly of what appeared to be an official stance regarding various ethnic groups.

There has not been any systematic maltreatment of so-called belligerents in the city with I think, one would have to say, displays of tolerance by our authorities, his aunt had initially explained. *From time to time we are, however, subjected to certain security measures such as the sealing up of some of the houses. They have also shipped out some occupants to a nearby island to keep them out of the sight of the visiting German Kaiser.*

He then learnt from his aunt that Armenians, Pontian Greeks, and Assyrian Christians had fallen into a different category entirely, along with their forced deportation.

It is a sickening affair if half the stories I hear are true ... his aunt has explianed before again changing the subject.

During their time together they shared news on many other matters of interest including Ahmed showing her his amulet, explaininh how he had come by it, but not mentioning having killed the thief who had been intent on taking it from him.

The demise of Peter the Jesuit

Turks smoke and drink coffee outside a Constantinople coffee shop

From a time following the first and second waves of Jewish immigration to Palestine from 1870, until the outbreak of war in 1914 every Jewish community or village (*yishuv*); farm (*moshava*); or cooperative or collective settlement (*kvutza*), had faced the need to protect itself. At the start protection had been mainly necessary to combat local Arab thieves or organised gangs, and it had been from these defensive beginnings that Jewish security organisations had evolved in several phases.

The Jewish settlement of Rosh Pina

At first, Jewish settlements had designated at least one person to be responsible for the security of the built-up area and, when necessary, the fields. This guard, armed with a personal weapon which in most cases had been a rifle, or a handgun, had operated by day and by night, on horseback or on foot. As time passed these guards hired Arabs for guard duty, especially at night. This method proved inefficient because it had not taken long before some of the Arab guards had begun to collaborate with the thieves and bandits. As a result in a few settlements like Zikhron Ya'akov young Jewish settlers had organised small groups for guard duty on a voluntary basis having learned the art of guarding and securing their settlements from the few professionals within their ranks. As a Jewish defence organisation in Palestine the Hashomer headed by a committee of three had been founded in April 1909, out of Bar-Giora. It would cease to operate after the founding of the Haganah in 1920.

The purpose of Hashomer was to provide guard services for Jewish settlements in the Yishuv, freeing them from dependence upon foreign consulates and Arab watchmen for their security.

Hashomer members - 1909

By 1913 the Hashomer leadership had established relations with the institutions of the Zionist Organisation in Europe, but this connection had been disrupted in August 1914 when war broke out. Hashomer, however, continued its security assignments in

Palestine as before, taking pains to deny the Ottoman regime any pretext to liquidate it.

The leading personality in Hashomer throughout its existence until 1920 was Yisrael Shohat, with the main figure in a Jaffa Group being Eliyahu Golomb. This second security organisation had also

come into being comprised of young people who provided security services for the Jewish community in Tel Aviv. It had also been founded in 1909 on the outskirts of the ancient port city of Jaffa.

Eliyahu Golomb

Palestinian Jews in the Turkish army

During the war several thousand Jewish residents of Palestine were inducted into the Turkish army, with a few trained and appointed as officers and NCOs. There was Moshe Sharett; Alexander Aaronson; Dov Hoz, who later deserted to the British army; and Elimelekh Zelikovich (Avner), who eventually became a senior commander in the Haganah.

Important Zionist developments had also taken place in the British army fighting against the Turks. The first of these occurred in Egypt in 1915 when the Zion Mule Corps was formed under the command of the Irishman, Lieutenant-Colonel John Henry Patterson. He was supported by Captain Joseph Trumpeldor. This Zion Mule Corps had joined the British Expeditionary Force. Landing on the Gallipoli Peninsula in May, 1915 it had seen action and offered valuable service until evacuation that December. Almost all the soldiers of this corps were Jews who had been expelled by the Turkish authorities from Palestine because of alien citizenship.

It was then only after relentless petitioning in British government circles in London by Jabotinsky, Rutenberg, and Trumpeldor, that the British War Office would eventually agree in September 1917 to the formation of a new infantry regiment based on nearly 100 veterans of the Mule Corps, who had arrived in Britain. They would be combined with Jewish émigrés from Russia who had settled in Britain and agreed to join a Jewish combat unit.

Known as the 38th Royal Fusiliers it came into being in southern England under the command of Lieutenant-Colonel Patterson, the former commander of the now dismantled Zion Mule Corps. It, however, would not be until February 1918 that the Fusiliers would be transferred to Egypt to take part in the last major British offensive in Palestine of September 1918. The regiment, then stationed in the Jordan Valley near Jericho would participate in crossing the Jordan river to the east in the direction of Es Salt, along with New Zealand and Australians. Vladimir (Ze'ev) Jabotinsky would be a deputy commander of this regiment, with the honorary rank of lieutenant.

Hashomer members – WW1

Avshalom Feinberg

Nestled in the mountains of Northern Palestine overlooking the Mediterranean, just 15 minutes north of Caesarea was the town of Zichron Ya'acov.

Above - Baron Edmond de Rothschild.

Right -French-born James de Rothschild, Edmond's son. He was educated at Trinity College, Cambridge. James shared his father's enthusiasm for Jewish communities in Palestine.

It had been founded in late 1882 when 100 Jewish pioneer members of the Hovevei Zion movement from Romania purchased land in Zammarin.

Difficulty in working the rocky soil and an outbreak of malaria had, however, led many of these settlers to leave before the year was up. Then in 1883, Baron Edmond James de Rothschild became the patron of the settlement and drew up plans for its residential layout and agricultural economy. As such Zikhron was one of the first Jewish agricultural colonies to come under the wing of the baron, along with nearby Rishon LeZion and Rosh Pinna. He would name Zikhron Ya'akov in memory of his father, Ya'akov (James / Jacob) Mayer de Rothschild.

Above - Ronya Datnowsky, Aaron and Sarah Aaronsohn as youngsters at Zichron Ya'acov before the war

Edmond de Rothschild visits Eretz Yisrael

By 1912 Zichron Ya'acov was also the home of the now famous Carmel Winery that had begun operations in 1886, as well as the home of Sarah, Rebecca, and Aaron Aaronsohn.

In the summer of 1908 a Bulgarian Jew by the name of Haim Abraham had left Rustchuk, Bulgaria, to come to Constantinople.

Along with his younger brother, Moritz, they had established and owned an import-export company going by the name of 'Abraham Freres', which sold cheap German metal goods such as razor blades all over the Levant.

Abraham Freres, letterhead, 1918

This business was very successful with Haim and Moritz described by 1912 as 'prosperous merchants', or well-to-do importers. The import side of the business required frequent travel, both to Germany and to various Levantine countries, often taking Haim away from Constantinople.

When back in the city he continued to be involved with a number of Jewish and Zionist organisations such as the The Maccabi Sports Organisation of Constantinople. This was the first Jewish sports organisation founded by Jews of German and Austrian extraction who had been rejected from participating in other social sport clubs.

Then in September, 1913 Haim attended the XI Zionist Congress in Vienna as part of his role with Maccabi. Here he was introduced by a friend of the Aaronsohn family to a young Jewish girl named Sarah Aaronsohn from Zichron Yaakov in Northern Palestine.

The Aaronsohn family, with a bearded Haim Abraham, in Zichron Yaakov.

Haim had heard about Sarah's family through his sister-in-law and expressed his desire in wanting to marry '*a girl from one of the real pioneers*' that had settled Palestine. Sarah agreed to a marriage proposal without really knowing him and after the wedding they had both travelled to Haifa where they had boarded a ship bound for Constantinople.

The couple lived in the suburb of Kandilli, next door to Ahmed's aunt, while Haim also had an apartment in Galata, (aka Pera); a neighbourhood on the northern European side of the city. The life Sarah now found herself in, however, didn't match her expectations at all, and it soon became clear to her that she and Haim were not meant for each other.

Haim Abraham and Sarah Aaronsohn were married on the grounds of the Athlit Station, under a velvet canopy on March 31st, 1914

With the arrival of the war Ahmed's aunt and Sarah had become firm friends, thinking alike about the suffering and persecution that was becoming evident around them. Being an impulsive

Sarah and Haim Abraham

young lady it had become obvious to Ahmed's aunt that Sarah had been at odds from the beginning with her wealthy businessman husband. Their marriage wasn't a happy one and it became clear that it wouldn't last. As the weeks progressed it had left Sarah wondering why she had decided to wed a man she had hardly known, if at all, and with whom she was not in love. The man she truly loved was a local Palestine Jewish lad by the name of Avshalom Feinberg; but so had her younger sister Rivka.

By the summer of 1915 Sarah regretted having stood aside to give her younger sister a chance at happiness, having also become homesick, depressed, and worried about her family who were suffering under Turkish rule. Then, unexpectedly, she learnt through a letter from Avshalom Feinberg that he had not married her sister Rivka after all. Rather, that her sister had gone to America, and that Sarah had been the one whom he was really in love with. Her heart soared for the first time that year and in the second half of August 1915, while Haim was away on a business trip to Germany and Vienna, Sarah started making arrangements to leave the city and return to Zichron.

With war raging in Europe, it had become too difficult for Haim to run his business from Turkey, and so with his marriage effectively over, he temporarily relocated to Germany where he would remain for two years.

Sarah Aaronsohn would return to Richon Yarkoov just before Christmas 1915, voicing her intention to Ahmed's aunt that she would return after a few months to tidy up a number of outstanding

Sarah Aaronsohn

matters. And so they had made their farewells and Sarah boarded her train feeling free and looking forward to getting back to Palestine.

Her excitement, however, was about to be curbed at a remote station on the Anatolian plain by an experience that would painfully be etched into her memory for the rest of her short life.

Part XVI

In 1913 a newly founded committee with the inspiring name of

'The Ottoman Committee of Union and Progress' had established the Teşkilat-i Mahsusa. A year later the Ottoman government had influenced its direction by releasing criminals from central prisons to make up central elements of a newly formed special forces unit in its name. There objective was to participate in the destruction of the Ottoman Armenian community.

Starting initially with 124 criminals, little by little into 1915, hundreds, then thousands of prisoners were freed to become members of this organisation. Dubbed as butchers of the human species by Vehib Pasha, commander of the Ottoman III Army these enthusiastic degenerates had then been charged with the escort the convoys of Armenian deportees.

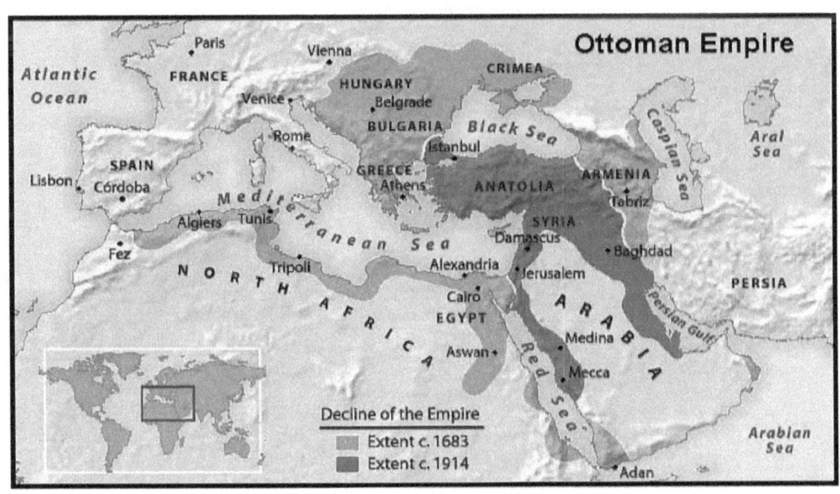

A map of the Ottoman Empire

By 1914 the Ottoman Empire was home to at least two million Armenians, most of whom inhabited the six provinces in Eastern Anatolia that separated the heartland of Ottoman Turkey from the Russian Caucasus. As a substantial Christian minority in a predominently Moslem empire, with their own vibrant culture and nationalist aspirations, the Armenians had endured an uneasy relationship with the Ottoman government for decades.

After the Ottoman Empire's entry into the war fighting between Turkey and Russia had quickly spilled into Eastern Anatolia. After a series of Ottoman military setbacks, most notably at Sarikamish in early 1915, the Armenians had been accused, in a few cases justly, of conspiring with the advancing Russian forces to ensure Turkish defeats. Accusations of 'Armenian treachery' gave the Ottoman government the pretext to sanction measures designed to remove all traces of the Armenian population from their empire.

Hanging Armenian males

This brutal state-sponsored persecution was designed to systematically exterminate the minority Armenian subjects. It would involve the wholesale killing of the able-bodied male population through massacre and forced labour, along with the deportation of women, children, the elderly and infirmed, on death marches to the Syrian Desert.

Other indigenous and Christian ethnic groups such as the Assyrians, the Greeks, and other minority groups had similarly been targeted for extermination by the Ottoman government. As part of the same policy of genocide this included the extermination of any in their way and as their guards saw fit.

Beginning in April, 1915 the Ottoman authorities rounded up tens of thousands of Armenian men and had them shot while hundreds of thousands of Armenian women and children were deported.

Armenian dead

By 19th April, 50,000 Armenians had already been killed in Van province alone, with tens of thousands being deported from neighbouring Erzerum. Similar acts took place throughout Anatolia during the rest of 1915. In Bitlis, 15,000 Armenians had been murdered during an eight-day period in June while a month later rampaging Turkish troops had massacred most of the 17,000 Armenians in Trebizond on the Black Sea. At that time the United States ambassador confirmed what was happening…

Scenes like this were common all over the Armenian provinces in the spring and summer months of 1915. Death in its several forms —massacre, starvation, exhaustion—destroyed the larger part of the refugees. The Turkish policy was that of extermination under the guise of deportation.

A dead Armenian mother and her children

It was an orchestrated policy of genocide that would later be dubbed 'ethnic cleansing.'

An Armenian merchant

While the shortest method for disposing of women and children concentrated in the various camps had been to burn them, other forms of extermination had been experimented with and practiced as directed by Nail Bey. From the main city in Trabzon province thousands of the children were loaded into boats and taken out to sea and thrown overboard, or capsized, in the Black Sea. Boat loads sent from Zor down the Euphrates River arrived at Ana 30 miles away, with three fifths of their passengers missing.

Armenian refugees being loaded onto a boat

Doctors were also directly involved in the massacres in poisoning infants, killing children, and issuing false certificates of death from natural causes. Dr. Saib stationed at a Red Crescent (Red Cross) hospital caused the death of children by the injection of overdoses of morphine. In the same location two school buildings were used to organise children and send them to the mezzanine to kill them with toxic gas equipment.

Deir ez Zor

Then in January 1916, when the spread of typhus was an acute problem, by order of the Chief Sanitation Office of the army innocent Armenians slated for deportation at Erzican were being inoculated with the blood of typhoid fever patients without rendering that blood 'inactive'.

Over the next six months the Inspector-General of Health Services, Dr. Tevfik Rushdu, would organise the disposal of the Armenian corpses using thousands of kilos of lime. For his efforts he would be appointed Foreign Secretary of a post war Turkey from 1925 to 1938. In excess of one million Armenians would perish in this attempted genocide, with its horrors impacting on the destiny of the amulet.

Armenian Genocide

Victims of the Armenian Genocide

Having disembarked while the train stopped on the outskirts of Ereğli, north of Konya, for its scheduled 30 minutes break to take on water and fuel, Sarah Aaronsohn made her way to the other

Ereğli Station

side of the station building to look at the landscape. Out in a field in front of her she was witness to Armenian refugees being herded like cattle toward a huge stack that looked like a funeral pyre.

At first her mind did not comprehend the significance of what she was taking in until she realised that those in line were being forced onto the already significant structure to be tied in place. With Turkish soldiers and

Ereğli Konya 1920

guards lashing out inhumanely at any women or child that took a wayward step it was a soul destroying sight. Sarah was transfixed as though time stood still watching helplessly as the last children were tied to the pile of living humanity that had been created over the foundation of timber and combustible material. Many had been propped up and tied to makeshift ledges while others stood, or were crowed above and around them. Continuing in a circular manner, five high and five deep, this living human tepee shaped structure now contained in excess of 500 souls.

The sound of the laughing of the armed psychopathic degenerate released convict guards carried on the wind, along with the moans and yelling of their victims, as the guards began to enthusiastically splash liquid from tins over the bottom rows of bodies. Totally lacking in principles or any sense of morality they were the Ottoman Empire's answer to the humanitarian treatment of refugees.

Obviously pleased with their work the guards then stood back to enjoy the fruits of their labours allowing others with lit rags on sticks to pock them through into the centre of the structure. In an instant the fumes caught, and realising that the liquid must have

been petrol, the flames quickly engulfed many of the lower, outer, writhing bodies while a horrific shrieking scream from within the blinding conflagration resonated through the air. Not being able to bear the horror, or her hopelessness in not being able to do anything to help, Sarah was forced simply to turn away praying for their redemption. Never considering that over the centuries millions of others had met their maker in a similar horrific manner in the name of religion, the scene of that mass of flaming screaming bodies would be etched into Sarah Aaronsohn's soul for eternity.

Sarah Aronnsohn

Ottoman guards

Another previous enlightened group who had at exploited the use of fire in the name of their God had been the Holy Roman Catholic Church. As a proponent of its use historically they had not just burnt at the stake in excess of 106 well known individuals accused of heresy, but thousands of others over the centuries. The recognisable few had simply been a scratch on the surface of their religious efforts in finding terrifying ways for mankind to confess his supposed sins.

Catholic persecution

In their records Sarah would have discovered that in a number of those cases the stripped naked accused had been forced to wear what was known as the 'tunica molesta'; a garment or shirt impregnated with a flammable substance such as naphtha, or liberally smeared on both sides with wax. They had then been fastened to a high pole above which the religiously inspired had continued to pour down, from above, burning pitch or lard. A spike fastened under the chin of the accused had prevented the excruciated victim from turning his or her head to either side in an attempt to escape the liquid fire until every part of their body was literally clad and cased in flame. Multitudes were destroyed by this one mode alone with the whole area of the Vatican circus round which they were impaled, inundated knee-deep with the fatty burning residuum of their bodies.

There are also thousands of other incidents of those condemned to death by fire hidden in the records of many other churchs since Judaism, Christianity, and Islam's Holy beginnings.

Hearing the chilling screams of the Armenians engulfed in flame, Sarah recognised that she had been blinded in thinking that man was intrinsically humane, even in times of war. Thankfully this fire, having become a large conflagration, had quickly sucked in and consumed the inner air. Death for many was now coming from carbon monoxide poisoning before the flames actually caused harm to their bodies. With the sight of the writhing engulfed forms still clear in her mind the victims' chilling massed scream, however, continued to hang in the air. The flames, now fuelled by human fat and a gentle breeze licked through the smoke reaching for the heavens. Sarah hoped the screams of the innocent would heard by all through St Peter's gate also, as this was not the work of a loving God.

Wanting to get as far away from the scene as possible Sarah returned to the train to try and shut the vision, the sounds, and the now pervading smell from her person. It was not meant to be but it would soon be replaced by a new found resolve that would give her a renewed inner strength. Sarah Aronnsohn was resolved to assist her brother and anyone wanting to put an end to Ottoman rule along with these atrocities, and in any way she could.

Since her trip back home to Palestine any alluding to the plight of the Armenians got Sarah physically and mentally upset. Unable to sit and do nothing she decided to assist her brother in his espionage activities.

Eitan Belkind

By early 1915 young men living around Zichron Ya'akov under Ottoman rule had formed an organisation called the Gideonites. This organisation had served as the basis for an espionage group created by Sarah's older brother Aaron, along with others including Eitan Belkind from Rishon LeZion. They would be joined in their efforts by Sarah; Naaman Belkind, who was Eitan's brother; and her cousin and the love of her life, Avshalom Feinberg.

Aaron Aaronsohn

Eitan Belkind had graduated from Turkish military high school and had participated in the team fighting locust invasions with Aaron. Together with other outraged citizens of the Armenian genocide and Ottoman rule such as Sarah, they had founded an organisation which would collaborate with the British against the Turks. It was known as the NILI, from the initials of *netzah yisrael lo yeshaker* - I Sam. 15:29, which translated, read ... *And also the Glory of Israel will not lie or have regret, for he is not a man, that he should have regret.*

From March to October 1915 a plague of locusts had stripped areas in and around Palestine of almost all vegetation. Worried about feeding their troops, at that time, the Turkish authorities had turned to Sarah's brother, the world-famous botanist and the region's leading agronomist Aaron Aaronsohn. His study in France had been sponsored by Baron Edmond de Rothschild and before assisting the Turks Aaron requested them to release his friend and assistant Avshalom Feinberg who they had been arrested on suspicion of spying.

Avshalom had been born in Gedera, Palestine, and had also studied in France before returning to work with Aaron at the agronomy research station in Atlit. With Avshalom's release the team fighting the locust invasion had been given permission to move around the country. With a dislike for Ottoman rule, and the Turks in general, they had taken the opportunity of collecting strategic information about Ottoman camps and troop deployments.

For months, however, the group would not be taken seriously by British Intelligence with attempts by

Avshalom Feinberg

Aaron Aaronsohn and Avshalom Feinberg to establish communication channels with the British in Cairo, and Port Said, failing. Even after Avshalom personally visited British Naval

Intelligence in Cairo at considerable risk to himself he was still not taken seriously. British arrogance just could not see what was being offered right in front of their up-turned noses.

In those formative months the NILI would continue to encounter opposition to their operations, in part from the British, but then largely from the members of the Yishuv who would come to regard their espionage activities as subversive and endangering Jewish settlements.

Back in Cairo Jehanne could not believe their stupidity and she had her say. As far as British Naval Intelligence was concerned she was simply seen as a mere woman who knew nothing of such matters. This was not something you did to Jehanne as she had a memory that stored such episodes as ammunition to exact retribution on any culprit at a later date. It was only after Aaron Aaronsohn arrived in London, by way of Berlin and Copenhagen, and by virtue of his reputation and a supporting communique to MI1 from Jehanne, that he was able to obtain cooperation from the diplomat Sir Mark Sykes. Here, unbeknown to Jehanne, he additionally circulated a memorandum which argued the case for a Jewish homeland that helped make the concept of a Jewish national home in Palestine part of British policy in Near East.

With Naval Intelligence in Cairo now grovelling to its masters in London, in Palestine Sarah was now overseeing NILI's operations operating from Zikhron Ya'aqov.

With the start of summer many wealthy people in Constantinople took advantage of their summer retreats along the waters of the Bosporus. Here, and on its various islands, they would escape the foul air in the city. There was no such luck for the majority of the local populace, however, for they had nowhere to go, and were by now additionally feeling the effects of the war.

On 12th April, 1916 Ahmed again visited his aunt. Being a warm Wednesday he suggested that they walk down to the foreshore so they could take in the sights and be refreshed by what breeze there was off the water. During their amble downhill his aunt explained that life was beginning to bite with increasing prices for food.

There was definitely a greater availability last year, she explained, *but shortages are now starting to be noticed. Rising prices are starting to make it increasingly difficult for those around where I live to sustain anything other than a subsistent living.*

Up until recently local residents had not had to pay for bread at fancy prices, however, over recent months there had been frequent price hikes. By August 1916 most would be in danger of having no bread, and then by January 1917 prices would be increasing twice daily. It was to cause an atmosphere of terror in the general populace.

In order to make ends meet many women were now forced to work, rent out their spare rooms, sell family valuables, or trade in furniture and clothes. At the same time the populace of Constantinople was starting to suffer from epidemics, water shortages, and rapidly spreading fires that increased psychological pressure on them at large. As they walked overlooking the sea another menace cast its shadow over the city in the form of the first air raid by British aircraft.

Looking up from the foreshore promenade Ahmed and his Aunt took in the shapes of two aeroplanes flying at about 2000 feet above them. Ahmed could make out the roundels under their wings and distinct lines that he instantly knew to be machines of the enemy.

Constantinople

These two aircraft had taken off from Imbros, and shortly after passing overhead they would drop 11 firebombs as well as propaganda leaflets over the city. The bombs were supposed to target the munitions plant in Zeytinburnu and the aircraft hangars at Yesilk

Air raid on Contantinople

Even though it was a small squadron with limited armament capacity and an aim of not inflicting damage on the city, it had definitely now sent the message to its inhabitants that even Constantinople was not untouchable.

While some of the streets in Ahmed Aunt's neighbourhood were wide, many of the important thoroughfares were mere lanes. They ran steeply up and down hill with small or large buildings, old and new, shouldering each other along the way. It was here lower down, closer to the water, that the first public Girls' High School in Ottoman Turkey had been intended to be opened prior to the war. It was to use the palace-like summer residence of Adile Sultan. The war, however, had forstalled that opening until recently when it had done so under the name of the Adile Sultan Imperial Girls School, *(Adile Sultan İnas Mekteb-i Sultanisi)*.

The fire that started in Kandilli close to the school while Ahmed and his Aunt were walking was begun, he was later advised, by an incendiary device from one of the enemy aeroplanes. It had supposedly exploded in an old warehouse building, however, Ahmed was not too sure about that as he had heard no explosion and he suspected other hands at work. He certianly hoped it had not been lit deliberately like several cases when he had been a boy when several professional arsonists had been active.

At that time they had been employed by the Constantinople Fire Brigade which had run profitable sideline business in burning down the mansions of the wealthy in order to extort rewards from their owners for saving the valuables within. Whatever the cause of this current fire, flames had leapt the lane directly opposite the warehouse and into a row of houses. Burning furiously, a number of these residences were quickly being engulfed. Fanned by an offshore breeze the fire was thankfully spreading away from the school where Ahmed and his Aunt stood.

Further up the hill in the tight older streets local residents were now rushing with determination to assist in firefighting, while dogs barked amongst a confusion of running shapes in the ever increasing smoke. Combating its spread up the hill would involve all members of the wider community, as not helping could mean homes further afield being consumed leaving theit occupants destitute also. For Ahmed it meant her Aunt's evacuation from the area while he was conscripted to help fight the blaze.

Men of the Constantinople Fire Brigade - an Ottoman army unit well-known in the 19th century for its corruption.

With the potential to cause ever increasing damage given the nature of the flammable building materials there was now a high degree of cooperation among the various ethnic groups who called the area home. Everyone capable competed desperately to stop the spread of the fire. In several areas citizen-formed 'bucket brigades' where their fire-fighting action competed with hand-pumped fire engines. The relatively primitive resources of most fire departments in Turkey generally made most fires difficult to control. Fortuitously being closer to the sea had its advantage in that it took a shorter time to pump, or carry, water in an attempt to contain the blaze.

The fire

It had only been three years since the first motorised fire engines had gone into service in the city and the bells on a number could now be heard as they approached from the east. Ahmed fought his way up a set of old timber stairs to break into an upper room to rescue a little girl who he had heard crying from one of its upstairs windows. Fire had caught its shingle roof, and with her clinging to his neck, one of her small hands grasped his amulet whose cord had accidentally broken. Ahmed carried her to safety through the sparks and smoke to exit onto a lane on the uphill side of the house just as a fire engine arrived. It was here that the child was handed over to an unknown lady. In the confusion of the moment the scared child retained the amulet.

Shifting possessions from the path of the fire

The fire would spread south away from them up the hill as far as a church which would be saved more through good luck than good management. While an attempt was made to stop progress of the flames by demolishing a vacant house with axes it was realised that the fire appeared to have run its course. For Ahmed seven hours of stinging smoke and heat was now replaced with exhaustion and a raging thirst, while the glow of embers and hot spots in the dark again brought back memories of those fearful times on Arafata Ridge when he had witnessed the demise of the wounded in the fires on Scimitar Hill.

Constantinople - WW1

Sitting exhausted he realised that he had lost the amulet. Resigned to the fact that it had been lost in the fire he would continue to help in dampening down the area.

As an outcome of the fire a section of the suburb nearer the sea had been devastated, while a number of stone structures such as a church had survived. Along with the school, and the forested areas further up the hill, they had thankfully not been affected. Fortuitously his Aunt's residence had also been saved. Thankfully there were few injuries and only one fatality. Saving 31 other homes with the meagre possessions of their hundred or so residents had, however, not been the case. These unfortunates' would be left to be supported by those around them, and in a time of war that was not going to be easy.

Whilst this fire, along with the previous carnage and lack of supplies Ahmed had experienced on the Gallipoli Peninsular, had been shocking, the plight of Armenians in Turkish society was becoming particularly soul destroying. It left him wanting to get on a train to get as far away from the degenerate bastards who treated people this way as soon as possible. He would rather face British bullets than experience the helplessness he now felt.

Having witnessed the mistreatment of several Armenians by a number of Labour Corp conscripts he had to wonder whether a modicum of compassion would not achieve a better outcome. Far be it for him to comment least he found himself in a similar predicament. He had experienced that war was often inhumane but deliberate inhumanity to others had no place in honest Islamic life. It would be different if these people had committed some crime or insult against Allah but that was not the case as far as he was aware. His simple faith in a compassionate Allah could not conceive of the treatment and scorn that had Armenian families being treated worse than animals. He could understand the unforgiving nature of military rules by his officers in demanding blind obedience in the face of the enemy but this was something entirely different. Witnessing deliberate mistreatment of helpless woman and children left him cold and furious.

Several of his fellow mehmets were of a similar opinion having all come from small close rural communities with an honest set of values and belief in the Qua'an. It was not these peoples' fault that they had been displaced, nor was this a Holy War on them or the teachings of Mohammed…. Peace be upon Him.

No longer clinging to the amulet as a symbol of faith he simply placed his faith in Allah the Compassionate that he would protect him and them, believing that in the fullness of time all would no doubt be revealed.

An Ottoman official teasing starving children with a piece of bread

The small hand that recovered the amulet from his younger sister several days later was that of a malnourished Armenian boy. Recognising that the object belonged to another, and with a sense of honesty that surmounted all those around him in sincerity and integrity, he had found the first adult he could to give his find to. That person had been Sarah Aaronsohn who was back in Constantinople tidying up her personal affairs while coordinating NILI activity with her friends, and in then visiting her old neighbour, Ahmed's Aunt. The boy's soulful eyes brought tears to Sarah's soft olive complexion. Taking the boy by the hand they went back to Ahmed's Aunt's home where he was given what food Sarah could afford for his mother and sister. When the boy saw the fresh baked bread being placed in the bag his eyes shone like long lost beacons of hope. There between the three differing ethnicities and two religions a simple display of shared humanity was exemplified through the gift of the amulet.

Boatmen at Galata Bridge,
Contantinople

Recognising the amulet as Ahmed's his Aunt had said nothing, allowing Sarah to keep it. With it again carefully cleaned it would be placed in Sarah's suitcase before she again headed south.

Hagia Sophia - Constantinople

Part XVII

For those like Jeanne Blanche, with an interest in the politics and history of the Near East, it could be construed that the Arab national movement has its roots in the literary revival which began in Syria in the 1850's. This revival had ultimately given birth to an Arab national consciousness in the Arab-speaking provinces of the Ottoman Empire and now for the political emancipation of those provinces from their Turkish yoke.

Stretching from the Black Sea in the north, to the Yemen in the south, the Ottoman Empire had existed for 600 years. From east to west it covered land from the Persian to the Greek frontiers, and below this, from the Persian Gulf to the Red Sea. Geographically at it's centre lay the Hejaz, a Turkish Arab Province containing the Islamic Holy cities of Mecca and Medina.

Building the Hedjaz railway

The Hejaz ran from the southern border of Palestine down two-thirds the length of the eastern coast of the Red Sea. It was a barren land consisting initially, from the coast, in five miles of scrub. This was backed by a range of stark mountains seven to eight thousand feet high that led to the burning and featureless 'empty quarter' of the Arabian Desert. With no proper roads the Ottomans had extended their railway line 820 miles from Damascus through Palestine, and then the Hejaz, to Medina. Ostensibly it was to carry pilgrims to the Holy Cities but it now supplied and supported Ottoman garrisons that were now spread throughout this part of the Empire.

It was here that rumblings of discontent had been evident for some time. A project using the Grand Sherif of Mecca as a kind of Caliph to counteract French influence in Egypt had first been discussed in 1860. With no real evidence of Arab support for the

The opening of the Medina railway station

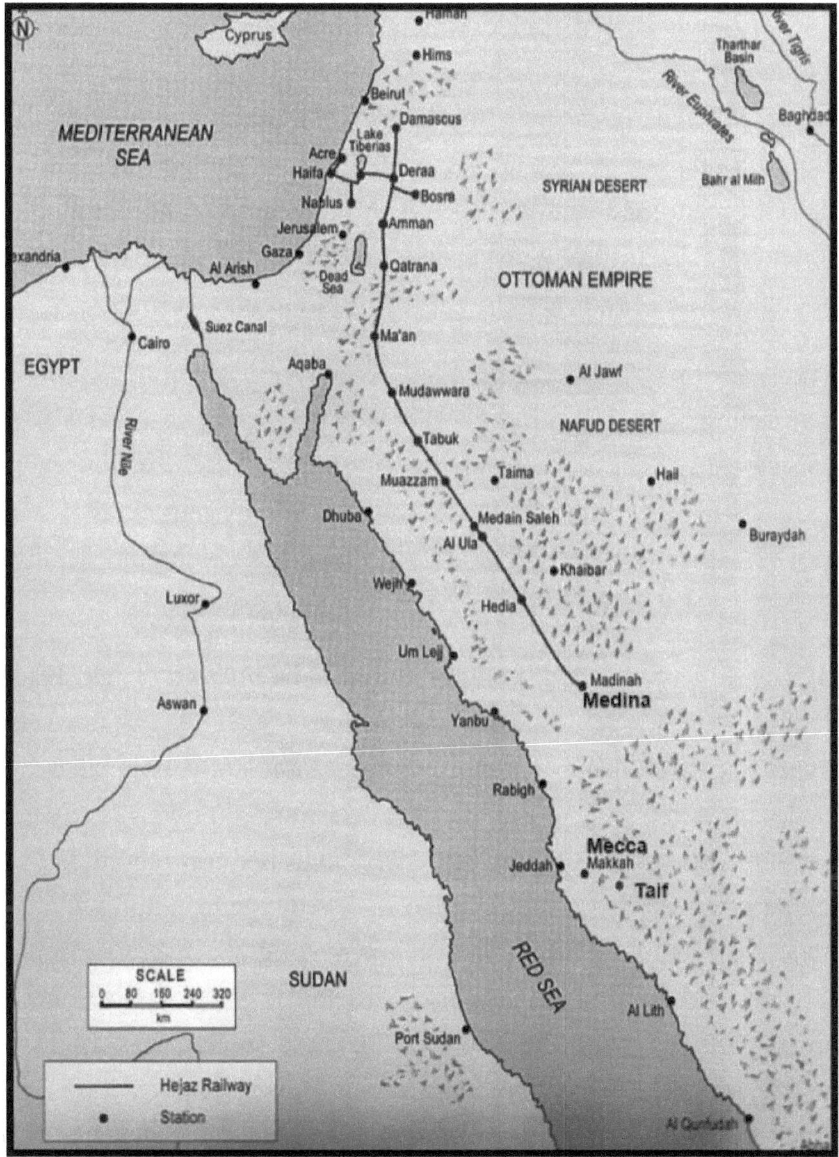

A map showing the Hejaz rail line from Damascus to Medina

idea at that time, later that year, the idea had been decisively vetoed by the then British Prime Minister, Henry John Temple.

Under the Tanzimat reforms of 1858 repressive new Ottoman

Land Law had been issued which offered legal grounds for the displacement of the Bedouin. This law had resulted in an unprecedented land registration process meant to boost the empire's tax base. Few Bedouin opted to register their lands with the Ottoman Tapu due to lack of enforcement by the Ottomans, illiteracy, refusal to pay taxes, and the lack of relevance of written documentation of ownership to their Bedouin way of life.

These reforms, to some degree had acted as a catalyst for Arabs to take action. The first stirrings of interest in an organised national consciousness had appeared between 1865 and 1880 when secret societies had been formed in Beyrouth and Damascus. In these, in the late seventies the Governor of Syria, the celebrated Midhat Pasha, was known to have lent some encouragement.

By the end of the 19th century Sultan Abdülhamid II had been settling other loyal Moslem populations, such as Balkan and Caucasus Circassians, among areas predominantly populated by Bedouin nomads and in the regions now known as Syria, Lebanon, Jordan, and Palestine. The Sultan had also attempted to create several permanent Bedouin settlements although the majority of them did not remain. Then making use of the Tanzimat reforms Ottoman authorities had initiated private acquisition of large plots of state land offered by the Sultan to absentee landowners, or effendis. Numerous tenants had been brought in, in order to cultivate the newly acquired lands that had come at the expense of Bedouin and other indigenous tribal land owners.

Renewed activity on a much larger scale had manifested itself in the years following the promulgation of the Ottoman Constitution in 1908. Arab literary societies, political clubs and other organisations for the promotion of racial interests had been formed in various centres in the years 1909 to 1914. The majority of these were established in Constantinople but they also had branches in Cairo, Beyrouth, Damascus, and, in some cases, Bagdad and Basra. A good many of them were secret societies in the sense that their members, while openly carrying on patriotic activities, were pledged never to disclose the existence of the organisation which directed their activities. These groups were composed principally of Druse and Moslems of Lebanon and Damascus that had, since the massacres of 1860, looked to Great Britain as their protector. They had approached the British Consul General in Beyrouth with a request that the British Government assist the Arabs in their struggle against the Turks.

A delegation of Syrian Moslem notables also visited Lord Kitchener, High Commissioner in Egypt, petitioning Great Britain to annex Syria to Egypt and to give Syria an independent administration. Like His Majesty's Government, Lord Kitchener was aware of the importance of extending British influence in western Arabia as well as on the coast of the Persian Gulf with lbn Saud. Such influence was essential if a Khalifat independent of Ottoman control, and of German influence, was to be created. It was also needed if the still nebulous project of a Trans-Arabia railway from Akaba to the Persian Gulf was to be realised. These advances by the Syrians and of Arab Nationalists had, therefore, been tactfully received.

Having experienced the Ottoman's cruel and repressive regime that subjected those who showed dissension to their rule harshly many tribes simply kept their heads down. By 1915, however, Arab dissension to Turkish rule originating in Syria had spread to be taken up enthusiastically by an Arab Revolt that would come to pass in the Hejaz in 1916.

With the worthy intent of creating an independent Arab Nation for the indigenous people of the land it was seen as a goal worth striving for.

The Hejaz Railway

Col. Mark Sykes

According to a Committee of Imperial Defence paper a section of the British Cairo Intelligence Department, known as The Arab Bureau, had been established to harmonise British political activity in the Near East. It had the added role of keeping the Foreign Office, the India Office, the Committee of Defence, the War Office, the Admiralty, and Government of India simultaneously informed on the general political landscape of Germano-Turkish Policy.

The Bureau had been constituted on the initiative of British Conservative Party politician and diplomatic adviser, Colonel Mark Sykes, in December 1915. He had reported to London at the time that following a recent tour of the Near East from Egypt to India that he had discovered that both the German and Turkish governments were widely distributing anti-British wartime propaganda. Sykes had been concerned because British command posts in the Near East seemed generally uncooperative and thus unable to successfully produce counter-propaganda. He had, therefore, proposed the creation of a London office under his auspices to gather, filter, and distribute intelligence on German and Turkish Near East policy.

One of this office's first initiatives had been recommended as co-ordinating propaganda in favour of Great Britain among non-Indian Moslems. Sykes' proposal had been welcomed by Gilbert Falkingham Clayton, the Director of Intelligence in Egypt, and the Sudan Agent. Clayton additionally believed that such an office

*Brigadier General
Gilbert Clayton*

might not only discover, and counter, enemy propaganda but also be capable of overseeing a wider collection of political and military information. This was information regarding the Near East that in turn would allow him to produce easily understood reports to inform policy-makers in Cairo and London regarding the Ottoman Arab territories.

Clayton's preference for locating the Arab Bureau in Cairo had initially met with resistance from the Government of India and the India Office. They had their own agendas and did not want interference in their control of territories around the Persian Gulf, particularly the Iraq provinces which they planned to occupy and

Jehanne Blanche

cultivate for grain production for India. Additionally superimposed over this were the newly discovered oil deposits located around the Northern Gulf that had brought further attention to the region.

*T E Lawrence and
Gertrude Bell*

Countering the India Office, the Director of Naval Intelligence in Britain, Captain Reginald 'Blinker' Hall, had supported Clayton's concept and urged government approval.

The result was a compromise and in January 1916 'The Arab Bureau' had been established as a section of Sudan Intelligence in Cairo under the overall authority of the High Commissioner of Egypt, Henry McMahon, and the Foreign Office. It was run by Gilbert Clayton, now Brigadier-General, as overall Director of Intelligence and staffed by Near East experts from Military Intelligence who shared Clayton's outlook. T.E. Lawrence would later describe Clayton's role as chief of British Intelligence in Egypt between 1914 and 1917, thus …

Clayton made the perfect leader for such a wild band as us. He was calm, detached, clear-sighted and of unconscious courage in assuming responsibility. He gave an open run to his subordinates. His own views were general, like his knowledge, and he worked by influence rather than by loud direction. It was not easy to descry his influence. He was like water, or permeating oil, creeping silently and insistently through everything. It was not possible to say where Clayton was, or was not, or how much really belonged to him. He never visibly led; but he was abreast of those who did....

Five of those who shared his outlook would be Colonel Stewart Newcombe, T.E Lawrence, Gertrude Bell, Harry Philby and Jehanne Blanche.

Following Colonel Newcombe's survey work in 1915, further front line service had followed with the Anzacs at the battle for Pozières Ridge on the Somme in France before he had been ordered to the Hejaz to rejoin Lawrence. With the majority of the Arab population within the Ottoman Empire now fighting with the Turkish forces, the Arab Bureau started to develop a strategy. They were aware that the German and Turkish inspired, instigated, and financed jihad had only partially succeeded, and not as a cohesive whole. A campaign, therefore, that supported breakaway-minded tribes and regional challengers to Ottoman centralised rule of their Empire may, on the other hand, pay dividends. If nothing else, it was determined, that as a diversion it would certainly require the Ottoman authorities to devote a hundred, or even a thousand, times the resources to contain the threat of an internal rebellion.

As the Allies' needed to sponsor it the question was what would be the bait? Would it be religiously, politically, or economically motivated; or a combination all three?

Ottoman 50 para stamp

Arab irregulars – Sherif of Mecca's forces

*Hussein bin Ali –
Sharif of Mecca*

Hussein bin Ali had been the Sherif and Emir of Mecca since 1908 when he had proclaimed himself, and was internationally recognised, as King of the Kingdom of Hejaz. For the British he had emerged as a hopeful leader to counter any likely Ottoman advances, religious or otherwise.

Hussein was a Meccan cleric with significant influence over other tribes on the Arabian Peninsula. The British believed that if he could insight an Arab revolt the Ottomans would be forced to reallocate their focus, and military, to maintain control over their empire as a result. Likewise their increasing pressure toward British passage through the Suez Canal would be removed.

*Above - Hussein bin Ali
Right - Henry McMahon*

As High Commissioner in Cairo, Henry McMahon was appointed the official correspondent to complete negotiations with Hussein before the Ottomans did likewise. In a series of ten letters from 24th October, 1915, to 1916, McMahon tried to attract Arab support against the Ottoman Empire. To set a lure in the jaw of this fish McMahon, with the approval of the British Government, had dangled the hope of supreme Arab leadership in an independent Arab state before Sherif Hussein and he had taken the bait.

T E Lawrence

By now T E Lawrence spoke passable Arabic and was sympathetic to the Arab desire to gain independence from the Ottoman Turks. He soon ingratiated himself with Arab nationalists who had a desire to revolt against Turkish rule, becoming a confidant and personal military adviser to Prince Feisal, the third son of Hussein Ibn Ali. Acting as liaison officer to Emir Feisal, whom he supported as the most likely candidate to take any nascent Arab Revolt forward in support of the British war aims in the region, Fiesel became a chief ally-of-convenience of the British.

Turkish soldiers

To Jehanne Blanche, the lanky diplomat, and soon to be knighted British High Commissioner, Lieutenant Colonel Arthur Henry McMahon, had seemed on first appearances to be an upstanding man. In her dealings with the opposite sex she had no preconceived ideas but she considered herself a good judge of character. Anyone who looked you straight in the eye and had a firm handshake deserved consideration, and this was the case with McMahon although being a diplomat she was under no illusion that he could no doubt change his position on any matter, at anytime, should it be politically expedient to do so. Having come to know him Jehanne had a fair idea that anything he agreed to would ultimately only be to protect, or secure, British interests, his own aggrandisement, or to cover his own butt. Whilst he was someone who could generally be trusted, in her mind he was deserving of being wary of.

As an extension of his diplomatic activities Jehanne was also aware of what McMahon was now attempting at the British Government's behest. With a British commitment and promise of the creation of an independent Arab state after the war, Hussein was being encouraged to attract support for the Arab people to rise up against their Turkish overlords. In so doing it might just split the Central Powers war effort effectively creating a third front.

In his first reply to McMahon, Hussein had called for the British Empire's written approval for nominated Arab countries rights to independence and self-determination after the war. This included the Arab countries whose boundaries consisted of Syria, Palestine, Lebanon, Iraq, and the Arabian Peninsula, and required Britain agreeing to the proclamation of an Arab Caliphate. Based on that British assurance in exchange Hussein pledged his assistance in a forthcoming Arab revolt against Ottoman rule.

In McMahon's reply to Hussein he intentionally left the boundaries vague for any future Arab Caliphate, which enabled the British Empire to maintain their strong oversight through the Near East. The clear promise, however, was of British support and commitment to the formation of an independent Arab state that included Palestine.

T E Lawrence

The wording of McMahon's reply would later hold special significance, and not just for Jehanne.

As for those regions lying within those frontiers wherein Great Britain is free to act without detriment to the interests of her ally, France, I am empowered in the name of the Government of Great Britain to give the following assurances and make the following reply to your letter:

(1) Subject to the above modifications, Great Britain is prepared to recognise and support the independence of the Arabs in all the regions within the limits demanded by the Sherif of Mecca.

(2) Great Britain will guarantee the Holy Places against all external aggression and will recognise their inviolability.

(3) When the situation admits, Great Britain will give to the Arabs her advice and will assist them to establish what may appear to be the most suitable forms of government in those various territories.

(4) On the other hand, it is understood that the Arabs have decided to seek the advice and guidance of Great Britain only, and that such European advisers and officials as may be required for the formation of a sound form of administration will be British.

(5) With regard to the vilayets of Bagdad and Basra, the Arabs will recognise that the established position and interests of Great Britain necessitate special administrative arrangements in order to secure these territories from foreign aggression, to promote the welfare of the local populations and to safeguard our mutual economic interests.

I am convinced that this declaration will assure you beyond all possible doubt of the sympathy of Great Britain towards the aspirations of her friends the Arabs and will result in a firm and lasting alliance, the immediate results of which will be the expulsion of the Turks from the Arab countries and the freeing of the Arab peoples from the Turkish yoke, which for so many years has pressed heavily upon them.

This McMahon-Hussein Agreement of October 1915 had been accepted by the Arabs as a promise by the British. A promise that Jehanne, along with all Arab Bureau personnel, clearly understood to mean that after the war land previously held by the Turks would be returned to the Arabs, with the exception of French interests and interests in Mesopotamian oil. This was unequivocally the land's return to the people who lived on that land, and who had done so as the indigenous peoples for millennia, and for them to control it politically and civilly achieving their own self determination. Disagreement had, however, rested over the word 'wilaya', or province. Husayn specifically requested, and was promised, Arab control over Palestine but the British would later subtly combine western Palestine with the northern Damascus district, leaving Western Palestine available for colonising. This would meet the needs of another later promise that would be manipulated using political pressure by Jews, out of the British.

As for McMahon, he obviously believed that deception was permissible if the overall goal was achieved; specifically the security of British interests in the region. As a legitimate ploy used by diplomats and solicitors, the word 'deception' would naturally be construed as a lie to by both Arabs and any honest man in the street. The gulf between McMahon's promise on behalf of his Government, and that Government's ultimate intentions based on that lie, would widen with the progression of the war. Regardless of whether they were going to default on their agreements and honour, both Britain and France would continue their duplicity by issuing more assurances to the Arab people, ever hopeful of retaining their continued allegiance.

The Hejaz

Gertrude Bell was only female political officer in the British forces, receiving the title of 'Liaison Officer - Correspondent to Cairo' having been assigned to work out of the Arab Bureau. It was here that she was reunited with Jehanne, becoming her field controller to teach her and another agent, Harry St. John Philby, the finer arts of behind-the-scenes political manoeuvring.

Gertrude Bell

Hejaz Railway - Zat ul Hajj station, 608 km from Damascus

It was subject that Jehanne did not really enjoy, as opposed to Harry Philby who would thrive on it.

'Harry' Philby

Hillary 'Harry' St-John Bridger Philby, would become known as Jack Philby, or Sheikh Abdullah by his Arabic name. He was an Arabist, explorer, writer, and British colonial office intelligence officer who would later state later that he had *become something of a fanatic and the first Socialist to join the Indian Civil Service* in 1907. He had been posted to Lahore in the Punjab in 1908, and from that time had acquired fluency in Urdu, Punjabi, Baluchi, Persian, and eventually Arabic languages. Philby had married his first wife, Dora Johnston, in September 1910, with his distant cousin Bernard Law Montgomery as his best man. He would later marry an Arab woman from Saudi Arabia. He had one son, Kim, later a British intelligence agent infamous as a double agent for the Soviet Union, and three daughters.

In late 1915 Percy Cox, chief political officer of the small British Mesopotamian Expeditionary Force had recruited Harry Philby. By 1916 he had been appointed head of the finance branch of theBritish administration in Baghdad with the title of Revenue

Sherif of Mecca's troops

Commissioner for Occupied Territories. It was a job which included fixing compensation for property and business owners.

Their mission was two-fold. Firstly to organise the Arab Revolt against the Ottoman Turks; and secondly to protect the oilfields near Basra and the Shatt al Arab, which was the only source of oil for the Royal Navy.

The revolt was organised with the same promise as espoused from Cairo, of the British offering the creation of a unified Arab state, or Arab Federation, from Aleppo in Syria to

Harry Philby

Aden in Yemen, when the war was won. With Gertrude speaking Arabic, Persian, French and German, and because both Lawrence and her had travelled the desert and established ties with the local tribes before the war, they had gained a unique perspective of the people and the land. As such the value of their expertise was realised.

Both Bell and Lawrence stood hardly 5'5", yet both could ride

with great determination and endurance through the desert for hours on end. Gertrude aptly described Lawrence to Jehanne as being able to … *'ignite fires in cold rooms'.*

On 3rd March 1916, after hardly a moment's notice, General Clayton sent Gertrude to Basra in Iraq. The town had been captured by British forces in November 1914 and her role was to advise the Chief Political Officer, Percy Cox, regarding an area she knew better than any other Westerner. In this position she would draw maps to help the British army reach Baghdad safely.

Melon Merchants

Part XVIII

Based on the Suez Canal at Ismailia Arthur Edgar Newcombe

along with others in his battalion had been granted leave and he had decided on a trip into Cairo by train to see the sights. In the evil-smelling crowded streets he quickly became aware of the immodesty of the people that were a part of a jostling mix of thousands from what appeared to be just about every country in the world. Some women wore veils while others did not.

Things were generally inexpensive for costing only 10 piastre, (worth about 2 shillings), he visited a French hotel for a late breakfast with others of his platoon, before striding out for the Cairo museum. By chance his fortunes would soar in meeting up with Jehanne Blanche whom he had last seen on the steps of another museum in what seemed to have been another lifetime.

The tram to Giza

Her smile was like a ray of sunshine to him and he forgot the war to gaze longingly again on her femininity. Arthur made enthusiastic small talk with her including asking about how she came to be in Cairo.

Jehanne could see that Arthur had changed. Whilst he had matured she sensed a war weariness as seen in others. It had aged him considerably along with an aloofness and loneliness even though he obviously did not want to see their conversation end. Jehanne told him she was employed working for the Foreign Service in a clerical capacity, and invited him to share a coffee. This offer he accepted without hesitation.

Not wanting to discuss the war, or that she was still in contact with the British Museum, Jehanne simply extended her genuine friendship, playing down her visit to the Cairo Museum as simply one of interest. In a tide of gossip that surrounded them, pervaded by the the aroma of Turkish coffee and pungent cigarettes,

The Nile River

Jehanne agreed to spend the afternoon with him visiting the pyramids about 10 miles away. It was the least she could do she thought; after all he was good company and she sensed he was lonely. With his longing looks that told their own story, he also made her feel needed in some way.

With the fare only 1½ piastres each for the tram trip across the Nile, they made small talk not dwelling on the war or what each had been up to. The picturesque appearance of the river, even though muddy and in partial flood, contrasted with Cairo's old appearance intermingled with its more modern buildings. For Arthur it was a chance to forget the tedium of battle and training, and to believe that life was normal. With his heart soaring and a growing ache in his loin he kept his feelings to himself being every bit the gentleman. They took a camel ride to look in awe at the pyramid of Giza before visiting the Sphinx. Here they stood in a large stone hollow where a high priest, or perhaps Pharaoh, had once talked to his people who thought him to be a God, and they then reflected on their time with Ernest Budge those two years earlier.

Caught up in his love for Jehanne and in having her photo taken for him, Arthur forgot to mention the amulet he had recovered at Suvla Bay, and had subsequently lost.

Jehanne at Giza

The evening's lovely sunset soon turned into the jaws of a heavy storm with wind, rain, lightning and thunder. For Arthur it had been one of most enjoyable afternoons of his life, but now it was as though God was signalling his return to the battlefield. Saved from only having a mental image of her the photo he now had, would be treasured to comfort him during many a cold night to come.

The pyramids at Giza

After making their farewells Arthur again met up with his fellow battalion mates to check out one or two of the local bars in the Birka. In the darker interior of the first bar it took them a few moments for their eyes to adjust to the light. Arthur had no sooner entered when an oversized Australian soldier tripped him, spitting out an insult about British soldiers being no better than wet nursed kids. As Arthur got to his feet to face his aggressor others behind simply pushed him further into the mass of military humanity to find a spare table. As he forced his way past, the Australian laughed and spat on the floor before returning to insult and intimidate one of the local Egyptian staff. Judging by the atmosphere in the place his arrogance and bullying had been the centre of attention in the bar for sometime without any of his fellow Australian reinforcement mates doing anything to stop him. The general consensus from Arthur's pals was that this thick fat slab of Australian beef was just another pig ignorant colonial. One verbalising his own thoughts …

What a bloody great ambassador for his country. I wonder whether their Prime Minister is as thick?

Up until this point their impression of colonial soldiers had been favourable. Whilst brooking no shit they considered New Zealanders to certainly be gentlemen, and what they had experienced of many of the Australians at Suvla had likewise been positive.

Little wonder the Gyppos' piss in their beer ….!

It was a comment offered up from another table nearby that was heard by one of the Australians leaning on the bar. No doubt wanting to see some free entertainment, yet avoiding getting involved himself, he reported the remark to the table where the oversized Aussie bully continued to hold sway. Infuriated by the insult the offensive Australian rose to his feet bristling with rage. He had replaced his desire at intimidating the locals with a new found contempt for the British Army. Yelling explicative's he cannoned at them from across the bar to be met by a kilted sergeant of the Royal Scots Lothian Regiment who, appearing from behind Arthur, held his ground. The bull-necked Australian loaded up with a round house punch that he directed at the Scot.

He simply side-stepped the intended blow, to level a well aimed kick of his own with his hob nailed right boot. It landed forcefully and sweetly between the Australians legs.

Careering two further steps the Aussie dropped gagging and screaming to the earthen floor. A simple stomp to his head would have completed the process but instead the sergeant simply raised his glass to the astounded Australians, welcoming any others that had an inclination to make a similar attempt.

The Australian

Having disgorged the contents of his afternoon's intake their cobber, if he had been that at all, continued to writhe in the expelled contents from his stomach while clutching his scrotum in agony.

Royal Scots

Arthur, along with other British soldiers in the bar had been on their feet in an instant ready for any ensuing fracas, which as it transpired, did not eventuate. Arthur knew it had nothing to do with the Australians not being game, so it had to be out of respect for the crude nature of justice having just been adjudicated on their bully of a mate. With the Scotsman standing aside three of the Australians dragged their still retching cobber from the bar to the cheers, whoops, and abuse from representatives of the other regiments present.

Who are you going to reinforce now…? followed by a final retort were the last words on the subject… *What an arsehole. I bet his mother's a whore and his father's a convict!*

A week later the story of the fray was still being celebrated not just by those who had witnessed it, but by many others; while the injured Australian walked around gingerly, bow-legged, with testicles the size and colour of dark purple damson plums.

Three months later it was reported that the Grand Sherif of Mecca had at last revolted along with his four sons. They had gathered together a large force of Arabs and attacked various Turkish garrisons and outposts in the Hejaz.

Sherif of Mecca's forces

On 16th June, 1916 it was reported that Jiddah had surrendered to the Sherifial forces and that the Emir was marching on Mecca which was then fairly strongly held by the Turkish garrison. It would not be until 10th July that Mecca would completely capitulate.

Abdullah, Hussein's eldest son, had in the meanwhile laid siege to Taif, while the other three sons were also busy. Several towns and fishing villages on the shores of the Red Sea fell, or rather surrendered their arms, including the towns of Yenbu and Umlejj. Being strongly held Taif, unfortunately, was a longer business with it not falling until 23rd September.

During this period of insurrection the Turks brought reinforcements down to Medina via the Hejaz railway, threatening an offensive on Mecca further south. Their progress, however, was slow as their line of communication, the railway, was being continually raided, while their convoys were harassed by Bedouin. Nevertheless Turkish forces pushed southwards and it became apparent that the town of Ragbegh would probably fall into their hands, to be utilised as an advanced base for an attack on Mecca.

Owing to the very mountainous nature of the country and the ignorance of the Arabs, the Sherif had great difficulty in estimating the numbers of the invading force, and their intended line of attack. Recognising this Colonel Stewart Newcombe was now put in command of a Hejaz military mission, to take part alongside Lawrence's tribal forces in mine-laying operations against the Turks' lifeline to the south; the Hejaz Railway. The Colonel's extraordinary exploits and courage, coupled with his seemingly inexhaustible supply of energy, would make him also a legend in the desert, causing the Arabs to complain that ... *'Newcombe is like fire as he burns friend and enemy'*.

In September 1916 a letter was received in Egypt from Hussein Ibn Ali, the 'Emir' or 'Grand Sherif' of the Hejaz, asking the British Government to provide aeroplanes to assist in their revolt against the Turks. The Middle East Brigade R.F.C. Cairo, was approached on the matter, and 'C' Flight of No.14 Squadron was fitted and equipped for Arabia. The concentration of this flight took place at Suez, and on 14th October, 'C' Flight under the command of Captain Albrecht M.C. embarked on the *S.S. Georgian* for Rabegh.

A fortnight previously the commander of No.14 Squadron, Major Bannatyne D.S.O., had left Egypt for Arabia to find a suitable landing ground. Captain Albrecht managed to communicate with him via *H.M.S. Dufferin* and came onboard in the Red Sea to direct them to Rabegh where they arrived on the morning of the 17th October 1916. No landing of troops would in fact be effected for at noon that day a wireless message was received from Cairo ordering the immediate return of the whole expedition.

It was the result, evidently, of there being too many Christians in the expeditionary party.

A month passed while Turkish forces pressed slowly southwards endeavouring continually to `buy in' further Arab tribes along the way. Not having any marked success it was decided that something must be done, so on 12th November 'C' Flight again embarked at Suez for Arabia. This time it was a smaller force in both personnel and materials with an suggestion that these were Christians well hidden. The Flight was under the command of Major A.J. Ross D.S.O. who had an excellent knowledge of Arabic that would eventually prove invaluable in support of T. E. Lawrence and fighters of the Arab Revolt.

The RFC personnel would discover that the conditions and terrain were somewhat harsher than the Western Desert, nevertheless, in six months of operations, 'C' Flight would provide valuable reconnaissance for Lawrence, as well as carrying out bombing attacks on Turkish facilities in the Hejaz.

Harry St John Philby

Jamal Pasha

At the start of the war the Turkish government had abolished Lebanon's semi-autonomous status and appointed Jamal Pasha, then minister of the navy, as the commander in chief of the Turkish forces in Greater Syria. Apart from his command of the 4th Army in Sinai Palestine, he received the rights of Commissioner Extraordinary, wielding absolute military and civil power with added special discretionary powers. Known for his harshness Jamal Pasha was nicknamed Al Jazzar, or 'The Butcher'.

Back in February 1915, frustrated by his unsuccessful attack on the British forces protecting the Suez Canal, he had initiated a blockade of the entire eastern Mediterranean coast to prevent supplies from reaching his enemies. With ongoing economic difficulties, along with the dislocation caused by wave of spontaneous discontent throughout Ottoman held territory south of Turkey, he had introduced martial law in the Arab provinces. Having

Jamal Pasha

additionally abolished the vilayet councils, and the civil court effectively destroying the mountain region's autonomy, he liquidated all the rights and privileges which had been granted to various religious communities on the basis of any international agreement. Jamal Pasha had then proceeded to persecute the Arab national liberation movement, conducting his policy of Turk rule with ruthless suppression of the Arab culture.

As Syria's, Lebanon's, and Palestine's economies began to struggle under his policies, along with the trials of the war, under the pretext of military necessity the Turkish authorities had also begun fleecing the civilian population. With the Lebanese having refused to acknowledge occupation, Jamal Pasha had responded by commandeering the peasants' cattle and food on a massive scale. By 1915 nine-tenths of the grain harvest in Syria and the Lebanon was being commandeered.

Simultaneously the Turks had been cutting down Lebanon's trees to fuel their trains. The outcome would be that their Ottoman forces had consumed more than half of Lebanon's forests, along with the country's fruit trees. Irrigation systems were now neglected with thousands of peasants having been forced off their land to work on all sorts of Ottoman military projects. The logical outcome had been that agricultural and industrial production had

Jemal Pasha with tribal leaders south of Bagdad

dropping sharply.

Even before the war there had been a shortage of home-grown wheat in Syria, and by now wheat imports were almost completely suspended. Turkish authorities took no measures to ward off approaching famine, continuing to arrange food exports to Germany. Naturally prices of essential goods had risen steeply with many commodities now unavailable. This was an environment where the flourishing kings of the 'black market' could make huge fortunes.

By 1916 hundreds of thousands of people in Syria, Lebanon, Palestine and Iraq, especially the inhabitants of the larger cities, had been on the verge of starvation. Lebanon had suffered more than any other Ottoman province with the blockade having resulted in a grave food shortage with swarms of locusts additionally invading the country. The outcome, unsurprisingly, had been famine, followed by plague, which had killed over a quarter of the population. Epidemics of typhus, and other diseases, had broken out here and there so that by the spring of 1915 / 16, tens of thousands of people had died in Syria and the Lebanon.

In Syria one-tenth of the population would die of hunger and disease, with no less than 100,000 people dying in the Lebanon alone. Under these conditions it is understandable why most Arabs adopted a hostile attitude towards the war. They hated the Turks and remained in-different to the Sultan's leaflets proclaiming the jihad as their combined Holy Moslem war. Previously there had been disturbances in several Syrian and Palestinian towns, where the people had demonstrated for bread and peace, and where small spontaneous uprisings had flared up. Now the Arabs were openly rejoicing at any Turko-German army defeat and readily responding to calls from émigré centres to sabotage Ottoman military efforts.

Supervised by German officers under Liman von Sanders', and the German military attaché to Damascus, Colonel Kress von Kressenstein's, command, Ottoman military operations in Syria, Lebanon and Palestine were being overseen from headquarters that had been formed in Damascus on 6th September 1914. In practice, however, von Sanders was the 4th Army's commander with Ahmed Jemal Pasha mainly engaged in securing the rear.

Completely unprepared for a long war, Jemal Pasha also suffered from the lack of good roads. With a need to keep nearly half his troops at the rear, since they might be needed in event of an uprising, he still had the problem that most were unreliable. Of three divisions, two were comprised of Kurds and Arabs from Mosul, with one of Syrians. Jemal had demanded the despatch of Turkish contingents but to date none had been forthcoming.

Jemal Pasha had promised his friends back in the capital that he would sail back to Constantinople via Alexandria. He had, however, been forced to begin his journey back through a sea of mud, and at the railway station in Aleppo he had to be carried out of the train on the soldiers' backs. The situation had been equally disheartening for him elsewhere.

Feelings against the war had spread quickly among the Arab soldiers of the Turkish army. There were cases of mass desertion, voluntary surrender, and even refusal to take part in the fighting, being common. Mutinies had also taken place in a number of towns including the Mosul garrison that had mutinied in April 1916. Northern Lebanon and Syrian Damascus guerilla detachments, known as Jebel-Druze, had then begun an armed struggle against the Turks. Anti-Turkish uprisings, that had previously flared up in the sacred Shi'a cities of Nejef and Karbala, broke out afresh in the spring of 1916.

To counter this insurrection, by early 1916 Enver Pasha had been forced to make several strategic changes in his armies. Other than sending armies to Galicia, Romania, and Macedonia, he reinforced his southern front in Palestine as the British began moves to extend their rail line across the Sinia. Traditional Ottoman forces depended on volunteers from the Moslem population of the empire which by this time, for Enver, had all but disappeared.

There were, however, several short-handed Turk regiments, including Ahmed's back in Constantinople, that had been retained and placed in training in preparation for redeployment as reinforcements to bolster the 4th Army's ranks in Syria and Palestine.

Ottoman Camel Troops of the bodyguard of Jamal Pasha in Barracks Square, Jerusalem, 1915.

Having shown an initial interest in the NILI, Jehanne Blanche was instructed to establish contact and determine the credibility, or otherwise, of their operation in Palestine. As a French girl who also now spoke a smattering of Arabic and Turk she was well placed to be able to circulate as a French volunteer from the International Committee of the Red Cross in Geneva, assigned to the American Red Cross Colony in Jerusalem.

The American Red Cross Society had done notable work for Turkey in 1913, and had a much wider field of activity than any of the other foreign branches of the Red Crescent working with the Turkish Army. Most of the Red Cross missions had confined their efforts to service on the battlefield during the war in

Jehanne Blanche

Thrace, and in the hospitals of Constantinople. Missions of physicians, nurses, and orderlies had also come from Great Britain, France, Germany, Italy, Russia, Japan, Egypt, India, Austria, Rumania, Switzerland, Holland, Belgium, Spain, Portugal, Norway, Denmark and Sweden.

Other than Jerusalem, the American Red Cross had equipped and maintained two wards of 60 beds each in the Tashliska barracks, Constantinople, which at the beginning of the war had been turned into a hospital of 1,500 beds. At that time, congregated outside the walls of that city there had been many thousands of refugees who had been refused entrance to the city owing to the prevalence of cholera in their midst. One particular American missionary had single-handedly prevented 12,000 of these refugees from dying of starvation, and for her brave heroic effort she had been awarded a decoration by the Sultan.

When the Ottoman Empire had entered the war as an ally of Germany an American Red Cross (Crescent) Colony in Jerusalem, known as the 'American Colony', had assumed a more crucial role in

Nurses with Turkish patients display the Turkish flag

supporting the local populace through their deprivations and hardships. The Turkish military commanders governing Jerusalem trusted the American Colony, even asking its photographers to record the course of the war in Palestine.

Travelling the short distance to Zichron Ya'acov Jehanne was charged with meeting up with Sarah Aaronsohn to validate the NILI's work and, if appropriate, to coordinate the relaying of intelligence back to Cairo. Armed with falsified papers Jehanne had been dropped just out of Haifa on the coast by a fishing vessel, and met by a NILI operative.

Sarah Aaronsohn

The beach south of Haifa where Jehanne came ashore

For Jehanne it would be a moving experience listening to Sarah's experiences along with her account of the plight of the Armenians.

During the course of their discussions she also managed to establish that several NILI contacts in Constantinople were currently planning to help more directly. Their intention was to hinder the activities of the Ottoman military by blowing up one of the Turks' munition trains before it had a chance to leave the station. Following this initiative Sarah suggested that she could work in having their Constantinople contacts liaise with British operatives in the city. Having just returned from Constantinople herself Sarah advised that the current planned operation was being handled quietly, and that while it may take some time to bear fruit, it would be worth the gamble.

Jehanne had easily gravitated to Sarah's positive attitude and her willingness to help. Unbeknown to Jehanne only two feet away in a closed box on the desk lay the amulet.

American and Turkish flags flying at the Jersusalem American Red Cross Colony.

After agreeing on a communication code and the process to be put in place, Jehanne made her farewells. Re-delivered uneventfully back to the coast she was collected by the fishing boat to be returned to Port Said two days later.

As for the American Colony of the Red Crescent that Jehanne had used as subterfuge, in April 1917 they would volunteer to administer six Turkish military hospitals in Jerusalem. It would be an offer that would help save the Colony's members from being deported after the United States joined the Allies in the war in the spring of 1917, with the Colony fortunately permitted to continue its relief efforts. During Ottoman occupation Izzet Pasha, the last Turkish military Governor of Jerusalem, had provided the nursing corps with all necessary assistance, including night passes that allowed their staff to move freely throughout the city. Then as the German and Turkish armies retreated before advancing Allied forces, the American Red Cross Colony would take charge of the overcrowded Turkish military hospitals which, by that time, were inundated with wounded.

Part XIX

Formed on 10th March, 1916 the Egypt an Allied Egyptian Expeditionary Force, (EEF), under the command of General A. J. Murray, was now made up of troops from the Mediterranean Expeditionary Force, along with Allied forces in Egypt in the Near Eastern theatre.

A Turkish Red Crescent doctor in the field

Initially created to guard the Suez Canal and Egypt, and provide reinforcements for the Western Front, it would subsequently fight the Senussi Campaign and the Sinai and Palestine Campaign. Included was the 53rd (Welsh) Division under the command of GOC Major General (temp) A. G. Dallas, that still included Arthur's 2/10th Middlesex Regiment, as part of it's 160th Infantry Brigade.

To allow a full military campaign in Palestine during April, 1916 the EEF had begun building the standard gauge Sinai Military Railway (SMR) from El Kantara on the Suez Canal, across Sinai. Borrowing rolling stock and 70 locomotives from Egyptian State

General freight train at Kantara on the Port Said to Cairo line

Railways by 1916 it included 20 Robert Stephenson & Co., 35 Baldwin, and seven small shunting locomotives, along with several saddle tanks of varying ages. The line would reach

Romani by May, 1916, El Arish by January, 1917, and Rafah in March 1917.

Presentation of colours to the 126th Turkish Regiment at Gaza April 1917

Since the beginning of the war the Egyptian police who had controlled the Sinai Desert up to that point had been withdrawn leaving the area largely unprotected.

By mid 1916, further north in Greater Syria, Turkish authorities had found evidence contained in Arab-French correspondence incriminating numerous Arab nationalists as traitors to the Ottoman Empire. As a show of vindictiveness Jamal Pasha had publicly executed 21 of these Arabs simultaneously in Damascus and Beirut for alleged anti-Turkish activities. The condemned had included ex parliamentary ministers, political leaders, a journalist and founder of the Homs-based newspaper, and even a poet.

Then in July a second joint German and Ottoman force had again advanced across the desert to threaten the Suez Canal. This force was defeated in August, 1916 at the Battle of Romani. After this

EEF victory the Anzac Mounted Division, under the command of the Australian Major General Henry G. Chauvel, had pushed the Ottoman Army's Desert Force out of Bir el Abd, and back across the Sinai towards El Arish near the southern border with Palestine.

Above - Ottoman troops defend El Arish

Right - A map showing the relationship of El Arish to Rafah. Gaza and Beersheba

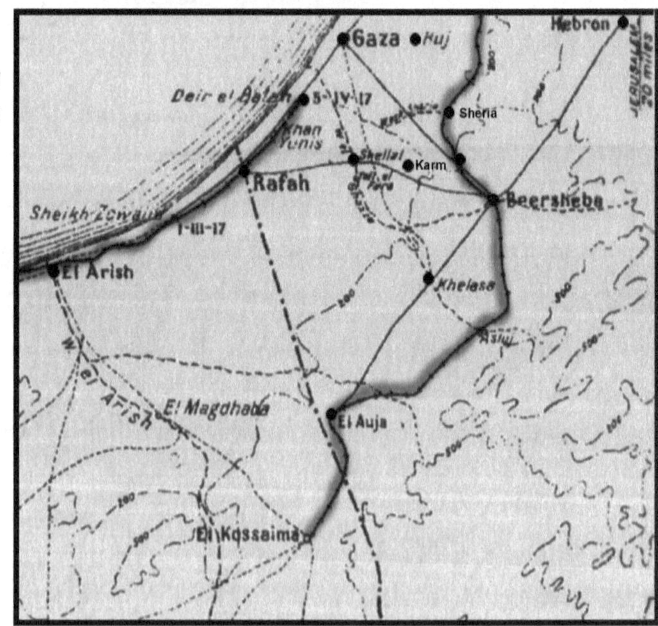

El Arish

The EEF built railway through El Arish

By mid-September the Anzac Mounted Division were pursuing the retreating Ottoman and German forces from Bir el Salmana, 20 miles along the northern route across the Sinai Peninsula to the outpost at Bir el Mazar. 50 miles south west of Romani, in the interior of the Sinai Desert, the Maghara Hills were also attacked in mid-October by a British force based on the Suez Canal. Although not captured at the time all these positions were eventually abandoned by their Ottoman garrisons in the face of growing British strength and pressure.

Part of the Australian Light Horse Brigade

Formed in Cairo on 18th October, 1916, with its headquarters at Ismailia, the Eastern Frontier Force, (also known as the Eastern Force), was commanded by Lieutenant General C. M. Dobell who had previously commanded the Western Frontier Force. Murray had his headquarters in Cairo to better deal with his multiple responsibilities although he had been based at Ismailia during the battle for Romani. Stationed at Kantara was one infantry brigade of the 53rd Division with 36 guns, along with the 3rd Light Horse Brigade detached from the Anzac Mounted Division. The balance of the division was at El Feradan station on the Port Said to Cairo line. This was in the northern half of the Suez Canal zone approximately eight miles east of Ismailia. Here there were many troops including Arthur who was were feeling the shackles of fatigue duty. This included the hauling of two massive chains which were the primitive means of propelling a giant punt that carried men, horses, and stores across the Suez Canal to the Sinai side where the Turks had been, but were no more. Ships were now also coming alongside to be unloaded and out of their holds a long single file of troops could be seen hefting massive quantities of stores. These goods included timber, compressed horse and camel fodder, sacks of dates, raisins, immense quantities of bully beef and biscuits, ammunition and various other necessaries for further EEF advances. With N.C.O.'s posted every ten yards or so, apart from the fact that they had no whips, the general feelings of Arthur and his mates' was that they were now no better off than the slaves of old.

With an an overall strength of 156,000 soldiers, plus 13,000 Egyptian labourers the EEF would establish garrisons along their supply lines that now stretched across the Sinai. Patrols and reconnaissance were regularly carried out to protect the advance of the railway and water pipeline that was still under construction by the Egyptian Labour Corps. These supply lines were marked by railway stations and sidings, airfields, signal installations, and standing camps, where troops could be accommodated in tents and huts.

Opposing them the Ottoman Army's Desert Force, commanded by Kress von Kressenstein, was being sustained and supported from their principal desert base at Hafir El Auja.

Hafir El Auja.

This base was located on the Ottoman side of the Egyptian - Ottoman frontier (Sinai / Palestine) and linked by rail to Beersheba, further to the north, and by road to Gaza to the NW, and also Palestine proper. As the major German and Ottoman base in the central Sinai, Hafir El Auja supplied and supported smaller garrisons in the general area towards El Arish with reinforcements, ammunition, rations, and medical support. It was also a rest location away from the front line.

For the British, if left intact, the Ottoman garrisons at Magdhaba and Hafir el Auja could seriously threaten the advance of the EEF along their more northern route towards southern Palestine.

Asluj Railway Station SE of Beersheba

An Ottoman Field Dressing Station at El Arish prior to the EEF gaining that ground

Now equipped with 233 camels and 94 mules by Christmas 1916 Arthur's 2/10th Middlesex Battalion would be on guard duty at Mazar, on the rail line from Kantara, approximately 25 miles WSW of El Arish. At the same end of 1916 London replaced Sir Henry McMahon in Cairo with the British Governor-General of the Sudan, General Francis Reginald Wingate.

Kress von Kressenstein and his officers at El Arish

General Francis Reginald Wingate

Wingate was a Scot, and 'straight-shooter', who had ascended from an impoverished background with a rudimentary education. Nonetheless, he had mastered several foreign languages including Arabic, and under his guidance, within a few months Sinai would be under British control.

By March, 1917 the railway and pipeline would reach Rafah, with an attack planned on Gaza.

Further afield in Mesopotamia British troops would capture Baghdad.

Above - Building the Sinai Military Railway
Below – Imperial camel Corp (ICC) camels travelling by rail

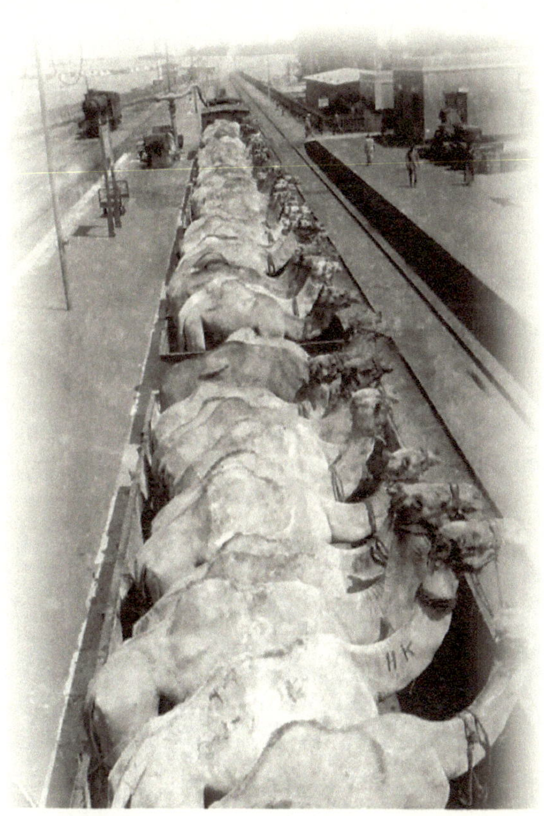

A Turkish officer
officer uniform

South from Hafir el Auja, on the Ottoman controlled Beersheba line, a railway extension had almost reached the Wadi el Arish. Whilst the railway bridge at Irgeig north-west of Beersheba had been bombed by Royal Flying Corps (RFC) aircraft on 22nd December, 1916, when bombs had actually hit their target, they had caused little damage. This solid strongly built bridge along with others on the line had as a consequence been discovered to be virtually indestructible from the air.

Between 7th to 14th May, 1917, during a raid on the wells south of Beersheba, two companies of the Imperial Camel Brigade (ICC), supported by a field troop and two motor ambulances, had successfully attacked the railway line between Beersheba and Hafir el Auja. The camels had been ridden out from their lines via Kossaima with their riders successfully blowing up wells and a stone bridge. They had also attacked a train near Hafir el Auja where five Ottoman railwaymen were captured. Intelligence gleaned from these prisoners indicated they had been ordered to pick up rails south of Hafir el Auja for use on a new branch railway line from Et Tine needed to supply the front at Gaza, leaving the railway between Hafir el Auja and Beersheba intact.

The 18 Arch Ashlar Bridge at Asluj

While the line south from Beersheba to Hafir el Auja remaining intact, it still represented a constant threat to the lengthy British lines of communication that now stretched from Egypt across the Sinai, via El Arish to 5 miles south of Gaza. During the Germans' and Turks' construction of the Beersheba to Hafir el Auja extension, the line crossed numerous wadis on fine arched bridges of dressed stone. An earlier May patrol had found and reported on these well constructed stone bridges, along with the buildings, barracks, hospital, and large water reservoir at Hafir el Auja. Whilst Kress von Kressenstein had been forced to abandon the location temporarily in January as the EEF had advanced up the coast to Rafa, with it now many miles behind the EEF front line, an Ottoman force could still be supplied and housed here with the Turks able to quickly transport large numbers of Ottoman troops to Hafir el Auja.

It, therefore, posed a serious threat and the simple solution was to destroy the railway that supplied it.

Given their previous successful experiences at destroying bridges and rail it was, therefore, decided that two attacking columns would be employed. The first would be under the command of Edward Chaytor. He commanded the Anzac Mounted Division, the Engineers in the 1st Australian Field Squadron (Anzac Mounted Division), and the Imperial Mounted Division Field Squadron. These would be escorted by the 1st Light Horse Brigade aand they would ride from Shellal via Khalasa to Asluj, 12 miles south of Beersheba.

The second column would be the Brigade Field Troop of the ICC escorted by their Camel Brigade, who would ride from Rafa for Hafir el Auja. This brigade would be required to navigate the Darb el Hager that ran along a plain between two banks of sand dunes. It was the only possible way for a large body of troops moving from Rafa. Their flank guards and patrols, however, would discover it difficult getting across the dunes as they rode along the boundary posts designating the frontier between the Egyptian Sinai peninsula and Ottoman held Palestine.

As a diversion, while the raid took place, the Imperial Mounted Division were to make a commotion to the southwest of Beersheba that would be supported by a wire-cutting bombardment directed on the Gaza defences.

By daylight on the 23rd May, 1917, the New Zealand Mounted Rifles (NZMR) Brigade had made it north of their planned demolition site. They were still in touch with the Imperial Mounted Division whose task it now was to hold the Beersheba line preventing any Ottoman troops attempting to stop the destruction of the railway. As it eventuated only a few snipers attempted to interrupt the work and Chaytor's northern column had reached Asluj at 7 am on 23rd May and within three hours they had set and were exploding their charges. This demolition would cut in half alternate rails on both sides of the railway line for a distance of seven miles while the 18-arch Ashlar Bridge at Asluj would also be destroyed with every second arch blown up.

With all demolition work for this first force complete by 1:00 pm the units made there way back to their bivouacs.

Meanwhile the ICC in following the line of the frontier to Hafir el Auja was delayed due to the dunes. They had not arrived until 11:45 am to begin demolitions along 13 miles of railway line that included seven bridges. To accomplish this each force led it horses

Laying the gun cotton charges on the railway line

*Damaged carriages and railway line blown up in the demolition raid
to destroy the railway line running south from Beersheba to Ashluj
and Auja.*

*The AMR at the Railway Station at Asluj - Men of the NZMR
preparing to blow-up the station. A team of Auckland Mounted
Riflemen have a hard working team lifting rails and sleepers from the
rail bed at the left of photograph- the rails are then heated over fires
to soften the steel and then bend the rail to make them useless to any
enemy repair squads who follow - two rails lie twisted in the
foreground.*

who were then followed by the two teams of dismounted demolition men moving in single file at walking pace. Setting the explosive charges began with the leading man placing a slab of gun cotton in the middle of a rail, and then missing a rail, he repeated his action, while the leading man of the second team put down a slab of gun cotton in the middle of the rail on his side, which paired with the rail missed by the other team. The next man of both teams then wired the gun cotton to the rail and walked on to the next prepared rail, while a third man put a detonator and fuse into the gun cotton. With the others moving ahead the fourth man lit the charge.

This squadron would blast a 12–15 inch piece of rail along their designated section of the line, with the bridges wrecked by placing gun cotton charges on alternate arches and firing the charges electrically.

Laying the gun cotton charges at the base of a pier of the Asluj bridge

Approximately one mile east of Auja, to within one mile of the Wadi Abiad Bridge, the ICC had fired their timed and instantaneous fuses together destroying approximately 7,600 yards of single track, with each rail destroyed at its centre. The six-span bridge over the Wadi Husaniya had been totally demolished while seven piers and eight arches of the 12-span bridge over the Wadi Abiad were in ruins. This work continued unhindered till 5.00pm when they to withdrew with their escorts.

The bridge at Asluj being blown.

The outcome was that a total of 13 miles of railway line, and six bridges, had been wrecked. The raid had been a complete success effectively isolating what remained intact of the railway to the south.

New Zealand Mounted Rifles

The 18-arch bridge at Asluj after demolition

Part XX

When Ahmed returned to Constantinople in early 1916 most Ottoman military motor transport was operated by German and Austrian troops. Included were the trains of the Anatolian Railway Company, that had continued under their control, along with wireless and telegraph communications. Admittedly these systems operated much more efficiently once the Germans had taken them over but there were still some inherent internal problems.

A carriage on the Hejaz line

Like a lot of things across the Empire the pre-war Ottoman rail system had been somewhat haphazard and internally corrupt. There were several gauges of rail in use with some tracks ending at difficult terrain, to resume on the other side, thus requiring mule or bullock transport in between. In other instances, such as at the Cicilean Gates through the Taurus Mountains standard gauge rails ended, and narrow gauge resumed until the difficult section was negotiated. Compounding the potential for problems was also the variety of rolling stock types and locomotives that not even German efficiency could not overcome problems with as spare parts became scarce. With bridges often badly built and track beds not able to carry full loads due to poor construction, it just added to their woes.

For Ahmed-oğlu Abdullah the army transport that he had become familiar with had predominantly been bullock-drawn. Whilst they had been terribly slow, affecting arrival times, it had not always been a disadvantage. In some of the worst terrain, like Gallipoli, the bullock teams had effectively been every bit as useful as any rail line or truck, or even more so. In using these the Ottoman army had continued the centuries-old system of supply of stores for their armies on the march. These bullock drawn wagons were designed so that when the stores were used up the wagons themselves became firewood for cooking and the bullocks, likewise, fresh meat on the hoof for the soldiers. This had meant that any Ottoman Army column that Ahmed had been a part of up until now, had got smaller as it progressed.

Additionally it was Ottoman Army practice to use those from within the empire whom they did not want, or who were unsuitable as soldiers, to do other tasks including running the bullocks and wagons. Christians, Armenians, Jews, Greeks, and Kurds all, therefore, either performed medical duties or ran and laboured on the transport systems. With the advent of rail those employed on the rail system naturally now came under the supervision of German and Austrian railway troops who ran the railways.

Building the Hejaz railway

On a section of line on the Berlin to Bagdad railway

On the Asiatic side of the Bosporus opposite old Constantinople the Golden Horn extended itself with thousands of minarets glittering in the sun. Here the neo-classical form of the Haydarpaşa Railway Station, that was northern terminus of the Baghdad and Hejaz railways, stood in all its splendour.

Constantinople

Haydarpaşa Railway Station

With the completion of the railway lines to both Damascus and Bagdad seen as a matter of vital importance to the German and Turkish armies, the German Government had advanced the necessary capital to the Turkish Government to complete the work. With increasing rail traffic, it had been earlier determined

Troops wait outside Haydarpaşa Railway Station

that a new and larger building was required, and it was this imposing structure that Ahmed now entered again with a sense of awe. With its blend of Western and Oriental architecture it had been built and inaugurated in early November 1909 for the anniversary of Mehmed V.

With the advent of the war to speed up construction on the railway it had been decided to build the remaining mountain rail section in southern Turkey to a narrower gauge of two feet, leaving its alteration to standard gauge to a later date. With the mountain ranges of the Taurus and the Caucasus having been pierced at the beginning of 1917 through communication had been established. The 750 odd miles southeast from Constantinople to Damascus in Syria now took around around two days to travel, and passed in the north through Konia, across the Anatolian table lands via Karaman and Ereğli, to the foothills of Taurus Mountains. It then negotiated the Gülek Pass, over the Çukurova plain, and through

Adana, Yenice, and the Amanus range, to Mouslimie Junction north of Aleppo in Syria. Here the line branched to Baghdad in Mesopotamia and south to Allepo in Syria. From Aleppo it was then onto Damascus.

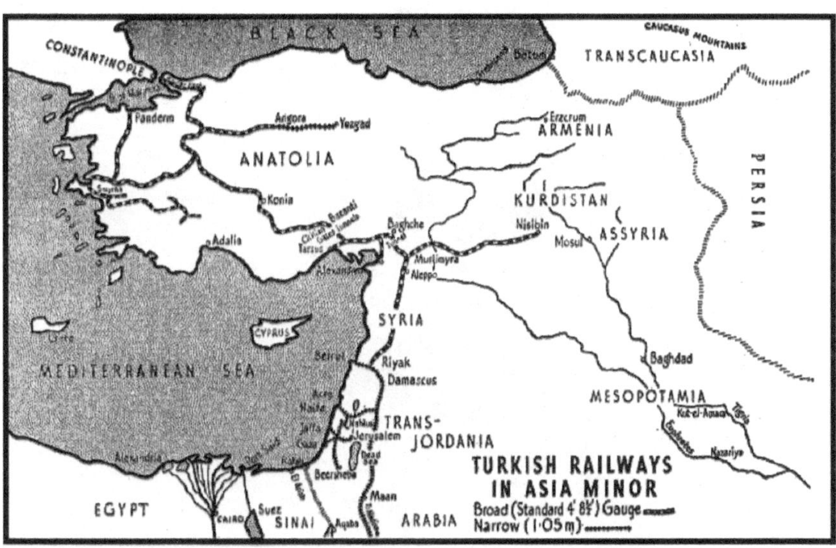

This was not a journey for those in a rush and with this being his first train trip, following their departure, Ahmed and his mehmet friends sat happily watching the olive groves, pistachio trees, and cattle pass the carriage windows. They took everything in while a local man playing the oud, or Arabic lute, added a certain romance to proceedings from the rear of their carriage until they heard a distant series of 'booms'!

Unbeknown to Ahmed as he looked out over the Turkish countryside NILI operatives had just detonated a number of bombs in the recently departed railway yards back in Constantinople. The explosions that occurred just outside the Haydarpaşa Railway Station would destroy several wagons full of arms and ammunition destined for the southern front. Whist

Ahmed and his fellow soldiers sat pondering what had occurred, it had been spectacular. The concussion of the initial blast had knocked platform passengers and passers-by on the street outside off their feet, shaken houses, and blown out windows. The detonation that was heard across the city also reverberated off the water of the Bosporus and Sea of Marama, to be carried for miles.

Following this initial detonation exploding ammunition would continue for several hours, placing at risk any unwitting soul who tried to extinguish the resultant fires. Having obliterated several wagons, along with killing and wounding a number of soldiers and railway officials, the blasts had destroyed a good section of the track. Along with the previous air raid this NILI inspired operation again sent the message that no one was going to be safe in their beds in Constantinople.

Turkish Intelligence would be at a loss to know, or to establish, who had been responsible. Initially suspecting the Greeks the Turks would finally conclude that it must have been local political activists, or the British. There would be repercussions for several suspects but with the explosion remaining a mystery they concluded that they were going to have to be more careful in future.

As for Sarah Aaronsohn her friends' loyalty and bravery had been truly validated, and as the sun set on that fateful day Ahmed was at peace. As the light began to fade he stuck his head out of his carriage window to see if he could see the front of the SLM Swiss built 2-8-0 class locomotive as it wound through the Turkish countryside. He was in his element with farmer waving at him from a field, and thinking that rail was a remarkably civilised way to travel, for it sure beat the hell out of marching.

Ahmed and his fellow mehmets enjoy a meal

Sustenance during the trip would be army rations along with the odd extra that could be obtained, if lucky, from the various stations en route. Ahmed knew, as well as any other soldier around him, that the Turkish army biscuit was as hard as a stone. When they had been in the field the biscuit had often been delivered by being thrown off the back of trucks, or from carts, as they rolled past the units being supplied. The mehmets reckoned bullets could bounce off them. As such they were jokingly referred to as 'armour' to be placed in a pocket before attacking the enemy. Soaked in water and then cooked on a fire, as was intended, the

biscuit was quite edible and certainly p r o v i d e d t h e Ottoman soldier a nourishing feed. Allied prisoners who learnt to use the biscuits the right way also found them OK.

If attempted to be eaten without cooking, however, the biscuit could break teeth with the consumer often dying of enteritis. If attempted to be eaten by breaking bits off after bashing these steely objects between rocks any unfortunate consumer of the pieces would wake in the night screaming in agony and frothing black at the mouth, to then die in great pain. With no cooking facilities on the train, other that a small stove they could use for boiling coffee, the soldiers were at the mercy of what stops the train made to allow them to boil a billy. Trying to allay his hunger Ahmed glanced at a brass dedication plate in Arabic at the end of the carriage concerning the 1908 construction of the Hejaz railway. It had no doubt been read already by hundreds of travellers and pilgrims as they too had raced over the tracks at the staggering speed of 40 mph.

The brass dedication plate

Knowing that they were heading towards Mecca evening prayers were held kneeling on the seats, or in the aisle of the carriage, facing towards the engine. As darkness fell the light of day was replaced by the strains of heavy breathing and snoring that comforted the few still awake. The brass bezelled carriage lights dimmed each time the load came on the steam engine, or flickered with any sudden movement over the tracks. Under the stars of a southern Turkish night the war seemed an eternity away, and eventually the methodical clacking of the train over the rail ties as the miles slipped by lulled Ahmed to sleep also.

At their first stop at Konia the bedraggled looking ravenous mehmets jumped down from the gently aging carriages looking for any vendor who still plied his trade to the passengers of passing trains. Before the war they could have loaded up with bread, sausage, hard boiled eggs and fruit, but that was obviously not the case now. As if forewarning them of some some future event, according to Mehmet Celal Bey the governor of Konia Province at the time…

Abdullah-oğlu Ahmet

Blood flowed instead of water, and thousands of innocent children, blameless elderly, helpless women and strong youths were flowing towards death in the flow.

Returning to the carriage hungry Ahmed again sat huddled in the cramped and close confines of the carriage.

A train stopped at Konia station

After their departure from Konia Station Ahmed again used his hat as a pillow against the timber window frame of the carriage as it again gently vibrated over the rails and ties. Close by another soldier eased the cheek of his backside to express a bodily need boldly with his flatulence. Its silent result would permeate with the combined smells of others in the hot atmosphere. Oblivious to its affects Ahmed was at peace, unconsciously shifting in his slumber with his shirt partly open due to the heat.

Several minutes later the carriage door behind him opened with a corresponding increase in rail noise to return to its lower toned repetition as the visitor closed the door behind him. Several soldiers facing to the rear studied his sneer and piercing eyes that indicated to them that this was someone with no interest in peace.

The vast empty spaces that comprised the Ottoman Empire made the aircraft an invaluable reconnaissance tool. Transported to Turkey along the famous Berlin to Bagdad railway this German aircraft is being unloaded for reassembly.

Having been set loose by their minders in Rome the first part of Simon the Redeemer and Peter the Jesuit's journey had involved

A locomotive of the Constantinople to Damascus railway

travelling on Church papers via Switzerland and into Austria before catching the train from Vienna to Constantinople. They had arrived in time to celebrate Christmas of 1916, but Peter had mysteriously gone missing. Unperturbed, and now in a different disguise, travelling with a diplomatic passport, Simon was making his way south by rail heading for Amman. Here, it was planned, he would meet up with Circassian rebel fighters from the village of Ain es Sir.

Circassian fighters

These Shapsough tribal people from central Europe had initially re-settled in the Moab Trans Jordan city of Amman in 1878. Loyal to the Turks several had managed to achieve high official status while others were involved in policing for the Ottoman Empire. All were generally despised by the Arab with each taking delight at the others death. Not religiously inspired, except to their own Muslim sectarian creed, the Jesuits would need to pay handsomely for their support. With gold in their purses the Circassians would not mind where they were going so long as it involved killing a few Arabs along the way.

Simon the Redeemer in disguise as a Turk

Simon pushed legs and bodies aside as he forced his way down the aisle to the other end of the carriage without taking heed to the remarks of those behind him. He was to return five minutes later. In the process of closing the carriage door his gaze met that of Ahmed, and then his open shirt, before it shifted to other soldiers as he forced his way past again to return to his seat in the rear carriage. Ahmed also instantly recognised him as no friend of Mohammed. This infidel, he thought, was no doubt another arrogant German. He reflected that it would be good when the war was over and they could return to a life of tranquillity … *Allah willing* …. After all there was only one God. Allah, and Mohammed was his prophet, and no German was going to replace him.

He looked out the window again at the flickering shadow of the train over the ground as they made the run from Konia to the

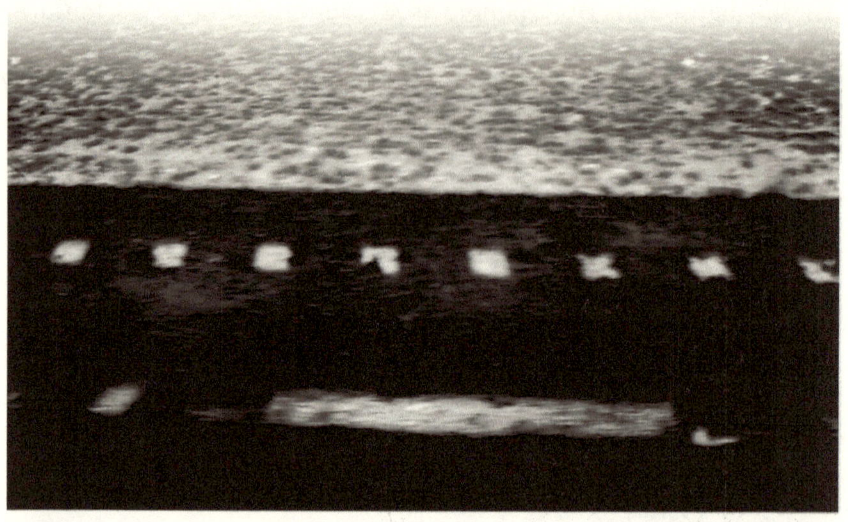

Taurus Mountains. This was a tableland over which thousands of Armenians had been force marched to Syria. Their fate in having avoided the mass killings in northern Turkey had been little better in the concentration camps that had sprung up along the sides of the train track, particularly between the cities of Konia and Gaziantep. Some had only been temporary transit camps while mass graves were dug, while others had been specifically built for those who had a life expectancy of a few days. Several had been vacated by the autumn of 1915 but there were still a few in existence under the command of Şükrü Kaya, one of the right-hand men of Talaat Pasha. The few that remained were situated near the Turkish - Syrian border where their occupants continued to attempt to defend themselves from bandits, starvation, and the wanton cruelty of there guards. Thousands had perished, while others who had flooded into Russia and the Mediterranean ports had faced starvation and disease, that still claimed further lives. An estimated 400,000 deportees had not survived the death march south towards Syria and Mesopotamia. Whilst the Turkish government supposedly ended their Armenian campaign of genocide in the summer of 1915 in the remaining camps, or anywhere they were found, soldiers and guards continued to be permitted to taunt, rape, brutalise, and kill remaining Armenians with impunity.

Turks rounding up Armenians

Having approached the Taurus Mountains on part of the railway only recently opened, the passengers were transferred onto the narrow gauge line. This section would negotiate the pass known as the Cilician Gates that allowed access from Anatolia to the Cicilean plains and its main centre of Adana.

The railway workshops at Belemedik erected for the building of the Baghdad Railway. The Taurus Mountains can be seen towering up in the background.

Above - A train exits one of the new tunnels

Back - Tunnelling work during the building of the railway

With the completion of the line to Bagdad seen as a potential shortcut to India it had brought pressure on the British in that it created a means of transportation between the two strategic areas of Anatolia and Mesopotamia thus negating the need to use the Suez Canal. The uncompleted line and tunnels, however, had created bottlenecks hampering the transportation of supplies from Anatolia to the Ottoman and German armies stationed in Mesopotamia and Palestine.

Tunnelling works had been accelerated, and the two feet width of the narrow gauge track that was laid for construction purposes had finally become operational through the two larger tunnels. The longest of these was a five mile tunnel between Ayran and Fevzipaşa which had been completed in early 1917. It now allowed the Turks to carry war supplies using a fleet of about one hundred engines that were supplied by Henschel. Being of narrower gauge troops and freight had to be unloaded on the standard gauge line and reloaded on narrower gauge wagons for the trip through the tunnels and over the viaducts to the Cicilean plains and on to Adana station. These tunnels would not be fully completed with a standard gauge line until a few days before the Mudros Armistice in late 1918.

Their train crosses one of the newly build viaducts

For Ahmed it was exciting in the open air wagons knowing that he was one of the first to travel the route although that feeling soon dissipated after the first of the close, pitch black tunnels, and then swaying precariously over a temporary viaduct with a sheer drop of hundreds of feet to the rocks below.

Onwards they were transported, to make a brief stop at Adana before negotiating the Amanus range. Having negotiated that obstacle they would continue to first steam through Mouslimiie Junction where the line branched off to Bagdad, and via the southern line to the main station of Aleppo.

Adana Railway Station

As the second oldest railway station in Syria Aleppo station was more commonly known as the Gare de Baghdad, however, it was not their stop.

Workers attempting to get a derailed train back on the track

RFC aeroplane shot down in Northern Palestine being transported to Turkey being transported north of Aleppo -1917. Below - Aleppo Railway Station 1917

Part XXI

Oudehi station

South of Aleppo they would arrive at Oudehi station where they were advised they were stopping for 30 minutes and where they could disembark to stretch their legs.

Make sure you are back on board five minutes before the departure time of 12.30 ... had been their final instruction.

Strolling to the end of the station Ahmed looked out over a grove of olive and orange trees in the direction he had been told there was an Armenian refugee camp. Seeing a line of what looked like women and children between the trees he walked, unobserved, in that direction. He was now away from the rest of the troops who were content to stay in the shade of the station, or try to get into its cooler confines.

The rural setting and upright healthy nature of the trees with their glossy green leaves brought back memories of home. He was about to walk further when he came across two unkempt Teşkilat-i Mahsusa guards cajoling a group of women towards a fence. One was lashing out with a stout stick. Ahmed knew of the Ottoman Labour Corp that used force labour along with released convict guards, but he had not experienced their hard pressed vindictive brutal behaviour before. He did not consider himself a devote Muslim by any stretch of the imagination but he did follow, as best he could, the teachings of Muhammad. For him it was the only way to achieve closeness to God and salvation in the afterlife. With no intermediary between Allah and man, by simply remembering Allah, Ahmed believed he could establish direct contact with Him. When dealing with others he always tried to bear in mind that Allah was watching over him. In order to avoid recrimination when his actions were ultimately weighed up on the divine scales of justice it was essential that he avoid, wherever possible, evils such as cruelty, dishonesty, pride, antagonism, jealousy, selfishness and callousness. If one feared Allah, one would not treat His creatures with disdain, for those who mistreated Allah's creatures should not expect kindness from him, or the Creator; only those who had treated others well would deserve good treatment.

Armenian refugees

That belief, however, did not negate one from supporting one of the most important tenants of the faith, and that was Al-Jihad, or 'holy fighting'. By abandoning Jihad he and his fellow soldiers believed that Islam would be destroyed by Muslims falling into an inferior position; with their honour lost, their lands stolen, and their rule and authority vanishing. Jihad was, therefore, an obligatory duty in Islam on every Muslim, and any who tried to escape from that duty, or did not in his innermost heart wish to fulfil that duty, would die with the qualities of a hypocrite.

Whilst he had been taught that women could be an evil omen and the most harmful thing for men, as written in the book of Mohammed, what he was now witnessing was not right and came as a shock to Ahmed.

Armenian mother and daughter with a dead child outside of Allepo

He reflected on the words of the prophet… *And, forbidden to you are, wedded women, those with spouses, that you should marry them before they have left their spouses, be they Muslim free women or not; save what your right hands own, of captured slave girls, whom you may have sexual intercourse with, even if they should have spouses among the enemy camp, but only after they have been absolved of the possibility of pregnancy after the completion of one menstrual cycle; this is what Allah has prescribed for you.*

Two of the Teşkilat-i Mahsusa released convict guards had dragged one woman from the group at bayonet point to a low waste high mud brick wall. While one pulled her arms across the wall with his feet wedged against it to hold them taught and extended, the other taller guard had positioned himself behind her. Spreading her legs forcefully with the aid of the bayonet and by kicking her insteps he positioned his boots so she could not close her legs. While his compatriot restrained her arms, grinning like a hyena at her wild terrified look, the taller mehmet sheathed the bayonet and lifted her skirts ripping at her undergarments to reveal her bare buttocks and femininity. Groping with his left hand between her legs he penetrated her with his fingers as he ripped at the buttons of his breeches with his other hand. Competing with the flies for her exposed under garment and flesh he exposed his now rigid penis. With his breeches around his knees he excitedly guided it with his hand to her vagina before thrusting it home with a force that

An Amenian woman

forced his captor against the wall. She let out a scream as he penetrated her. This only egged both soldiers on, as the one perpetrating the act continued to forcefully ride up inside her. With her continuing to cry out in vain his thrusting eventually peeked after several minutes with his climatic ejaculation inside her.

Satisfied with his few minutes of pleasure he slipped out of her to return his manhood to his breeches before walking away doing up his buttons. The other sneering guard released the victim's arms, pushing her to the ground before strolling off in the opposite direction without a word or backwards glance.

He was off to select one of his own.

An Ottoman guard

Ahmed was aghast. This rapist's self-guided life was unprincipled. Unconcerned about the nature of reality or the effect on others his efforts were all centred on worldly gain and his own debauched desires. Having developed into the selfish, cruel person that he was, it was the opposite of what Allah and His prophet would like to see. His behaviour sickened Ahmed as he spoke quietly to himself … *There is no one worthy of being served save Allah, and Muhammad is His messenger.*

Watching the perpetrator retire to the shade of a nearby tree to light a cigarette, Ahmed moved towards him silently. The guard had his back to him oblivious to his presence in his now relieved and relaxed state. With Ahmed's hand suddenly clamping the guard's mouth he quickly and forcefully drove his bayonet in through the guard's back, piecing a kidney, and through his stomach to exit just under his diaphragm. With the quiet words, *Allah is merciful...* he let the body slump to the ground. In his simple way of thinking this infidel had broken the code of Muhammad and deserved to die. The woman was not his slave to do with as he desired; she was a slave of the Empire.

Quickly making his way back to the station under cover of a small embankment Ahmed skirted the station master's structure to look back down the track. Most of the soldiers, and other passengers, were at the other end of the station near the rear of the train. Ducking across the track he made his way past the engine and up the far side of the line of carriages until he came to the one he was travelling on. Mounting the footplate he quickly entered the carriage to be back in his seat a moment before their young officer started herding the balance of the troops back onboard. Ahmed feigned sleep and appeared to wake as others crowded around him. The officer looked down on him and asked if he had been off for a break to which Ahmed indicated he had simply disembarked to relieve himself before returning to secure a more comfortable seat. The officer grinned…. *Better four hours of comfort than 20 minutes of fresh air and a sore bum ... heh?* Ahmed simply smiled and nodded his head.

Further south a rail connection had been made to the Hejaz line through Rayak. This had effectively extended the reach of the Ottomans to the Suez Canal and served as a symbol of the growing influence of Germany in the Middle East at the time. As such all these considerations for the British weighed in favour politically in helping to endorse the war.

With a heavy clunk of the couplings the engine's drive wheels slipped and squealed before biting into the rails as the train got under way. Their next stop was Damascus; Headquarters of the IV Army, and where they were due to leave the train. They would run through Hama and Homs to Rayak Junction in the Lebanon Valley, where the line branched to Damascus, and to the Hejaz line. From Rayak Junction the final part of their trip

Abdullah-oğlu Ahmet (right)

would run ESE on the Beirut to Damascus line.

Off to the west, on the coast, lay Beirut with its good, if small, port, that was connected also by road with Damascus. In sharp contrast to its surroundings the great green plain in which the largest urban settlement in Syria lay came into sight like a Nile Delta. The brown rocky country about it was like desert sand beside the rich belt of green fed and purified by the rushing Adana and Pharpar rivers. Hidden in the forest through which only its noblest features were seen from a distance was this the most ancient of cities, Damascus. For Ahmed he did not see its towers

Above - Baramke railway station - Damascus
Below -Abdullah-oğlu Ahmet marching through Damascus

until they were just about upon it. He had made out a number of outer suburbs that climbed up barren ridges of clay on the surrounding hillsides, as they had got closer.

Without incident they entered the city proper, at 6:00 pm on 3rd March, 1917, to pass Serai Square and pull in at the Baramke Railway Station, close to the Baramke Army Barracks.

Damascus

Turkish troops - Damascus

With their gathered stores and equipment on the platform, Ahmed slung his rifle over his shoulder and looked back at the train as it departed on its continued trip heading for the Hejaz line. The last passenger his eyes came in contact with was that of Simon the Redeemer. His piercing stare made him uncomfortable for some inexplicable reason, and it struck him that he was glad that he had nothing to do with him.

With a population that was singularly proud, conservative, and jealous of western interference, in this city the tarbush–wearing Syrian was the most common. Ahmed would learn that on the city's north western edge, in and around the main suburb of Salahiyeh, that there were Kurds, Algerians and Cretan Moslems. One fifth of those living in the city were Christians, of all denominations, including the odd remaining Armenian and some Jews of very ancient settlement. Almost all of the remainder were Arab Moslems. As for the tented Bedouin Arab nomads they were predominantly located in an oasis lying to the east. They had been advised to be wary of them and to steer clear.

Ottoman troops with an ammunition tender in Damascus

Sandjakdar - Damascus

Troops of the Mevlevi Regiment – Damascus 1917

These Bedouin had made the environs of Damascus less safe to live in than the desert, being more likely to steal, loot, or join in an attack on the city than to help its defence. As one of the most independent of mankind's groups, they acknowledged no authority, only taking orders from those who were able to exact obedience from them by force of arms. Counterpointing this the inner city had trams and electric light, with most of the buildings of the variety one might have seen in certain small towns on the Riviera. While beautiful gardens surrounded the place, most of the country outside was bare and stoney.

Ahmed now joined other troops in the streets and through the narrow bazaar alleyways, between Salaniys and Amara, where on his time off he could enjoy a coffee in one of the small cafes.

A young Ottoman soldier deals with a local Damascus merchant.

The most interesting building to Ahmet was the Great Mosque. It was an enormous place and one of the few edifices where both Christian and Islamic services were held under the same roof; with one half of the building being reserved for the Christians and the other for Mohammedans.

At the end of August 1916 another battalion of regular recruits had been added at Damascus to support an already 800 strong dervish battalion, to form the Mevlevi Regiment. The original battalion had been formed in December 1914 in Konia, and sent to Damascus at that time to also serve under the command of 4th Army.

The town square - Allepo

A Turkish Railways' belt buckle

Part XXII

Continuing to be engaged in active espionage for Britain under the leadership of the agronomist Aaron Aaronson, by now the NILI were achieving results. In her brother's absence Sarah Aaronsohn, along with her sister Rebecca and their friend Avshalom Feinberg, had continued to operate with others from their Jewish agricultural community and village. Coded messages were received intermittently from Sarah by pigeons that had been smuggled ashore and into Zikhron Ya'akov.

Atlit

NILI's independence from mainstream Zionist politics had, by now, made it controversial but the group had maintained its activities. With Aaron having begun travelling more between Europe and Cairo, and Avshalom Feinberg having disappeared in 1916 in an aborted expedition to Egypt, things had been left to Sarah.

From the end of 1916 until October 1917 Sarah Aaronson would coordinate and manage the NILI's activities in Palestine and the Lebanon area, handling a core of about 40 agents, its larger circle of supporters and informers, and the organisation's finances. She decoded and sifted information, encoded it and communicated with British Intelligence headquarters in Cairo; making contact from their Atlit station located south of Haifa. This location had originally been an outpost during the Crusades, and then in 1903 a Jewish village had been founded here, again under the auspices of Baron Edmond de Rothschild.

When he arrived in Palestine, Yosef Lishansky had sought to join Hashomer, but being denied membership, he had founded a rival organisation, known as Hamagen. Then in 1916 he had joined the NILI.

From February to September, 1917, the British warship *HMS Managam* regularly sailed to the Palestinian shore near Atlit. It was from here that Yosef Lishansky would swim out to the ship to deliver NILI information, and return with Jewish American money that had been converted to gold. The presence of German submarines operating out of Jaffa, however, had made these trips too risky and so the group had switched back to the use homing pigeons.

At Zikhron Ya'akov Sarah supervised the transmission by NILI agents of the Jewish American gold that was also used to aid a Jewish population that was by now suffering destitution, hunger and dislocation. Unaware of more subversive underground activities Sarah additionally liaised with the Turkish authorities, along with the increasingly hostile community of her native colony, and the formal leadership of the Yishuv, which by now had distanced itself from their NILI organisation.

German U-boat Jaffa harbour 1917

Following the success of the attack on Contstantinople rail using Sarah's contacts, Aaron Aaronsohn now had an idea for a far bolder plan. He recommended to the British that they should make an overall plan of attack through Beersheba. It was a plan that would ultimately be used by Allenby, and its intent was to break the Gaza to Beersheba line allowing the capture of Jerusalem by Christmas 1917.

Due in large measure to information supplied by NILI to British Intelligence in Cairo concerning the locations of oases in the desert, General Edmund Allenby was now able to plan to mount a surprise attack on Beersheba, unexpectedly bypassing the now strong Ottoman defences at Gaza.

The spoils of war.... A captured Ottoman flag

For the next planned attack which was on Gaza, it was proposed there would be six brigades involved, and all were going to require sustenance. With a brigade of Australian Light Horse, New Zealand Mounted Rifles, and Bristish Yeomanry each consisted of approximately 2,000 soldiers and horses at war establishment, it was obvious to their commanders that it would be a vast undertaking keeping supplies up to them. In this regard in January 1917 the British War Office in London agreed to British infantry divisions being re-equipped with wheeled transport instead of camels. This was, however, on the condition that any personnel to operate them had to be found locally, as none were available from elsewhere.

By the end of February, 1917, 388 miles of railway had been laid by the British towards Palestine, 203 miles of metalled road, 86 miles of wire and brushwood roads had been layed, along with 300 miles of water pipeline. Transport was, therefore, reorganised so that the horse-drawn and mule-drawn supply columns were combined with the camel trains to support this Eastern Force who were by now operating at about a day's journey north beyond the railhead.

British infantry marching on the wire road across the desert between Bir el Mazar and Bardawil in February 1917

The wagons of the Anzac Mounted Division were pulled by teams of mules; two in the pole and three in the lead, and driven by one man from the box. These wagons and mules did such excellent service that the five-mule team was now prescribed for the complete EEF, ultimately almost superseding the British four, or six, horse ride-and-drive teams.

By the 1st March the railhead had reached Sheikh Zowaiid, 30 miles south of Gaza, and by the middle of the month they had reached Rafa, 12 miles from Deir el Belah. It was here that the Royal Navy undertook to land stores on the beach to additionally help. This landing area was well within range and more suited for an attack on Gaza by mounted troops and infantry.

After their losses in the battle of Rafa, on 5th March, the Ottoman Army had retreated from Shellal to a line on the north side of the Wadi Ghuzzeh that ran from Gaza, not far from the Mediterranean Sea. They were discovered to be 14 miles to the north and northeast, having extended their line between Gaza and Beersheba; with additional support 12 miles to the northwest at Tell es Sheria where the railway to Beersheba crossed the Wadi el Sheria.

Horse lines at El Arish

In preparation for the assault on Gaza bombing attacks were now being carried out by the Royal Flying Corps (RFC) on Beersheba,

Tell es Sheria, and on the junction of the Beersheba and Jaffa–Jerusalem line.

As Commander-in-Chief of the EEF, Murray had agreed with his Eastern Force commander, Dobell, on a plan to attack the coastal town of Gaza at the end of March. Despite the delay he considered an early surprise attack to be essential otherwise it was widely believed the enemy would withdraw without a fight.

Above - Aircraft of the RFC at Rafa.
Right - British tent line

On 20th March Dobell moved his headquarters from El Arish to Rafa where, with due celebration, a Rafa railway station was opened. Then on the 21st with trophies having been ordered from Cairo and a programme printed, a Rafa Horse

Race Meeting was held. Complete with an enclosed paddock, totalisator, jumps, and a marked course, each race was contested by Yeomanry, Australians, and New Zealanders.

New Zealand Mounted Rifles in sight of 'Jacko'

After this grand day out at the races preparatory moves to put the plan to attack Gaza began. All roads and tracks possible for wheels were carefully reconnoitred as far as Deir el Belah, with each allotted to the different formations. As a result of the advance to Rafa, and the lengthening of the EEF's lines of communication along the coast, these tracks now overlapped with the Ottoman lines of communication further inland and it was consequently necessary to strongly garrison this territory.

On the 24th Dobell issued orders for the forthcoming battle. By this stage the railhead had reached Khan Yunis where, fortuitously, an almost unlimited supply of water had been discovered that could be exploited. There was still insufficient transport, however, to support operations at any considerable distance from the advancing railhead. To help relieve this shortfall the Egyptian Camel Transport Corps was augmented with horse-drawn wagon trains from the infantry divisions.

British artillery at Deir el Belah - March 1917

Private Arthur Newcombe's 53rd Division were designated to lead the attack on Gaza on the 26th. They had been assigned to the Desert Column under the command of Lieutenant General Chetwode, with their division remaining under the command of Major General A.G. Dallas, and Arthur's brigade under the command of Brigadier General V. L. N. Pearson.

While Arthur and his battalion mates were preparing for the forthcoming battle, back in Cairo Gertrude Bell had been summoned to Baghdad as 'Oriental Secretary.' Her work would later be specially mentioned in the British Parliament, and she would be awarded the Order of the British Empire (OBE). Arthur would be promoted to Lance Corporal which to him, personally, was a distinction no less lofty.

On 25th March, 1917, the Anzac Mounted Division moved out of their bivouacs in two columns. The first column consisting of the New Zealand Mounted Rifles Brigade, and 22nd Mounted

Yeomanry Brigade, marched up the beach from Bir Abu Shunnar at 2:30 am. They had been designated to go out in front to

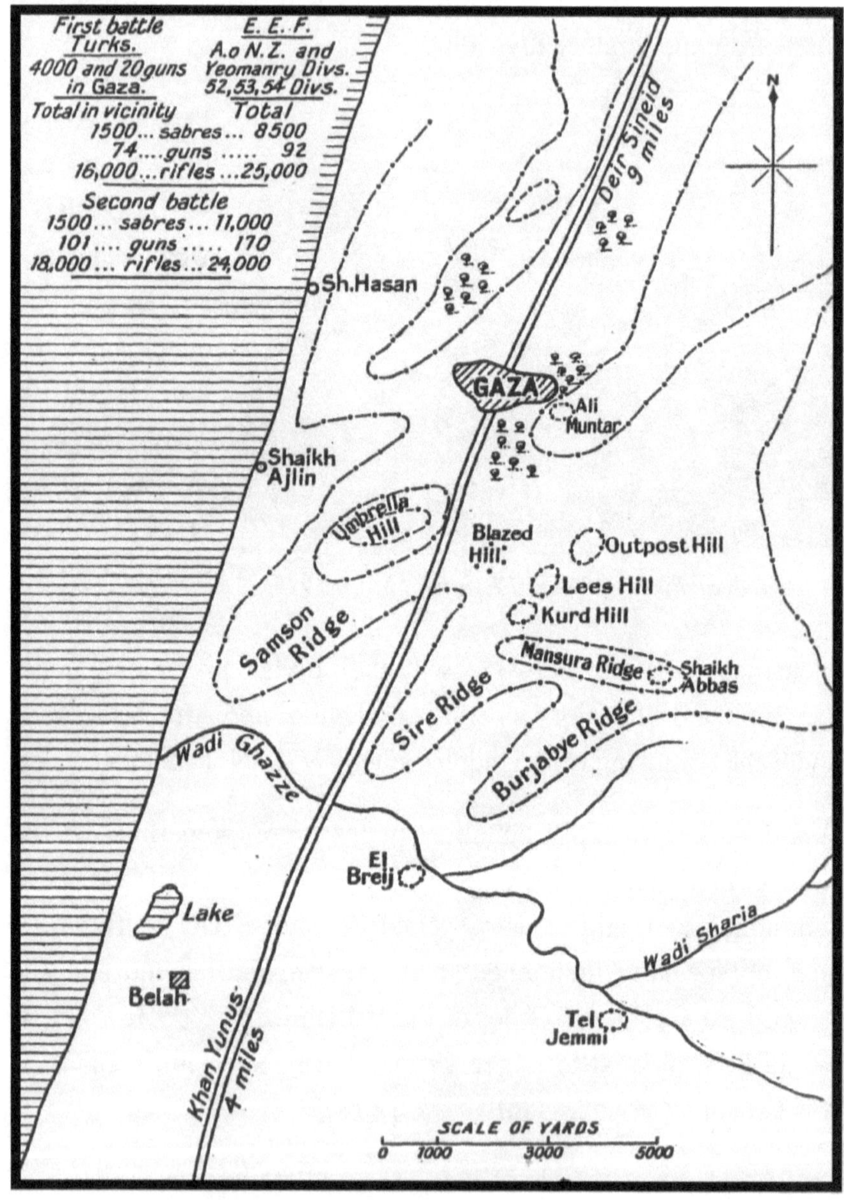

Map showing general location of features pertaining to the Gaza attacks - First and Second Battles of Gaza - March & April 1917

establish a line just south of the Wadi Ghuzzeh and to find the best place to cross this formidable deep dry wadi, for both the infantry and mounted troops.

The second column consisting of Anzac Mounted Division's Divisional Headquarters, Signal Squadron, Field Artillery, and 2nd Light Horse Brigade as Divisional Reserve, arrived southwest of Deir el Belah, where they were ordered to water and bivouac. By 10:00 am both Chauvel and Chetwode had established their Divisional and Desert Column Headquarters on a hill designated as Hill 310.

Troops wait in Wadi Ghuzzeh

While the Ottoman army positions at Gaza had been reconnoitred and photographed from the air, it was still necessary to carry out reconnaissance of the Wadi Ghuzzeh in person. In the afternoon possible crossings were carefully reconnoitred and an intended crossing point finally chosen and marked near the Wadi Sheria.

The mounted force commanded by Chauvel and Hodgson was to

pursue any enemy force that showed signs of retiring, and if necessary to support the main assault on Gaza that was to be made by the 53rd Division under the command of Dallas. They would be reinforced, if necessary, by the 161st Brigade.

By 5.00 pm on the evening before the attack, Anzac and Imperial Mounted Divisional Commanders, along with Dallas, had received their orders. Dallas's orders directed Arthur and his fellow foot soldiers to begin crossing the wadi at 3:30 am the following morning and to advance up the Burjabye and Es Sire Ridges. Another two brigades were to follow them across the wadi and remain on the opposite side until further orders were received.

By 3.50 am Arthur and the Desert Column had marched from Deir el Belah in increasing fog that had begun to develop. By the time they were close to the wadi the fog had become so thick that the expectation of an unknown enemy in its depths led to uneasiness in the troops. With a positive belief in the ability of his commanders Arthur crossed quiet happily. As far as he was concerned the fog was his friend and the longer it lasted the better. He reasoned that what he could not see, could not harm him, even if it was the same for Johnny Turk. At least they weren't facing hidden snipers behind trees as they had experienced at Suvla Bay. Any thought of the amulet had long since been forgotten so why it returned to his thoughts during the crossing of the wadi was strange. Maybe it was his heightened sense of awareness, or was it that subconsciously he thought he needed a good luck keepsake?

Concentrating on their advance any thought of the amulet slipped from his mind once more. By this time most of the infantry had crossed around dawn at 5:00 am the fog was so dense that objects could not be seen 20 yards away. It had been with them for about four hours now but it was now appeared to be starting to lift.

While Arthur had been comforted by the fog it had made it impossible for his Divisional Commander, A. G. Dallas, to reconnoitre the proposed battleground. He waited at El Breij for it to lift more, while Arthur and his fellow soldiers continued to move slowly forward.

By about 7.30 am visibility started to improve and by 7.55 am the fog had lifted sufficiently for heliographs to be used to communicate with headquarters. It was around this time that Arthur heard the distinct sound of aircraft overhead. The fog had meant that all aircraft in No. 1 Squadron AFC that had moved forward to a new landing ground at Rafa for the opening attack, had to turn back as the ground could not be seen from the air.

With the lead battalions supposedly approaching Sheikh Seehan without having come in contact with any Ottoman force, and the fog having lifted further, the quiteness of their situation was rudely interrupted. Appearing out of the gloom the twin orange winking eyes of an enemy DIII fighter plane's oncoming machine guns stitched a tapestry of death across the sand. Diving for cover Arthur made it behind a low sand dune, while on his right his friend Private John Richard Bestonso did likewise; and just in time. Sand spewed up across the low ridge that sheltered them as another machine roared overhead before banking and returning to administer a similar dose of its lead medicine. Sustaining only minor casualties by 8:55 am the hostile planes had departed, out of ammunition.

German Albatros DIII fighter aeroplanes – Palestine 1917

Albatros DIII fighter

When higher ground was reached the lead battalion of the brigade discovered that they were still two miles from their main objective; that of the commanding height of Ali Muntar that overlooked Gaza.

A German Albatros DIII fighter

It was now 9:30 am and the advance infantry were just under a mile north of 53rd Brigade Headquarters at Mansura. With the troops spread out of position it was considered that a proper plan of attack could not be formulated until further reconnaissance had been carried out. Dallas decided to meet with his Brigade Commanders, however, during this time he would be out of communication with Chetwode for two hours while his headquarters was also moved forward.

At 10.50 am Dallas contacted Chetwode advising that the loss of time in him not having communicated was in fact due to the difficulty of bringing the artillery forward, but that he would be prepared to attack at 12.00. Unbeknown to him the artillery was in fact already in position between the Burjabye and Es Sire Ridges. Although artillery communications had not been established with any order received to commence firing, those in the artillery had taken it upon themselves to do so at 10.10 am.

While the fog had made navigation difficult for the infantry it had positively shielded movement of the two mounted divisions, with the Imperial Camel Corps Brigade commanded by Chetwode. They had rapidly intercepted traffic on the roads leading to Gaza from the northeast, effectively isolating the garrison of the town in a 15 mile long cavalry screen.

Ottoman artillery in action from the hedges outside Gaza

The first Ottoman forces had been encountered at 8:00 am by an Australian Light Horse Regiment near Sheikh Abbas, which they had attacked. Shortly after they engaged an enemy aircraft that directed machine gun fire on the leading mounted troops causing a number of casualties. Then as their mounted unit crossed the Gaza to Beersheba road, they cut the telegraph lines. Further along the road one patrol captured 10 wagons while another captured 30 German pioneers and their pack-horses. With Gaza completely surrounded by 11.30 am Desert Column Headquarters had become aware that infantry in the 53rd Division was practically stationary, and a message was sent to Dallas.

I am directed to observe that you have been out of touch with Desert Column and your own headquarters for over two hours; no gun registration appears to have been carried out; that time is passing, and that you are still far from your objective; that the Army and Column Commanders are exercised at the loss of time, which is vital; you must keep a general staff officer at your headquarters who can communicate with you immediately; you must launch your attack forthwith.

Having been in fact been in position awaiting orders for three to four hours after advancing towards Esh Sheluf, the 53rd Division received Desert Column orders to launch an attack on the hill that was Ali Muntar. This they did at 11.45 am. Not having been in action since Gallipoli they made their direct attack from the south-

Turkish artilleryin the cactus of the Labyrinth

west along Es Sire Ridge. They were now about two miles from their objective with patrols well forward.

A further message was received from GHQ at 12.00 am and increased artillery bombardment began immediately, however, with the Ottoman defences not having been identified, there was still no artillery programme. Not having received any reports of enemy reinforcements moving towards Gaza in support of the Ottoman garrison, HQ sent a message to Chauvel and Hodgson to prepare to despatch a brigade each to assist the infantry in their attack on Gaza.

By now Arthur's battalion's line of advance was over completely open ground and it was here that they met with stubborn opposition. The determined German and Ottoman defenders were firing from strong entrenchments, while the British artillery support still hadn't come to grips with what they were attempting, and again proved inadequate. The brigade was sustaining very high numbers of casualties and by 1.10 pm Dallas requested the support of the 161st Brigade which had been waiting at Sheikh Nebhan since 11.15 am, to reinforce them.

By 1.30 pm the Imperial Mounted Division had established itself north of the Gaza to Beersheba road, near Kh er Reseim, with the 5th Mounted Brigade on their right. The mounted British Yeomanry reported Ottoman patrols now visible from Huj to Tel el Sheria. It was reported there were approximately 150 Ottoman soldiers holding the ridge along the 400 contour with a column of smoke towards Hareira, and dust moving south from Tel el Sheria. Aerial reconnaissance of the battlefield reported progress of the attack to Divisional Headquarters. This included monitoring any Ottoman Army reinforcements advancing towards Gaza from Mejdel, Huj, Tel el Sheria, or Beersheba; providing strengths and dispositions of any columns. With the planes not having reported any signs of large bodies of Ottoman reinforcements moving from any direction Chetwode now ordered both mounted divisions to supply one brigade each to move towards Gaza to assist the infantry attack.

Ottoman anti-aircraft gun – Huj 1917

The infantry attack in fact was progressing. On the left the 53rd Brigade had advanced rapidly and by 1.30 pm they had captured the Labyrinth; a maze of entrenched gardens due south of Gaza. It was here that Arthur and his friend John had established themselves on a small grassy hillock.

Their next objective was a maze of small fields running slightly uphill separated by dense cactus hedges. Progress was now slow. Exposed to the sun, and cactus thorns that were worse than wire, while being shot at by Turkish machine guns and snipers, was not Arthur's idea of fun. Machine gun fire ripped through the cactus beside Arthur and John, killing one soldier and injuring two others. They hit the hard stone impregnated ground together as a further spray of bullets whizzed over their heads.

Bloody hell... Allah got a bit close that time! ... and then a moment later from John, *... But as the man said before we came to this forsaken country .... God is on our side!*

Turks communicating with a field telephone

For all their nervous joking this was just as deadly as Suvla Bay with all of them knowing that it only took one bullet to meet their maker. Arthur rolled on his back, and with his rifle alongside him, he looked up wistfully at the neat little holes that had perforated the cactus stems and thickened leaves. Several looked like green Swiss cheese, he thought to himself, before whispering, *... God, we could do with that fog now ...* and with that thought he rolled back ready for the next dash forward.

The stress of warfare, in shooting at others and being shot at, had previously had Arthur's nerves standing on end. Now, somehow, he seemed to be coping better mentally and he felt more relaxed. Whether it was fatalism, or the thought of his afternoon with

Jehanne that came to mind whenever he was in a tight spot, he was unsure. He knew he had a job to do and he wasn't going to let his mates down. While the machine gun concentrated on one area, troops in another stealtherly made their way ever closer to the hill. Once the gun shifted its aim it was his squad's turn again, and gathering up his fortitude Arthur leapt forward to be ripped by the spines on the cactus hedgerow in front of him. The cactus was not known in Arabic as 'sabr', which stood for 'patience', for no reason. As at Suvla they were all suffering from a lack of water, and when they reached the cactus south of Ali Muntar they allowed the other battalions to come up on their right. From here their brigade would slowly fight its way forward towards Clay Hill.

One of the cactus hedge the men had to fight their way through.

By 3.50 pm they had succeeded in entering the enemy's trenches in two places east of the Ali Muntar mosque, capturing 40 Germans, Austrian and Ottoman soldiers. At 4.45 pm, and only 600 yards from Ali Muntar, the 53rd Division reported the successful capture of Clay Hill.

Then at 4.23 pm the high ridge east of Gaza was captured by the New Zealand Mounted Rifles Brigade, with the 22nd Mounted Brigade on their left capturing the knoll running west from the ridge. The New Zealander's headquarters took up a position on the ridge, on a knob later called 'Chaytor's Hill', while their Wellington and Canterbury Regiments pressed on towards Gaza. Only four machine-guns were attached to each of these regiments, with their remaining four held in reserve.

Finally one squadron of the Canterbury Mounted Rifles Regiment swung south against Ali Muntar to enter the enemy trenches just after the 53rd Division. By 6.30 pm the position had been completely overrun with the Ottoman defenders retreating back into the town centre.

God it had been a torrid afternoon.

Turk defenders

The Wellington Mounted Rifles and the 2nd Light Horse Brigade were now well into the northern outskirts of the town, while the Canterbury Mounted Rifles, and part of the 53rd, were in the trenches at Ali Muntar. The balance of the division, including

Arthur and John, deployed south of the town and north of the Labyrinth, and by nightfall this combined force was consolidating its positions.

Gaza - 1917

It was only on the south-western side of Gaza, in the sand hills, that the attack had not been completely successful. At 5.00 pm they reported back advising that they urgently needed more ammunition and water, and unless they were reinforced that their position would become untenable. They were simply ordered to consolidate their position and persevere.

Unfortunately back at GHQ General Dobell was not aware of the extent of the territory gained. Believing that a Turkish relief force had almost reached Gaza he now, unwisely, ordered a general withdrawal. For those in the advanced trenches it seemed bloody unbelievable that their hard fought for ground was now being ordered to be given up to the Turkish garrison in Gaza who were virtually on the point of surrender.

It was likewise amazing that the oncoming Turkish relief forces had also been stopped by their commander who assumed the town was already in British hands.

Defenders of Gaza prior to the first attack

As dutiful soldiers of the King, Arthur Newcombe and John Bestonso, with the rest of the dumbfounded 53rd Division fell back as ordered, continuing their fighting retreat the next day. By the 28th March they had retired back across the Wadi Ghuzze to Sheikh Reshid. Their losses were 4 officers and 14 other ranks killed, plus 5 officers and 108 other ranks wounded. A further 26 were declared missing in action.

Sitting in the sun they each took turns at sharing a pair of tweezers they had acquired from a medical orderly, and with a needle they prized what cactus spines they could from their lacerated bodies. Knowing that any left in would cause an irritation, and would likely fester, they probed with the needle until the last of the offending objects were removed.

Natives of Gaza

I hope the bloody artillery knock the shit out of those hedges before we try that again..... It's bad enough having to fight Johnny Turk's defences as well as nature's to boot.

Yeah... but I bet the buggars are ready for us next time. Why did we have to retire anyway? We were bloody well right on top of them! It was a valid question that would not get a statisfactory answer.

John Bestonso sat up to re-apply a bandage on his arm. *I wish we had that amulet of yours now Arthur, as we could wave it at Jacko and let him know that Allah is on our side also... After all he is supposed to be merciful isn't he?*

*British burying their dead
after the battle*

Scratched and bleeding they would apply some foul smelling antiseptic balm that had been issued, before settling down to clean their rifles and then sleep the sleep of the dead.

Part XXIII

While Ahmed-oğlu Abdullah had bided his time in Damascus, Ottoman forces in Palestine had launched a second attack across the Sinai with the objective of destroying or capturing the Suez Canal. This investment in manpower and resources by the Turks had been just as unsuccessful as the attack the previous year, though not costly by the standards of the Great War. The British had then proceeded with their offensive, attacking east into Palestine. They had now come to a halt denting their armour in their failed attempt to capture Gaza.

A few months earlier it had been decided by the Ottoman commander in Damascus that all battle seasoned reinforcements should be put into the field immediately. Consequently on 17th February Ahmed had been transferred as a reinforcement replacement to the 48th Regiment, 16th Division, XX Corps, of the Fourth Army, based in Beersheba, Palestine.

Loading equipment and stores – Damascus 1917

Along with other Ottoman reinforcements he had again found himself boarding a train that would connect with one on the Beersheba line.

Travelling initially through the southern suburb of Damascus they had passed a number of large ammunition dumps, and a large German wireless installation at Kadem Station. Next had come what had looked like numbers of toy houses and wooded gardens before they had skirted Pharpar stream 10 miles from the city. The further south they travelled an unseasonal spike in temperature had the thermometer in the carriage recording 115°F. Hot and sticky their perspiration had run freely, adding its smell to the already close atmosphere.

Heading south

The Ottoman held railroad to Beersheba was part of what was referred to as the Egypt branch of the Hejaz railroad. It had been opened for traffic by the Turks in the middle of October 1915 and just nine months from the start of its construction. Originating off the main Hejaz line it branched at Afula in Northern Palestine, to run via Tul Karem, Lydda, Tel es Sheria, Beersheba, the extention onto Uja-el-Hafir had been extended to run down to Kseima in the Sinai. This section had been established to support further Turkish assaults on the Suez Canal.

Above & below - The opening of the Beersheba line – Beersheba 1915

Beersheba Railway Station - 1917

The station building at Beersheba, like many others along the Hejaz railroad, had been designed by Meisner Pasha in typical European style; with red roof tiles and a balcony. Its welcoming sign in Arabic read, *Bir-a-Saba*. Inaugurated at the end of October 1915 with a fancy celebration participated in by the Jerusalem Governor, Jemal Pasha, its surrounds now included a residence house for the station master.

Also located nearby, was a stone constructed water tower base that supported two metal tanks. These were filled with water pumped from the wells at Beersheba's wadi and used for the locomotives steam engines.

On the southern outskirts of the town a 20 arc railway bridge spanned the Wadi Saba. It was considered the longest in Palestine and it had recently been completed by a group of 120 Jewish builders. Unfortunately during their nine months of work they had suffered from disease, hunger, floods and other hazards in doing the bidding of their masters. It was typical under Ottoman rule where life was expendable.

Further south was an oasis and watering point alongside the ancient road from Beersheba to Sinai where there was a Bedouin village. It was known as Bir Asluj, or the 'well of honey'. This well would have the honour of being the last watering point of the Desert Mounted Corps before their march to attack Beersheba that would come later in the year.

The seven span railway viaduct at Tel es Sherif

Two days after embarking at Damascus Ahmed, along with 54 other reinforcements, had been dropped from the train at Tel es Sheria station to the north of Beersheba. That morning had blazed with an unseasonal suddenness with the haze of the horizon lost in the shimmer of scorching heat. The sun had hardly risen yet the heat had already close and muggy. Rushing up to them a fat, leather-slippered, Arab porter shuddered to a stop to bow before their young company officer. Instructed to get out of the way and back to the other end of the train where he was required to help unload, he instead remained squatting. Ahmed remembered that the Arab's teeth had chattered out a reply that was lost on a sudden wind that followed his arrival creating its own whirlwind of stabbing sand.

Tel es Sheria

Noticeably quivering under his birkah he looked up at the officer who looked back at him. Their young officer then became conscious of what the furious rush of that first hot, stinging, wind signified. In the chaos of the disembarkation none had noticed the descending dark cloud on the horizon that descended on them from behind the station and its outbuildings. Since their arrival it must had grown rapidly as an overcast cloudy veil, before covering the awakening sky.

Pushing the Arab out of the way the officer yelled through the rising noise of the increasing maelstrom for the reinforcements to all to get back on the train. As the morning light faded the clouds of burning sand mercilessly flogged all living things as several managed to clamber back onboard while covering their heads. In the carriage the whistle of the wind dominated all other sounds. With the suffocating heat becoming unbearable it seemed that even the air was turning against them. With the densest concentration of sand and dust bouncing close to the ground outside, several of their number who had lain exposed in the open lost consciousness even with their heads covered in what tight clothing they had. Lasting only 20 minutes this unforeseen phenomenon had been unusual especially at this time of the year. It had strangely appeared to have also been localised over a track of about a mile, with the station directly in its path. The wind dropped as fast as it had arrived with the sky returning to its blazing glory. Those onboard shook themselves off to descend once more, to help the less fortunate and to survey the damage. For the survivors like Ahmed he saw it as a sign and warning from Allah…. but a warning of what?

Sand storm

Following the strange event it had not be long before they all acquired traditional Arab headdress. Known as the keffiyeh it was fashioned from a large square of cotton material, and it was commonly worn in arid regions. It would offer them protection from direct sun exposure as well as them being able to protect their mouths and eyes in future from blown dust and sand.

Ottoman troops on the move – Palestine 1917

Turk soldiers wearing their keffiyehs

As part of their orientation Ahmed and his fellow mehmets were shown a map displaying the locations of the overall Ottoman force commanded by Kress von Kressenstein. On it they could see that the Ottoman line extended over 10–12 miles. Supported by well concealed and sighted guns that began on their right flank away in the distance on the Mediterranean coast around Gaza it wended its way west to Beersheba, and was now entrenched. They were informed that the country to the east of Gaza, to the sea, was dominated by wired trenches situated on rising ground, while the line towards Beersheba was less strongly held. Well sited redoubts, however, covering the wider gaps providing mutual support. These, they were advised, enabled a large reserve force outside the danger zone to be available to take advantage of counterattack opportunities.

Of the 25,000 German and Ottoman troops in the area; 8,500 were deployed at Gaza, 4,500 east of Gaza, 2,000 in the Atawineh redoubt 8 and 10 miles away on the Gaza to Beersheba road,

German and Turkish officers at Tel el Sheria in 1917

6,000 at Hareira, with additional reinforcements at Tel el Sheria where Ahmed now was, located slightly north, about half way between Gaza and Beersheba. Those who had moved to reinforce Gaza during the first defence of the town had remained to garrison it, along with the area to the coast. Regiments of the infantry division involved were made up of four battalions with two machine gun companies each, in addition to any machine guns with the actual regiments. They were supported by four batteries of field artillery that included Austrian mountain howitzer batteries and a 5.9 in howitzer battery.

Ahmed's division, comprising the 48th regiment, was being held in reserve at Tel es Sheria, and it was here on the evening of 17th April that 1,500 swords of the 3rd Cavalry joined them.

Imperial Camel Corps

Ottoman troops at Tel es Sheria

Part XXIV

British dead - Gaza

U nfortunately, in attempting to report on the brighter aspects of the failed attempt to capture Gaza, General Murray had sent a very positive report about his exploits of his troops in this regard to London. He was so successful in his report writing that it encouraged the British War Cabinet to demand a quick advance through Palestine to capture Jerusalem.

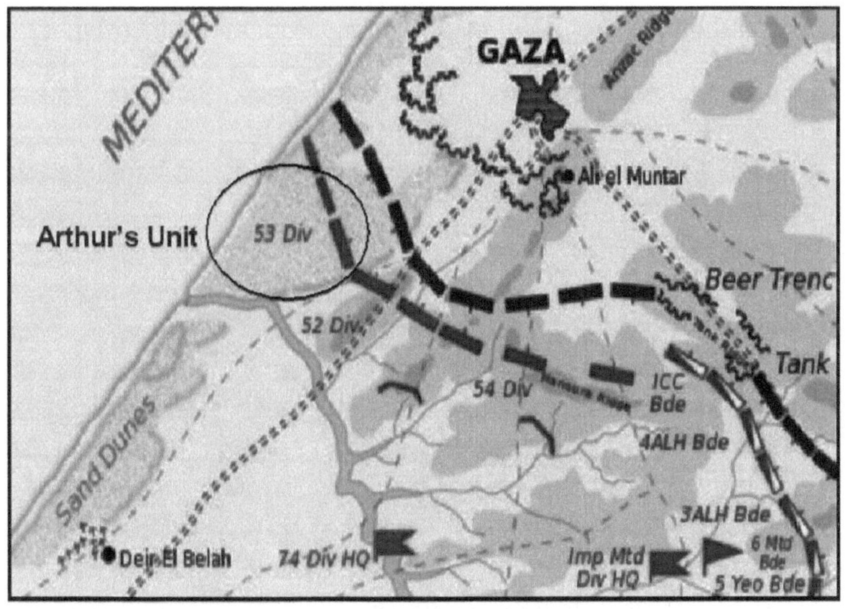

Map showing the location Arthur's unit at Gaza

Murray requested forces but was told to advance immediately, so just three weeks later a second attempt to take Gaza would take place. Naturally by this time the Turks had reinforced their positions around the town; including in the east towards Beersheba to avoid any flanking attack. With additional regiments brought into the town the moral of their troop's was also naturally buoyed by their added strength and recent victory.

Ottoman troops in Gaza

Against this improved defence General Dobell this time decided on a conventional frontal attack on Gaza, supported by 170 artillery pieces, a limited number of tanks, and by the use of naval guns firing from monitors offshore.

53rd Division lads with Arthur Edgar Newcombe - (Third from right as viewed)

It would be the only time that poison gas was used in this theatre of war.

Three divisions would be employed in the attack. Two of these, the 52nd and 54th, were to again attack from the south up the ridges leading to Ali Muntar. The mounted units of the desert column would occupy the Turkish forces to the east of the town, while Arthur, in the ranks of the 53rd, was destined to advance through the sand dunes along the coast. At least in in his mind there would be no damn cactus to contend with.

The two inland divisions began their moves on the 17th April, successfully crossing the Wadi Ghuzze and establishing their positions ready for the main attack.

The Wadi Ghuzze

With this first phase successful, Dobell was to make his main attack from Mansura and Sheikh Abbas in the east, with the objective of capturing Ali Muntar and then striking left into Gaza. His intention was to create a gap for his Desert Column to break through, while on the coast side of Gaza in the sand dunes, the

53rd Division was designated to capture any Ottoman defences in that area.

Of the five tanks that had arrived to be attached to 'Eastern Force' two were alloted to 53rd Division, while the Mounted Yeomanry Division would remain in reserve.

The battle began at 5.30 am on the 19th April with a two-hour artillery bombardment during which the French coastguard ship *Requin*, protected by a screen of drifters and trawlers and escorted by two French destroyers, fired at Ali Muntar. One monitor fired on the 'Warren' on the western side of the ridge, while another monitor fired on the 'Labyrinth'. Coming under the orders of Eastern Force divisional commanders, who controlled its fire, the heavy artillery was directed in counter-battery fire against strong points which could hold up the infantry attack. This barrage was conducted with the exception of three brigades of 18-pdrs that were being held back for the infantry attack.

For the first 40 minutes the field howitzers fired gas shells at the Ottoman's battery positions, and on a woodland area southwest of Ali Muntar. These guns were supplied with 500 rounds per 60-pdr and 6-inch howitzers, 400 rounds per 8-inch howitzer, and 600 rounds per 4.5-inch howitzer. The 18-pdrs were allocated 600 rounds.

Ten minutes before the infantry were due to attack at 7.15 am the 18-pdrs began their fire. Then at 7.30 am the ships were ordered to shift their fire to the north and NW of Gaza, and north and NE of Ali Muntar, to avoid firing on the infantry.

At 7.15 am the 53rd Division, now under the command of Brigadier General S. F. Mott, began their advance in extended line order across the sandhills from Tell el Ujul, between the Mediterranean coast and the Rafa to Gaza road. They had proceeded 15 minutes before the 160th Brigade on their right, and who had been ordered to capture Sampson Ridge.

With the 159th Brigade on their left ordered to capture Sheikh Ajlin on the sea shore, things progressed fairly well for this Brigade. They advanced until they were 800 yards from Sheikh Ajlin where their orders required them to wait for the capture of Samson Ridge, due to the possibility of any enemy remaining their exposing their right flank.

Advancing towards Sampson's Ridge it soon became clear to Arthur and his fellow 2/10th Middlesex Battalion chums that their artillery fire had not silenced the defenders' artillery. In reality there had not been enough guns to cover the 15,000 yard front, with only one gun deployed every 100 yards compared with one every 36 feet on the Western Front. The light field guns were also

Officers of the 2/10th Middlesex Battalion

not producing a sufficiently dense bombardment even when strengthened by barrages by the naval guns. For Arthur and his fellow soldiers the whole situation was starting to look tenuous at best.

The Ottoman Order of Osmanieh

Powered by a 105 horse power engine, including dynamos and differentiator, the British Mk I tank had a top speed of just under four mph. Manned by an officer who sat beside the driver who viewed his track through a periscope; two greasers; and four gunners on bike seats, the tank was armed with four Hotchkiss guns firing through loop holes, and two larger auxiliary side guns.

Mark I British tank

Being very slow and notorious for frequent mechanical failures both of these facts made it vulnerable to enemy field artillery if the opposing gunners held their nerve and engaged the tanks with direct fire.

Tanks had first been used in France in September 1916 and Palestine would be the only other theatre of the war where they were employed. Eight from the Tank Corps, or Heavy Section of the Machine Gun Corps, had reached the Palestinian front along with 4,000 rounds of 4.5-inch gas shells. These, it had been decided, had seemed to offer the best chance of a successful frontal assault. Not of the latest type, these tanks had arrived in January 1917 to be used initially for instruction. Arthur had witnessed them attacking a practice position through the sand which, though fairly heavy, did not seem to interfere with them in the least.

In fact they worked well in sand so long as they were not greased.

British troops with a tank – Gaza 1917

To Arthur they buzzed along most satisfactorily. He thought that if they could only get the Turks to make a stand he felt that the tanks would frighten them out of their wits.

Ottoman machine gun corps at the Tel el Sheria - Gaza line, 1917

This detachment of tanks, however, was now being misused by senior officers who, having no battlefield experience with them, deployed them in pairs widely separated apart. As such they were positioned along the front advancing across open country where it was considered they would give shelter to the infantry advancing behind them.

In reality they simply became targets around which the infantry would also suffer. Expectations had been that the enemy would flee before them, and the affect of their gas bombardment. But the prevailing summer west wind, blowing across the front off the sea, nullified the effects of the gas while Turkish artillery would range in on each in turn.

Walking steadily behind the tank allotted to his brigade, Arthur's 2/10th Middlesex regiment had initially been sheltered from direct frontal light arms fire. The incoming Turkish artillery fire, however, was now taking its toll on the surrounding the troops. Then, suddenly from his the right machine gun fire from the woodland area on Sampson's Ridge that had been bombarded by gas shells with little effect, took out several men around Arthur. He hit the sand along with several casualties as bullets struck the tank with dull thuds to ricochet and wine off into oblivion. The staccato sound of the distant machine gun on the wind was followed again by a further fusillade that stitched its dance across the sand to his side. There was nothing he could do other than shelter behind the dead soldier beside him whose blood was now seeping into the sand of Palestine.

With their advance slowed by the machine gun fire it would not be eased until the 1/4th Sussex eventually reinforced their right flank. Delayed, Samson Ridge would not be captured by the 160th until 1.00 pm when a bayonet charge would take the ridge again with heavy casualties to capture 43 Turkish soldiers and 2 officers. Many officers and NCOs fell in the combined attacks that morning, and at the conclusion of the fighting for Samson Ridge one battalion that was commanded by a 2nd Lieutenant recorded....

The 54th Division on the right again, and the 53rd among the sand dunes had, for the most part, their attacks shattered by machine-gun fire, while the Imperial Mounted Division and the Desert Column, fighting in a line half-way to Beersheba, had failed to produce anything like a break through. The Turk, forewarned, was little troubled by British artillery fire, and held his positions with the tenacity which had long ago made his reputation as a defensive soldier.

Arthur and his Middlesex pals had consolidated their position with a gap on their right being filled by the 1st Herefords. On their left the 159th Brigade continued to push forward to just north of Sheikh Ajlin, while they fought off a Turk counter-attack on the ridge.

By the afternoon of the 20th April what remained of the 2/10th Middlesex Battalion were relieved and moved back to the shore just north of Wadi Ghuzze. Their losses had been 2 officers killed and 7 wounded, plus 27 other ranks killed, with 8 more dying of their wounds; 6 were missing and 132 were wounded. By the time they were back on the beach the 159th Brigade had captured Sheikh Ajlin without difficulty.

Ottoman cavalry ready to charge

The Division had suffered 600 casualties during the morning's advance and fighting. They were also unable to advance further until the 52nd (Lowland) Division came up to protect their right flank. Attacks by the 54th and 52nd Divisions had not been successful due to the effective defence by the Turkish forces and the lack of adequate supplies of artillery shells. This left the final occupied line running from Sheikh Ajlin south-east through Sampsons Ridge, Heart Hill, and Lees Hill to Sheikh Abbas Ridge. To add to the confusion during the afternoon several ships were targeted by a German submarine that had fired a torpedo at *Requin'*, just missing her stern. On shore the inevitable trench warfare that existed on the Western Front now set in until a third attack on Gaza could be made.

That attack would not take place until late October.

On 20th April an Ottoman counter attack was anticipated when German aircraft bombed EEF camps and Ottoman cavalry massed at Hareira. This threat did eventuate after the Ottoman cavalry were bombed by three B.E.s and two Martinsydes. Although no general counter attack occurred there were numerous local attacks. One of these attempted an advance down the Wadi Sihan, and was stopped by British artillery.

The defeat, or at least stalemate over the EEF, again boosted the Ottoman Fourth Army's morale, and within weeks Kress von

Ottoman cavalry

Kressenstein was reinforced by two further divisions.

As for the EEF, their strength which had supported their advance into Palestine prior the two battles for Gaza, was now decimated. Dug in on Sampson's Ridge the 160th Brigade would remain looking forlornly at the outskirts of Gaza receiving artillery fire from the Turks whenever they deemed it appropriate. Of the eight tanks that took part in the battle two had been successful in reaching their objectives; one had slipped off a bank; another had broken down; while three had been destroyed by enemy artillery fire. Those destroyed were named *HMLS Sir Archibald*, *HMLS War Baby* and *HMLS Nutty*.

British Tank - Palestine

B y the Second Battle of Gaza NILI operatives had been working behind the Ottoman lines secretly gathering intelligence for British commanders. One of their original group was a Jew named Naaman Belkind, and Sarah had given him the amulet to wear as a symbol of good luck, along with helping authenticate his appearance as a Bedouin. Naaman's role had been to spy north of the Gaza to

Naaman Belkind

Beersheba line, across to the Hebron Road north of Tell es Sheria, gaining intelligence on Ottoman troop movements.

With his camel held by its reins Naaman walked through country north of Tell el Sheria. A hot wind swirled the sand in the open and off the ridges of the low dunes. Its squalling effect raised dust that to some extent camouflaged his existence by cutting down observation at a distance. Infused with the partial sunlight the atmosphere created an eerie patchwork of shifting light over the ground. All was going according to plan with his first pigeon released when he had the misfortune to run into a Turkish patrol. He had just slipped past one Turk rear guard patrol but was completely unaware of another that was on the opposite side of a gently rising ridge that had hid their presence from him.

Close to the Hebron to Beersheba road Naaman was spotted by this second patrol just as he spotted it. Whilst he may have looked to be Bedouin to the Turkish soldiers they had been warned about spies and so they now quickly moved diagonally east to cut him off. Naaman was in the process of mounting his camel to make his escape when he dropped the leather shoulder bag he was carrying. He had not heard the report of the rifle shot but he now certainly felt the bullet that had hit him in the right arm.

Sending forward three soldiers to investigate, Ahmed remained prone with two other mehmets to offer cover the three out in front. Once they got to the spot where the Bedouin had been last seen, he was gone. All they had to show for their efforts was his leather shoulder bag that contained an old amulet, a map of the area, and a copy of the Qur'an. One of the mehmet's who had also been at Suvla Bay immediately recognised the amulet as the same design as one Ahmed had lost at Gallipoli.

So much for it being an ancient relic that a museum would want to display, quipped the soldier, *as these amulets are obviously not as uncommon as Ahmed believes…* He held it up for the other two to see. *Why don't we surprise Ahmed and present it to him as a replacement before handing the rest of the bag's contents in?* suggested another, and they all agreed.

Standing in front of Ahmed one the returning mehmets brought the amulet out from behind his back and started swinging it on its goat's leather cord between his forefinger and thumb.

Allah be Praised… Where did you get that from…?

To Ahmed it was obviously his amulet, but confusion was evident in his expression. He was rooted to the spot unable to move in not comprehending how it could have appeared out of desert's wastes, unless his friend had retained it all this time. Being handed it, he cradled the artefact in his hands and then turned it to reveal the initial he had scratched on its back after he had first recovered it at Gallipoli. He half expected it not to be there, but it was; shining out at him brighter than ever. It simply added to his confusion, and falling to his knees he could only comprehend that in the shifting sands of time, that this was no coincidence. It was the hand of almighty Allah who had delivered it back into his safe keeping.

He could only utter…

Allah be Praised… Allah is Merciful….!. Its deliverance will not be questioned, just protected.

That night Ahmed would receive his first visit from a 'dabe mukhatat', or striped hyena. Generally regarded as the physical incarnations of jinns by the Arabs, this 'dhubba' unusually held its ground. In ordinary circumstances the hyena was often considered a cowardly animal being extremely timid around humans. This one was different for some reason. Ahmed had learnt that as a scavenger it would be prepared to protect its rights in disputes over food, yet there was no food on offer and still it stayed silhouetted in the moonlight directly in front of him.

Being nocturnal he also knew that it only typically emerged in darkness and would be quick to return to its lair before sunrise. With dawn not far off Ahmed sat staring at the animal as it stared back at him. In the half light he could make out its large ears and recessed close beady eyes. Its presence and behaviour was strange. It stared at him out of the darkness with its ears pricked high and nose raised, no doubt sensing all surrounding smells both good and bad. With a slight shift in the light at around 5.00 am the hyena vanished just as fast as it had arrived, and its disappearance left Ahmed with a queer feeling he had not experienced before.

The hyena

Hey, Ahmed....where's your friend? We saw it sitting staring at you and wondered whether you had something special to eat that

we were unaware of. Your aunt hasn't sent you a cake you have been keeping to yourself, has she?

General Archibald Murray

Rail tracks across the desert

In late June General Edmund Allenby replaced General Archibald Murray as commander of the EEF, reorganising this force shortly afterwards to place himself in direct command of three corps. In the process Allenby deactivated Chetwode's Eastern Force giving him command of XX Corps, while XXI Corps would be commanded by Lieutenant General Edward Bulfin. The Desert Column was renamed Desert Mounted Corps and continued to be commanded by Lieutenant General Henry Chauvel.

About this time the Ottoman IVth Army was also reorganised with the establishment the new Yildirim Army Group commanded by the German General Erich von Falkenhayn, along with the formation of the Ottoman VIIth and VIIIth Armies.

As the stalemate continued through the terrible conditions of summer EEF reinforcements began to arrive replacing the huge numbers of casualties they had suffered at Gaza.

Ottoman troops on the move

On the 7th May on returning to the front Arthur had cause to visit the Welsh Field Ambulance. Shortly before entering their dugout he had taken a few moments to relieve himself behind a stores dump. He was only 20 yards away at the western end of Sampson Ridge when a Turkish shell landing directly in the dugout he was heading for killing the medical orderly inside outright.

Ottoman artillery in action

British dugouts

Harold Newcombe

Then on the 4th July one of his battalion cobber's advised Arthur that a soldier by the name of Harold Newcombe in the 52nd Division had been murdered a few days earlier. The grape vine concerning the event had spread like a scrub fire, along with the fact that the soldier's dying words had been that his killer had been looking for an ancient amulet of some kind.

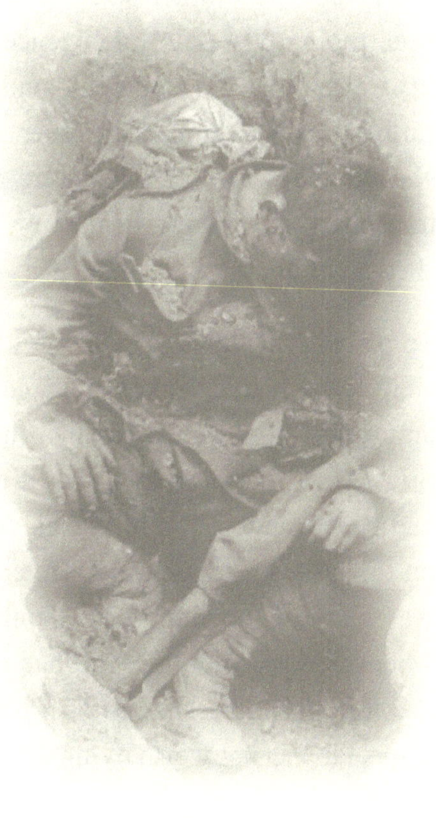

Thankfully the perpetrator had been shot dead through the upper spine while trying to escape. Evidently he had been caught in the act of torturing Harold some distance from his camp. Unfortunately, before attempting his escape, he had shot Harold Newcombe who had subsequently died. For those who were now investigating the murder nothing made sense until they searched the clothing of the Circassian killer. Under his thawb, in the bloody pocket of his shirt, they had discovered a tattered piece of paper with a note that read in Arabic … *Recover amulet piece by whatever means necessary for gold. British*

soldier named Newcombe identified with it.

The note had added little to what had transpired other than in explaining that a soldier by the name of Newcombe was being targeted by persons unknown for some kind of amulet. The note along with a roll of film of the killer, and the murder scene, had been promptly sent to Intelligence in Cairo for development and  further investigation. All other soldiers with the surname of Newcombe in any division were also being advised of what had transpired, along with them being interviewed to see if they could shed any light on the matter. This naturally now included Arthur.

To his way of thinking whilst Turkish machine guns and artillery were to be feared, this was whole new turn of events…. Was the amulet being searched for the one he had recovered and lost at Suvla Bay? If it was then that it dawned on him that this soldier had been murdered in his stead, and that he was likely to be next on the killers' shopping list. He could not grasp, however, what it was that was so important about that particular amulet, or that whoever was searching for it had not ascertained that he no longer had it in his possession. Still, if it was that amulet, whatever made it special was not worth dying over.

His prior ownership of the amulet now took on a whole new meaning. Having opened the diplomatic pouch he suspected he might also be in serious trouble if he admitted having retained

Government property, and then lost it. That was especially now that it had resulted in the death of a fellow soldier. It was hard to admit, but fortunately the majority of the other soldiers that had known of its discovery by him at Suvla were all now dead. He had to wonder, however, whether one of those had anything to do with the amulet as, on reflection, one had been a suspicious death also. He would check with his friend John Bestonso as the only other one who knew of Arthur having had the amulet in his possession.

General Allenby

Respected as a valuable and brave soldier by the Lieutenant who interviewed him, Arthur simply advised him openly that he had heard about the murder. He then acted puzzled and dumbfounded when an object named a 'hirz' was mentioned. He asked what a 'hirz' was, to be told that it was a Moslem amulet that contained a message; usually a prayer with brief extracts from the Q'uran.

No I have not come across one of those… he had jokingly replied, and I'll keep my head down, and let you know, if I do.

This seemed to satisfy the officer, who simply advised him to keep alert. Just prior to parting he then unexpectedly advised Arthur that he was being promoted to the rank of Acting Corporal.

Lieutenant General
Philip Chetwode

After the EEF defeats at the first and second battles of Gaza in March and April Lieutenant General Philip Chetwode, commanding the EEF's Eastern Force, and Kress von Kressenstein's Ottoman Empire force had again ended up in a stalemate in southern Palestine.

Entrenched defences, more or less on the lines held at the end of the second battle were strengthened, and regular mounted reconnaissance into the open eastern flank was undertaken by both sides. July came to a close with the 2/10th Middlesex taken off the front line on the 13th August to rest.

As the stalemate continued through the terrible summer conditions, on the northern edge of the Negev Desert EEF reinforcements began slowly to strengthen the depleted divisions which had suffered more than 10,000 casualties in the first two battles for Gaza. Both the EEF and the Ottoman Army were now conducting ongoing training for all units while continuing their primary function of manning the front lines and patrolling their open flanks.

Turk Machine Gun Line

*Turks displaying their
divisional colours – Gaza 1917*

In northern Palestine at Zikhron Ya'akov Sarah Aaronsohn continued to supervise the transmission by NILI agents of the Jewish American gold to aid the Jewish population. Aware of the NILI's underground activities she additionally liaised with the Turkish authorities, an increasingly hostile community of her native colony, and the formal leadership of the Yishuv, which had distanced itself from the organisation.

Old trenches

Following the British success in Constantinople earlier in the year using Sarah's contacts, Aaron Aaronsohn re-outlined the idea he had earlier couched. This was a far bolder plan and it was again recommended to the British that their primary overall plan of attack should be through Beersheba, instead of solely concentrating on Gaza. It was a plan that would now be used by Allenby in an attempt to break the Gaza to Beersheba line and hopefully allow the capture of Jerusalem by Christmas 1917 as the politicians still seemed hell bent on having him achieve.

Due in large measure to information supplied by NILI to British Intelligence in Cairo concerning the locations of oases in the desert, General Edmund Allenby was able to plan to mount a surprise attack on Beersheba, unexpectedly bypassing the now strong Ottoman defences at Gaza. It was during this period of planning that the Ottoman defenders also received reinforcements.

Both sides had conducted ongoing training for all units while the primary function of manning the front lines was maintained. Following the second British attempt at taking Gaza, Ahmed and his 48th regiment, had been ordered to Beersheba. He and his fellow mehmets were pleased with their posting expecting little activity.

Beersheba

Ahmed could see that the natural features around the town favoured defence. Located on a rolling plain devoid of trees or water to its west, it was dotted with hills and tells to its north, south and east. These features had been strengthened by a series of entrenchments, fortifications, and redoubts, including well-constructed trenches protected by wire, and with fortified defences in the northwest, west, and southwest of the town. This semicircle of entrenchments included well-sited redoubts on a series of high points extending out to four miles.

Defending the east of Beersheba was redoubt on a hill named Tel el Saba. It overlooked the town and was now manned by a battalion of Ahmed's 48th Regiment, along with a machine-gun company. Two other regiments of the 3rd Cavalry Division were deployed on high ground to the northeast in the foothills of the Judean Hills. They guarded the Jerusalem road with the role of keeping Beersheba from being surrounded.

To the west and southwest of the town, three infantry regiments were deployed in a fortified semicircular line of deep trenches and redoubts strengthened by barbed wire.

Ottoman cavalry

These regiments consisted primarily of Arab farmers from the surrounding region. Although they were inexperienced fighters the Ottoman officers knew they had incentive in defending their own fields. Two battalions of the 2nd Regiment of Anatolian riflemen from Chanak, commanded by German officers, were deployed in trenches defending the southeast, facing the open plain south of Tel el Saba. As for Ahmed, his battalion was also positioned in the southeast, now protecting part of this line.

Part XXV

A mile or two inland from Deir-el-Belah Arthur was bivouacked with the 53rd Division. The distance from the sea made bathing a bit of a toil but otherwise it was a good camp. All that, however, was about to change. By mid October, while Arthur's XXI Corps had maintained the defences of the Gaza sector, Allenby's preparations for manoeuvre warfare, with attacks on the Gaza to Beersheba line were nearly complete with the arrival of the last of his reinforcements.

Australian Light Horse

With it necessary that the Beersheba plan be concealed from the Turks until the assault went in, a series of deceptions would now be instigated. This included an apparent seaborne attack north of Gaza that would be divulged to the enemy by badly concealed naval intelligence. In this regard Arthur's prowess in swimming was again called on with him finding himself in a selected group of soldiers singled out for special training. They were all expert swimmers and they would be given training in amphibious warfare. Told nothing of any overall intentions as to how they were to be used they were allowed to speculate, with such speculation leaked to the enemy. Notably this included it being made known that their training was being carried out for a forthcoming raid on a Turkish coastal battery. It was never command's intention of see any amphibious raid materialise, but it did keep Arthur on edge as a member of what could legitimately be construed as the first commando group ever organised by the British Army.

British engineers create a cutting across a wadi

As well as swimming training in the surf Arthur and the others in the special unit received ongoing demonstrations and practice in wire-cutting, smoke screens, bangalore torpedoes, and practising co-operation with aeroplanes. For all other units there had been frequent night marches by compass, combined with digging in, followed by procedures for attack or advance at dawn. It was very practical training for the task which they were about to undertake.

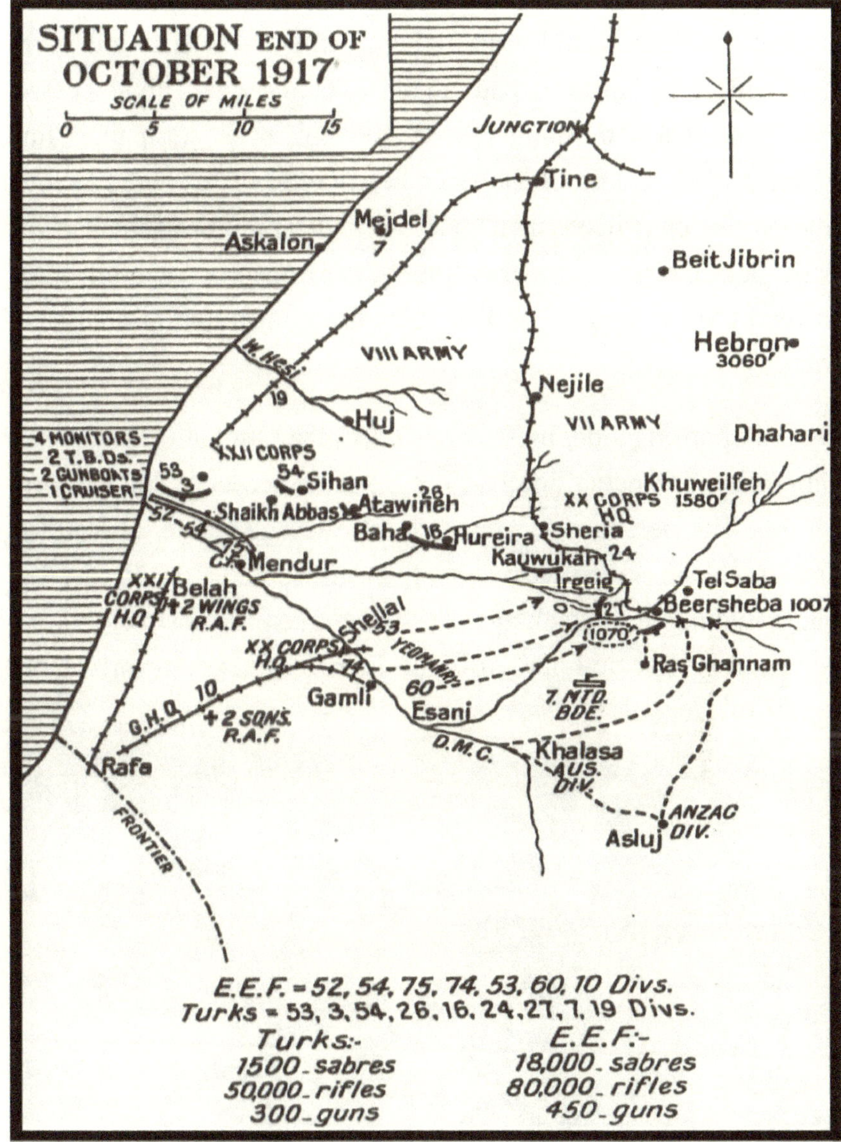

In order to additionally minimise the chance of anything going wrong with the plans for a third attack on Gaza, along with the concentration and attack on Beersheba, several officers of the division was given the chance of making a reconnaissance as near as possible to the Turkish positions. These incursions were commenced in the east from a location in the Wadi Ghuzzeh, about 15 miles inland from where Arthur and his unit were stationed. Their officers had ridden over there the night before, and in the early morning cavalry moved out to push their line within a mile or two of the Beersheba defences. Covered by this line parties of officers then rode out and familiarised themselves with the sector in which their unit was to operate, enabling them to report so as brigade staff could allot concentration areas and routes.

On the opposing side, by October 1917, the Ottoman VIII Army's supporting defensive line had been established at Huleikat, north of Huj. The defences at Atawineh, at Sausage Ridge, at Hareira, and at Teiaha supported each other overlooking an almost flat plain, making any attack against them almost impossible. Ahmet had been given two hours off with the rest of his company before

Ottoman cavalry at Tel el Sheria

they were redeployed to the conical hill that was Tel el Saba. He visited the Postal and Telegraph office in Beersheba to post a letter to his aunt in Istanbul wishing her well and informing her of his mysterious recovery of the amulet. Outside several of the town's garrison lazed in the sun watching four mehmets on fatigue duty unloading cases of ammunition from an old dray that had arrived by rail. Stepping inside the coolness of the post office was a pleasant change from the pervasive heat outside. Behind the desk a telegrapher was carefully ripping apart perforated stamps and placing them in a labelled tin with the particular stamps face

An Ottoman soldier

Beersheba

value. He paid little attention to Ahmed as he took an envelope from the desk stand and retired to a short wall desk to fill it out and enclose his letter. As he wrote an officer outside swore at some miscreant who had just dropped one of the crates. Ahmed thought it a stupid time to be involved in heavy labour as an attack on them was not imminent. The clacking of the teletype machine interrupted his thoughts in the silence of the room. The telegrapher turned in his chair reading the first part of the tape. As soon as it had stopped he ripped it from the machine and in one motion rushed for the door without a sideways glance, or word.

Finishing his letter Ahmed enclosed it without sealing the envelope, knowing that the telegrapher doubled as the town's military censor and that he would need to check it. He dropped it in the 'outward mail' tray on the desk before glancing up at the old station clock on the wall and leaving the office, closing the door behind him.

Covering all approaches to Beersheba the Ottoman garrison defending the town was deployed in a mix of trench lines supported by isolated redoubts on earthworks and hills. Ahmed noticed that several pieces of artillery had been relocated to a new trench line that was being dug facing the plain to the southeast. It was no doubt being positioned in case any attack over came the their series of field works that was mutually supported by artillery, machine guns and rifles, and that extended westward towards Gaza, four miles from Beersheba.

British preparations were also well in hand for their planned attack on the town with an outpost line having been designated for establishment some miles east of Karm and El Buggar. This was to be held on the left by Arthur's 53rd Division, with another division on their right. Then came the Imperial Camel Corps (IIC), and finally south of the Wadi Saba where it was much more lightly held, by a mere line of cavalry observation posts. These cavalry posts were to offer cover slightly in advance of the positions selected for 'Battle Headquarters' for the two divisions.

Turk commanders at Tel el Sheria

During this period of British concentration the plain lying between Shellal and Beersheba was now a scene of great activity. Karm had been selected as the position for a forward supply dump with both light and broad gauge railways being pushed out towards it at top speed.

Once things were ready movement towards these allotted areas would start on 25th October with a very dusty and tiresome march. Word then came in that the Turks were attacking the British outpost line at El Buggar some 10 miles out, so a battalion was urgently moved at a moment's notice in it's support.

For Arthur and his foot slogging mates the march through the sand and heat of the afternoon was trying with perspiration soaking through their karkis. The preliminary arrangements for troop movements had gone like clockwork, and so too were the approach marches to the troops positions of deployment. At the appointed time on 30th October Divisional H.Q. moved up the five or six miles to its selected battle station. There was no sign of crowding or confusion with the only indication that there was anything unusual occurring being the occasional dust cloud which had been seen here and there.

Arthur now suspected that the main attack would be pushed home south of the Wadi Saba by the two divisions. He was not aware that it was HQ's intention that the enemy's extreme left flank would be turned by the cavalry at the same time. Unbeknown to him and the Turks they were currently making a wide detour through very difficult and waterless country to attack Beersheba from the east. If possible it was intended that they would also cut off the retreat of the garrison from the Beersheba area.

Before dawn on the 31st October Acting Corporal Arthur Edgar Newcombe, along with the rest of his 53rd Division and a supporting brigade of Irish, would be deployed WNW of the Wadi Saba and Beersheba awaiting further orders. They were spread out over a seven mile long line stretching west back towards Gaza, and about a mile from the Karm railway station. Arthur was on the extreme east of this line closest to Beersheba, and he and his fellow 'diehards' had been ordered to watch for a counter-attack from Hareira to the north. They were also ordered to capture any of the Beersheba garrison if they attempted to retreat along the road to Gaza, or to the north.

Meanwhile to the north-east of Beersheba the Anzac Mounted Division were charged with cutting the road from Beersheba to Hebron, which continued on to Jerusalem.

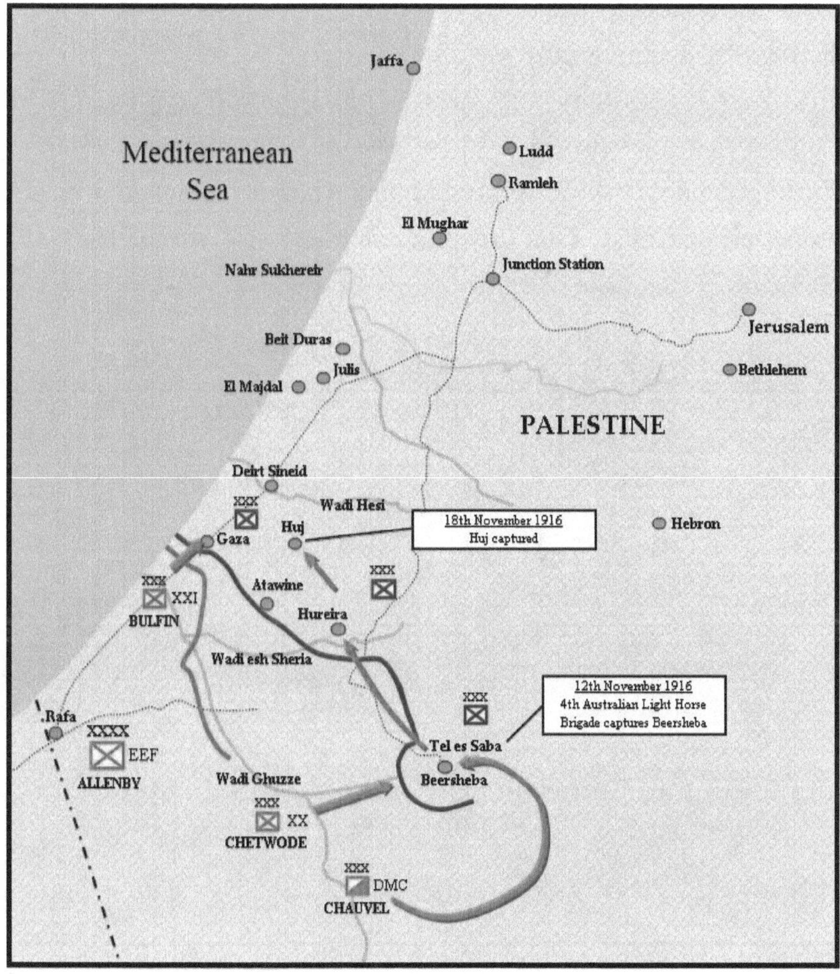

Map showing troop movements relative to the attack on Beersheba

Australian Light Horse on the move

Four days prior, on the 27th October, 1917, Allenby had opened his offensive against the Turkish positions at Gaza with a combined barrage of accurate gun fire from his artillery and British gun ships off the coast. The ongoing barrage was directed by airborne observers and at times the crescendo of high explosive and shrapnel reached western front proportions. This historic moment had been No. 113 Squadron's first taste of battle.

Beersheba 1917

On the 28th Ahmed, as one of the 1200 rifles in his regiment, had been ordered to take up a position NW of Beersheba at the base of the conical hill that was Tel es Saba. For the next two days they had dug trenches and made themselves at home as best they could. They expected little activity with Gaza obviously being the stumbling block for the British.

Looking back up the hill Ahmed could make out the sun reflecting off a heliograph or binoculars before returning his gaze to once

Turks defending from prepared trenches

more ponder over who had made his amulet. With Allah in his heart it certainly gave him a feeling of comfort. With the sun on his back his eyelids drooped and he almost fell asleep. Snapping back to reality he realised the consequence if he was found sleeping on duty and he again focused, this time to the southwest. In the distant heat haze he thought he saw rising dust and reporting his suspicion along the line. All his fellow mehmets were now alert to what appeared to be a body of troops, or mounted infantry, out in those wastes and moving across their front to their right. Behind them a heliograph began communicating with their fellow regimental members on Tel el Saba who were also aware of the dust. A distant bugle called all those in the town to general quarters

If they were mounted infantry they are going to be short on water and they will be in for a hot time in more ways than one…, commented a soldier to Ahmed's left.

In the early hours the 31st October, as Ahmed's eyes began to droop again miraculously the hyena returned to sit out in front of him once more. Two of his friends appeared by his side and they all looked from their trench at the animal as it sat only 20 yards away, clearly visible under the well lit night sky.

A depiction of the hyena

The mehmet who had seemed quite knowledgeable when this hyena had appeared on the first occasion offered ….

One thing I forgot to tell you about this scavenger … In Africa some tribes say that the soul of a man can enter a hyena which

then attacks the man's enemies... The Arabs on the other hand generally regard striped dhubbas as physical incarnations of jinns. Interestingly, given this animal's need to seem to want to visit you, the Arabs also believe that there had once been a tribe of 'dabe mukhatat people' that believed that if one in their line was in a group of 1000 people, a dabe mukhatat could pick him out!

I guess you should now be referred to as 'hyena man', from the tribe of the dabe mukhatat people'.

Beersheba

They all laughed quietly their mirth was followed a moment later by a howl that broke the silence of the night. The hyena's interjection startled them, along with other mehmets further along their line, one of whom had accidently wet his pants. The hyena sat for almost two hours out in front of Ahmed before offering up a final howl before vanishing around 4.00 am back into the open wastes southeast of the town.

When dawn broke on 31st October, 1917, the first blow was launched at the defences of Beersheba which faced west extending north and south of the Wadi Saba. These wired defences occupied a commanding position and 30 British light and heavy batteries opened fire on the trenches between Wadi el Saba to the Beersheba - Khalasa road, that was held by the Turks, including Ahmed's 48th Regiment. Without warning Ahmed and his fellow mehmets were under fire. With their line and the surrounding landscape erupting in shrapnel bursts thankfully for Ahmed and his friends they were only smothered in clouds of dust.

In the town Ismet Bey and his staff were likewise taken completely by surprise. Messages delivered by friendly Bedouin from Ottoman pilots, and handed to Ismet Bey that morning, were only now being read. They stated that during the night two divisions of the enemy's mounted infantry had marched through Iswaiwin and Khashim Zanna.

*British artillery
in action*

Under pressure to react Ismet sent his Cavalry division to the heights northeast of Beersheba with orders to prevent an encirclement of the town by enemy Light Horsemen. The conical hill of Tel el Saba that controlled the surrounding area was strengthened by a battalion of Ahmed's regiment that consisted of 300 rifles and six heavy machine guns. Having worked on the assumption that the English would not proceed against Beersheba's southern and eastern fronts, especially those of Tel el Saba, the Turks had not prepared any significant defence there.

Ahmed, with the remainder of his regiment and the two remaining reserve battalions were immediately ordered to quickly close the broad three mile gap between the left wing of their prepared position at Tel el Saba, to defend south of the town from the Khalasa road to Ras Ghannam. It would not be until much later in the day that Ismet was able to create a new reserve by withdrawing some companies out of the quiet section between the railway and Wadi Saba.

To the northwest the British had by now commenced bombardment on Ottoman advanced positions to the west on the hill they had recorded as Hill 1070, and with good effect. It was under the cover of this fire that two of the British divisions developed their attack. They were aware from intelligemce that between their front line and the Wadi el Saba there were weaker enemy forces. Further east 'Smith's Detachment', that was an infantry brigade strengthened by the Imperial Camel Brigade (ICC), had been ordered to threaten the Turkish positions rather than attack. At Bir Esani Arthur's battalion was ready to advance east and northwards, if required, to Tel es Sheria.

The westerly bombardment by the British was followed by the

first assault on Hill 1070 at 8.30 am. 15 minutes later it was in British hands.

Between 8 and 9:00 am British troops stormed the Turkish artillery observation outpost on the southwest of the perimeter, and its small detachment was also forced to surrender after putting up courageous resistance.

Then over the next hour all the remaining advanced positions fell, with it even reported that the enemy were evacuating portions of their main line. By this time Beersheba was virtually encircled by the two infantry divisions, and the two mounted divisions who had worked their way SE. Supporting artillery again moved forward to bombard the main Ottoman trench line in an attempt to break the wire for the attack on the town garrison's main positions.

Ottoman artillery in action

Displaying a cool ability the Turkish batteries, however, laid fire over the British infantry as they worked themselves into a position about 400 - 600 meters in front of the Turk trenches. During this period the British infantry suffered from enemy shelling.

Much of this was enfilade fire from positions northeast of Wadi Saba towards Beersheba. It was, theefore, with relief that they finally received the order to proceed with the main attack. With the sun at its highest point in the sky the British began storming the enemy's trenches which led to heavy fighting and considerable losses. In about 40 minutes all the trenches opposite 60th Division were captured, with the adjoining division on their right completing their task 20 minutes later. Only one brigade had struck difficulty owing to incomplete wire-cutting.

By 2.00 pm Arthur had advanced some way beyond the captured trenches towards Beersheba, while soldiers of the other division had managed to cross the Wadi Saba to clear trenches northward to a barrier on the Fara-Beersheba road. Whilst they forced remnants of one Turkish division to retreat back towards the Wadi el Saba, they did not follow the retreating Turks but rather remained in their captured trenches to establish their own defensive perimeter.

Due to a lack of water for the horses General Allenby wanted Beersheba to be taken and occupied by the Desert Mounted Corps. While Arthur had been part of the infantry attacks the mounted infantry who had manoeuvred themselves into position in the southeast, assailed the eastern front of Beersheba from the direction Wadi el Imleih to besiege Tel el Saba.

A short time later a British cavalry regiment was in the area of Khirbet um Butein and had reached the Beersheba to Hebron road.

The main hill and defences on Tel el Saba, east of the town, that overlooked its southeast and northeast approaches, was the key to taking the outpost township of Beersheba. No advance could take place across the desert floor corridor towards the town while the Turks strategically held this high ground. With Turko-German weaponry dug in over-looking the township from it's trench defences, it had to be in the hands of the Anzacs before a frontal attack on the town could take place.

On Beersheba's southern front two battalions of Ahmed's 48th regiment had hurriedly dug in even further and stayed put with only a weak body of enemy cavalry appearing, to depart just as quickly.

During the morning while British forward patrols were feeling out the defences of the Ottoman Cavalry Division, the New Zealand Mounted Rifles (NZMR) Brigade, with some assistance, commenced it's frontal assault against Tel el Saba. They had bravely begun their advance from the southeast knowing that the Turk defenders on the hill were well protected by the rocky terrain with not one tree impeding their view of the oncoming New Zealanders. With that open area leading to the hill providing no cover Turk machine gun fire brought the first attack to a standstill, while Ottoman pilots caused further losses to the New Zealand cavalry by bombing their horsemen.

Tell el Saba

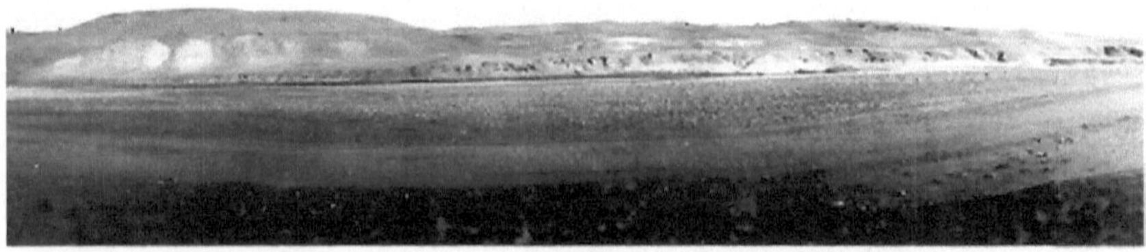

It was now obvious that the capture of the hill would take much longer than had been hoped. Further resolute attacks by the New Zealanders would come under continued heavy fire all day. As a consequence any secondary attack planned for the Australian Light Horse was held up until the threat of the machine guns on Tell el Saba could be cleared.

Given the overall situation units of the Ottoman 48th Regiment with Ahmed would have have the distinction of the first Turks to retire. Those remaining in the two battalions were ordered to withdraw from their position between Ras Ghannam and Tell el Saba, to positions behind Wadi el Saba, in the direction of Beersheba.

New Zealand Mounted Rifles on Tel el Saba

After intoducing fresh forces in a coordinated attack against both the north and south flanks of the hill, eventually, shortly before 3:00 pm the New Zealanders succeeded in taking Tel el Saba by storm. The under strength Turk battalion of Ahmed's fellow mehmets entrusted with its defence had doggedly held out with great courage for as long as they could, holding up two British cavalry divisions for six hours, along with preventing any outflanking manoeuvres around the Beersheba-Hebron road. With darkness approaching the overall outcome was that Anzac position was now in a critical state with those in the overall attack in desperate need of water for the horses and men. With the only water source available in the town itself it was at this eleventh hour that Australian General Harry Chauvel took a gamble ordering a mounted charge across the open ground into the enemy garrison town. With the 3rd Light Horse Brigade having been sent to reinforce the Anzac Mounted Division and with the swords of the 5th Mounted Brigade being retained as Corps reserve, the only brigade available was the 4th Light Horse Brigade. It, therefore, fell on their colonial shoulders to capture Beersheba.

Members of the Auckland Mounted Rifles gather on Tel el Saba after its capture from the Turks.

Shortly before their move, and fortunate for them, Ismet Bey who commanded the Beersheba garrison, had ordered a general retirement north from Beersheba at 4:00 pm. In preserving his own person he had wisely decided to withdraw his headquarters to that of a regiment located about six miles north of Beersheba in the Judean Hills.

Australian Light Horse on the move

Turkish troops with machine gun and range finder in the Wadi el Saba defending Beersheba.

At the same time Ottoman divisional engineers were ordered to destroy the Beersheba water supply.

Turkish defenders

Starting at a canter over the plain the mounted infantrymen of the Australian 4th Light Horse would employ a charge at full gallop once they were within artillery range. For Ahmed lying prone in Wadi el Saba the oncoming sight was awe inspiring. Normally they would have dismounted and attacked on foot but this was a full blown cavalry charge. Through the fall of artillery fire they rode with a rumbling thunder over the ground that had grown in intensity to peak as the first of them cleared the Turks' trenches.

Australian Light Horse charge towards Beersheba

On their extreme left flank Ahmed fired at an oncoming trooper. Unseated in the growing clouds of dust he fell sideways to bounce on the ground as his horse thundered on. Ahmed only got off one more shot before the outer flank horsemen were on top of them. As one horse jumped the mound he was sheltering behind its rider slashed out with a bayonet narrowly

Ottoman dead in trenches on Hill 1070

missing him. In that instant Ahmed realised that these cavalry troops had no swords and it dawned on him from the white plumes in their hats, with their rifles slung over their backs, that these were Australian Light Horse. Instead of stopping they had simply jumped their shallow wadi to gallop on with renewed energy towards Beersheba.

It was a sight to behold; lines of mounted soldiers, now camouflaged to some degree by the airborne sand and dust, continuing to charge towards the redoubt and entrenchments to the east of the town. A few minutes later those of the 4th Light Horse on the right were jumping the Turk trenches on the town's outskirts before turning to make a dismounted attack on the

Ottoman infantry in the trenches, gun pits and redoubts on rising ground to the east. Most of the 12th Light Horse Regiment on the left had ridden across the face of the main redoubt to find a gap in the Ottoman defences. Their squadrons were now riding on through the now sparsely spread defences, over the railway line and into Beersheba, where they would fortunately discover that the destruction of the wells that had been ordered by Ismet had only partially been accomplished.

Australian Light Horse riding into history

Camouflaged by the dust it had been immediately after the last horsemen had passed the Wadi Saba that Ahmed's squad made a dash to the northwest to bypass Beersheba to head for Tel es Sheria. Breaking through the thin Turkish lines the mounted troops had charged into history while the British were now capturing a good number of the fleeing garrison before the sun set. Although the Beersheba garrison had suffered many casualties stubborn fighting by strong Ottoman rear guards would delay the EEF who had been holding the remainder of the Gaza line.

Ahmed along with his squad had moved from their forward position on the wadi just prior to the 60th Division advancing to cross the wadi to clear trenches northward to the barrier on the Fara-Beersheba road.

The British Vickers machine gun

As fate would have it Ahmed, with remnants of the Ottoman 48th Regiment, retired directly into the path of the waiting 2/10th Middlesex Regiment who had moved also to the east in line with the EEF advance. As they came into view a warning burst from a Vickers machine gun suggested to the Turks that it would be wise to surrender. They chose to fire back while attempting to find cover. Several Lee Enfield's, Arthur's included, fired immediately while their machine gunner liberally sprayed the retreating soldiers. Several of the enemy fell in the fusillade of lead as Arthur worked the bolt on his rifle to fire again.

The Gallipoli Star

Below - The retreating Turks open fire

Arthur watched as the Turk he had aimed at was hit in the chest. The impact spun him sideways and fell to lie still. It was all over in half a minute, as without any natural cover 14 others deciding that surrender was preferable to suicide immediately dropped their weapons and raised their arms. Given the order to advance and secure these prisoners Arthur and four others leapt from cover to quickly close the distance between their line and their unarmed enemy. With their prisoners covered by four rifles they started back across the wadi. They had not gone far when Arthur came across the dead soldier he had hit, along with a young dead Turkish officer a few feet away. Initially he thought he was hallucinating as exposed lying on the sand, still hanging from the neck of the Turk mehmet, was his amulet. Arthur stood transfixed for a moment before quickly reaching down to remove it from around the dead soldier's neck.

An unfortunate end to a valiant Turk

On the spur of the moment as if to justify his action he also leant over the young officer to search pockets for intelligence. Removing his map case he also claimed his enamelled Gallipoli Star award from his tunic before catching up with the file of prisoners. Back with the battalion they handed over the enemy captives to be marched to the rear, while Arthur handing over the map case with its leather shoulder strap.

Ottoman prisoners

Even when he was back in position on the front line, with the amulet and Gallipoli Star both in his pocket, he still had difficulty focusing on what had just transpired. In a quiet moment he brought the amulet

out to study it. It was definitely the one he had lost two years earlier at Sulva Bay with its small icons depicting frogs on each half. There was no disputing its authenticity but it seemed an amazing coincidence that made him feel uneasy. The only thing he could think of was that the dead Ottoman soldier must have been

British troops on the move

fighting against him on Chocolate Hill to have had it on his person. Yet he still wanted a more rational explanation and the more he thought about the real reason in him being reconnected with the amulet the more he felt nervous.

Austrian troops march through Jerusalem

During the preceding three days EEF's XXI Corps who had been holding the Gaza section of the line had adopted a passive role until the night of 1st / 2nd November when determined night attacks had taken place on Gaza's defences. They had only partially succeeded due to the new strength of the Gaza garrison.

To the northeast the Ottoman III Corps new headquarters, since their withdrawn from Beersheba to Tel es Sheria, had moved back

The Imperial Camel Corps Brigade outside Beersheba, 1st November 1917

to support the defence of the road to Hebron and Jerusalem, at Dhahriye. They were now followed by a fresh regiment along with 1,500 rifles of the former Beersheba force that had been reorganised at Tel es Sheria. The latter group would then move to reinforce the defence of Tel el Khuweilfe several miles north of Beersheba.

Part XXVI

Having shifted to Jerusalem Simon the Redeemer was closing in on his two remaining candidates with the surname of Newcombe. Supplied to him on a short list by the ever resourceful SP the first was a Private Charles Newcombe in the Devonshire Regiment, with the second being Arthur. Simon had been fortunate in having had Arthur identified in a recently discovered Middlesex battalion photo that had been taken back in England shortly after his enlistment.

On 6th November the British bombardment of Gaza intensified. That night and the following morning successful attacks were launched on several trench systems defending the town. Then later that morning Gaza was found to have been evacuated during the night.

The Gaza to Beersheba line had then collapsed with the Ottoman armies now in full retreat. It was the first two steps along a road which would see the EEF capture Jerusalem six weeks later.

Jerusalem

Stewart Newcombe

The 1st November had also been a fateful day for Colonel Stewart Newcombe who had contributed a daring scheme to the military activity of the offensive. His had been behind enemy lines north of Beersheba where he had attempted to cut the Ottoman's communication lines, and their line of retreat.

The Ottoman command at Tel es Sheria

The Imperial Camel Corp (ICC) force on the move

Commanding the heavily-armed Imperial Camel Corp (ICC) group, Newcombe had become encircled and outnumbered by superior forces. With his casualties increasing he had no alternative other than to surrender. With German Intelligence having become aware of the activities of the Church in Rome, and thinking they were a lot more astute, they had worked on the premise that Colonel Stewart Newcombe was the 'Newcombe' the Catholics were after concerning the whereabouts of the amulet. They patiently waited their opportunity and now they had him in the bag, even though they were themselves retreating. To their autocratic German way of thinking, having served at Gallipoli as an officer of distinction, Stewart Newcombe had to be the British soldier who knew the whereabouts of the amulet and its messages.

Unfortunately for them it soon became patently clear that the colonel did not know *what the hell they were talking about!'* Stewart Newcombe would, however, endure some harsh treatment

Ottoman cavalry

Beersheba Railway Station after the attack

in the process, before they came to the conclusion he was telling the truth, and that he was actually ignorant of any artefact that held an ancient message.

Following his interrogation while captivity with the Ottoman Empre for an officer of Stewart's rank afforded some degree of comfort, his men fared a lot worse being forced to march to prison camps in Anatolia. Many would die en-route. For the colonel the following months were to be full of danger, intrigue, and more surprisingly, romance, but he would never forget his men.

As for Arthur Edgar Newcombe he was again wearing the amulet still trying to figure out the odds of what had occurred in him getting it back. With a heightened sense of foreboding he had lain in his bivouac that night with his mind racing. Was it fate, or if not who was pulling the strings? He was trying to think of some rational explanation, as deep down inside he could not accept that it was some coincidence. What were the odds of that soldier first having faced him at Suvla Bay, to then recover the amulet, and then be the one in the middle of another battle some 1,500 miles away that he had the fortune to shoot and virtually trip over. It all seemed a bit surreal. Maybe in the great ethereal gift that was life there was some sort of intended plan for him, even if it was beyond his comprehension.

Ottoman dead

Arthur had considered himself normal but now he was starting to wonder. He needed an explanation that made some sort of sense, but instinctively he knew he was not going to find one. The combination of events, and coincidences, combined with the vagaries of war were just too mind boggling to keep trying to fathom. One thing he did know was that the amulet was dangerous with others obviously willing to kill for it, so he applied his thinking to something he could control. Recent experience told him that all was not right and he knew he had to figure out what he should do. Knowing that his friend Budge back at the British Museum had some interest in the artefact he decided he would hide it and keep quiet about its coincidental recovery in the meantime.

Escorting Turkish prisoners

Following the capture of Beersheba British engineers, who had at initially reported that the water supply and wells had been captured intact, would be proved wrong. Within 48 hours a shortage of water would be severely felt.

After Beersheba had been secured an advance northward had begun headed by the 53rd Division with others taking over their outpost line. One of this division's brigade groups advanced in a northerly direction to the west of Ain Kohleh while the remainder, including Arthur and the 2/10th Middlesex Battalion, advanced in a north-easterly direction on Kuweilfeh. This northerly advance was successful with a line established on their desired objective; a ridge running east and west some five or six miles north of Beersheba. The advance involving Arthur was not so fortunate with them encountering strong opposition, while something had also gone wrong with their supply of both water and ammunition.

After the fall of Beersheba the Turkish Seventh Army had retired to the stronghold of Tel es Sheria commanded by German commander Kress von Kressenstein's Eighth Army. Panicked there by another diversionary attack to the east by a 70-strong camel company, the Turkish defenders had begun to scatter believing it to be a large-scale flank attack by the British. In so doing they left the flank of the Seventh Army exposed. To complicate matters a Turkish division sent to reinforce forces the Ottoman's believed were still defending Beersheba had been redirected to Kuweilfeh in anticipation of an attempt by the British to turn their extreme right flank. The 53rd were now keeping them busy and in so doing stopping them being able to send any serious force back to support Sheria.

It was impossible country to campaign in; practically without tracks, and very much broken up with wadis and rocky precipices making it difficult to maintain communications, even though a mounted brigade had been thrown in to help the 53rd. No great progress was being made, with them managing to get through most of their water and ammunition. Located some three miles N.W. of Beersheba it would be an anxious day with them now in dire need to replenishment. With Arthur clutching his amulet for luck there was now considerable doubt in view of the general scarcity of water whether it would be possible to carry on with their part in the campaign involving rolling up the Sheria and Kuwauka defences from the east.

To relieve the situation, on the afternoon of the 5th, Allenby rapidly issued orders for an attack next day on the Sheria defences and the Kuwauka system. As most of the troops destined for the Sheria attack were at this time in the outpost line it meant a concentration and deployment by night over unknown country where map reading would be very difficult indeed. For all of that the mission was successfully carried out and by dawn on the 6th November the British struck north splitting the two Ottoman armies.

By midday the complete line of the Sheria defences were in British hands. With this success in the bag another British division now took over, advancing to attack the wells and railway station at Tel-el-Sheria. By this time it was getting dark and unfortunately direction was to some extent lost. The Turks and Germans put up a good fight, and it was not until the morning of the 7th that the wells and station were in British hands.

Ottoman Prisioners WW1

Allenby had hoped to trap Kressenstein's Eighth Army at Gaza but the Turks had retreated in some haste further up the coast; with them finally abandoning Gaza on 6th and 7th November, 1917.

The Turks now fell back to establish themselves in Jerusalem preparatory to making a stand once more against the British.

Both Simon and his Circassian rebel guide were frustrated in being forced to bide their time in Jerusalem while Ottoman forces fought futile rear-guard actions. Simon tried to console himself that at least the two suspects they were looking for were heading

The ruins of Gaza 1917

their way. Whilst he had learnt to restrain his tendency in displaying his aggressive nature unless he was alone with a candidate for redemption, he could not just sit and wait.

As for Arthur and the other Middlesex's battalion survivors they had been withdrawn back closer to Beersheba. From here they could see Turkish dumps blazing all night off to the north indicating that Johnny Turk had made up his mind to opt for a general retreat.

The 53rd Division, would remain in the vicinity of Beersheba for almost a month. Plagued by ill health and deprived of their transport that had been taken by other divisions due to supply difficulties, it would be here that the division re-gathered needed supplies slowly. It was during this period that Arthur requested to be ordered back to Deir el Belah as one of the escorts of Ottoman prisoners, and to secure needed supplies.

Nine miles south of Gaza, and six miles north of Khan Yunis along the coastline of the eastern Mediterranean, lay Deir al-Balah. It had been captured by the British following the surrender of Khan Yunis back in February, and been the launching point for the

Deir al-Belah cemetery

Ottoman prisoners

Wire – Gaza 1917

British forces against Gaza and Beersheba to its north and northeast respectively. Arthur knew it well, along with the 724 marked graves that had been dug there back in March. Then in April it had also become an aerodrome and army camp with an established Field Post Office. The cemetery where Private Harold Newcombe was buried was located neraby and it now became part of an idea that Arthur now considered prudent.

Deir al-Belah airfield

Without letting on what he was considering Arthur had made a request of his Lieutenant that he be allowed to accompany the stores'

The registered envelope addressed to Jehanne Blanche

detail back to the coast, to visit both the Field Post Office at Deir al-Balah and it's cemetery. With his application granted, and knowing he would get two hours spare before his detail needed to return to the front, he put his plan in action. With a small trench shovel he first visited the cemetery to look down on the grave of Private Harold Newcombe. As far as he was aware nothing further had transpired by way of intelligence concerning his murder back on the 4th July. Checking that no one was in the vicinity he quickly dug a foot down at the head of the grave to bury the amulet in an oil paper wrapping. Covering up his excavation he placed a small rock over it before smoothing out the sand to remove all traces of his visit. Discreetly retiring from the area he next visited the censor at the Deir al-Balah Field Post Office to write to his friend Jehanne Blanche. He suspected that Jehanne had contacts with Cairo Intelligence, and independent of that, she was the only person he trusted and whom he had an address for in Eygpt. Additionally Jehanne knew Ernest Budge, and Arthur knew that she would do the right thing should anything untoward happen to him.

His short message to her read… *Dear Jehanne,*

I trust this finds you well. As one of the last of our original battalion intake remaining I have a fear of not making it through. I have hidden a piece of Mr Budge's property and note under Pte Harold N. (my name) grave Deir al-Belah cemetery. You may want to recover for him soonest. If I do get to the end I look forward meeting with you to share a smile and hear what you have been doing.

Yours, Arthur.

In September, 1917, the NILI operative Eitan Belkind had set out for Egypt to look into the circumstances regarding his friend Feinberg's death earlier that year. Caught by Bedouin in the Sinai he had been handed over to the Turks and transported to Damascus.

Unfortunately that autumn one of the NILI's message carrying pigeons had also been caught by the Turks who had been able to decrypt the Hebrew, Aramaic, French, and English NILI code within a week. As a result they had been able to unravel NILI's spy network. Even with Ottoman forces in retreat, and with the writing to some degree on the wall, the leadership of the Yishuv and the Hashomer still disassociated itself from NILI and its actions. One by one the NILI group began to be discovered and captured; which hastened as some gave others up under the stress of torture. Wanted by the Ottomans for his activities Yosef Lishansky had escaped capture several times previously. This included being wounded but managing to reach British lines. Continuing his activities he was now betrayed by Hashomer when he sought refuge with them. He was also captured, along with Na'aman Belkind who reportedly revealed secret information about the group. The prisoners were now 

Yosef Lishansky

incarcerated in Damascus with Yosef Lishansky sentenced to be hanged in the public square.

By mid-October the Turks had surrounded Zichron Yaakov where they arrested numerous other people including Sarah who surrendered to spare her aging father from torture by the Turks. Sarah was 27 years of age and her end was not a pleasant one with her eventually managing to commit suicide after four days of torture. The Turks had been planning on transporting her elsewhere for their continued pleasure and she had requested to be taken home to change her clothes. It was here that she had shot herself with a pistol hidden in her bathroom, to die several days later.

Sarah Aaronsohn

Other prisoners were also incarcerated in Damascus.

Earlier in the year Chaim Weizmann had sent NILI's founder and leader, Aaron Aaronsohn, on a political campaign to the United States. It was while he was there that Aaron learned of NILI's carrier pigeon having been intercepted that had led to the demise

Deir al-Belah lagoon

of the group, along with the arrest and death of his sister.

Following the Balfour Declaration of November 1917 Aaron Aaronsohn would become increasingly active in the campaign to

Hangings in the public square in Damascus

increase British and Zionist relations. In the spring of 1918 he would return as a member of the Zionist Commission, but remain in Cairo until the end of the war.

As for Lloyd George's instruction to General Edmund Allenby that the British people expected the capture of Jerusalem before

Ottoman troops outside Jerusalem 1917

A crashed RFC BE2c in the Palestine hills around Jerusalem - Nov 1917. The Germans are a crew from the local Field Ambulance paying respects to a fallen enemy.

Charles Newcombe's Devonshire Regiment advancing towards Jerusalem

numbers by RFC bombing and strafing. All the while British artillery directed by No. 113 Squadron aircraft had added to the confusion as the British gave chase. When the retreating Turks were out of range, naval gunfire had taken over, also using aerial spotting for the fall of shot.

On the 20th November the British again attacked the enemy's positions, meeting very strong resistance around Beirtunia some four miles short of their objective. Included in this attack was a battalion of the Devonshire Regiment with one of their 'rank and file' being a Private Charles Newcombe. He was no close relation to Arthur and he had been with his regiment since their assembly at El Arish the previous March.

The Devonshire regimental badge

Charles's last occasion with his mates would be a hurried meal on the evening of the 22nd November. In the early hours, the following morning, he was abducted unseen from within British lines. He would be interrogated and murdered further up the Nablus to Jerusalem road by Simon the Redeemer and his associate, before his body was discovered and reported later that day.

With Arthur oblivious to Charles demise General Chetwode had organised two forces for his attack on Jersuslam, with the main attack to be made on the city from the west. The other would be made by Arthur's 53rd Division to which were now attached another supporting battalion, a heavy artillery battery, and a light armoured car battery.

Known as Mott's Detachment they had been given orders to begin their move north. Whilst the Turks had withdrawn northwards it was not known how far they had gone, although it was known that there were active patrols as far south as Hebron. The plan of advance was explained to commanders in a meeting on the 3rd December.

Anticipating that the detachment would likely face a well developed series of enemy redoubts and trenches, the overall 'speed of march' was set as that of Mott's Detachment. It was known that the anticipated Ottoman redoubts had been completed a year earlier, and that they had recently been strengthened. Therefore, if the Turks moved to block Mott's force, the plan was for the other divisions to attack north of Jerusalem. The ideal scenario was still to take the city from the south and west, with Mott's Detachment closing in from the south while the main attack came from the west.

British infantry on the move

The 53rd Division's role with the detachment was to advance

northwards along the Beersheba to Jerusalem road to take Hebron and Bethlehem before moving eastwards to secure the road from Jerusalem to Jericho.

On the 4th December Arthur and his battalion began their 50 mile march up the narrow, poorly formed, Hebron road. Progress was slow with them still having to haul their own supplies from Gaza by a variety of methods that included rail, trucks, camels, and mules. Mott's desire to advance with extreme caution, however, delayed progress with them not reaching, and passing through, Hebron until the 5th. At this point orders were received for them to proceed at full speed until shot at, and without bothering with reconnaissance. Mott, however, again hesitated continually believing reports from uninformed locals while Chetwode impatiently ordered him onwards to get into a position three miles south of Jerusalem by the morning of 8th December.

The poorly formed road north

At Mott's insistence the detachment's advance guard again moved tentatively during the night of 5th December to three miles north of Hebron. By the 7th they had made contact with the Ottoman position defending Bethlehem where bad weather prevented any further advance. Despite being under direct orders of GHQ, they were still on the Hebron road south of Bethlehem, four miles short of their objective. Whilst they had managed to capture Solomon's Pools to the south of Bethlehem they were supposed to have advanced northwards in time to cover the right flank of the 60th (London) Division in the attack on Jerusalem, and to cut the road from Jerusalem to Jericho.

On the morning of the 8th Ottoman artillery began firing on a road junction they were required to negotiate, and with shells bursting amongst them with monotonous regularity Arthur clung to his rifle wondering if he would ever get to see the Holiest of cities. Like Stopford and Suvla Bay Mott continued to dither unable, it appeared, to advance, or retaliate, against the accurate shell fire from the Ottoman battery near Bethlehem. Around noon the

Ottoman artillery – Judean Hills

detachment was again ordered to get moving with the order couched in plain English. This time it seemed to have the desired effect with them finally getting to attack their main objective at Beit Jala at 4.00 pm that afternoon. As for their enemy the Ottoman Army had in fact already retired, and so it was not until that evening that they continued their advance to find the way completely clear of Ottoman defenders.

As it transpired, however, at the crucial moment Mott had been unable to cover the southern flank of the 60th (London) Division and as a consequence they had been forced to pause during daylight as enfilading fire made any advance even more costly than it already had been. Needless to say with the 60th's casualties mounting Chetwode was by now justifiably in a foul mood with Mott.

By the 8th December, 1917, in almost continuous rain, Jerusalem ceased to be protected by the Ottoman Empire and Chetwode launched his final advance taking the heights to the west of the city that day. The defending Ottoman army retreated that evening and the city attempted to surrender the following morning when the mayor of Jerusalem, Hussein Salim al-Husseini, delivered the Ottoman Governor's letter to two sergeants of a London Regiment who were located just outside Jerusalem's western limits. The sergeants who had been scouting ahead of Allenby's main force refused to take the letter and it would be eventually be accepted by Brigadier General C.F. Watson, commanding the 180th Brigade.

Jerusalem was now almost entirely encircled by the EEF, although, Ottoman Army units briefly held the Mount of Olives on 9th December before being overwhelmed the following afternoon.

On 14th December, 1917, Allenby reported to the War Cabinet that the rainy season would prevent any further operations for at least two months after Jerusalem was secured. Now paralysed by a breakdown in logistics it would force Allenby to send the Anzac and the Australian Mounted Divisions, along with the Imperial Camel Corps Brigade, to the south of Gaza to shorten their lines

The surrender of Jerusalem to the British, 9th December 1917

of supply. He wrote… *I can't feed them, with certainty, and even now, a fortnight's heavy rain would bring me near starvation.*

Any further advance had come to a halt.

A move into the Judean Hills would rely heavily on the ability of supply lines keeping the front line troops provisioned with food, water and ammunition. Already operating at considerable distances from their railhead and base, the advance was forced to pause on 17th November to enable supplies to be brought forward for the infantry. This was carried out by columns under corps control that had been sent back to the railhead. With the Turks having destroyed as much of their infrastructure as they could during their retreat, transporting needed supplies forward was a slow yet continuous 24-hour-a-day business.

Landing stores at Wadi Sukereir

Supplies were also being shipped by sea and landed at Wadi Sukereir, as they would later be at Jaffa. This latter port town had been occupied by the New Zealand Mounted Rifles Brigade on 16th

November, however, Ottoman troops forced out of the town were still able to interdict shipping and harass troop movements from their new defensive positions on the northern bank of the Yarkon River at Nahr el Auja.

Further east, before Jerusalem could be truly secured fighting would continue in the Judean Hills to the north and east of the Hebron–Junction station line. As part of these Jerusalem operations there were also successful second attempts on 21st and 22nd December to advance across the Nahr el Auja. With a lack of infrastructure at Jaffa, however, all supplies brought via ship still had to be unloaded into surf boats, which then were unloaded on the beaches. Naturally, these operations were heavily dependent on the weather, so the eventual amount of supplies transported by sea was limited.

Landing supplies at Jaffa

Trucks of the British Army Service Corps (ASC) Motor Transport companies, along with camels of the Egyptian Camel Transport Corps, continued to use the single, narrow, poorly metalled road from Gaza to Junction Station. Between Gaza and Beit Hanun, however, the unsealed road was deep in sand making it difficult for trucks to proceed even with only a light load of one ton.

For the Turks the loss of Jaffa and Jerusalem, together with the loss of 50 miles of territory during the EEF's advance, constituted a grave setback for the Ottoman Empire and their army. It had been an advance that had included the capture of Beersheba, Gaza, Hareira, Tel es Sheria, Tel el Khuweilfe, Mughar Ridge, and Jaffa. As a result of these victories British Empire forces had eventually captured Jerusalem to establish a new strategically strong fortified line.

Austrian troops leaving Jerusalem

This new line now ran from north of Jaffa on the coastal plain, across the Judean Hills to Bireh north of Jerusalem, and from there, east of the Mount of Olives. With the capture of the road from Beersheba to Jerusalem, via Hebron and Bethlehem together with substantial Ottoman territory south of Jerusalem, the city was effectively secured.

An older section of Jerusalem

General Edmund Allenby respectfully entered the Old City through the Jaffa Gate on the 11th December, and in a show of respect for the Holy city he had done so on foot, instead of on horse or in a vehicle. He was now the first Christian in many centuries to control Jerusalem and his success was seen as a great moral victory for the British Empire. With God obviously on his side the Prime Minister of the United Kingdom, David Lloyd George described the capture as *a Christmas present for the British people…*

Allenby simply remarked… *The wars of the crusaders are now complete*!

General Sir Edmund Allenby enters Jerusalem – December 1917

Jewish soldiers in the British army in a camp near Jerusalem

To the inhabitants of Jerusalem the Blessed, and the people dwelling in its vicinity.

The defeat inflicted upon the Turks by the troops under my command has resulted in the occupation of your city by my forces. I, therefore, now proclaim it to be under martial law, under which form of administration it will remain so long as military considerations make this necessary.

However, lest any of you be alarmed by reason of your experience at the hands of the enemy who has retired, I hereby inform you that it is my desire that every person pursue his lawful business without fear of interruption.

Furthermore, since your city is regarded with affection by the adherents of three of the great religions of mankind, and its soil has been consecrated by the prayers and pilgrimages of multitudes of devout people of these three religions for many centuries, I make it known to you that every sacred building, monument, holy spot, shrine, traditional site, endowment, pious bequest, or customary place of prayer, of whatsoever form of the three religions, will be maintained and protected according to the existing customs and beliefs of those to whose faith they are sacred.

Guardians have been established at Bethlehem, and on Rachel's Tomb. The tomb at Hebron has been placed under exclusive Moslem control.

The hereditary custodians at the gates of the Holy Sepulchre have been requested to take up their accustomed duties in remembrance of the magnanimous act of the Caliph Omar, who protected that church

Ottoman troops Nablus Road, Jerusalem

On New Year's Day of 1918, the Australian Mounted Division began moving back through the rain and slush to Deir el Belah, south of Gaza.

The Anzac Mounted Division did not move back quite so far; with two brigades moving to Esdud, while the New Zealand Mounted Rifles Brigade bivouacked near Ayun Kara, or Rishon Le Zion, just south of Jaffa.

Grain boat – Dead Sea 1917

On 3rd January two Australian aircraft discovered Ottoman boats carrying corn and hay moving from Ghor el Hadit and Rujm el Bahr at the northern end of the Dead Sea. They were bombed and sprayed with bullets repeatedly until the enemy boat service stopped.

Australian Flying Corp – early 1918

On the 10th, as part of the preparations for the attack on Jericho, six aircraft dropped 48 bombs on Amman and Kissir. This latter place was

The Royal Flying Corp (RFC)

a railway station six miles to the south of Amman on the Hejaz. The aircraft's efforts resulted in several direct hits on rolling stock, station buildings and troops.

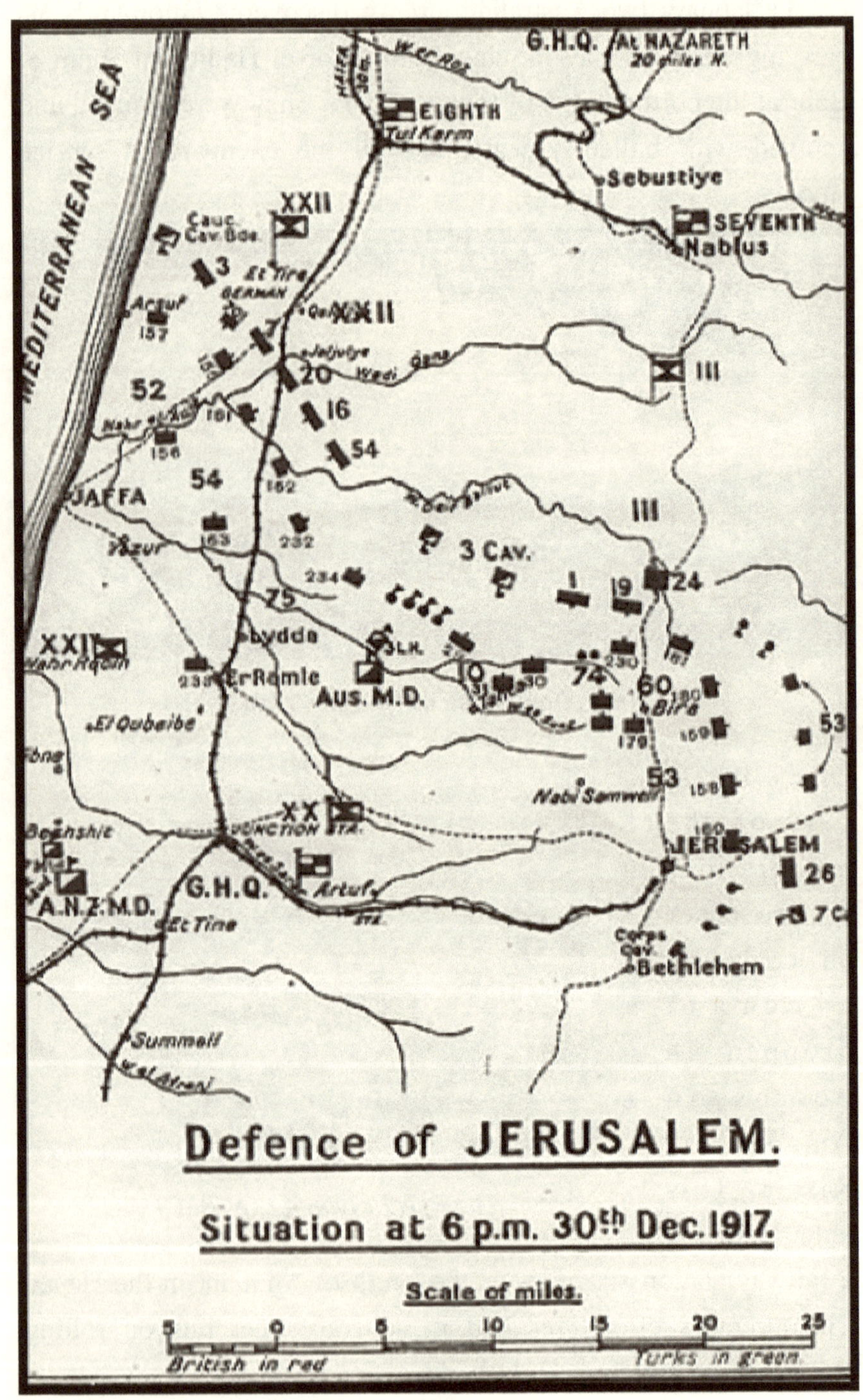

MEDITERRANEAN SEA
G.H.Q. At NAZARETH
20 miles N.
W. er Ret
HAIFA Jan.
EIGHTH
Tul Karm
Sebustiye
SEVENTH
Nablus
XXII
Cauc. Cav. Bde.
3 Et Tira
GERMAN
Acsur
157
Ge. XXII
Jeljulye
20 Wadi Gana
52
16
Nahr el
156
54
54
162
III
JAFFA
163
232
II. Deir Ballut
75
3 CAV.
234
1
9 24
III
lydda
75
S.L.H.
230
81
XXI
Aus. M.D.
74 60 180
Nahr Rubin
233 Er Ramle
Biré
El Qubeibe
230
179 159
53
Ebna
53 158
Nabi Samwel
XX
160
JUNCTION STA.
JERUSALEM
Beershit
26
G.H.Q.
Artuf
7C
A.N.Z.M.D.
Et Tine
Artuf STA.
Corps
Cav.
Bethlehem
Summell
W. el Afranj

Defence of JERUSALEM.

Situation at 6 p.m. 30th Dec. 1917.

Scale of miles.
5   0   5   10   15   20   25
British in red   Turks in green.

Part XXVII

Standing on its rocky plateau, bounded on the east by the valley of the Kidron and on the west and south by the Wadi Er Rababi, or valley of Hinom, Arthur looked at the city that was Jerusalem. As the location of the First Temple built by Solomon, the site of Jesus Christ's crucifixion and purported resurrection, and the destination of Muhammad's night journey and ascension, it bore more religious significance to the three Abrahamic faiths than any other. Whilst he knew it was steeped in the principal sacred narratives of Christianity, along with its strong Islamic association, it continued to be the political and spiritual hub of Judaism. Shared with the other Abrahamic faiths he was unaware, however, that the first Moslems had directed their prayer toward this city rather than towards Mecca.

With his love of history and antiquity Arthur Newcombe would enter the ancient city through its western Jaffa Gate as Allenby had. The Jaffa Road that led to the gate negotiated its way through a valley between the northern hill of the Acra and the southern hill of Mount Zion. This road, and the valley it followed, continued eastward down into the Tyropoeon Valley that bisected the northern and southern halves of the city. It was here that the Christian and Muslim quarters lay to the north, with the Armenian and Jewish quarters to the south.

Passing through the Jaffa Gate he discovered a small square with entrances leading off it to the Christian Quarter on the left and the Moslem Quarter, as part of the 'suq' or marketplace, directly ahead. From his small map he could see that the Moslems

The Temple Mount and the Jewish Quarter

bordered the Christian Quarter and the Temple Mount in the east. while the Armenian Quarter was to his right. It included the distinctive landmark that was the Tower of David that was believed to have been built on the site of Herod the Great's Tower of Phasael.

Bordering this quarter to the southeast was the Jewish Quarter of the old walled city, located on a higher hill before the Temple Mount itself. With a Jewish population in the quarter of around 20,000 it was not homogeneously Jewish but rather a mix that had neither been desired by its Jewish inhabitants, or been enforced by its previous Ottoman rulers. Most of the homes in the quarter were in all reality leased from Moslem property owners. This had resulted in growth of buildings west of the city walls since land

outside the city was considered 'mulk', or freehold, and easier to acquire. Most residents, however, still preferred to live near members of their own community, and with Moslems living in the Jewish Quarter and Jews living in the Moslem, there was intense overcrowding.

Arthur had immeditely noticed this mass of humanity along with the dusky Bedouin merchants. They had toted their assortment of boxes and bags into the city and assumed, he could only surmise, their usual market places. With faces framed by various coloured and white head-coverings they were selling fresh figs, grapes, and okra amongst oranges and other produce. One carried a huge golden teapot on his back from which he sold a strange cold liquid tasting like old tea mixed with liquorice. None looked out of place, other than the visiting British soldiers, and one other.

Simon the Redeemer was only a short distance from the gate when Arthur came face to face with him. There was something in the shift of his eyes, and his piercing glare, that immediately told Arthur that he was in trouble.

As for Simon he had quickly taken in Arthur's regimental cap

Inside the Jaffa gate

badge and his facial features, memorised from the earlier battalion photo, and he knew instantly that he had been delivered an unexpected opportunity. In a split second he grabbed Athur's left arm with a force that belied his build. To Arthur this priest was now proven to be no gentle soul, in fact, judging by his eyes and his smell of garlic, he doubted whether he had a soul at all. Pulling back Arthur attempted to free himself from Simon's grasp but he could not. In that instant he suspected that this individual had something to do with the Ernest Budge's amulet. If that was the case then this representation of the anti-Christ must have had something to do with the deaths of others of his name.

Being steered forcibly through the crowd by his gripped arm Arthur's mind continued to race quickly concluding that guile was going to be his best form of escape. Judging that he might throw his captor mentally off balance if he surprised him, he waited for an opportunity.

They were almost alongside an outdoor merchant's display of religious icons and artefacts when Arthur cried out ….

STOP!.. STOP.. The amulet you want is on the table on your left!

Outdoor merchants

The statement had an immediate effect on his captor whose penetrating gaze instantly swept the table to his left. It was in that instant, with his mind momentarily focused elsewhere, that Arthur suspected he was likely to unconsciously loosen his grip.

Arthur reacted … Chopping down with all his strength on his

captor's wrist, he ripped his arm free. The priest's reaction was quick but not quite quick enough, while Arthur had an instant of luck. Ducking under a shop display of Turkish rugs the priest's hand only missed grasping his collar by his fingertips. Tripping over a basket of oranges, to send them cascading down a set of steps, Arthur jumped another. What had started as an historic outing was now replaced by only a glance at an arch, doorway, or minaret, while every step brought him closer to the tangible remains of long since decayed dramatic chapter in Jewish history.

Inside the city from the Jaffa gate

Darting between the alleyways he would miss many sites and surprises that could have turned his visit into something special. In the heart of the Jewish quarter he exited down steps onto the main street of the city, the colonnaded Cardo. Here, he was forced to again change direction by the nearby remnants of Jerusalem's West Wall, from the time of the First Temple that had fallen to the Babylonians with its destruction in 586 BC. Passing those against it at prayer he turned right back into another less crowded alleyway, and without a backward glance, ducked into a carpet store where he leapt two kneeling workers stitching a rug on its floor. Tripping on the end of the carpet he was catapulted out into the alley beyond.

Jerusalem's West Wall – The wailing wall

Scrambling amongst a mass of legs he was dragged to his feet by Simon's Circassian guard as several dirty looking street urchins and rabbis looked on in amazement. Arthur lashed out with his left elbow catching the Circassian below the ribs before grabbing his birka to hip throw him to the stone cobbles. Free from his grasp Arthur again disappeared through the gathering throng to eventually find sanctity and freedom in another alley alcove two streets over.

He had turned sharply right behind a stack of bales to duck through an open Parisian style gate of a residence to hide in the cool darkness of its portico. Looking back through the gate latch opening he witnessed the Circassian run past. There was no sign of the priest, who, unbeknown to Arthur, had resigned himself to having to resort to other means to catch his elusive quarry. From the shadows, with his mind was still racing, Arthur quickly reflected on what had just transpired.

Judging by the evil looking priest's eyes they had definitely shown murderous intent. He had reacted instantly to his mention of the amulet, and he had also

obviously recognised him to make the wild lunge at him the way he had. His mind went back to Gallipoli and the dark figure that he had narrowly avoided on the beached destroyer in Suvla Bay. Putting the pieces together in his mind he then remembered the suspicious murder of Harold Newcombe back at Gaza. Given what he had gleaned from the interview at the time it now became obvious to him that all of these occurences had been connected. Now convinced it was his amulet these murderers were after he wished he had not sent the letter to Jehanne considering that it may also place her in harm's way.

A number of Arthur's fellow soldiers

He was definitely in danger in the city and it was obvious he was going to have to watch his back. Not being able to trust anyone other than his battalion associates, he realised it would pay for him in future to stick close to them, both in and outside of camp, until the situation could be resolved.

Wailing wall, Jerusalem, with military visitors - 1918

Mount of Olives - Jerusalem

Arthur's 53rd Division camp east of Jerusalem

The first British guard at the Jaffa Gate - Jerusalem

With Arthur remaining safely in the confines of his camp aircraft patrols were now directed to fly over Jericho and Shunet Nimrin, on the western and eastern sectors of the Jordan Valley, on alternate days. These patrols closely watched and reported the enemy's tactical moves; including the number of tents and camps, the state of supply dumps, the conditions of roads, tracks, and traffic on the railway.

On patrol

As a member of the Imperial War Cabinet, General Jan Christiaan Smuts had been sent to confer with Allenby regarding the implementation of a French qualification to the War Office's Joint Note No. 12, in that no troops from France could be redeployed to the EEF. Smuts was on his way back to London in February when the first step was taken to accomplish a plan to cross the Jordan River.

On 25th January Allenby had recorded his intention to extend his right flank to include Jericho, and the land north of the Dead Sea, thus removing the threat to his right by pushing the enemy across the Jordan River and in securing the Jordan River crossings. It would also prevent raids into the country to the west of the Dead Sea and provide a narrow starting point for operations against the Hejaz Railway.

The country on the eastern side of the Judean Hills falls into the Jordan Valley in a confused mass of rocky ridges and deep narrow valleys. With the main wadis running from west to east, often with steep high banks, tributaries join from all directions that break up these ridges, making the hills almost impossible to cross. At the time of these operations most tracks ran along the narrow beds of ravines where progress had to be made in single file.

Further north closer to Jericho, at Jebel Kuruntul and the Mount of Temptation, the mountains ended abruptly in a 1,000 foot cliff. This meant that any attacking parties would have to haul themselves, and each other, over abrupt cliffs to be in a position to fight at close quarters at the top.

Three Ottoman armies were now deployed to defend their front line. The first, defending the Mediterranean section, was head-quartered at Tul Keram; another was at Nablus, defended the Judean Hills sector; while a third was head-quartered at Amman, defended the eastern Transjordan section of their line. 3,000 to 5,000 Ottoman troops of two Turkish infantry divisions defended the area on the western edge of the Jordan Valley. They garrisoned a series of hill-top defences from Tubk el Kaneiterah, near the Dead Sea, through Talat ed Dumm, to the Wadi Fara. Here the remainder were entrenched at Ras um Deisis, and El Muntar Iraq Ibrahim astride the Jericho road. There was also at least one regiment in the Jordan Valley near the Wadi el Auja.

Turkish defenders behind trees north of Jerusalem

By February, logistics had sufficiently developed to support the Allied advance towards Jericho, and Allenby ordered Lieutenant General Philip Chetwode's Corp to capture the town as soon as the weather cleared. While the remainder of the EEF held the front line and garrisoned the captured territories in southern Palestine, Chetwode's Corps was to make the attack towards Jericho. His effort was to be supported by the 53rd Division with one other infantry brigade on their left. The latter's objective was to move towards the Wadi el Auja, that flowed eastwards into the Jordan River.

Concurrent with this move, Chauvel's Desert Mounted Corps, made up of brigades from the Anzac Mounted Division, were to cover the right flank of Chetwode's infantry with one company advancing towards Rujm el Bahr on the Dead Sea.

The plan was for an infantry division to advance to Mukhmas, eight miles north-north-east of Jerusalem, and to then move forward six miles east, through El Muntar Iraq Ibrahim and Ras et Tawil. This division's left flank was to be covered by Arthur's 53rd Division, who were designated to capture the high ground at Rammun, three miles north of Mukhmas, while their right was being covered by the Anzac Mounted Division.

Turks in retreat

The second stage, and final advance, was to then take them to the edge of the ridge overlooking Jericho and the Jordan Valley, with no plan for them to enter the valley until that objective had been achieved. Each infantry column was to be supported by a 6-inch artillery battery, a Field artillery brigade, and a field company of Royal Engineers.

On 14th February, preliminary operations were carried out with one infantry division advancing to Mukhmas eight miles north-north-east of Jerusalem, while on their left flank the 53rd were designated to capture the village of Deir Diwan.

At this time Chauvel's Desert Mounted Corps were at Ayun Kara. They had marched out for Bethlehem arriving there on 17th and 18th February. While the infantry attacks were progressing along

Signal Post Ayun Kara

the road between Jerusalem and Jericho on 19th, the two brigades of the Anzac Mounted Division were to move in a flanking movement towards Nebi Musa.

Ottoman troops on the move

They were to make their way down into the Jordan Valley towards Rujm el Bahr to cut off enemy retreat from Jericho, and drive the remaining Ottoman defenders to the eastern side of the Jordan River.

On the night of 18th February Arthur was resting in his bivouac in camp with his 2/10th Middlesex Regiment on the outskirts of Deir Diwan, when a bayonet was noisily swished under his tent canvas. Hurriedly rising to face the threat he was unaware whose hand it was that clamped over his mouth, or delivered the blow that knocked him unconscious. Kidnapped by the Catholic SP agent Simon the Redeemer and his Circassian guide, Arthur was stealthily carried from the camp past the unsuspecting pickets to be transported north strapped to a horse saddle. Carried to an olive grove on the outskirts of the village of Et Taiyibe he was brought back to consciousness by the flaying of a stick that bit into his still bound arms.

Asked continuously in English, ….. *WHERE is AMULET?*... he held out until a red hot wedge was forced under one of his finger nails, with the nail then forcibly extracted with a set of pliers. He screamed the scream of the dead jabbering out the hidden location of the amulet as being buried in a grave at Gaza. With further nail removals the pain intensified as he willingly stammered out all the details of any question he was asked.

The torture, however, did not stop there as Simon the Redeemer, with a new found delight, perpetrated any indignity he could on the now still form of Arthur Edgar Newcombe. Considering his victim suitably religiously purged of his sins Simon, along with his Circassian guide, left him hanging in a tree. With the information they needed as to the whereabouts of the amulet they stealthily once more made their way southeast. Their plan was to get back across the Jordan River into Turkish held territory to the Circassian Moab village of Es Sir where they could plan the recovery of the amulet.

From nearby Amman, Simon could also communicate in code with Rome by telegraph if it was still operational.

'X' marks the location where Arthur Newcombe's body was found

As Simon and his Circassean associate evaded British positions in the early hours of Tuesday 19th February, 1918, Arthur was reported missing. With the 53rd Division in the first stages of a new advance there was little that could be done. That morning their infantry advanced with the New Zealand Wellington Mounted Rifle Regiment covering their right flank. Being early spring the area was covered by wild flowers including cyclamen, anemones, poppies and tulips.

At Ras et Tawil they suffered 50 casualties in attacking 300 entrenched Turks; capturing 25 prisoners and two machine guns, before the Ottoman troops abandoned their position. To the north-east of El Muntar Iraq Ibrahim, during a further advance by the infantry along a narrow ridge on the south bank of the Wadi Fara, they captured the high ground suffering 66 casualties. On their left flank Arthur's brigade captured Rammun, where the 2/10th Middlesex Regiment had some hard fighting on the heights to the south.

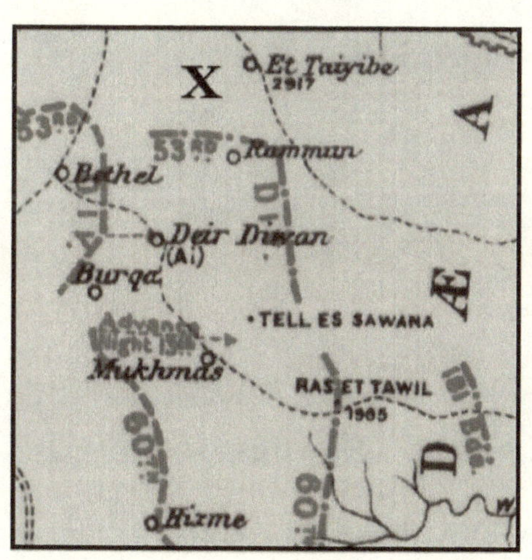

'X' marks the approximate location where the body of Arthur Edgar Newcombe was discovered.

Preliminary operations the same day, along the brigade's line of advance, to identify better gun positions to the north of Rammun, resulted in the discovery of the body of Acting Corporal Arthur Edgar Newcombe. Operating behind enemy lines a small forward reconnaissance party had stumbled onto his mutilated form in the tree late on the 19th.

Arthur's arms had been tied behind his back. With a rope tied to his wrists he had been suspended in the air until it had dislocated both his shoulders. It must have been incredibly painful, including the whipping he had received to his front with what looked like barbed wire. It was not until they cut him down that they noticed the extraction of the victim's finger nails. Judging by the burns something red hot had been forced up under them before their removal. They had never witnessed anything so cruel. Whilst they knew the Turks to be murderers involved in genocide, this was torture on a whole new scale. The significance of the find was such that they returned in haste to Brigade HQ to report their discovery. Personally they all wanted the killer, or killers, found and they wanted them dead.

Act' Cpl. Arthur Edgar Newcombe's demise

With the discovery of Arthur's body questions were now starting to be asked. Had Arthur Newcombe been kidnapped for intelligence, and if so what intelligence could he have had? It did not make any sense before it dawned on the Brigade's Intelligence Office that given the murder of Private Harold Newcombe at

Gaza, that someone was trying to track down a particular soldier with the name of Newcombe who obviously had important information regarding an ancient artefact. To negate further demotivation in the ranks the hunt was now on for that killer, or killers.

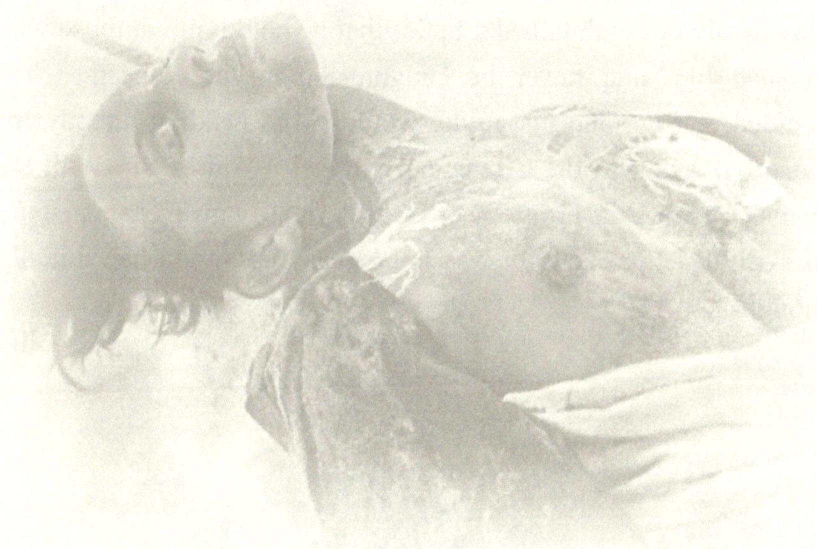

Back at 53rd Brigade HQ Intelligence personnel had also gleaned from a recently captured Arab that the culprits they were more than likely looking for were in fact now heading for the Dead Sea. The captured Arab had proudly stated to his new found British friends that there were two of them; a Circassian guide from the heights of Moab, and an unknown Italian. With the route via Jericho likely closed off the Circassian guide had asked the Arab about making a crossing of the Dead Sea, and fortuitously, yet unwittingly, the Arab had bought the British some time.

I help Briteesh. I point tem southeast of Jerusalem to cross Dead Sea by boat. I tell tem Jericho and river in Briteesh hands.

His beaming smile revealed smoke stained, decaying teeth, and knowing now that he had likely added days to their journey back to Ain es Sir, he finished with.....

I help Briteesh... I no like Circassea, at which he spat on the ground. *If you catch him, can I kill heem?*

Having always maintained a belief that he could outwit those who pursued him and never be caught, Simon the Redeemer had decided that he, and his guide, would avoid heading directly for Gaza but rather to the Circassean village of Ain es Sir. With the British advance in progress towards Jericho, however, managing to skirt all Allied activity was not as easy as Simon had initially thought.

Advance towards Jericho

When he had first been appointed to his command earlier in 1917, Brigadier General Sir Edmund Allenby had turned to the commander of the 67 Squadron RFC, Squadron Leader Richard Williams, to disrupt water-born traffic on the Dead Sea. At this time that squadron had been better known by its unofficial title of 1st Squadron, Australian Flying Corps (AFC).

RFC aerodrome

On the 3rd January two Australian aircraft had discovered boats carrying corn and hay moving from Ghor el Hadit behind Point Costigan, and Rujm el Bahr at the northern end of the Dead Sea. Following the Dead Sea being identified as a route used by the Turks to support their troops, initial bombing raids against the Dead Sea Ottoman port at El Bahr, with aerial strafing attacks on the boats themselves had caused little effect. The boat skippers had learned to zigzag, and had often escaped, with the result that

Turkish troops continued to get their needed grain.

In a moment of brilliance Squadron Leader Williams had instructed his mechanics to strip the wings and tail from an obsolescent Martinsyde

The amphibian known as Mimi

bomber and replace its wings with floats. Slow and clumsy as an aircraft the Martinsyde had proved itself a fast and agile catamaran as the weirdest craft ever seen on those age-old waters. Christened '*Mimi*', this Australian amphibious aircraft had gone into action effectively at a depth below sea level on the Dead Sea that would crush a submarine. At various times *Mimi* was piloted, or rather helmed, by either Captain J. A. D. Dempsey or Captain P. D. Drury, with their crew chief being a 1st Air Mechanic named Doig.

Through Mimi's activity, the grain fleet had been sprayed with bullets repeatedly until the boat service had been placed in such sore straits that reinforcements were sent to it from the far-away Bosporous. Bigger, faster and better-armed motor boats had been transported by rail, to then carried by road to Jericho and on to the Dead Sea. And then, just when Mimi was proving too good even for these reinforcements, Allenby had settled the whole Turkish grain problem with the capture of Jerusalem.

Now, in late February, a further attempt was being made to smuggle the Circassian guide and an unknown assassin back across the Dead Sea.

The first either Simon the Redeemer or the Circassean guide knew of a threat to their person was an increasing noise hidden in a cloud of mist that was moving fast towards them. Initially the Jesuit thought he was witnessing God's hand at work. In fact he was, in so far as pure justice was concerned; for as they looked on in awe, riding on a swirling mass of salt foam Mimi's inspiring form appeared out of the spray to bear down on them.

For Mimi's pilot and observer their quarry was easily overhauled so they could run parallel with the escaping boat. The Jesuit and the Circassian, along with the boat crew, were then aghast to see

Mimi on the move - Dead Sea

Mimi's observer stand up and open fire with his Lewis gun. The bullets stitched the boat's hull above the waterline as the apparition that was Mimi thundered past. A final salvo smashed

Lewis gun with mount

the cockpit of the boat, killing the helmsman and skipper outright. With a single pass the bullets that penetrated the port side of the boat, at waist height, found their mark.

Ottoman Dead Sea Fleet

Of the three rounds that hit Simon the Redeemer, two found his groin to effectively castrate him, while the third passed through his stomach into his spine. He now lay in the bottom of the boat screaming in agony and bleeding to death. Likewise another two rounds had found the Circassian who was also gut shot. He would also die an hour later.

For the 2/10th Middlesex Battalion an action at Tell 'Asur would commence that night of 2nd March when infantry from the 53rd Division advanced west of the Nablus road, over a three mile front, from north-west of Rammun to south-west of Bir ez Zeit. On the night of the 6th they would occupy the village of Taiyibe, close to where Arthur had been murdered, with the artillery being brought up.

Above - Dead Sea - Rujm el Bahr and Ottoman naval personnel.

Right - Motor boat in transport to the Dead Sea.

Below - Ottoman troops.

FIELD SERVICE
TOP SECRET
PASSED BY CENSOR
No 3743

Part XXVIII

In Cairo, off to the left of Shepheard's Hotel the 'Wazzir', or 'Wozzer', was still doing a roaring trade with British troops continuing to come and go when they were quartered in Egypt, or moved through as reinforcements. In its much frequented Ezbekiya fleshpots, where everything could be had for the right amount of coppers, they also continued to suffer the inevitable 'casualties'.

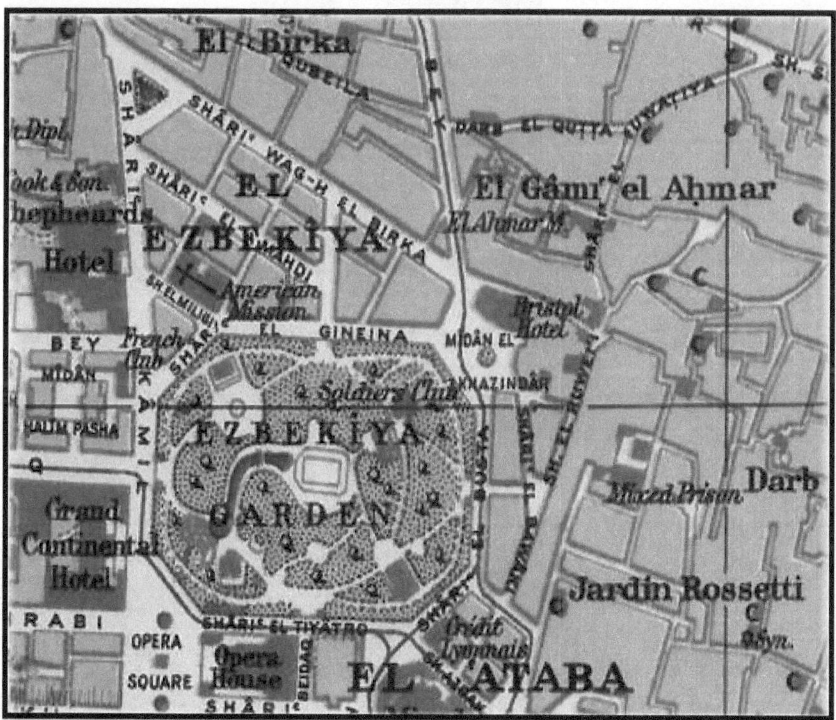

Shepheard's Hotel, however, still held its own among world-famous hostelries in spite of the more gorgeous, modern, larger European-like structures. These had sprung into social prominence in the neighbourhood since Cairo had become an international rendezvous for travellers between the West and East, a half century or more earlier.

For Jehanne and the officers, in residence at Shepheard's, however, they got a different view of exotic life in Cairo from the orchestra seats on the terrace that still overlooked one of the original streets in the city.

Obove - The Terrace at Shepheards, and a further view of the hotel below

Many had previously observed that as a d i v e r s i f i e d amusement nothing quite took the place of the 'Terrace' at Shepheard's in the height of tourist season. Prior to the war that season had been about February. Now it was not quite as often that a band played, while the chairs before the little wicker tea tables under the previously gay

Egyptian hangings, hosted occupants of a different kind. Out of bounds to non commissioned ranks the hotel had by now become a popular meeting place for officers of all services and nationalities. Predominantly clothed in khaki, rather than all degrees of brilliance, they took tea to discuss matters of a military and territorial nature.

On the terrace the few officer's present gossiped oblivious to the multi-coloured population of the city that drifted ceaselessly past, or to Jehanne's emotional state. This day was a low point in her life for after filing a request for news on Lance Corporal Arthur Edgar Newcombe via Army Intelligence, following his one and only letter, Jehanne had just received news of his death. According to the reply whilst his demise had been suspicious, he had been recorded as 'Killed in Action' (KIA), to not draw attention to it.

Jehanne with a nurse from El Arish hospital in Gaza

The circumstances surrounding his death were also still being investigated to establish the likely reason. Jehanne, however, knew what that reason had been, and that whoever had carried out the deed had no doubt tortured him also to establish the whereabouts of the amulet. They would be sorely disappointed as she has recovered it from the grave in which it was hidden a month earlier, on the pretext of visiting the hospital at El Arish to interrogate a double agent being held in the town.

Above - The war cemetery

Right - A destroyed British tank - Gaza

During her two day visit she had taken time out to walk the town's outskirts before expressing an interest in visiting the graves of British dead at Deir al-Balah. No one had seen her locate Harold Newcombe's grave site and recover the small oil skin package, and this was information she had kept to herself. With the amulet safely in her possession, with no one aware where it was, Jehanne realised it was the best outcome. Her intuition told her that if the amulet surfaced again that her life would be placed in danger, along with the lives of others.

More importantly she now suspected it also meant that the amulet's ancient messages would be used to blackmail others. It was a ploy she knew the British would definitely employ if they had the artefact in their possession. It certainly seemed to her as though fate had been trying to have it find its way back into her hands, and she was not going to take that lightly.

Her wartime experiences had changed her in clarifying her

The entrance to Shepheards Hotel

thoughts, particularly on religion, and as she sat in one of the lounge areas of Shepheard's Hotel her next move became clearer.

The death of Arthur sickened her, along with the deviousness of

British politics, and the hypocrisy of the Christian and Judean Churches. Each had changed her perspective and opened her eyes; not just to the danger of the Roman Catholic doctrine and intent, but also to a flawed Jewish faith, and the now obvious manipulative politicking of people like Sir Henry McMahon and his cronies back in London. They, along with other Government ministers and officials of supposed integrity were prepared, she now suspected, of letting the Arabs down at the end of hostilities. Jehanne suspected Lawrence was blinded ideologically, however, she was starting to see through British 'modus operandi' suspecting they were going to break their promise to Hussein that had been given on behalf of the British government to gain Arab support in the war.

Jehanne also correctly deduced that the French in Syria would cause a problem, as would the Italians, the Catholic Church, and particularly the Jews who she knew were lobbying in London using their religion as a wedge for their own state in Palestine; continually pushing their false agenda that it had been bequeathed to them by Jehovah. With the Allied capture of Jerusalem, Jehanne could now see that they wanted their hooks in the Holy Land. It was not too hard to surmise, therefore, that Palestinian, Syrian and Jordanian lands would not be freed up in entirety to create any independent Arab state. Someone was going to be disappointed, and this realisation brought her to the conclusion that it was going to be the Arabs.

Fate, however, was about to draw Jehanne an unexpected 'card' in the form of 2nd Lt Robert Polaschek, an Australian pilot of Polish descent. He had recently been appointed to the Hejaz Expeditionary Force stationed at Rabegh, Arabia. Due to report as a pilot to No.14 Squadron, Arabia Detachment, and destined for Suez the following morning, he had observed Jehanne's forlorn look from across the balcony in Shepheard's Hotel. Courteously introducing himself he had asked politely if she was by herself. It would be the beginning of a relationship that would again change the course of history, and it started with him offering to buy her dinner.

The dining room at Shepheard's Hotel

Asked about his views on the Middle East, and what he thought was likely to occur after the war, Rob had openly expressed his views.

I hope genuinely that all inhabitants receive their freedom, self determination, both politically and civilly, and that they prosper ... He had then felt the need for some reason to qualify his initial comment by stating that whatever religion or belief they followed, it should be respected as their own without discrimination.

Whatever the outcome, Britain has to allow the rightful inhabitants the ability to preserve their land, independence, and control.

It may have sounded idealistic but it was what Jehanne needed to hear. At heart Rob was a humanitarian who did not label people, or condemn them for their beliefs, and she took that to mean her also. In that regard he reminded her of an older version of the innocent Arthur Newcombe who she knew had forlornly looked at her during the lectures in the British Museum those years earlier. The

Arthur Edgar Newcombe

war had taught her a lot about human nature, the greed of mankind, and about religion and its politics. Invariably it was the innocent who were the victims, like Arthur in his simple desire to help Ernest Budge. Looking at this handsome pilot who was approximately her age, it was obvious he liked her, and not just her quick wit and understanding. He had asked if he might call on her again to take her out when he returned to Cairo on leave and her answer had been a rather hurried… *Yes!*.

Jehanne wanted to hold and kiss him right there in Shepeard's lounge but she restrained her desire. Something stirred within her she had not felt before, and it made her feel good.

Ottoman Troops Attack

When orders were received in the middle of March 1918 for the New Zealand Mounted Brigade's next move forward, both men and horses had been fit. Since their return from Jericho into a temperate climate on the coast with plenty of green feed beneficial to the horses, they had been ready for action once more. It was fortunate that they had been for the operation that they were to embark on would prove to be one of the most trying of the campaign; testing the powers of endurance of man and beast to the limits.

This was an operation to cut the enemy line of communication along which the Turks were feeding their forces engaged across the Jordan against the Sherifian troops led by T. E. Lawrence, in the Hejaz. Additionally they had been ordered to co-operate with these Sherifian forces operating to the east and south-east of the Dead Sea.

Besides the Anzac Division other troops for the raid into the Land of Moab included the Imperial Camel Corps, the well tried 60th Infantry Division with whom the Jericho operations had been carried out, along with artillery and bridging trains.

Later the Australian War Museum (AWM) would write that for Lawrence personally the move north had provoked in him a crisis. Information from Cairo and a recent visit to Wejh by Sir Mark Sykes had convinced him that Britain's promises to the Arabs were paper-thin. He realised that from now on his role in the deceit would be much greater. He had won the Arabs' confidence and they were much more willing to trust someone they knew than a distant foreign government. Taking his assurances at face value they had fought, with many more killed or wounded. He had tried to limit casualties, but their sacrifice and Britain's deceit would be forever on his conscience.

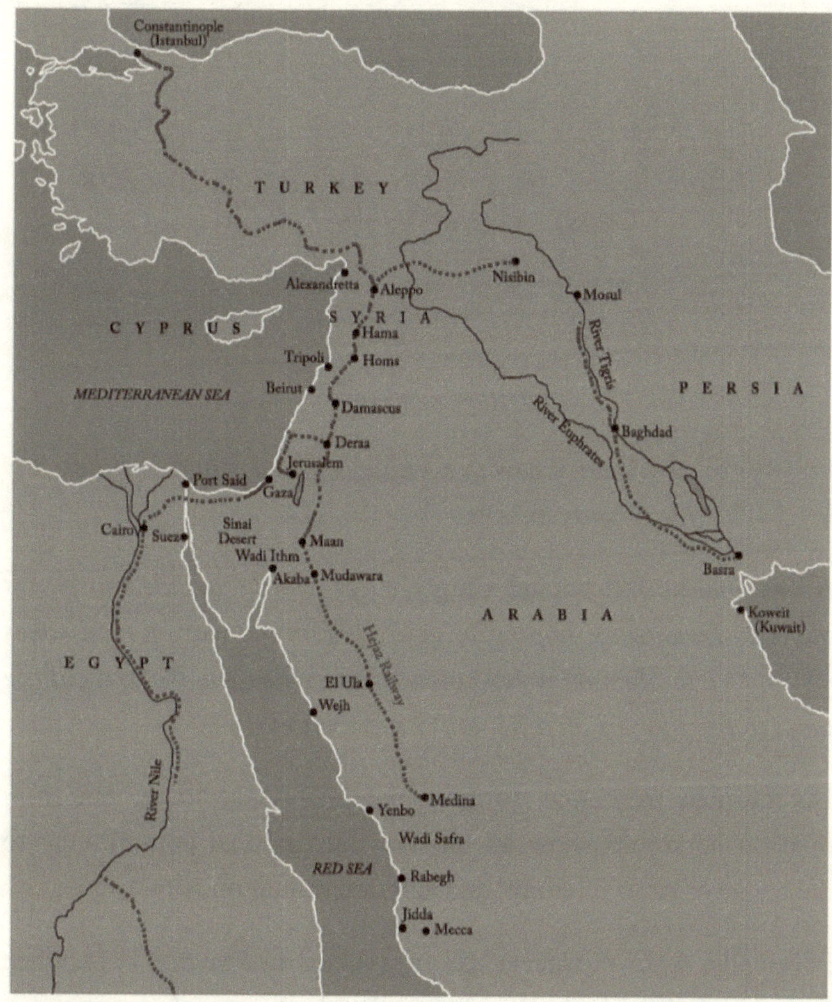

The full horror of his position came home to him during his journey to Akaba. Notes in his wartime diary record his deepening distress.

On 13th May Lawrence wrote - *Near Abu Raga in a valley with Themail. The weight is bearing me down now. Auda last night, and pain and agony today.*

Ottoman prisoners

Finally, on 5th June Lawrence wrote - *Can't stand another day here. Will ride N and chuck it.*

A message he left behind simply reads ... *I've decided to go off alone to Damascus, hoping to get killed on the way: for all sakes try and clear this show up before it goes further. We are calling them to fight for us on a lie, and I can't stand it.*

He returned from that northern reconnaissance alive, but from then on he would show an unswerving personal commitment to the cause of Arab freedom, and self determination.

Politically, Arab prospects had brightened in January 1918 when American President Woodrow Wilson's speech enunciated 'Fourteen Points' for post war world order. In this it was the 12th point that demanded sovereignty for the Turks, but that other nationalities which were under Turkish rule should be assured an undoubted security of life and an absolutely unmolested opportunity at autonomous development. The statement had understandably thrilled the Arabs who felt they had a friend in

America, untainted by colonial scheming.

Meanwhile Allenby's success in Palestine had been fully exploited with Feisal's Arab Northern Army assigned a key role in harassing the Ottoman forces east of the Jordan River, to then push north to Damascus and beyond.

T E Lawrence

Feisal had assembled a force of tribesmen who had been supported by Indian Gurkhas, the Egyptian Camel Corps, and Algerian artillery. In all there had had been about 1,000 fighters, and they had gone on to blow up railway lines, attack station houses, and destroy bridges.

The Arab revolt that had begun in June 1916 had first seen an attack by half-armed and inexperienced tribesmen upon the Turkish garrisons in Medina and about Mecca. They had met with little success and after a few days' effort had withdrawn out of range to begin a blockade. This method had forced the early surrender of Mecca; the more remote of the two centres.

Medina, however, was linked by railway to the Turkish main army in Syria, and the Turks had been able to reinforce the garrison there. The Arab forces that had attacked it had been forced to fall gradually back and the campaign had stood still for many weeks.

The Turks had then sent an expeditionary force to Mecca to crush the revolt at its source, moving an army corps to Medina by rail. While Arab regulars were still being trained the Turks had suddenly begun their advance on Mecca.

They had broken through the hills in 24 hours; to prove the second theory of irregular war - that irregular troops are as unable to defend a point, or line, as they are capable of attacking it.

With Allenby in command it was surmised that perhaps it had

Sherif of Mecca troops - Fiesal's fighters

been the threat of attack by the Arabs upon the Turkish northern flank which had made the enemy hesitate for so long.

The Turkish flank at that time had run from their front line to Medina, a distance of some 50 miles; but it had been reasoned that if the Arab force moved towards the Hejaz railway behind Medina, it might stretch its threat and accordingly, the enemy's flank as far potentially as Damascus 800 miles away to the north. Such a move would force the Turks onto the defensive, allowing the Arab force to regain the initiative.

King Fiesal, Sherif of Mecca's fighters

The January 1917 plan had acted like a charm. The Arabs had done nothing concrete but their march had recalled the Turks all the way back to Medina. One-half of the Turkish force had taken up an entrenched position about the city, which it would hold until after the Armistice. The other half had been distributed along the railway to defend it against the Arab threat. For the rest of the war the Turks would, therefore, stand on the defensive while the Arabs would go on to win advantage over advantage till, when peace finally came, they would have taken 35,000 prisoners, killed and wounded about as many, and occupied about 100,000 square miles of the enemy's territory, at little loss to themselves.

T E Lawrence with the reporter Lowell Thomas

In late January, 1918, in Shepheard's Hotel, one of General Allenby's staff officers had told an American reporter named Lowell Thomas about T. E. Lawrence's guerrilla activities along the Hejaz railway. Thomas had then requested and received permission to follow Lawrence, with the Arabs. It was this conversation that helped turn Lawrence into the world-famous figure called 'Lawrence of Arabia', and at the same time launch the reporter's own career as one of the most successful broadcasters in America.

By stretching the limits of conventional journalism, and public entertainment, to offer cutting-edge, multimedia, lecture-performances, in true American style Thomas would take a fascinating story and turn it into a legend.

Akaba

Below - T E Lawrence (centre) and friends at Akaba

With substantial material support from Britain, Feisal and Lawrence had reorganised the Arab forces gathered to oppose Turkish garrisons in Medina and Mecca. Lawrence had then gone on to lead guerrilla raids against the Turks, risking his life on several occasions. His raiders had disrupted the Hejaz railway, the main transportation route for Turkish reinforcements; interfered with enemy lines of communications; and captured the Red Sea city of Aqaba.

As early as late 1916 Turkish and German forces aligned against the British had been offering huge bounties for Lawrence — dead or alive. Even before Thomas put Lawrence on the map a story in 'L'Echo de Paris' had noted ... *The name of Colonel Lawrence will become historic in Great Britain.*

Thomas and his invaluable cameraman, Harry Chase, had left for Europe in August, 1917. By then the conflict in Europe had bogged down into bloody trench warfare and the Allies were finding it increasingly difficult to produce optimistic coverage of the battlefields. Thomas had initially hoped *to find an appealing young doughboy and follow him into action,* but foul weather and the grimy realities of war had soon disabused him of that notion.

When Thomas learned that General Edmund Allenby had been given command of British forces in Palestine, he had recognised a ready-made propaganda opportunity and had applied to the War Office in London for permission to travel to the Holy Land to highlight the Middle East struggle. He credited good luck for his success in gaining access to Allenby's army, but in fact he underestimated Britain's interest in having the dramatic campaign for the Holy Land publicised in the United States. For whatever reason British officials considered Thomas's mission both timely and important, and whenever possible they had expedited his travel arrangements. Whether by luck, or by design within the British War Office, Thomas and Chase had finally arrived in the Middle East in early 1918.

A destroyed Ottoman train – Hejaz railway

By the time Jehanne became aware of British complicity in allowing the Press to promote Lawrence's activities, she had met the effervescent reporter Thomas in Shepheard's Hotel, where he and his cameraman were also staying. For two weeks they had remained in Egypt before a military transport plane had flown them to Palestine where they had arrived in time to cover the capture of Jericho on 21st February 1918. Then, after a journey that had taken Thomas and Chase back to Cairo; up the River Nile to Khartoum; across the Nubian Desert to Port Sudan; and north on the Red Sea aboard a steamer, they had finally reached Lawrence in Aqaba.

It was 29th March, 1918.

In the weeks that followed, Thomas wrote, … *I slowly came to learn the story of Lawrence's astonishing desert campaign. He is 5 feet 2 inches tall, blonde, blue sparkling eyes, fair skin; too fair*

Shepheard's Hotel, Cairo

even to bronze after seven years in the Arabian desert; bare-footed, and wears the costume of a Meccan Sherif. Though we grew to be friends I got little enough of it from him; he...remained difficult to draw out about himself.

Instead of pushing Lawrence, Thomas relied on the accounts of people around him to piece together a story about his increasingly significant and colourful military role as British liaison officer to the Arabs.

T E Lawrence

Section of destroyed Hejaz railway

Jehanne had been a reluctant contributor that Thomas had paid little heed to, instead embroiling himself in his own hero creation, with little interest in the real issues.

Col. Lawrence - remarkable man ..., Thomas noted in his diary. *Well versed on any subjects from astronomy to aerial gunnery, from archaeology to dietetics, from literature to handling and making high explosives. Natives are crazy about him...Goes alone always ...usually smiling.*

Lawrence officially introduced the Americans to Prince Feisal, the revolt's charismatic leader who would later become king of Iraq. Feisal arranged for them to take rare photographs and film footage of the Sherifian army. As a young journalist, Thomas had, in newspaper terms,

Lawrence of Arabia

Lawrence with his Arabs on the move

As Allenby's 1917 reorganisation had proceeded, as part of the Arab Revolt, the Arab Northern Army had continued to operate east of the Jordan under the overall leadership of the Emir Feisal. At that time Feisal's headquarters had been at Aba el Lissan, about 15 miles south-west of the Ottoman position at Ma'an, with his army receiving support from the British through the port of Aqaba. This assistance had included liaison officers; detachments of armoured cars; Indian machine gunners, and a French Algerian mountain battery; 2,000 camels from three disbanded battalions of the Imperial Camel Corps Brigade; weapons, ammunition and above all money, almost always in coin. This financing had started as a monthly subsidy of £30,000 in mid-1916, and by the time Allenby launched his last Megiddo offensive in September 1918, the amount would have grown to £220,000 a month.

British armoured cars

The Bristol FE2b fighter

In late September, 1917, Lieutenant Colonel T E Lawrence had called for air assistance for his Arab army that, at that time, was being constantly attacked by German aircraft. Led by Captain R. Smith, three pilots from No 1 Squadron had aided Lawrence, shooting down several German invaders. Colloquially knick-named the 'Biff' or 'Brisfit', their new Bristol FE2b fighter aircraft had dominated the air, being faster, better armed, and more capable than the German machines.

While Allied supply lines were less extended than the Turks, logistics in getting petrol oil and bombs to these aircraft in the Hejaz was still a major hassle. Here the situation was far more difficult as they could not work desert areas, east and southeast of Amman, without supplies.

The 4,000 regular soldiers of the Arab Northern Army had

maintained a blockade of the Ottoman garrison at Ma'an after an unsuccessful attack at Al-Samna earlier in 1917. They were commanded by Jaafar Pasha, formerly an Ottoman officer who had been sent to lead a rebellion against the British by the Senussi in Egypt, but had joined the Arab Revolt after being captured. Most of these regulars were former Arab conscripts in the Ottoman Army who had deserted or,

T E Lawrence

like Jaafar, had changed sides after becoming prisoners of war.

With spring having come for the Arabs of the Hejaz, war had started again in earnest. Provided with transport and everything else they wanted, except enough guns, a large number of Arab irregulars had gone to Atara, 70 miles due north of Bair to await news of Allenby's attack on Amman 50 miles to the north-west. Lawrence had gone too with his body guard.

On the 4th April, 1918, the Arab army had started with its train of 2000 baggage camels and reached Atara four days later without loss.

Camel Corp cameleer

Nearing sunset, and with everything seeming peaceful enough, Lawrence rose up the embankment to cross the railway line when his camel's footing slipped in the loose shingle ballast, and out of the long shadow of a culvert to his left rose a Turkish soldier. He looked wildly at Lawrence, who had a pistol in his hand, and then with sadness at his own rifle yards away out of reach. Lawrence stared at him and said softly … *Allah is merciful.* The Turk new the sense of the Arabic phrase and a look of incredulous joy came over his fat, sleepy face, however, he made no answer. Lawrence pressed the camel's shoulder with his foot, and she went carefully over the metal rails and down the bank on the other side. The Turk had enough good feeling not to shoot him in the back, and he rode away with warmth of heart that a man always has to a life he has saved. When at a safe distance he looked back and the Turk had his thumb to his nose, 'twinkling' his fingers in farewell.

At Atara everything was green and fresh with spring and the camels were enjoying themselves greatly. News initially came that Amman had been taken and that the Arabs further north were making a move to join them, when further news reported it lost again, so the Arabs had again turned south.

First, however, Lawrence had gone spying into Amman in the company of three gypsy women, with his body guard Farraj disguised like himself as one of them. He had a good look round but decided the place should be left with it being too strongly defended for any Arab attack. As they were returning a number of Turkish soldiers had stopped them and attempted to make love to them. They only escaped by running away at high speed. From that point on Farraj was a changed man, and Lawrence forthwith decided to only go disguised in future in full British uniform.

The Hejaz railway

In the weeks following the failure of Allenby's second attack across the Jordan, Lawrence and his Arab irregulars again went to work. They carried out demolitions on a 80 miles stretch of line around Mudawara, due east of Aqaba. effectively closing the line for a month and ending Ottoman operations around Medina at the end of the railway.

The fortress of Qasr el 'Azraq

The large fortress of Qasr el 'Azraq, that in the 16th century had held an Ottoman Turk garrison, now held strategic significance for the Arab irregulars advance north. Located roughly 62 miles east of Amman this ancient 12th century desert castle lies in the middle of the Azraq oasis was the only permanent source offresh water in approximately 4,600 sq. miles of desert. It had become T. E. Lawrence's desert headquarters during the winter of 1917, with his office in the chamber above the entrance gatehouse.

The fortress of Qasr el 'Azraq

For the AFC pilots the flat, hard desert nearby had made an ideal place to build an airfield and so they had set up a forward base here as part of British support for the Arab cause. It was from here that Der'aa was attacked on 16th and 17th September, 1918, by British aircraft, when sections of the railway to the north and west of the Der'aa junction were bombed.

The railway south of the junction was then attacked on 17th September by an Arab irregular column supported by British armoured cars and a French mountain battery. They had also left Qasr el 'Azraq with the aim of destroying a bridge and a section of the rail line.

Early on the 19th, 2nd Lieutenant Rob Polaschek, and another AFC Bristol FE2 pilot, reported that all Ottoman camps in the area to the east of the Jordan River were quiet. After attacking a mass of cavalry at Ain es Sir they had returned to base by flying over the Wadi Fara road. Here they had dropped their remaining bombs on a column of 50 motor lorries moving eastwards along the road towards the Jisr ed Damieh bridge over the Jordan River. A direct hit on one of the trucks now blocked the road. Later that afternoon another two Bristol Fighters continued this attack.

Attack on Turk transport in the Wadi Fara

Allenby's report 15:00 19th September, 1918

On the E. of Jordan, the Arabs and the Druses are up; and they have cut the Hejaz railway, N.S., and W. of Der'aa. Der'aa is the junction, where the railway into Palestine leaves the Damascus–

Medina line; so, Liman von Sanders has lost his only railway communications with the outer world. I really don't know what he can do; and I am beginning to think that we may have a very great success. The weather is perfect; not too hot, and very clear.

Handley Page 0/400 bomber

To add to their strength No1 AFC squadron had recently received a new twin engine Handley Page 0/400 bomber aircraft.

During the evening of 19th September, and early the next morning, Ross Smith in the Handley-Page bombed the Jenin aerodrome and railway station, leaving the aerodrome looking like a rubbish-heap. A second dawn patrol reported a column of about 200 vehicles spread along five miles of the Wady el Fara road moving from Nablus in the direction of the Jisr ed Damieh bridge. This column was now bombed by the Bristol FE2s, with three making direct hits on the transport which again blocked the road. Another five bombs were dropped on this target as well as machine gunning those on the ground, which created mayhem.

Early morning reconnaissance flights on the 20th reported the effects of the previous day's bombing, in particular between

Anebta and Deir Sheraf, where all Ottoman camps were reported as either burnt or empty. From this region northwards, Ottoman troops were seen retreating along the road and railway towards Jenin. At Messudie railway station two trains were being loaded, while from Burka northwards the road was full of carts, camels and soldiers.

Aerial attacks had begun at 9:00 am. on the Samaria to Afulah road. Five aircraft would drop 40 bombs and fire 4,000 machine gun bullets at several retreating columns, and after 24 hours Afulah was a blackened wreck. Four lines of carriages without engines had been in the Afulah station, while at the aerodrome four German aircraft had being preparing for flight. All had been destroyed.

Insert- Albatros D.VA Serial 7416/17 with white/black/ white stripe and intermediate type national insignia captured at Jenin

Between Burka and Jenin nearly every bomb fell among retreating congested bodies of troops. They suffered terrible casualties, and when the aircraft ran out of ammunition they returned for supplies before repeating their bombing and machine gunning near Arrabe. Those who survived the aerial attack to continue their retreat towards Damascus would be captured later that night at Jenin by the 3rd Light Horse Brigade.

The last reconnaissance of the day reported fires burning at Nablus and at the Ottoman army's dumps at Balata, indicating the whole Ottoman line from El Lubban to the Jordan was in retreat.

Allenby described the destruction in a letter to his wife on 20th September.

I was at Tulkaram today, and went along the Nablus road. It is strewn with broken lorries, wagons, dead Turks, horses and oxen; mostly killed and smashed by our bombing aeroplanes. The same bombing of fugitives, on crowded roads, continues today. I think I ought to capture all the Turks' guns and the bulk of his Army.

By 23rd September communications to the west between Deraa and Samakh, and to the north of Deraa, had been restored. With Azrak requiring petrol, oil, ammunition, and parts to be constantly flown in supply lines were again stretched. This was particularly the case for the AFC supporting Lawrence and his Arab irregulars further afield near the railway junction at Der'aa, 60 miles north of Amman. The normal line of supply via Akaba on the Red Sea was now useless so the Handley Page was pressed into service to meet Lawrence at Um es Surab.

Taking off to arrive just before dark on 23rd September, 1918, and escorted by the two Bristol FE2's the bomber was used to transport petrol, oil, bombs and ammunition.

As it transpired the twin engine bomber was so big and inspiring it was the best recruiting agent the British could have had with the Arab irregulars.

When it landed they celebrated its arrival by firing their guns in the air while racing around the aircraft on their horses.

The Handley Page 0/400 bomber at Um es Surab

Arabs celebrate the bomber's arrival

Loaded up with flammable liquid and explosives, this behaviour naturally made the pilot extremely nervous. The two Biffs had gone on to bomb the enemy aerodrome at Deraa to distract attention from the arrival of the larger transport. They also knocked down two German aircraft the same day which meant the

718

irregulars enjoyed local air superiority and in not having to worry about further attacks from the air, courtesy of the AFC.

As a consequence Deraa was captured on 27th September, 1918.

Sherif of Mecca's troops

The capture of Jenin including 20,000 Turks and the aerodrome

Since his incarceration in late 1917 Colonel Stewart Newcombe had been anything other than a passive prisoner of the Turks, making several attempts to escape. He had now finally succeeded with the help of a brave, young, woman of French parentage named Elizabeth Chaki.

Known as Elsa he had befriended her while he was recovering in hospital in Istanbul from smallpox. The pair had fallen in love and after his escape from the prison camp at Bursa, Colonel Newcombe had remained undercover in the city. Here he had liaised on possible Allied peace terms with various members of the emerging political powers which rose and fell during the turbulent weeks leading up to the Armistice. Colonel Newcombe would finally get away from the Turkish port of Smyrna, but was too late to be able to witness the signing of the Armistice that took place on *H.M.S Liverpool,* and so he returned to Cairo.

As for Jehanne, Lawrence, Fiesel, and Hussein, they correctly continued to interpret correspondence given to Hussein by McMahon as a clear indication that Palestine would be given to the Arabs once the war had ended. Sir Henry McMahon's promises, on behalf of the British government, were being disputed, however, by British politicians and other vested interests playing on the fact that they were open to interpretation. They claimed that any land definitions were only approximate and that a map drawn at the time excluded Palestine from land to be given back to the Arab people.

With a map that had not been drawn by McMahon, or a member of the British delegation, it was now used by the British to twist the truth. Their solicitors additionally then picked on one small phrase in the correspondence between McMahon and Hussein, that stated that the '*land cannot be said to be purely Arab*'. As a consequence it had been excluded from the agreement, as far as the British were concerned.

On the other hand, Hussein and very many Arab people considered Palestine to be '*purely Arab*'.

After the British had defeated Turkish forces and occupied Palestine in late 1917 they had set up a military administration across former occupied Ottoman territory, with the land remaining under British military administration for the remainder of the war.

Outside pressure, however, was now forcing the British to view Palestine differently, as the Turks had before them. While they had been masters over Palestine they had allowed other religious groups to exist in Jerusalem – hence their belief that Palestine '*cannot be said to be purely Arab*'. It was a spurious religious distinction, not an ethnic one, and by the end of the war in November 1918 two distinct schools of thought had developed regarding the land.

The first was the position that Lawrence and Jehanne took that the British had promised Palestine to the Arabs after the war in return for their support to the Allies during the war. The second was that the British had agreed to give their support to the Jews for a homeland in Palestine as laid out in the Balfour Declaration of 1917. This was a religious based decision that was also politically supported by Gertrude Bell.

Saad Zaghlul

In Cairo on 13th November, 1918, the Day of Struggle, or Yawm al Jihad, the Al Wafdal Misri, or Wafd as it is known, was formed headed by Saad Zaghlul, a prominent member of the Egyptian Umma Party.

Zaghlul, together with other members Abd Al Aziz Fahmi and Ali Sharawi met the British High Commissioner Sir Reginald Wingate, and demanded independence. They also asked permission to go to London to present their case before the British Government, but this request was rejected by the British. Then in early March 1919, Zaghlul and three others were arrested by the British and thrown into Qasr an Nil prison, before being exiled to Malta. The arrest and subsequent deportation stirred up a wave of resentment among the Egyptians that led to an Egyptian Revolution against the British.

Demonstrations and strikes were organised in major cities such as Cairo, Tanta and Asyut, that caused major disruptions in communications and utilities services.

Eygptian and British troops - Cairo

Demonstrators went further cutting railroads and destroying telegram lines. With its population united in its opposition against the British, for a moment Egypt came to a standstill. Many Egyptians, young and old, in various cities, joined in the revolt. Both Moslems and Christians also showed their agreement in a show of unity by carrying crescent and cross banners during their demonstrations. The revolution peaked on 16th March with the biggest demonstration, when some 10,000 civil servants, students, teachers, lawyers and workers marched to Abdin Palace.

Many such strikes were also started in other areas such as Al Mansurah, Al Fayyum, Alexandria, Tanta and Damanhur. Even women, who were usually excluded from political activities, participated in the public demonstrations. They were instigated by Zaghlul's wife Safia Zaghlul, when 150-300 women in veils protested against the British occupation.

In other parts of Egypt, women demonstrated with men, and even organised strikes and boycotts. Violence, often fierce, broke out

A Cairo demonstration - 1919

amongst Egyptians and Europeans as the British attempted to bring down the demonstrations using force. It resulted in many casualties with as many as 800 Egyptians, 31 Europeans, and 29 British killed, not including the extensive damage done.

For Jehanne it was simply a portent of things to come as British politicians, in their arrogance and vested interests, could not see the writing on the wall.

Female nationalists demonstrating in Cairo, 1919.

Part XXIX

Emir Fiesal

On the 3rd January, 1919, Emir Feisal, son of Sherif Hussein of Mecca, and leader of the Arab movement, met in Aqaba with Dr. Chaim Weizmann, the head of the Zionist Commission to Palestine. Later at the Paris Peace Conference the two negotiated and signed an agreement which spoke of full cooperation in the development of an independent Arab state in present-day Syria and Iraq, as also promised by the British to Feisal.

Additionally, in a spirit of compromise by Fiesel, they agreed and included a Jewish home in

Emir Feisal bin Husain al

*Dr Chaim Weizman
with Emir Fiesel*

Palestine based on the 'Balfour Declaration' that would encourage the large scale immigration of Jews into Palestine. This came with a proviso in the declaration that all other people in existing non-Jewish communities in Palestine, as designated Palestinians and existing people of the land, would have their civil and religious rights protected, as Balfour's original agreement had stipulated and been agreed upon.

Gertrude Bell

In late January 1919, Gertrude Bell was assigned to conduct an analysis of the situation in Mesopotamia. Due to her familiarity and relations with the tribes in the area she had strong ideas about the leadership needed in Iraq. She spent the next ten months writing what was later considered a masterful official report, titled… '*Self Determination in Mesopotamia*'.

At the time there were different ideas of how Iraq should be run. One scenario preferred an Arab government under the influence of British officials who would retain the real control. Gertrude, was asked to remain in Bagdad and continue on as Oriental Secretary, acting as liaison with this forthcoming Arab government. Being widely travelled and a fluent Arabic speaker, her influence in Persia would be significant, with her playing the role of mediator between the Arab government and British officials.

The various groups included a majority population of Shi'a Moslems in the southern region, Sunnis in central Iraq, and the Kurds mostly to the north, who wished to be autonomous. Keeping these groups united was essential for political balance in Iraq and for British imperial interests. Iraq not only contained valuable resources in oil but would act as a buffer zone, with the help of Kurds in the north as a standing army in the region to protect against Turkey, Persia (Iran), and Syria.

Finally there was a qualification by the Emir Feisal in the agreement with the Zionist Commission to Palestine that confirmed that …. *If the Arabs are established, as I have asked in my manifesto of 4th January, addressed to the British Secretary of State for Foreign Affairs, I will carry out what is written in this agreement. If changes are made, I cannot be answerable for failing to carry out this agreement.*

British officials in London, especially Winston Churchill, were highly desirous of cutting heavy costs in the colonies, including the cost of policing tribal in-fighting. They, however, quickly realised that their strategies in governing were adding to those costs. Iraq would be cheaper as a self-governing state as it had been promised, along with Palestine.

The Cairo Conference of 1921 was held to determine the political and geographic structure of what later became Iraq and the modern Middle East. Significant input was given by Gertrude Bell in these discussions, making her part of its creation. Jehanne was present in her capacity as a female operative working outside of the conference's proceedings.

Attendees at the Cairo Conference with Winston Churchill, and Gertrude Bell on the left.

At this conference both Bell and Lawrence recommended Faisal bin Hussein, and former commander of the Arab forces that had helped the British during the war. He had recently been deposed by France as King of Syria, and so British officials at the Cairo

Conference decided to make him the first king of Iraq. They believed that due to his lineage as a Hashemite, along with his diplomatic skills, that he would be respected and have the ability to unite the various groups in the country. Shi'as would respect him because of his lineage from Prophet Mohammed; while Sunnis, including Kurds, would follow him because he was Sunni from a respected family.

Keeping all groups under control in Iraq was essential to balance the political and economic interests of the British.

A rare photograph at the Cairo conference with Jehanne Blanche, Winston Churchill, Gertrude Bell and others in front of the Sphinx

Throughout the early 1920s Gertrude was an integral part of the administration of Iraq while Jehanne remained in Cairo. Upon Faisal's arrival in Bagdad in 1921, Gertrude then advised him in local questions, including matters involving tribal geography and local business. She also supervised the selection of appointees for cabinet and other leadership posts in the new government. The new Hashemite monarchy used the Sherifian flag, which consisted of a black stripe representing the Abbasid caliphate, green stripe representing the Umayyad caliphate, and a white stripe for Fatimid Dynasty, and lastly a red triangle to set across the three bands symbolising Islam. Gertrude felt it desirable, if not essential, to customise it for Iraq by adding a gold star to the design.

Soldiers of the Arab Army in the Arabian Desert carrying the Flag of the Arab Revolt.

Faisal was crowned king of Iraq on 23rd August 1921, but he was not completely welcomed. Utilising Shi'ite history to gain support for Faisal, during the holy month of Muharram,

Gertrude Bell in Iraq

Gertrude compared Faisal's arrival in Baghdad to Huysan, the grandson of Prophet Mohammed.

Gertrude Bell

Gertrude Bell's first love, however, had always been archaeology, and she did not find working with the new king easy..... *You may rely upon one thing, I'll never engage in creating kings again; it's too great a strain,* she quipped.

British Occupation stamp - Iraq

Picnic at Ctesiphon 1921- approximately 22miles south of the city of Baghdad

A quarter of a century earlier in 1896 Theodor Herzl, a Jewish journalist living in Austria-Hungary, had published Der Judenstaat, or 'The Jewish State'. In it he asserted that the only solution to the 'Jewish Question' in Europe, including growing antisemitism, was through the establishment of a Jewish State.

Theodor Herzl

Political Zionism had been born at that time, and a year later, Herzl had founded the Zionist Organisation (ZO) which at its first congress had called for *the establishment of a home for the Jewish people in Palestine secured under public law.* Serviceable means to attain that goal had included the promotion of Jewish settlement there, the organisation of Jews in the diaspora, the strengthening of Jewish feeling and consciousness, and preparatory steps to attain those necessary governmental grants.

Chaim Weizmann

During the first meeting between Chaim Weizmann and Arthur Balfour in 1906, Balfour had asked what Weizmann's objections were to the idea of a Jewish homeland in the Uganda Protectorate in East Africa in the British Uganda Programme, rather than in Palestine.

Mr. Balfour, supposing I was to offer you Paris instead of London, would you take it?

He sat up, looked at Weismann, and answered …. *But Dr. Weizmann, we have London.*

That is true, Weizmann said, *but we had Jerusalem when London was a marsh*…..completely disregarding the fact that Jeruslaem was in ancient kingdom of Judea and not the kingdom of Israel, or that London has once been Londonium under Roman rule, but that did not mean it was was still owned by Italy. Balfour had then said two other things which Weismann remembered vividly. The first was…. *Are there many Jews who think like you?* … to which Weismann had answered … *I believe I speak the mind of millions of Jews whom you will never see and who cannot speak for themselves.*

Vera Weizmann, Chaim Weizmann, Herbert Samuel, Lloyd George,
Ethel Snowden, Philip Snowden

To this Balfour had replied…. *If that is so you will one day be a force.*

Two months after Britain's declaration of war on the Ottoman Empire in November 1914, Zionist British cabinet member Herbert Samuel had circulated a memorandum entitled *'The Future of Palestine'* to his cabinet colleagues. In this memorandum it stated,

I am assured that the solution of the problem of Palestine which would be much the most welcome to the leaders and supporters of the Zionist movement throughout the world would be the annexation of the country to the British Empire.

At that time the British had been busy making promises.

The downfall of the Czardom of Russia, that had started with the first revolution in February 1917, was considered one of the greatest events in the world's history that seemed to bring with it all the blessings of right and liberty. The restrictions affecting nationalities, and creeds had been removed, but far from destroying Zionism, the new liberty had given it an immense stimulus. At Odessa a Zionist demonstration had taken place, where entire battalions of Zionist soldiers had carried blue and white banners through the town, with the motto… *Liberty in Russia - Land and Liberty in Palestine.* 150,000 men had followed these banners, to which the Military Governor of Odessa had insisted on showing honour publicly. At Kieff, when the procession approached the Town Hall the Zionist flag had been raised on the balcony, where the *Hatikvah,* - The Hope, - and now national anthem of Israel had been played by a municipal orchestra.

The first Zionist Congress flag – 1897
Blue stripes on white background with yellow Star of David

Then at a War Cabinet meeting, held on 31st October, 1917, Arthour Balfour had suggested that a declaration, favourable to Zionist aspirations, would allow Great Britain *to carry on extremely useful propaganda both in Russia and America.* The cabinet had believed that expressing support would appeal to Jews in Germany and America, and help the war effort. It had also been hoped that it would encourage support from the large Jewish population in Russia. Britain had promoted the idea of a national home for the Jewish People in the hope that Britain would implement it and exercise political control over Palestine, effectively freezing out France, and anyone else, from any post–war presence in Palestine.

David Lloyd George

British Prime Minister David Lloyd George had, therefore, supported the creation of a Jewish homeland in Palestine because *it would help secure post-war British control of Palestine, which was strategically important as a buffer to Egypt and the Suez Canal.*

In addition, Palestine was to later serve as a terminus for the flow of petroleum from Iraq via Jordan; the three former Ottoman Turkish provinces that had become British League of Nations mandates in the aftermath of the war. Oil would officially flow along the Mosul-Haifa oil pipeline from 1935-1948, and unofficially up until 1954.

The Balfour Declaration, dated 2nd November, 1917, was a letter from the United Kingdom's Foreign Secretary Arthur James Balfour to 2nd Baron Rothschild, Walter Rothschild, a leader of the British Jewish community, for transmission to the Zionist Federation of Great Britain and Ireland.

In it was stated …

His Majesty's government view with favour the establishment in Palestine of a national home for the Jewish people, and will use their best endeavours to facilitate the achievement of this object, it being clearly understood that nothing shall be done which may prejudice the civil and religious rights of existing non-Jewish communities in Palestine, or the rights and political status enjoyed by Jews in any other country.

The records of discussions that led to the final text clarifies some details of its wording. The phrase *'national home'* was intentionally used instead of *'state'* because of opposition to the Zionist programme within the British Cabinet.

Following discussions over the initial draft Cabinet Secretary,

Mark Sykes, had met with the Zionist negotiators to clarify their aims. His official report back to the Cabinet had categorically stated that in fact the Zionists … *did not want to set up a Jewish Republic or any other form of state in Palestine, or in any part of Palestine.*

He would, however, later write to Faisal I of Iraq in which he expressed the following view

Mark Sykes

of the Jews, ... *that this race, despised and weak, is universal and all powerful, and cannot be put down.*

Both the Zionist Organisation and the British government would devote efforts over the following decades, including Winston Churchill's 1922 White Paper, to denying that the formation of a 'state' was the intention. In private, however, many British officials agreed with the prevailing interpretation of the Zionists by that time, that a state would be established when a Jewish majority was achieved.

The initial draft referred to the principle *that Palestine should be reconstituted as the National Home of the Jewish people.* In the final text the word, '*that*' was replaced with '*in*', to avoid committing the entirety of Palestine to this purpose. Similarly, an early draft did not include the commitment that nothing should be done which might prejudice the rights of the non-Jewish communities. These changes came about partly as the result of the urgings of Edwin Samuel Montagu, an influential anti-Zionist Jew and secretary of state for India, who was concerned that the declaration, without those changes, could result in increased anti-Semitic persecution. In this his foresight was rather prophetic.

Following the draft being circulated during October, 1917, the British government had received replies from various representatives of the Jewish community. At that time Lord

James Balfour with British Prime Minister Lloyd George

Rothschild had taken exception to the new proviso on the basis that it pre-supposed the possibility of a danger to non-Zionists, which he denied, yet this is exactly what would occur.

Immediately following the publication of the declaration Germany had entered negotiations with Turkey to put forward counter proposals. A German-Jewish Society had been formed known as the Vereinigung jüdischer Organisationen Deutschlands zur Wahrung der Rechte der Juden des Ostens (V.J.O.D.). Then in January 1918 the Turkish Grand Vizier, Talaat, had issued a statement which promised legislation by which *all justifiable wishes of the Jews in Palestine would be able to find their fulfilment.*

James Balfour and the 2nd November, 1917, Balfour Agreement letter

By November, 1918, the Arabs, however, could see the writing on the wall when at a parade marking the first anniversary of the Balfour Declaration, the Jews carried new white and blue banners with two inverted triangles in the middle. The Moslem-Christian Association protested drawing the attention of authorities to the serious consequences of the political implications in raising the banners.

Later that month, on the first anniversary of the occupation of Jaffa by the British, the Moslem-Christian Association sent a lengthy memorandum and petition to the military governor protesting once more on any formation of a Jewish state. In November 1918 a large group of Palestinian Arab dignitaries, and representatives of political associations, addressed a petition to the British authorities in which they denounced the declaration.

This document stated…

We always sympathised profoundly with the persecuted Jews and their misfortunes in other countries... but there is a wide difference between such sympathy and the acceptance of such a nation... ruling over us and disposing of our affairs.

A British mobile machine gun platform - 1919

Chaim Weizmann and Nahum Sokolow, the principal Zionist leaders based in London, had asked for the reconstitution of Palestine as 'the' Jewish national home. The declaration may have fallen short of Zionist expectations, but British public and government opinion was becoming increasingly less favourable to the commitment that had been made to Zionist policy.

In February 1922, Winston Churchill telegraphed Herbert Samuel asking for cuts in expenditure, noting…

In both Houses of Parliament there is growing movement of

hostility against Zionist policy in Palestine, which will be stimulated by recent Northcliffe articles. I do not attach undue importance to this movement, but it is increasingly difficult to meet the argument that it is unfair to ask the British taxpayer, already overwhelmed with taxation, to bear the cost of imposing on Palestine an unpopular policy.

Chaim Weizmann

As history proves the Zionists 1919 agreement with Emir Fiesel over Palestine was another agreement not honoured, following the League of Nations giving Palestine to the British to govern as a mandate. It effectively left the Arabs rightly feeling that they had definitely been betrayed by the British government and the Zionists.

Around the same time many Jews started entering Palestine as a result of what they believed the Balfour Declaration had offered them. The British would be left to ensure law and order was guaranteed; something they would find increasingly difficult to do. The formal objective of the League of Nations Mandate system had been to administer parts of the defunct Ottoman Empire…. *until such time as the people are able to stand alone.*

The League of Nations

No one had suggested only Jews lived in Palestine; a geographical term which has existed for millennia. The governing League of Nations that developed *'The Palestine Mandate'* document stated, among other things …

that there was recognition of the historical connection of the Jewish people with Palestine and to the grounds for reconstituting their national home in that country.

It was flawed thinking in so far as much of what was being promoted in the name of Zionism, and espoused since the formation of Judaism and the Jewish church, was based on fictitious religious legend, and not even myth.

It went on to espouse that… *an appropriate Jewish agency shall be recognised as a public body for the purpose of advising and co-operating with the Administration of Palestine in such economic, social and other matters as may affect the establishment of the Jewish national home and the interests of the Jewish population in Palestine, and, subject always to the control of the Administration to assist and take part in the development of the country.*

The Zionist Organisation, so long as its organisation and constitution are in the opinion of the Mandatory appropriate, shall be recognised as such agency. It shall take steps in consultation with His Britannic Majesty's Government to secure the cooperation of all Jews who are willing to assist in the establishment of the Jewish national home.

The Administration of Palestine, while ensuring that the rights and position of other sections of the population are not prejudiced, shall facilitate Jewish immigration under suitable conditions and shall encourage, in cooperation with the Jewish Agency referred to in Article 4 - close settlement by Jews on the land, including State lands and waste lands not required for public

Sherif of Mecca's troops

purposes.

The Administration of Palestine shall be responsible for enacting a nationality law. There shall be included in this law provisions framed so as to facilitate the acquisition of Palestinian citizenship by Jews who take up their permanent residence in Palestine.

The British had not honoured their original agreement to Hussein and neither were they destined to honour the Balfour Agreement.

The Zionists, also, would not honour their agreement to Fiesel, having tabled a carefully worded new document that gave them the opportunity to take the high ground. They would also not honour the terms of the Balfour Agreement over Palestine.

As Jehanne would later correctly reflect …

The United Kingdom agreed in it's Hussein-McMahon Correspondence that it would support Arab independence if they revolted against the Ottomans. It is now said that the two sides had different interpretations of this agreement although that is not true in Fiesel's case. The British, on the other hand, had underhandedly not told Fiesel of their true intent, nor of their political manipulation for other reasons. As it transpired the United Kingdom and France have both reneged on the original deal and divided up the area in ways that the Arabs felt was unfavourable to them under the 1916 Sykes-Picot Agreement.

Further confusing the issue is the Balfour Declaration of 1917, which promised support for a Jewish 'national home' in Palestine, but based as a 'home' not a 'state', with it unequivocally agreed and stated – 'with it being clearly understood that nothing shall be done which may prejudice the civil and religious rights of existing non-Jewish communities in Palestine'.

What was it that Thomas Jefferson said regarding enlightenment that applies equally well regarding Israel…

Yet we have not advanced one inch towards uniformity. What has been the effect of coercion? To make one half the world fools the other half hypocrites.

As for the Hejaz region of western Arabia, it became an independent state under Hussein's control, until 1925, when it too was abandoned and isolated by British policy which shifted its allegiance to the al Saud family in favour of oil, having become Saudi Arabia. Oil has talked along with Western expediency; where honour has been traded at the expense of others, no matter what has previously been promised.

As such it is simply the betrayal of the native inhabitants of these lands….!

New Zealand Mounted Rifles

Part XXX

Rob Polaschek

From the time Jehanne had first met 2nd Lieutenant Rob Polaschek their relationship had developed into something much more than a simple friendship. Her feelings had literally taken flight and for the first time in her life she had fallen in love. With no conditions, or apprehension Jehanne now simply submitted to the inner joy of wanting to be with her pilot whenever he was on leave. He jokingly referred to her as his *'Blonde Jane'* without knowing about her Bureau nickname, or her work for British Intelligence.

From Shepheard's Hotel it was walking distance to the American Comosgraph picture theatre; to the Salle Kleber which also showed films; to the Cairo British Recreation Club, and to the Obelisk Hall on Emad al-Dine Street. Diagonally opposite Shepheard's Hotel, to the right, were the Ezbekiya Gardens that were more

than just an urban park built with forethought by Khedieve Ismail. He had commissioned their rebuilding to follow in the style of Parisian parks. He had also ordered its builder to transform the park into the first botanical gardens in Eygpt that included collections of plants and trees from all over the world. The result was a beautiful garden stretching over 20 feddans, (acres), with four gates, an artificial grotto and waterfalls, a small mountain cultivated with cacti, and a marble fountain decorated with botanical motifs. Water pumps were installed to irrigate the profusion of greenery that comprised some 27 families of trees, plants and shrubs, and the 13 species of palm trees, succulents, perennial herbs and climbers that were also represented. When not sitting on the terrace at Shepheard's, or enjoying the sights of Cairo, Jehanne and Rob enjoyed strolling in the gardens.

It was during one of these outings that Jehanne had told him about her work for British Intelligence, the amulet, and her desire to see it returned to its rightful owners when the opportunity presented itself.

Rob Polaschek

Ezbekiya Gardens

With her eyes having been opened to those who were supposedly upstanding, respected, and honourable, only to discover the majority were not, Jehanne had personally matured in many ways.

Additionally she had come to abhor British arrogance in the field, with its inane ability to rub her up the wrong way.

More striking, however, was the witnessed corruption, hypocrisy, and murder in the name of Christianity by the Holy Roman Catholic Church, along with the hypocracy of the Jews, that really sickened her. There was nothing 'Holy' about either and they both reeked of self interest.

On this day Rob wanted to travel by ghary, or horse-drawn coach, across town to the Comfort Committee's Headquarters at Bab al-Louk in downtown Cairo. The Australian Comforts Fund (ACF) had been formed in 1916 to raise money through various activities back in Australia to buy, or make, items and food that could be sent to the troops. They also ran small canteens like the one Rob wanted to visit that served food supplies and provided other items such as primus stoves, clothes, sporting equipment, games, newspapers and magazines.

Jehanne had just learnt that the Roman Catholic S.P., that had flourished in a world engulfed by war, had slowed its momentum with the publication in 1919 of documents

recovered from the archives of the German secret service that had revealed the extent of the Catholics involvement and acceptance of German funds for political ends. With Germany on the losing side the Roman Catholic Church was a financial winner but, once again, its credibility and its crown had been tarnished.

Good ... she thought, *The pigeons are coming home to roost! Hopefully the masses will wise up to the corruption that is inherent in its ranks and the lie that has been promoted that their supporters all believe in, and live by.*

Her thoughts then switched to the Jews who were now flooding into Palestine based on the flawed premise that it was their promised land. She thought again on Ernest Budge's words on religion, reflecting on the fact that the British had been duped politically. A political ruse using an age old religious myth that had usurped their previously given promise to the Arabs;.... or was it a family connection with Winston Churchill and the attraction of the banking prowess and association with the Rothchilds?

Jehanne wondered how many coincidences had occurred with the amulet without any rational explanation, since she had been involved with it. She had a strange feeling that there was more to this artefact than met the eye; or that had been revealed in its messages. It was a sensation she also could not explain and it only seemed to manifest itself when it was in her presence. Out of interest she had read several of the Books of the Old Testament for the first time so she could more fully understand the significance of the amulet's messages. Appreciating more fully Ernest Budge's thoughts she could now see that the biblical accounts were simply old legendary stories that had been placed in a historic context with local identities. They were accounts that had highly likely been created with the knowledge, or auspices, of the Jewish temple hierarchy at the time, that more pointedly promoted a desired genealogy linking the Israelites to God with them holding sway over the land of others as its central theme.

In that regard the Jewish account was different than the amulet's message, or was it? Further finds in time would no doubt clarify the situation. In the meantime Islam would hold sway.

The term 'Peace be upon Him' sprung to mind. It always seemed at odds with the concept of Holy war, or jihad, and simply another form of gaining power and control. Peace was definitely upon anyone like the dead young Arthur Newcombe, but that was not its intent, surely. In reality humanity had not advanced in its understanding since the days of Abraham, Christ, and Muhammad, with mankind still fighting wars and killing one another with impunity in the name of religion.

It was obvious that based on religious ideals mankind had not learnt much since the days when a distant ancestor first discovered that fire could burn. It was also obvious to her that fundamentalist extremists, and others with their own agendas, would continue to use religion to gain power and control.

Whilst the old biblical values were true and honest as worthy rules for life many who professed to uphold them were not. They were simply mortal like the rest; no better and no worse in extolling their morality by placing their conditions on others that ultimately encouraged, or created, conflict. While the small man and dweller on the land had his story, lineage, and rights, once again they were being swept away on a tide of western manipulation; like pawns on a chess board. Because of religion, not instead of it, Jehanne could see that these Middle Eastern countries would continue to be a pyramid of conflict where the three religions of Judaism, Christianity, and Islam met at its apex to fight over which was closer to God.

In the infinity of time and space mankind had not crawled an inch with him still kissing stone walls, or the ring of a mortal Pope. It was simply absurd, and as a French citizen she reflected that even her country were now behaving like pigs at the trough over Syria, stomping their colonial foot on Arab interests over any promised self determination.

With the United States also joining in to secure their share of the spoils of war in the form of regional resources, particularly oil, it was highly likely that the people of the land would once again become slaves to be exploited, like those of old who had been used to create Babylon's Hanging Gardens? If that was the case how long would their empires' last, as inevitably there would be reciprocity that would likewise seal their fate and their posterity?

Jehanne smiled inwardly when she reflected that most lives were still simply dedicated to selfish ideals. In the greater scheme of things she could now see that it was short term thinking. Any empathy to their fellow man and the development of his self esteem was accordingly lost, unwittingly confused with the quest for wealth, and quite often, once more, at the expense of others.

To some degree she realised that her life had been like that also, however, to achieve fulfilment, she comprehended she needed more. Life should be celebrated and nurtured with equality and respect; not sacrificially uprooted on some capitalistic or religious alter of earthly desire. In truly accepting the gift of life that existed in all living creatures she had come to comprehend and believe in universal love, empathy, honesty, understanding and simply being kind.

Knowing now that her focus and guide should be the truth and in doing something good each day, she was transcending any earthly desires for peace. Jehanne had finally comprehended that her mind was the developer of any inner faith and as such the true temple of God, not some institutionalised Church professing false piety and salvation with exclusivist values, gold clad trappings, and its baubles of office.

Again Ernest Budge's words came to mind… *Is it not our freedom of choice that we should be fighting for?*

Intuitively she knew that if everyone understood that, without any labels or preconditions, and they learnt how to share, conserve, and help each other, that the world would be a better place.

Reflecting that any journey started with a first step, with a new found clarity born out of her experiences and association with the amulet, she sat and wrote her resignation to MI6. Other than that there was only one final thing to attend to, and that was more personal.

Located in the Wadi Rabigh, roughly 112miles from both Mecca and Medina and inland of the town of Rabigh, lies Ghadir Al-Khumm, or the 'Pond of Khumm'. Located in the most arid part of Arabia on the Incense Route between Syria and Yemen it is here that travellers have replenished their resources of water for millennia. Fed by several permanent freshwater springs it is unique on the Tihamah north of Jiddah. Mentioned also in the 'Hadith of the pond of Khumma', here also was the Mosque of the Prophet lying between thick trees and the spring.

With their Bristol Fighter having a range of 369 miles they had more than enough fuel for the round trip back to Rabigh aerodrome.

Jehanne in the rear cockpit at Rabigh aerodrome

This stop and interlude had been Rob's idea. He had set the aeroplane down just north of the wetland where Jehanne was now standing enjoying the untouched beauty of these surroundings. It all seemed appropriate in some way, and with an inner peace she returned to where Rob was arranging rugs for her in the rear seat of the Bristol to make it more comfortable on the next leg of their trip. Standing in the Phragmite reeds that fringed the edge of this natural wetland and lake, Jehanne watched several pink-backed pelicans with their distinctive pouches under their beaks going about their business in the shallow water. Feeling totally relaxed for the first time  in years she reflected on her fortune in having met Rob in Cairo those years earlier.

Aware that faithful Moslems were expected to face the venerated shrine of Allah in Mecca during their prayers each day, Jehanne had learnt that the direction facing it was called the *Qiblah*. Turning to where she thought its direction was now she thought of the shrine itself that was known as the *Kaaba,* and that in facing it every believer faced their destiny no matter where they were located in the world.

For Jehanne it seemed like her destiny had been ordained in some way with this as a final entry in a chapter of her life. Knowing that to confirm their faith that one of the five pillars of Islam required every Moslem to perform the Hajj pilgrimage to Mecca at least once in his or her lifetime if able to do so, it had set her on her current mission. Once there, she also knew that the faithful were required to partake seven times in the *Tawaf,* or counter-clockwise circumambulation around the Kaaba's high, black, silken-shrouded sides. This, she had been told, was also a ritual performed by pilgrims during the *Umrah*, or lesser pilgrimage. They were not going to be able to do that, she thought, but this was her pilgrimage of sorts, in an odd sort of way.

*Jehanne and Rob study their
proposed flight route*

Standing together at the front of the still warm engine Rob showed her where they were on the map, and the route they were about to take.

The Kaaba in Mecca

One hour, 15 minutes, later, as Jehanne's file was being sealed by MI6 back in London, the Bristol F2 fighter flew low across the outskirts of Mecca. Below them upturned faces of native Arab inhabitants stared back from under their kūfiyyāt looking at peace in the mid afternoon sun. In the aeroplane's rear observer's cockpit Jehanne reached down for the timber floor and picked up a small folded silk parachute attached to an oil skin package. It was addressed to Hussein bin Ali, Sherif and Emir of Mecca. Enclosed was the amulet with a covering letter…

Al Munquiz Al A'zam -
H.M. Hussein ibn 'Ali,
Caliph al-Islam,
King of the Hijaz,
Commander of the Faithful, Grand Sherif and Amir of Mecca,

Tawak –kalto –ul-Allah

Enclosed is a valuable item of property that once belonged to Muhammad, Salahlahu Alaihi wa salaam, and which belongs to the Arab people. Maybe this in some way compensates your people for the frailties and unfulfilled promises of the Western powers. May the light of truth ultimately be revealed.

From a sympathetic friend…

SubhanAllahi azim wa bihamdi,
Fi-umman-allah

Whilst the rights of the indigenous inhabitants of the land were being usurped, more important to them was their religion as Moslems that was now ultimately validated. As people who believe in the Oneness of God, and the six articles of faith as true brothers and sisters in Islam, unity as an *Ummah* was very important. The rejoined unity and messages of the amulet were a gift richer than any Arab homeland, or any amount of gold. Transcending borders and confirming their beliefs it would be kept for a time when the world was ready for the true light of Allah. The West's materialistic life, that simply took it from one point to the next in an endless turbulent journey, did not offer true inner happiness, or eternal happiness in any possible life to come. In due course the amulet's message would be revealed as the true 'reality' to a repentant world. In the name of Allah the Merciful all religions would then be exonerated by the omnipotent one, however, *grace would not conflict with perfect justice!*

For Jehanne she had no such fears…

View (taken by Jehanne Blanche) of Mecca, with the Kaaba, (between the gun magazines), taken from the rear cockpit of the Bristol Fighter.

By the time Jehanne Blanche's resignation had been received at the London telegraphic address for MI6 things had already been changing. Decoded British Intelligence telegrams from its other agents abroad continued to show just how volatile Europe had become at the end of hostilities. MI5 and MI6 now needed to maintain a close watch on revolutionary movements. For them Bolshevism had replaced German militarism as the principal problem facing Britain, its Empire, and its intelligence community.

Robert Polaschek

For Jehanne the tenderness of Rob's love making had a soothing effect. With her emotional and physical surrender it had stimulated an inner sensuality in her for the first time in her life. It again rose in its intensity to overwhelm her in a flood of ecstasy; an intense feeling that burst open as a massive wave of overwhelming pleasure. As the feeling dissipated she lay there complete and at peace. From some far off mosque minaret a muezzin reciting the adhan called the faithful to prayer. With an eerie honesty its sound resonated, intermingling with the fragrance of frangipani and bougainvillea that wafted in through the open window shutters on the breeze. It was the closest Jehanne had ever come to understanding the simplicity of eternity. Maybe one day mankind would be resurrected and united under one true God.

In early July 1927, the Sacred Congregation of the Holy Office of the Roman Catholic Church in Rome would issue a response to a doctrinal question. It was whether it was permissible for Catholics to be present at, or to approve of, gatherings of non-Catholics that sought to procure the unity of all Christians. The Holy Office response would be… *in the negative.*

They additionally declared that a decree that had been issued by the same Congregation in July 1919, prohibiting the participation of Catholics in the 'Society for the Union of Christendom', was '*absolutely to be observed*'. This decree, in turn, had reiterated the binding force of two instructions promulgated by the Holy Office under Pope Pius IX back in 1864, and 1865. Things were not going to change to threaten their church.

In the infinity and wonderment if the firmament, man had not learnt much; in hardly scratching the surface of enlightenment for it to again be tarnished by man's propensity for power, control, greed, and dishonesty. It was still a world where invented doctrines and religions encouraged an environment of 'them' and 'us'.

In a corner of the Kaaba, is a sacred black stone, a meteorite that Muslims believe was placed by Abraham and Ishmael as symbol of God's covenant with Abraham and Ishmael and, by extension, with the Muslim community itself. Unbeknown to all of them, or the millions of pilgrim believers visiting the Kaaba, hidden in another corner, hanging round the neck of a statue of the deity Hubal, is an amulet. Burdened with their lies, religious hypocrisy, political manipulation, materialism and greed, one day Rome and the West were going to experience the straw that would break their camel's back.

The WW1 medals of A/Corporal Arthur Edgar Newcombe
held in trust by the author

It isn't until you come to a spiritual understanding
of who you are – not necessarily a religious feeling,
but deep down, the spirit within – that you can begin
to take control.

Oprah Winfrey (b) 1954

Epilogue

The earliest writing systems evolved independently, at roughly the same time, in Egypt and Mesopotamia; but current scholarship suggests that Mesopotamia's writing appeared first. That writing system was invented by the Sumerians, and it emerged in Sumer around 3500 BC.

c 3000 BC Sumarian clay tablet

The tools these Sumerian scribes used were styluses with sharp triangular tips making it easy to leave markings on the clay; the clay tablets themselves came in a variety of colors such as bone white, chocolate, and charcoal. Pictographs had begun to appear on clay tablets around 4000 BC, and after the later development of Sumerian cuneiform writing a more sophisticated partial syllabic script evolved that, by around 2500 BC, was capable of recording the vernacular, or everyday speech of the common people.

The Akkadian Empire was the first ancient Semitic-speaking empire of Mesopotamia, centered in the city of Akkad and its surrounding region, (also called Akkad in ancient Mesopotamia in the Bible). The empire united Akkadian and Sumerian speakers under one rule. The Akkadian Empire exercised influence across Mesopotamia, the Levant, and Anatolia, sending military

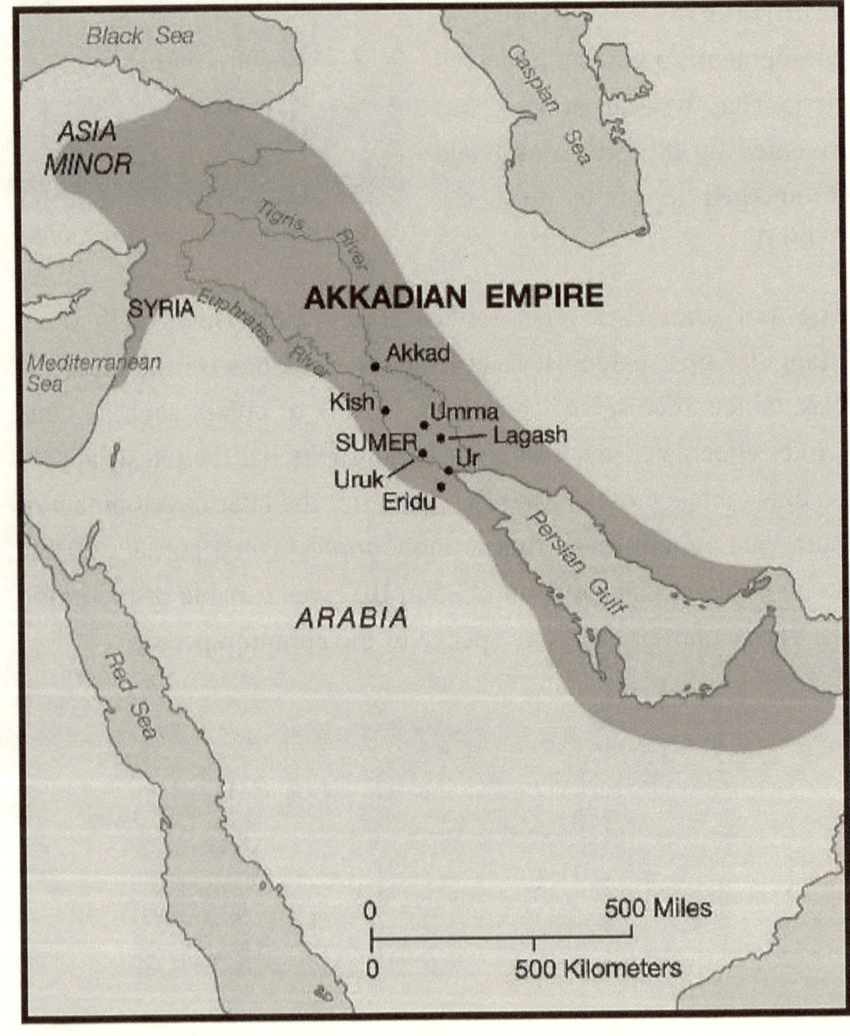

expeditions as far south as Dilmun and Magan (modern Bahrain and Oman) in the Arabian Peninsula.

During the 3rd millennium BC there developed a very intimate cultural symbiosis between the Sumerians and the Akkadians, which included widespread bilingualism. Akkadian gradually replaced Sumerian as a spoken language somewhere between the 3rd and the 2nd millennia BC. The Bible refers to Akkad in Genesis 10:10, which states that the beginning of Nimrod's kingdom was in the land of Akkad. Nimrod's historical identity is unknown, but some have compared him with the legendary Gilgamesh, founder of Uruk.

The Akkadian Empire reached its political peak between the 24th and 22nd centuries BC following the conquests by its founder Sargon of Akkad. Under Sargon, and his successors, the Akkadian language was briefly imposed on neighboring conquered states such as Elam and Gutium. Akkad is sometimes regarded as the first empire in history, though the meaning of this term is not precise, and there are earlier Sumerian claimants.

The empire was bound together by roads, along which there was a regular postal service. Clay seals that took the place of stamps bear the names of Sargon and his son. A cadastral survey seems also to have been instituted, and one of the documents relating to it states that a certain Uru-Malik, whose name appears to indicate his Canaanite origin, was governor of the land of the Amorites, or *Amurru* as the semi-nomadic people of Syria and Canaan were called in Akkadian. It is probable that the first collection of astronomical observations and terrestrial omens was made for a library established by Sargon. The earliest 'year names', whereby each year of a king's reign was named after a significant event performed by that king, date from Sargon's reign. Lists of these 'year names' henceforth became a calendrical system used in most independent Mesopotamian city-states. In Assyria, however, years came to be named for the annual presiding *limmu* official appointed by the king, rather than for an event.

After the fall of the Akkadian Empire, the people of Mesopotamia eventually coalesced into two major Akkadian-speaking nations: Assyria in the north, and, a few centuries later, Babylonia in the south.

Today, scholars have documented some 7,000 texts from the Akkadian period, written in both Sumerian and Akkadian. Many later texts from the successor states of Assyria and Babylonia also deal with the Akkadian Empire.

Semites, Semitic people or Semitic cultures (from the biblical

'Shem', as one of the sons of Noah in the Hebrew Bible as well as in Islamic literature), was a term for an ethnic, cultural or racial group who speak, or spoke, the Semitic languages that include Hebrew, Arabic, and Aramaic, and certain ancient languages such as Phoenician and Akkadian, constituting the main subgroup of the Afro-Asiatic family.

The terms 'anti-Semite' or 'antisemitism' came by a circuitous route to refer more narrowly to anyone who was hostile or discriminatory towards Jews in particular.

The concept of the Promised Land is the central tenet of Zionism, whose discourse suggests that modern Jews descend from the Israelites and Maccabees through whom they inherit the right to re-establish their 'national homeland'. Palestinians also claim partial descent from the Israelites and Maccabees, as well as all the other peoples who have lived in the region.

If the promised land in the Bible was that geographic area God gave to a chosen people, as the descendants of Abraham, then it should apply to Moslems as they are his descendants, from his son Ishmael, and the children of Keturah, Abraham's third wife who are supposedly represented by the Arab tribes who lived south and east of Palestine. The Bible, however, records that God told Abraham that he would establish his covenant through Abraham's son Isaac, and when Abraham inquired as to Ishmael's role, God answered that Ishmael has been blessed and that He …

….will make him fruitful, and will multiply him exceedingly; twelve princes shall he beget, and I will make him a great nation.

The United Monarchy is the name given to the ancient Israelite kingdoms of Israel and Judah, during the reigns of Saul, David and Solomon, as depicted in the Hebrew Bible. These kingdoms are traditionally dated between 1050 BC and 930 BC. On the succession of Solomon's son, Rehoboam, around 930 BC, the biblical account reports that the country split into two kingdoms; the Kingdom of Israel, including the cities of Shechem and Samaria, in the north, and the Kingdom of Judah containing

Jerusalem, in the south.

In contemporary scholarship the United Monarchy is generally held to be a literary construction and not a historical reality, pointing to the lack of archaeological evidence. Some scholars argue that there is historical evidence to support its existence. It is generally accepted, however,' that a 'House of David' existed, but many believe that David could have only been the monarch or chieftain of Judah, which was likely small, and that the northern kingdom was a separate development.

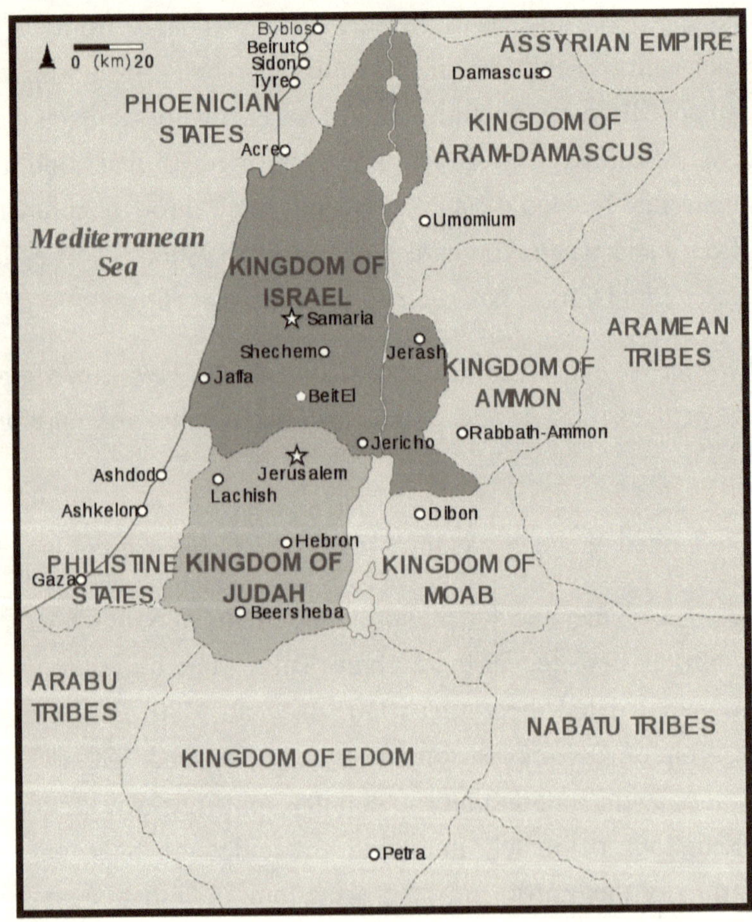

The Kingdom of Judah was an Iron Age kingdom of the Southern Levant. The Hebrew Bible depicts it as the successor to a United Monarchy, but, as mentioned, historians are divided about the veracity of this account. In the 10th and early 9th centuries BC, the territory of Judah appears to have been sparsely populated, limited to small rural settlements, most of them unfortified. Jerusalem, the kingdom's capital, likely did not emerge as a significant administrative center until the end of the 8th century; before this the archaeological evidence suggests its population was too small to sustain a viable kingdom. In the 7th century its population increased greatly, prospering under Assyrian vassalage, but in 605 BC the Assyrian Empire was defeated, and the ensuing competition between the Twenty-sixth Dynasty of Egypt and the Neo-Babylonian Empire for control of the Eastern Mediterranean led to the destruction of the kingdom in a series of campaigns between 597 BC and 582 BC, the deportation of the elite of the community, and the incorporation of Judah into a province of the Neo-Babylonian Empire.

The Maccabees were a group of Jewish rebel warriors who took control of Judea, which at the time was part of the Seleucid Empire. They founded the Hasmonean dynasty, which ruled from 167 BC to 37 BC, being a fully independent kingdom from about 110 BC to 63 BC. They reasserted the Jewish religion, partly by forced conversion; expanded the boundaries of Judea by conquest, and reduced the influence of Hellenism and Hellenistic Judaism.

In Judaism, the theological importance of the Old Testament book of Genesis centers on the covenants linking God to his supposed chosen people, and the people to a supposed Promised Land. Christianity has interpreted Genesis as the prefiguration of certain cardinal Christian beliefs; primarily the need for salvation, as a hope or assurance of all Christians; and the redemptive act of Christ on the Cross as the fulfillment of covenant promises as the Son of God.

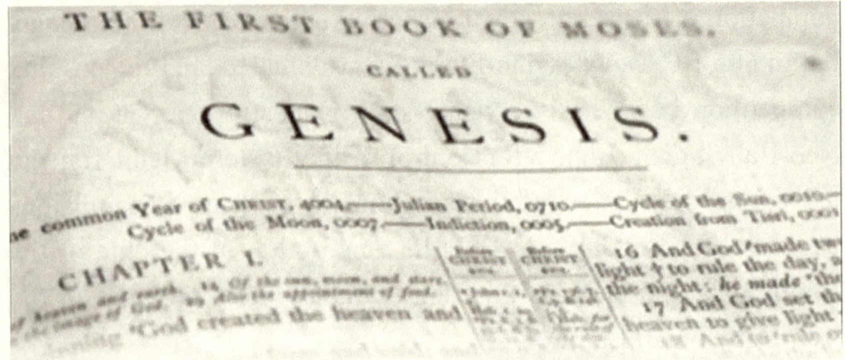

Genisis can be divided into two parts, the Primeval history and the Ancestral history. The Primeval history sets out the author's (or authors') concepts of the nature of the deity and of humankind's relationship with its maker in which God creates a world which is good and fit for mankind, but when man corrupts it with sin God decides to destroy his creation, saving only the righteous Noah to re-establish the relationship between man and God.

What most do not realise, however, is that the story of Noah is in reality the much older Sumarian mythological account of King Gilgamesh and the Flood. The Ancestral History of the Old Testament that supposedly tells of the prehistory of Israel, from

Noah as God's chosen people is, therefore, proven as flawed from the outset.

In the Genesis account, at God's command, Noah's descendant Abraham journeys from his home into the land of Canaan, supposedly given to him by God, where he dwells as a sojourner, as does his son Isaac and his grandson Jacob. Jacob's name is changed to Israel, and through the agency of his son Joseph, the children of Israel suppossedly descend into Egypt. There were purportedly 70 people in all with their households and God promises them a future of greatness. Genesis ends with Israel in Egypt, ready for the coming of Moses and the Exodus. The narrative is punctuated by a series of covenants with God. These successively narrow in scope from 'all mankind' as the covenant with Noah, to a special relationship with 'one people' alone, namely Abraham and his descendants through Isaac and Jacob.

Tradition credits Moses as the author of Genesis, as well as Exodus, the Book of Leviticus, Numbers and most of Book of Deuteronomy, but modern scholars increasingly see them as a product of the 6th and 5th centuries BC. Whatever the age of the compilation of stories that make up the Old Testament it is clear, that at the very least, the story of Noah and the Great Flood is a re-work of the ancient Sumerian mythical account portrayed in the Epic of Gilgamesh that originally dates from sometime after an actual flood in Sumer in 2900 BC, that was recorded at least by 2100 BC.

Likewise any associated promises, or promised lands are also fictitious.

The *Epic of Gilgamesh* is an epic poem from ancient Mesopotamia that is often regarded as the earliest surviving great work of literature. The literary history of Gilgamesh begins with five Sumerian poems about Gilgamesh, king of Uruk, and of Enkidu, dating from the Third Dynasty of Ur around 2100 BC.

Enkidu embodies the wild or natural world that was formed from clay and water by Aruru, the goddess of creation, to rid Gilgamesh of his arrogance. Though equal to Gilgamesh in strength and bearing, Enkidu acts in some ways as an antithesis to the cultured, urban-bred, warrior-king.

In the second half of the epic, distress over Enkidu's death causes Gilgamesh to undertake a long and perilous journey to discover the secret of eternal life. From this he eventually learns that ...

'Life, which you look for, you will never find. For when the gods created man, they let death be his share, and life withheld in their own hands'.

More relevant, however, is what the immortal man Utnapishtim told Gilgamesh about the Great Flood.

Early Mesopotamian flood stories concern the epics of Ziusudra, Gilgamesh, and Atrahasis. The Sumerian King List relies on the flood motif to divide its history into preflood and postflood periods. The preflood kings had enormous lifespans, whereas postflood lifespans were much reduced. The Sumerian flood myth found in the Deluge tablet was the epic of Ziusudra, who heard the gods' plan to destroy humanity, in response to which he constructed a vessel that delivered him from great waters. In the Atrahasis version, the flood is a river flood.

In the Akkadian version that was compiled sometime between 1300 and 1000 BC from earlier texts, Gilgamesh observes that Utnapishtim seems no different that himself, and asks him how he obtained his immortality. Utnapishtim explains that the gods decided to send a great flood. To save Utnapishtim the god Ea told him to build a boat. He gave him precise dimensions, and it was sealed with pitch and bitumen. His entire family went aboard together with his craftsmen and 'all the animals of the field'. A violent storm then arose which caused the terrified gods to retreat to the heavens. Ishtar lamented the wholesale destruction of humanity, and the other gods wept beside her. The storm lasted six days and six nights, after which 'all the human beings turned to clay'. Utnapishtim wept when he saw the destruction. His boat lodges on a mountain, and he releases a dove, a swallow, and a raven. When the raven fails to return, he opens the ark and frees its inhabitants.

A much later story of Noah and the Mesopotamian flood myth,

closest to that in Genesis, is found in a 700 BC Babylonian copy of the epic.

Finally in the 4th century Genesis mythology of the Hebrew Bible, Yahweh decides to flood the earth because of the depth of the sinful state of mankind. Righteous Noah is given instructions to build an ark. When the ark is completed, Noah, his family, and representatives of all the animals of the earth are called upon to enter the ark. When the destructive flood begins, all life outside of the ark perishes. After the waters recede, all those aboard the ark disembark and have Yahweh's promise that he will never judge the earth with a flood again. He causes a rainbow to form as the sign of this promise.

As for the dating of any likely flood that are depicted by the eralier accounts, excavations in Mesopotamia have revealed evidence of localised flooding at Shuruppak and various other Sumerian cities. A layer of riverine sediment that dates to about 2900 BC, interrupts the continuity of settlement, and extends as far north as the city of Kish, which took over hegemony after the flood. Pottery from the Jemdet Nasr period of 3000–2900 BC has also been discovered immediately below the Shuruppak flood layer. This flood seems to have been a localised event caused through the damming of the Karun River through the spread of dunes, flooding into the Tigris, and simultaneous heavy rainfall in the Nineveh region, spilling across into the Euphrates.

A more likely theory, however, is that about 12,000 years ago, toward the end of the Ice Age, the Earth began growing warmer. Vast sheets of ice that sprawled over the Northern Hemisphere began to melt. Oceans and seas grew deeper as a result. Towards the end of this last Ice Age, about 7,000 years ago, the Black Sea may have been an isolated freshwater lake surrounded by farmland. The Mediterranean Sea swelled with seawater pushing northward, slicing through what is now Turkey. Funneled through the narrow Bosporus, the water hit the Black Sea with 200 times the force of Niagara Falls. Each day the Black Sea rose about 15 centimeters, and coastal farms were flooded. Seared into the memories of terrified survivors, the tale of the flood may have been passed down through the generations to eventually become the Noah story.

In the areas known to have been the ancient Kingdom of Israel, and Kingdom of Judea, there is no such evidence of a widespread flood. Given the similarities in the Mesopotamian flood story and the Biblical account, the only conclusion that can be drawn is that they have a common origin in the memories of the Shuruppak account. More-over a world-wide deluge, such as that described in Genesis, is incompatible with any current understanding of natural history, especially geology and paleontology.

The eastern Mediterranean seaboard of the Levant stretches 400 miles north to south from the Taurus Mountains to the Sinai Peninsula, and 70 to 100 miles east to west between the sea and the Arabian Desert. The coastal plain of the southern Levant, broad in the south and narrowing to the north, is backed in its southernmost portion by a zone of foothills, the Shfela; like the plain this narrows as it goes northwards, ending in the promontory of Mount Carmel. East of the plain and the Shfela is a mountainous ridge; the 'hill country of Judah' in the south, the 'hill country of Ephraim' north of that, then Galilee and Mount Lebanon. To the east again lie the steep-sided valley occupied by the Jordan River, the Dead Sea, and the wadi of the Arabah, which continues down to the eastern arm of the Red Sea. Beyond the plateau is the Syrian desert, separating the Levant from Mesopotamia.

To the southwest is Egypt, to the northeast Mesopotamia. The location and geographical characteristics of the narrow Levant made the area a battleground among the powerful entities that surrounded it.

Canaan in the Late Bronze Age was a shadow of what it had been centuries earlier. Many cities were abandoned, others shrank in size, and the total settled population was probably not much more than a hundred thousand. Settlement was concentrated in cities along the coastal plain and along major communication routes; the central and northern hill country which would later become the biblical kingdom of Israel was only sparsely inhabited although letters from the Egyptian archives indicate that Jerusalem was already a Canaanite city-state recognising Egyptian overlordship. Politically and culturally it was dominated by Egypt, with each city under its own ruler, constantly at odds with its neighbours, and appealing to the Egyptians to adjudicate their differences.

The Canaanite city state system broke down during the Late Bronze Age collapse, with Canaanite culture then gradually absorbed into that of the Philistines, Phoenicians and Israelites. The process was gradual and a strong Egyptian presence continued into the 12th century BC. While some Canaanite cities were destroyed, others continued to exist in the Iron Age.

The discovery of the remains of a dense network of highland villages, all apparently established within the span of few generations, indicated that a dramatic social transformation took place in the central hill country of Canaan around 1200 BC. There is no sign of violent invasion or even the infiltration of a clearly defined ethnic group. Instead, it seems to have been a revolution in lifestyle. In the formerly sparsely populated highlands from the Judean hills in the south, to the hills of Samaria in the north, far from the Canaanite cities that were in the process of collapse and disintegration, about 250 hilltop communities suddenly sprang up.

It is here we find the first Israelites.

As for the name Israel it first appears in the Merneptah Stele of c. 1209 BC, where it states, *'Israel is laid waste and his seed is no more.'* This 'Israel' was a cultural and probably political entity, well enough established for the Egyptians to perceive it as a possible challenge, but still an ethnic group rather than an organised state. It was likely that a population group began to identify itself as 'Israelite', differentiating itself from its neighbours via prohibitions on intermarriage, and an emphasis on family history, genealogy, and religion.

The Kingdom of Israel and the Kingdom of Judah were related kingdoms from the Iron Age period of the ancient Levant. The Kingdom of Israel only emerged as an important local power again around 1000 BC before falling to the Neo-Assyrian Empire in 722 BC. Israel's southern neighbour, the Kingdom of Judah, emerged in the 8th or 9th century BC and later became a client state of first the Neo-Assyrian Empire and then the Neo Babylonian Empire, before a revolt against the latter led to its destruction in 586 BC.

As for the Old Testament accounts, the combined weight of

evidence now tells its own story. Taking into consideration that many of these accounts are proven, or likely to have been old mythology accounts from previous times and empires; and with no evidence of a Jewish people having ever migrated from Eygpt with Moses, or of them ever being a chosen people with land being promised to them by any God, the credibility of the whole current State of Israel is brought into question. With Jerusalem not having been in the original Kingdom of Israel, combined with evidence of the early 1200 BC hill settlements of the original Israelites with their change in lifestyle and religion at that time, it confirms at least two things. The first is that mankind, in his underlying nature, is still gullible, manipulative, devisive, and not very intelligent. The second confirms the idealogical Jewish religious scam that continues to be perpetrated on the ill-informed in the name of Judeism. With land theft continuing to be orchestrated by the State of Israel at the expense of the indigenous peoples on the land known as Palestine, it is all about power and control by those who promote state sponsored religion.

A Jewish believer at the old west (wailing) wall in Jerusalem

As Ernest Budge eloquently extolled it … *I for one would rather be an enlightened heretic than a brain dead believer.*

Arthur Newcombe

Following his death on the 19th February 1918 at the tender age of 20 years, Lance Corporal Arthur Edgar Newcombe No. 290898 - Middlesex Regiment, was buried just over 2.5 miles north of the walled city of Jerusalem. The cemetery lies on the neck of land at the north end of the Mount of Olives, to the west of Mount Scopus. Known today as the Jerusalem War Cemetery, Yerushalayim (Jerusalem Dist.), Israel, Arthur rests in Plot: M. 48.

Lying only 10 rows away in Plot C. 47 is Private Charles Newcombe, No. 241158, Devonshire Regiment, who had been killed on 23rd November, 1917.

The Jerusalem War Cemetery, Yerushalayim, Israel

Jehanne Blanche

Jehanne Blanche resigned from British Intelligence in June, 1925, with her file sealed by MI6. As Mrs Polaschek she would migrate to Australia where she lived in the outback of the Northern Territories with its heat and windswept terrain that was similar to the land where she had first met her pilot husband. A related descendant Robert Polashek II, who I have conversed with regarding his family history, lives in Christchurch New Zealand.

Gertrude Bell

Returning briefly to Britain in 1925, Gertrude Bell found herself facing family problems and ill health. Her family's fortune had begun to decline due to the onset of post-war worker strikes in Britain and economic depression in Europe. Gertrude returned to Baghdad and soon developed pleurisy. When she recovered, she heard that her younger brother Hugo had died of typhoid. On 12th July 1926, Gertrude was discovered dead, of an apparent overdose of sleeping pills.

Ernest Budge

Egyptologist, Orientalist, and philologist Ernest Budge was knighted in the 1920 New Year Honours for his distinguished contributions to Egyptology and the British Museum. He died on 23rd November, 1934, as Jehanne Blanche's respected friend, and one of only two people that 'Mike', the famous cat of the British Museum, would allow to feed him.

*Stewart
Newcombe*

Within a few months of the war's end Colonel Stewart Newcombe and Elsie Chaki were reunited. They married on 16th April, 1919, in St. Margaret's, a small church nestling in the shadow of Westminster Abbey, London. If he wanted to impress his young bride he could not have selected a more stunning location, situated as it was, at the political epicentre of the Empire he had served as a loyal and dedicated agent.

*Aaron
Aaronsohn*

By 1919 Aaron Aaronsohn, NILI's founder and leader, had drafted a map of Palestine, not based on arbitrary borders, but on topographical features that would permit the development of a viable Jewish state. He carried this map with him as a member of the Jewish delegation when his plane went down in the English Channel on the 15th May, 1919, on his way to the Paris Peace Conference. The circumstances surrounding the crash and untimely death were unclear and, at the time, quite controversial, with the finger of blame pointing in several directions, but most notably to the British government.

Jehanne was shocked and suspicious surrounding his death and it just added more weight to her already flagging faith in British intentions.

The seal of Mossad - The Institute for Intelligence and Special Operations

"Where no counsel is, the people fall, but in the multitude of counsellors there is safety." (Proverbs XI:14)

Arab opposition to British rule and Jewish immigration would lead to the 1920 Palestine riots and the formation of a Jewish militia known as the Haganah. The Israeli Mossad, short for Ha Mossad, or 'Institute for Intelligence and Special Operations', is the national intelligence agency of Israel. It is one of the main entities in the Israeli Intelligence Community, along with Aman (military intelligence) and Shin Bet (internal security).

Today Mossad is responsible for intelligence collection, covert operations, and counterterrorism, as well as bringing Jews to Israel from countries where official Aliyah agencies are forbidden, and in protecting Jewish communities. Its director reports directly to the Prime Minister.

Enver Bey

Since 1922 Turkish denial of the genocide of 1.5 million Armenians has been driven and constant. It is purportedly state-funded, with special departments in overseas missions whose sole purpose is to attempt to minimise and counter and reference to the events surrounding the genocide of Armenians, Pontian Greeks and

Assyrian Christians in Asia Minor from 1914 to 1922. In reality it was an Ottoman government execution of a scheme to annihilate the Armenian, Greek and Syrian Christians of Turkey. It was a campaign of outrageous terrorizing and cruel torture; the driving of women into harems, and the debauchery of innocent girls with the sale of many of them at 80 cents each; the murdering of hundreds of thousands, along with deportation and starvation in the desert of many hundreds of thousands and the destruction of hundreds of villages, and many cities.

Enver Bey was tried in absentia in the Turkish Courts-Martial of 1919-20 for crimes of plunging the country into war without a legitimate reason, forced deportation of Armenians and leaving the country without permission and was, as a consequence, condemned to death.

George Mansfield Smith-Cumming

During World War I the Secret Service Bureau (SSB) had under its umbrella 19 military intelligence departments designated from MI1 to MI19. MI5 and MI6 would become the most recognised and are the only two to have remained active to this day.

Agents who worked for MI6 during the war included, Augustus Agar, Gertrude Bell, Jehanne Blanche, John Buchan, Paul Dukes, Compton Mackenzie, W. Somerset Maugham, and Sidney Reilly.

On Sunday, 21st November 1920, the Headquarters Intelligence

Staff of the IRA, and its special Counter Intelligence Branch known as 'The Squad' under the leadership of IRA Intelligence Chief and IRA Adjutant General Michael Collins, mounted a successful operation to assassinate 14 of Smith-Cumming's case officers. While many more appear to have escaped the IRA execution squads that morning, Whitehall feared that more of its professional agents would be identified and suffer the same fate. This prompted the hasty withdrawal of most of the remaining SIS agents from Ireland in the days that followed. It was the single greatest catastrophe in the history of the British Secret Service, and Smith-Cumming was forever after reluctant to involve the SIS in Irish operations.

As head of MI6, Captain Sir George Mansfield Smith-Cumming, KCMG CB would die less than two years later on 14th June 1923.

A British Girl Guide

Following a small group of girls having gate-crashed the first Scouts Rally in Crystal Palace in south London in September 1909 asking for a group of their own, they had been fortunate in being permitted to lobby Scouting chief Robert Baden-Powell at that event.

While serving with the army in India Robert Baden Powell had been impressed with local guides who helped with dangerous expeditions, and using the notion the name conjured up, he formed the Girl Guide Association the following year, asking his adventurous sister Agnes to take charge. No doubt worried about their daughters frolicking in tents with boys in the remote countryside critics denounced 'girl scouting' as a *mischievous new development; a foolish and pernicious movement and an idiotic sport.*

By 1912 Girl Guide badges on offer to teenage girls included air mechanic, cyclist, electrician, sailor, telegraph operator and even tailor. By the start of the First World War, two years later, the Girl Guide movement was 300,000-strong and Government departments began contacting the Girl Guides and the Boy Scouts, seeking teenagers to work as messengers and backroom staff to assist the war effort. MI5 had specifically spotted qualities in the Girl Guides earlier and several were now being put to good use.

As 10 shilling a week messengers working undercover for H Branch of MI5, Girl Guides passed on highly classified information during WW1. It was the last thing they, or anyone else, would have then expected. All the 90 teenage girls who worked for MI5 between 1914 and 1918 were required to be aged from 14 to 16, be of good standing, quick, cheerful and willing. They were so trusted by MI5 bosses that they were allowed to relay some of the messages verbally.

At the start of the war Boy Scouts had been used but it quickly became clear that Girl Guides were more efficient because they were less boisterous and talkative and could adapt to periods of inactivity between their duties. Working at Waterloo House, and two other offices in central London, they were divided up into five or six Guides under a patrol leader, with each allotted to a floor, and each patrol leader responsible for the work, discipline and good behaviour of her patrol. The Guides were allotted marks each day for good work by their patrol leaders and at the end of the month the room which has proved most generally satisfactory was awarded a prize picture for the following month.

Initially engaged on three month probation period with an initial rate of pay of 10 shillings a week with dinner and tea included. Guides who completed special work, or who had special responsibilities, received a higher rate of pay, and those who helped in the kitchen received extra duty pay of four shillings and sixpence per month. Observing a strict dress code which stipulated that their blue skirts must be no more than eight inches off the ground, and that they had to wear a belt with their distinctive hat at all times, they sallied forth to deliver their top-secret messages, either in written form or verbally. It often involved them going out of the buildings in which they were employed; into a public domain that had a small, yet increasing, number of clandestine espionage and counter espionage agents.

If the character of the girl is developed, she will discipline herself not to 'blab' and will 'play the game' not for herself and her own glorification — but in the interests of her side, that is of her country or her employer.

One later Girl Guide would be none other than Stella Rimington, MI5's first woman director.

Francis Aidan Gasquet

Cardinal Francis Aidan Gasquet had a slight stroke shortly after his 80th birthday from which he never fully recovered. He died at the Palazzo San Calisto, Rome, on 5th April 1929, from pneumonia, having suffered for many years from a weak heart. He was buried in the abbey church at Downside, where a monument was erected to his memory.

Gilbert Falkingham Clayton

Before the war Brigadier-General Gilbert Falkingham Clayton had served Sir Reginald Wingate, Governor General of Sudan, as Director of Intelligence in Sudan and agent in Cairo. With the outbreak of war he became Director of Military Intelligence at the British Headquarters in Cairo, head of the Arab Bureau, and eventually chief political officer of the Egyptian Expeditionary Force and military Governor of Palestine.

After the war Clayton was knighted and still played an active role in Palestinian, Arabian and Mesopotamian affairs in the 1920s. As a colonial administrator, he helped negotiate the borders of the countries that later became Israel, Jordan, Syria, Saudi Arabia and Iraq. From 1928, he was High Commissioner for the British Mandate of Mesopotamia (Iraq). In this role, Clayton had been involved in negotiations over a new Anglo-Iraqi Treaty. His unexpected death, from a heart attack, in September 1929, delayed matters somewhat.

Wilhelm Wassmuss

Wilhelm Wassmuss survived the war. For a time, Wassmuss had been dazzlingly successful in Iran, but tribal support for him began to fade when it became obvious to the tribal leaders that Germany was not defeating Britain. After the war, Wassmuss, whose network had spread through Afghanistan and as far as India, and for whom the British had offered a $500,000 reward, was imprisoned by the British. He was released in 1920 and made his way back to Berlin. Once there, the same man who had so eloquently lied to the Persian tribesmen on Germany's behalf struggled to persuade the German Foreign Office to honour his pledges and pay the money he had promised to the tribes.

As the post-war years went by, Wassmuss could not forget his promises. He returned to Bushehr in 1924 and, purchasing cheap farmland, promised to repay the tribesmen from the profits he hoped to make from farming. The farm failed. After legal squabbles over money with some of the tribal chieftains who once been his friends, Wilhelm Wassmuss returned to Berlin in April, 1931. A broken man, he died virtually forgotten and in poverty in November, 1931, but with his honour intact.

Feisal Hussein

Feisal Hussein, eldest son of Hussein, Sherif of Mecca and King of Iraq and Syria had agreed to Jewish settlement according to British Mandate in 1918 based again on promises that were broken. He led the Arab intifada against Turkey (1916-1918) and was designated king of Syria.

Feisal was at first sympathetic to a Jewish homeland from which he hoped to receive aid in building his future kingdom. He met Dr. Weizmann in Jordan in 1918, and in Paris in 1919, where they reached an agreement on mutual aid, conditional on the implementation of British promises to the Arabs and under the terms of that agreement. Later, owing to his expulsion from Syria by the French after a reign of only four months, the breaking of the agreement by the British and the Jews, along with the influence of other Arab leaders, his attitude naturally became hostile.

He was appointed King of Iraq from 1921 with his reign lasting to 1933. In July of that year, right before his death, Faisal went to London where he expressed his alarm at the current situation of Arabs that resulted from the Arab-Jewish conflict and the increased Jewish immigration to Palestine, with the Arab political, social, and economic situation declining. He asked the British to limit Jewish migration and land sales … *for fear that otherwise in the near future the Arabs would either be squeezed out of Palestine or reduced to economic and social servitude.*

King Faisal died on 8th September 1933, at the age of 48. The official cause of death was a heart attack while he was staying in Bern, Switzerland, for his general medical check up. Many questions arose over his sudden death.

T E Lawrence

The legend of Lawrence of Arabia was stimulated first by public lantern shows in Britain and America, and later by T. E. Lawrence's writings on the Arab revolt that resulted in a growth of public interest in Arabia. Although the Arab revolt had only minor military significance, it formed the basis of legend. A myth based on a natural affinity between the British Empire and Arab desert warriors, countered by the betrayal of true Arab nationalism by duplicitous British diplomacy. Both legend and fact would exercise a powerful subliminal influence on Anglo - Arab attitudes ongoing, including a genuine dislike by Moslem's.

Suffering from depression Thomas Edward Lawrence was fatally injured in a motorbike crash in Dorset in 1935, only two weeks after leaving the service.

Edmond James de Rothschild

Before Baron Edmond James de Rothschild died in Paris in 1934, he indicated that he wanted to be buried in the Holy Land. After the establishment of the State of Israel, the baron's son would have his body, along with that of his wife, both reinterred near the town on Ramat Ha-Nadiv; the Heights of the 'Benefactor', as the name given to Rothschild.

Today, the tombs are set in beautiful gardens filled with the varieties of plants that Rothschilds' helped develop.

Sir James Rennell Rodd

Sir James Rennell Rodd, the British Ambassador to Italy had been appointed Companion of the Order of the Bath (CB) in 1897, Knight Commander of the Order of St. Michael and St. George (KCMG) in 1899, Knight Grand Cross of the Royal Victorian Order

(GCVO) in 1905. He was appointed to the Privy Council in 1908, and raised to Knight Grand Cross of the Order of St Michael and St George (GCMG) in 1915.

He left the Diplomatic Service in 1919 but nonetheless served on the mission to Egypt in 1920 with Lord Milner, and was British delegate to the League of Nations from 1921 to 1923. He also sat as Unionist Member of Parliament for St Marylebone between 1928 and 1932. He was made Knight Grand Cross of the Order of the Bath (GCB) in the 1920 New Year Honours, and in 1933 he was raised to the peerage as Baron Rennell of Rodd in the County of Hereford.

Lord Rennell died in July 1941, aged 82, and was succeeded in the barony by his second but eldest surviving son who later served as President of the Royal Geographical Society.

Gabriele D'Annunzio

With Italy entering the war in 1915 Gabriele D'Annunzio had volunteered and achieved further celebrity as a fighter pilot, losing the sight of an eye in a flying accident. In February 1918 he took part in a daring, if militarily irrelevant, raid on the harbour of Bakar helping to raise the spirits of the Italian public, still battered by the Caporetto disaster. On 9th August 1918, as commander of the 87th fighter squadron 'La Serenissima', he organised one of the great feats of the war, leading nine planes in a 700-mile round trip to drop propaganda leaflets on Vienna. This is called in Italian 'il Volo su Vienna', or the Flight over Vienna.

In 1924 he was ennobled by King Victor Emmanuel III and given the hereditary title of Principe di Montenevoso. In 1937 he was made president of the Royal Academy of Italy.

D'Annunzio died in 1938 of a stroke, at his home in Gardone Riviera. He was given a state funeral by Mussolini and was interred in a magnificent tomb constructed of white marble at Il Vittoriale degli Italiani.

Sir Henry McMahon

Sir Henry McMahon is remembered for his famous, much-debated, correspondence with Emir (Sharif) Hussein. Lawrence would comment that he had *shrewd insight and a tried, experienced mind that understood our design at once and judged it good.* Sir Henry died in 1949.

Reginald Wingate

General Reginald Wingate held the post as High Commissioner in Egypt until 1919. He was not a successful administrator in the very different political climate in that country, and was made a scapegoat for the riots incited by Saad Zaghlul and his party that plagued Egypt. Angry at his treatment, Wingate refused to actually resign, even after he was officially replaced by Lord Allenby, and threatened to embarrass the British Government.

He was made a knight of the Venerable Order of St John in 1919. He was refused a peerage or another appointment, although he was created a baronet in the 1920 King's Birthday Honours, gazetted as Baronet Wingate of Dunbar, in the County of Haddington, and of Port Sudan. He never held another public or military office, retiring from the Army on 1st February 1922. He died in 1953.

Arthur Balfour

Arthur James Balfour, 1st Earl of Balfour, KG, OM, PC, FRS, FBA, DL was a British statesman of the Conservative Party who served as Prime Minister of the United Kingdom from 1902 to 1905. As Foreign Secretary from 1916 to 1919, he issued the Balfour Declaration in November 1917 on behalf of the cabinet. '

Nothing matters very much and few things matter at all', was one of Arthur James Balfour's quips.

Being aloof, privileged, and extremely wealthy, even his contemporaries had trouble working him out. As a product of Eton and Cambridge, he clearly liked power and being at the center of things, without liking the boring detail of hard work. As a member of the Conservative Party, throughout his political career he served as Chief Secretary for Ireland, Secretary for Scotland, Lord Privy Seal, First Lord of the Admiralty, Prime Minister and Foreign Secretary; the position he was holding when he signed the Balfour Declaration.

He once uttered that *'enthusiasm moves the world',* without showing many signs in demonstrating that himself, with perhaps Zionism being an exception. One biographer wrote that he *'has said nothing, written nothing, done nothing which lives in the hearts of his countrymen. To look back on his record is to see a desert ...'* Yet as a lifelong bachelor, Balfour still fathered one disturbed child, … the state of Israel; that Palestinians, the Middle East, and the world generally, have had to live with the consequences of ever since.

Visiting Palestine in the 1920s for the laying of the foundation stone of the Hebrew University, he moved on to Damascus, and could not understand why the locals were angry. Besieged in his hotel room by demonstrators he saw nothing of the city, had to be surreptitiously whisked out of the hotel by a side door before being driven at speed across back roads to Beirut, from where he took passage on a ship and sailed away, still unable to understand why his visit had caused such a fuss among the Arabs.

In the end, soon after receiving a visit from his friend Chaim Weizmann, Balfour died on 19 March 1930.

Sir Winston Leonard Spencer- Churchill

Sir Winston Leonard Spencer-Churchill, KG, OM, CH, TD, DL, FRS, Hon. RA was a British politician who was Prime Minister of the United Kingdom from 1940 to 1945; that is, for most of WWII, and again from 1951 to 1955. Widely regarded as one of the greatest wartime leaders of the 20th century, Churchill was also an officer in the British Army, a historian, a writer, and an artist. He is the only British Prime Minister to have received the

Nobel Prize in Literature, and was also the first person to be made an honorary citizen of the United States.

Churchill was born into an aristocratic family as the grandson of the 7th Duke of Marlborough. His father, Lord Randolph Churchill, was a charismatic politician who served as Chancellor of the Exchequer; his mother, Jennie Jerome, was an American socialite. As a young army officer, he saw action in British India, The Sudan, and the Second Boer War. He gained fame as a war correspondent and wrote books about his campaigns.

At the forefront of politics for 50 years, he held many political and cabinet positions. Before the First World War, he served as President of the Board of Trade, Home Secretary, and First Lord of the Admiralty as part of the Asquith Liberal government.

Clementine and Winston Churchill – 1915

During World War One, he had continued as First Lord of the Admiralty until the disastrous Gallipoli Campaign caused his departure from government. He then briefly resumed active army service on the Western Front as commander of the 6th Battalion of the Royal Scots Fusiliers. He returned to government as Minister of Munitions, Secretary of State for War, and Secretary of State for Air. After the War, Churchill served as Chancellor of the Exchequer in the Conservative Baldwin government of 1924–29, controversially returning the pound sterling in 1925 to the gold standard at its pre-war parity, a move widely seen as creating deflationary pressure on the UK economy.

Also controversial was his opposition to increased home rule for India, and his resistance to the 1936 abdication of Edward VIII.

Winston passed from this mortal earth on 24th January, 1965.

Hillary 'Harry'
St-John
Bridger
Philby

In November 1917, Hillary 'Harry' St-John Bridger Philby CIE had been sent to the interior of the Arabian peninsula as head of a mission to Ibn Saud. This Wahabbi chieftain, and bitter enemy of Sherif Hussein, had been sending raids against the Hashemite ruler of the Hejaz, leader of the revolt.

For more than 700 years the non-Turkic Hashemite dynasty had held title as Sharif of Mecca. Philby secretly had begun to favour Ibn Saud over Sherif Hussein as 'King of the Arabs'. This was at odds with British policy which had been promising support for the Hashemite dynasty in the post-Ottoman world. On his return Philby completed the crossing from Riyadh to Jeddah by the 'backdoor' route, thus demonstrating Ibn Saud was in control of the Arabian highlands, whereas Sherif Hussein could not guarantee safe passage.

On 7th November 1918, four days before the Armistice, Britain and France had issued the Anglo-French Declaration to the Arabs assuring self-determination. Philby felt the betrayal of this assurance, along with the Balfour Declaration, Sykes-Picot Agreement, and other diplomatic manoeuvres had broken faith with the promise of a single unified Arab nation in exchange for aligning themselves with the Allies in the war against the Ottoman Turks and Central Powers. In this he was not out of step with Lawrence and Jehanne.

Ibn Saud

Philby, however, argued that Ibn Saud was a democrat guiding his affairs by mutual counsel as laid out in the Quran, in contrast to Lord Curzon's 'Hussein policy'. After the Great Iraqi Revolution of 1920 Philby was appointed Minister of Internal Security in the British Mandate of Iraq. He roughed out a democratic constitution complete with elected assembly and republican president.

In November 1921, Philby was named chief head of the Secret Service for the British Mandate of Palestine, or what is now the region of The Hashemite Kingdom of Jordan and Israel. He worked with T. E. Lawrence for a while, but did not share

Lawrence's views on the Hashemites. Here he met his American counterpart, Allen Dulles, who was stationed in Constantinople.

At the end of 1922, Philby travelled to London for extensive meetings with all involved in the Palestine question. They included Winston Churchill, King George, the Prince of Wales, Baron Rothschild, Wickham Steed, and Chaim Weizmann as head of the Zionist movement.

Philby was of the view that both British and the Saudi family's interests would be best served by uniting the Arabian Peninsula under one government from the Red Sea to the Persian Gulf, with the Saudis supplanting the Hashemites as Islamic 'Keepers of the Holy Places' while also protecting shipping lanes on the Suez–Aden–Bombay route of the British Empire.

Following the war the British sought to set up legitimacy for their continued control of the region of Palestine. This was achieved and formalised with League of Nations' consent in 1923 under a 'British Mandate' for Palestine which covered two administrative areas. The land west of the Jordan River, known as Palestine, would be under direct British administration until 1948, while the land east of the Jordan, as a semi-autonomous region known as Transjordan, would be under the rule of the Hashemite family from the Hijaz, until it gained independence in 1946.

From 1920 until 1948 Palestine would operate as a geo-politic entity under British administration with its prescribed area carved out of Ottoman Southern Syria after World War I.

Philby was forced to resign his post in 1924 on differences of allowing Jewish immigration to Palestine. He was found to be in unauthorised correspondence with Ibn Saud, which carried with it the connotation of espionage by sending information he gained in his post to Ibn Saud. In the parlance of the day he had in fact 'gone native', however, the British Secret Service continued to pay Philby for another five years.

Shortly after Philby's resignation, Ibn Saud began to call for the overthrow of the Hashemite dynasty, and Philby was able to advise Ibn Saud on how far Saud could go in occupying all of Arabia without incurring the wrath of the British government as the principal power in the Middle East.

By 1925 Ibn Saud had brought unprecedented order into Arabia, and Philby was put in charge of arranging

Ibn Saud

Ibn Saud's coronation as king of the newly-created state of Saudi Arabia. Philby now settled in Jeddah, becoming a partner in a trading company, and over the next few years he became famous as an international writer and explorer. He personally mapped on camel back what is now the Saudi–Yemeni border on the Rub' al Khali, then in 1932, while searching for the lost city of Ubar, he was the first Westerner to visit and describe the Wabar craters.

In his unique position he became Ibn Saud's chief adviser in dealing with the British Empire and Western powers. He converted to Islam in 1930. In 1931 Philby invited Charles R.

Crane to Jeddah to facilitate exploration of the kingdom's subsoil oil. Crane was accompanied by noted historian George Antonius, who acted as translator.

In May 1932, Standard Oil of California (SoCal) sought out Philby in its quest to obtain an oil concession in Saudi Arabia, ultimately signing Philby as a paid advisor to SoCal. Philby, in turn, recognising that competition by foreign interests would get a better deal for his friend the Saudi King, Ibn Saud, made contact with Dr. George Lees, Chief Geologist of the Anglo-Persian Oil Company, in order to alert him to SoCal's interest in gaining oil exploration rights in Saudi Arabia.

Anglo Persian was one of five international partners in the Iraq Petroleum Company (IPC), through which it pursued its interest in the Saudi concession.

In March 1933, IPC sent a representative, Stephen Longrigg, to join negotiations with the Saudi government in Jeddah. However, Philby's primary loyalty was to the Saudi King and, although he was being paid by SoCal, he kept the arrangement a secret from Longrigg. In May 1933, IPC instructed Longrigg to withdraw from Jeddah, leaving SoCal free to conclude negotiations with the Saudi Arabia for a 60-year contract to obtain the exclusive concession for exploration and extraction of oil in the al-Hasa region along the Persian Gulf.

Kim Philby

Meanwhile, at Cambridge, Philby's son, Kim, was being recruited by the OGPU of the Soviet Union. In recent years the theory has been suggested that Kim was recruited in particular to spy on his father, who had such a powerful influence over the founder of the Saudi state and its connections with Britain and with American oil interests.

By 1934, in an effort to safeguard the port of Aden, Britain had no fewer than 1,400 peace treaties with the various tribal rulers of the hinterlands of what became Yemen. Philby had undermined British influence in the region, however, by facilitating the entry of United States commercial interests, followed by a political alliance between the United States and the Saud dynasty.

In 1936 SoCal and Texaco pooled their assets together east of Suez into what later became ARAMCO (Arabian–American Oil Company). The United States State Department describes ARAMCO as the richest commercial prize in the history of the planet. In this Philby represented the Saudi interests.

In 1937 when the Spanish Civil War broke out, Philby arranged for his son, Kim Philby, to become a war correspondent for The Times. Later Philby began secret negotiations with Germany and Spain, concerning Saudi Arabia's role in the event of a general European war. These discussions would allow neutral Saudi Arabia to sell oil to neutral Spain, which then had it transported to Germany. John Loftus, who worked in the United States Department of Justice Office of Special Investigations Nazi-hunting unit, claims Adolf Eichmann, while on a mission to the Middle East, had met with Philby during the mid-1930s.

St John Philby ran for election to the House of Commons for the British People's Party declaring, ... *no cause whatever is worth the spilling of human blood* and *protection of the small man against big business*. He lost soon after World War II began, and because of his activities, he was arrested on 3rd August 1940 under

Defence Regulation 18B, on a visit to Bombay, India. He was deported back to England and briefly imprisoned. Following his release from custody, Philby recommended his son, Kim, to Valentine Vivian, MI6 deputy chief, who unwisely recruited him into the British Secret Service as an outside informer, on retainer, with the assignment to spy on his father.

When Harold Hoskins of the U.S State Department visited Ibn Saud with Philby in August 1943 regarding the resettlement of Palestinian Arabs he asked if the king would be willing to have an intermediary meet with Chaim Weizmann. In anger Ibn Saud responded he was insulted by the suggestion that he could be bribed for £20 million to accept re-settlement of Arabs from Palestine. Hoskins told him that Weizmann had also confirmed that the promise of payment would be *guaranteed by President Roosevelt*. A month later Weizmann wrote…

It is conceived on big lines, large enough to satisfy the legitimate aspirations of both Arabs and Jews, and the strategic and economic interests of the United States;... properly managed, Mr. Philby's scheme offers an approach which should not be abandoned.

On 29th November 1947, the United Nations General Assembly recommended the adoption and implementation of the partition plan of Mandatory Palestine.

On 14th May 1948, David Ben-Gurion, the Executive Head of the World Zionist Organisation and President of the Jewish Agency for Palestine, declared .... *the establishment of a Jewish state in Eretz Israel, to be known as the State of Israel,* and as a state independent upon the termination of the British Mandate for

Palestine, on 15th May 1948.

Below - Palestine / Israel with Jordan (right), and Syria (top) taken from on high, clearly showing the Dead Sea and the Jordan River to the Sea of Galilee.

With the formation of the State of Israel the local indigenous inhabitants as Palestinian Arabs were effectively left with nothing. Whilst they could live on the land they had no state and effectively little control should the State of Israel want to dictate the terms. A huge injustice had been perpetrated, this time by the United Nations. Realising this, the day after Israel declared itself an independent state, neighbouring Arab armies invaded Palestine, fought the Israeli forces, and lost.

After Ibn Saud's death in 1953 St John (Harry) Philby openly criticised the successor King Saud, saying the royal family's morals *were being picked up in the gutters of the West*. He was exiled to Lebanon in 1955.

In exile he wrote…

The true basis of Arab hostility to Jewish immigration into Palestine is xenophobia, and instinctive perception that the vast majority of central and eastern European Jews, seeking admission . . . are not Semites at all. . . . Whatever political repercussions of their settlement may be, their advent is regarded as a menace to the Semitic culture of Arabia... the European Jew of today, with his secular outlook... is regarded as an unwelcome intruder within the gates of Arabia.

While in Beirut St John (Harry) Philby reconciled with his son Kim, and the two lived together for a time. He helped his son's career further by introducing him to his extensive network of contacts in the Middle East, including President Camille Chamoun of Lebanon. Both were sympathetic to Nasser during the Suez Crisis of August 1956. Between Harry's access to ARAMCO and Kim's access to British intelligence there was little they did not know about Operation Musketeer, the French and British plan to capture the Suez Canal. With Kim's duplicity the Soviet Union exposed the entire plan in the United Nations and threatened Britain and France with long-range guided missiles equipped with atomic warheads.

In 1955 Harry Philby returned to live in Riyadh. In 1960, on a visit to Kim in Beirut, while in bed with his son at his side, he reportedly exclaimed ... *God, I'm bored, ... and died.*

Some have summarised Harry Philby as a British traitor and an anti-Semite. They suggest that he never forgave the British government for ending his civil service career due to sexual misconduct. Once recruited by MI6, according to these sources, he used his intelligence assignment to take revenge on the British government. With the extensive contacts he acquired as a British agent, Harry had continued to betray British policy and resist all efforts at creating a Jewish homeland throughout his life. Philby disclosed classified British intelligence to Ibn Saud as King of Saudi Arabia, during wartime; he secretly helped secure American oil concessions in Saudi Arabia, double-crossing British competitors; he created economic partnerships, allied against British interests and in favour of Nazi Germany, with the help of Allen Dulles (later CIA Director); and worked with Nazi intelligence to sabotage efforts at creating a Jewish homeland.

How much of this is Jewish Israeli propaganda I will let you decide.

Israel has since fought several wars with neighbouring Arab states, in the course of which it has occupied the West Bank, Sinai Peninsula (between 1967 and 1982), part of South Lebanon (between 1982 and 2000), Gaza Strip and the Golan Heights. It has annexed portions of these territories, including East Jerusalem, with borders such as the West Bank disputed and with the Israeli state continuing to occupy land belonging to the indigenous Arab inhabitants.

In March 1977 the Palestinian Liberation Organisation (PLO) executive committee member, Zahir Muhsein's, definition was that....

The Palestinian people do not exist. The creation of a Palestinian state is only a means for continuing our struggle against the state of Israel for our Arab unity. In reality today there is no difference between Jordanians, Palestinians, Syrians and Lebanese.

Only for political and tactical reasons do we speak today about the existence of a Palestinian people, since Arab national interests demand that we posit the existence of a distinct 'Palestinian people' to oppose Zionism.

The term 'Palestinian,' as it is used today is, therefore, a political choice not a national name. Palestine is just one name for a land that never was a homogenous group, or a distinct nation of people. Other people who lived on this land had called it other names over the millennia. The people who live on it were, and still are, ethnically diverse, however, most accept that when one refers to a 'Palestinian' they mean the Arabs of Palestine. In that sense they are not Jews, (which is a religious term), Romans, Turks, Druze or any of the other people of the land of Israel and Palestine, referred to by names other than Palestinian.

The Arabs of Palestine speak the same language and share the same customs and history. They even have the same genetics of the Arabs of Jordan, Syria, Lebanon, Egypt and Saudi Arabia, and the Jews who were of Arab descent. Palestinians are not a national group in the political or ethnic sense, although they may become a nation in the political sense some day, if they ever attain political sovereignty and autonomy without a Zionist tag.

Bedouin bints and baby

Likewise, the term Jew is a religious tag making the State of Israel little more than a religious politicised state. The continuing dispute is in reality between the two largest groups - the Jews and the Arabs - of Palestine who are separated by religion. They can both be considered 'Palestinian' as they both live on what can be construed as Palestinian lands. They can also both be construed as Arabs as this is from whom they are both originally descended. In that sense they are fighting a civil, and to some degree religious, war over the land. Once again power, money, religion, politics, self determination and outside interests, are the drivers rather than any belief in honesty, equality, humanity, or addressing the original injustices.

With the US backing Israel for its own political ends and the Jews forcing Arabs off their land it is little wonder that the non Jewish indigenous local inhabitants have a genuine axe to grind. Efforts to resolve the Israeli–Palestinian conflict, therefore, will not result in peace until the original injustices are addressed, or the wrath of a true just God addressess the balance.

In the words of the author and prophet Kebir Clinton mhic Aonghais… *In the name of any God who is Merciful, all words in this account are true other than those that are not* ... take from it what you may.

Assalamu alaikum.

The end is never the end; it is only the beginning...

FIELD SERVICE
TOP SECRET
PASSED BY CENSOR
No. 3743